Also by Patricia Haley

Chosen

PATRICIA HALEY

POCKET STAR BOOKS

NEW YORK LONDON TORONTO SYDNEY

POCKET STAR BOOKS
A Division of Simon & Schuster, Inc.
1230 Avenue of the Americas
New York, NY 10020

This book is a work of fiction. Names, characters, places, and incidents either are products of the author's imagination or are used fictitiously. Any resemblance to actual events or locales or persons, living or dead, is entirely coincidental.

This Pocket Star Books paperback edition November 2009

POCKET STAR BOOKS and colophon are registered trademarks of Simon & Schuster, Inc.

For information about special discounts for bulk purchases, please contact Simon & Schuster Special Sales at 1-866-506-1949 or business@simonandschuster.com.

The Simon & Schuster Speakers Bureau can bring authors to your live event. For more information or to book an event, contact the Simon & Schuster Speakers Bureau at 1-866-248-3049 or visit our website at www.simonspeakers.com.

Cover design by John Vairo Jr.
Cover photograph by Glowimages/Getty Images

Manufactured in the United States of America

10 9 8 7 6 5 4 3 2

ISBN 978-1-4165-8066-9
ISBN 978-1-4165-8350-9 (ebook)

Chosen is dedicated to the ones I love.

*Thank you for your endless support,
encouragement, love, and prayers.*

*Let the purpose for which God created you be the
driving source of inspiration in your life.*

"My son . . . , the one whom God has chosen, is young and inexperienced. . . . Do not be afraid or discouraged, for the Lord God, my God, is with you."

—1 Chronicles 29:1, 28:20

chapter

1

The best way for Don Mitchell to describe this moment was that it felt like clawing up a wall of loose dirt while standing in a pool of quicksand. How many more times would he set himself up for heartache and disappointment? Once the recommendation was handed down from the almighty Dave Mitchell, the one whose bloodline he shared, the board of directors wasted no time in fulfilling the directive. Six votes in favor, two opposed, with one abstention. As easy as that, little brother Joel, barely out of diapers and teething rings, was running the company. Twenty-three years old. Don sat quietly with no retort, unlike his mother, Madeline, who wanted a recount. He slowly packed his belongings, trying not to make eye contact with the board members as they scattered from the room amidst a cloud of chitchat, with his mother in relentless pursuit, nipping at their heels and hurling accusations.

To onlookers, the vote was a simple executive decision. For Don it was more profound, yielding yet another rip in the veil of affection he'd worked so hard to keep mended with his father. Every time a bud of kinship sprang forth in their relationship, some unforeseen act squashed the bonding. This time he wasn't four years old, crying himself to sleep for a father who wasn't coming home. He was a thirty-one-year-old man who wasn't looking to be fathered. He wasn't even looking to be loved, the basic benefit that should have come freely from his father at birth. At this point, a dash of respect would be sufficient, yet it continued eluding him.

His mother came back into the room after chasing everyone else away. "Don't you worry," she consoled with a pat on the back. "I'm not going to stand for this. You are the rightful heir to your father's company. I don't know what your father and that little conniving gold-digging wife of his were thinking, but when I'm through with them, you'll be in charge. That's a promise, if it's the last thing I do. Sherry's not getting her hands on anything else of mine and that includes your place as head of this organization. When your father was only working with a handful of churches, I was there, back when he was struggling to make the leadership training ministry a viable business. Now that DMI is worth more than a billion dollars, she wants it, too. I can't lose everything to her, not again, not without a fight. I mean a real war this time." Her voice faded for a second, but Don could tell his mother was putting on a brave face guarded by a steel disposition. Others saw her as a shrewd businesswoman, but his image of her was padded by the countless childhood memories he had of her crying when she thought no one was looking. Loss after loss spread over two decades was bound to wear her down.

Don reflected on his options. This would be the time when a practical person would evaluate the defeat and assess what went wrong. No need. He already knew the source of his problem, and it began with his birth. "Mother, it's done," he said while fumbling with the stack of papers in his portfolio. "Dave Mitchell made his choice," he said, hesitating, "and it wasn't me." He braced both hands against the giant mahogany table and let his head bow with eyes closed. "It never is." When Dave Mitchell gave away his favorite classic Porsche, the one Don dreamed of owning, the car went to Joel. When his father needed someone from DMI to represent him at the international summit of leaders, Don wasn't chosen. In his mind, he never was.

"Don, don't you worry. I'll take care of this. I'm going to see your father right now. He has to answer to me. I might not be in a full-time marketing role any longer, but I'm still on the board of directors and a key member of the executive team," she said, pausing for a moment, regaining strength in her voice. "I've helped keep this place running. There's no way I'm going to stand by and let that woman and your father destroy you. It won't happen again. Dave owes me. He has to do right by at least one of my children, and you're the only one I have left."

Steering clear of the conversation surrounding his siblings was the best approach to take with his mother, given the fresh layer of defeat she was experiencing yet again at the hands of Dave and Sherry Mitchell. "Mother, don't bother." Every time there was peace and a chance for his mother to consider releasing the anger she harbored about the divorce, something new came up to make her madder. Felt like every year or at least every other year there was new trouble with Sherry and Dave, making the divorce seem as if it was yesterday—plenty of fresh cuts on an old scab. His mother's unabridged anger was the proof.

Don's heart sank deeper, which he didn't think possible. Madeline was a good mother. Commitment to her family was undeniable. She was sixty-two. He wanted her to begin living her life outside the clutches of Dave and Sherry, but he didn't know how to help her make the transition when he couldn't help himself.

She squeezed his shoulder tight and pushed her cheek next to his. "Too late, darling, I'm already on my way to see your father. I'll talk with you later."

Don blew out a deep breath as he watched his mother leave the boardroom. He wanted to be demanding and stop her from confronting his father. On the other hand, he wanted someone to do something, but in the end he knew no one could. Even at this moment, he couldn't garner enough contempt to hate his father. There were many reasons why he could, but his heart wouldn't take the plunge into that abyss. His father, the mighty man, the shot-caller, had dubbed baby brother Joel top dog and that was the end of it. No sense fretting any longer. He might as well go and congratulate the chosen one. Don plucked his portfolio from the table and went into the hallway, where he ran into Joel. He hadn't expected to see the new leader quite so soon.

"Don," Joel said, panting for breath, "I got this envelope from Dad's office. I'm supposed to cast this vote in his absence."

"Too late, little brother, the vote has already been taken and everyone is gone."

"But I didn't get to cast Dad's vote," Joel said, holding the small sealed envelope.

"Didn't need to, little brother, nope, no need at all," he said letting his glance graze the floor before mustering enough dignity to regain eye contact with his father's favorite. "Dave Mitchell's vote was just extra reinforcement in your back pocket. Don't worry. You're the new chief executive officer."

"Me—what are you talking about? I thought you wanted the job."

"I did, but the position wasn't offered to me," Don said.

The enthusiasm in Joel's eyes fizzled. Maybe he was shocked and remorseful or maybe he really was that selfish spoiled-rotten kid who was good at pretending to be sincere when it benefited him. Either way, Don would maintain a semblance of dignity. He planted his feet solidly, pleading unsuccessfully with his soul not to let an inkling of his disappointment be exposed, not to run the risk of giving Joel extra gratification. "That's right. You're the new man in charge. You were chosen to run his business," Don said, and let the realization have a few moments to soak in. "The board went along with it, although I'm the oldest and the most legitimate."

Don was very familiar with the controversy surrounding his parents' divorce, followed by his father's marriage to Sherry and the birth of their son Joel. Right or wrong, Joel was obviously loved enough to gain control of their father's prized possession without merit.

Joel took a step back.

Don felt good letting the wind out of the chosen one's sails, but the innuendo about Joel's legitimacy must have stirred a hornet's nest, judging by the cutting look he was giving. It seemed best to calm the brooding waters before the awkward conversation got out of hand.

"I'm not trying to say that you stole my position. I'm not saying that at all."

"Then what are you saying, Don? I had nothing to do with this decision. This came from our father. I don't know why he chose me, but he must have a reason," Joel said, his back stiffening.

Conscious of the escalating tension, Don quickly acted to defuse it. "If our father and Sherry deem you the most suited to run my family's business, then that's the way it is."

"Leave my mother out of this."

"That's pretty hard to do." Before Joel became too defensive, Don shifted the focus back to the business. "Regardless of whose decision this is, I'm willing to support you as the head of this organization." He heard the words squeak through his teeth and wondered from where they'd come. They sounded good, the right words to say. If only they were true. "Do you want me to stay on as senior vice president managing the East Coast?"

"I don't see why not. Obviously Father wants you in the role. Why shouldn't I?"

Don was a half-smashed bug under Joel's feet, hoping the crushing weight would leave enough of his ego intact for him to crawl away, balancing a load of dejection on his back. This wasn't his brother. His real brothers were dead. Joel was no more than an unwanted relative wedged into his world. Don conjured up as much gratitude as his pride would allow and slung it at his father's son for the extended grace. "Great, that's good to hear. So this means I'll keep my office on the East Coast and stay out of your way. The rest of the country is all yours, yours and that mother of yours."

"Don," Joel raised his voice and spewed, "you are

welcome to stay on, so long as you leave my mother out of this."

The passive approach wasn't working. Don had to harness his disapproval in Joel's presence. Before he could move two more feet, the new leader threw more words his way.

"Because if you don't," Joel hurled at him, completing the message by jerking his closed fist and extended thumb backward over his shoulder before snarling, "brother or not, you'll have to leave."

In the silence, Don let his glaring eyes meet Joel in the center of the hallway, confirming the warning was duly received. Any room for misinterpretation was eliminated. Joel's need to defend Sherry wasn't surprising. After all, the feuding between the two families had lasted Joel's entire lifetime. Joel had been taught to believe that Madeline was the culprit. In Don's world, Sherry was undeniably the culprit, which is why he believed her to be the mastermind behind this play for power. Joel didn't know Sherry the way Don and his mother did. Her reign as Mrs. Dave Mitchell had led to the perpetual and merciless annihilation of his family. Rehashing the past with his father's other son was a waste of time. Don walked away, praying every step of the way that he could control his burning distress. What was the point? Joel wasn't the source of his despair. Baby brother didn't have any more control over being the chosen child of Dave Mitchell than he had of ending up second best. Don had become the placeholder for whatever was left, but hating his half brother for always getting the best couldn't come close to alleviating his rage.

chapter

2

Sherry sat in the sunroom staring into the distant morning sky, remembering the time, which seemed like eons ago, when plans for her family were fueled with naiveté, back when she felt like a giddy schoolgirl skipping into wedded bliss with the one man she intended to love for a lifetime. How could she have known back then that her fairy-tale relationship would become a source of torment?

Those who knew the whole story behind her marriage to Dave had constantly gossiped about it. Sherry believed they saw her as the scheming secretary who seduced her boss, intentionally got pregnant, and forced Dave to leave his wife of ten years and their four little children—a common thief. That's what Madeline believed, and there were plenty of others, too. Many hadn't acknowledged her as Dave's legitimate wife. It didn't matter today. Joel Mitchell was visible to everyone as an authentic and bona-fide member of Dave's family, a label she had never possessed. He was finally, officially Dave's legitimate heir, not just legally as he'd always been, but in a way that really counted, in the public's opinion. With the endorsement, no one needed to ever again question the worth of her offspring. Joel wasn't a sin or the product of some lustful mistake. He was the beloved son, the keeper of his father's legacy. He had a purpose for living. There would be opposition from Don and his mother, but adversity was something Sherry knew intimately. Marrying Dave had been a moment of overflowing joy in her life, but she had never figured on the degree of respect and integrity that had to be sacrificed. It had been the price of marrying and creating a family with the man she loved, the one who shouldn't have been hers, since he was legally and spiritually committed to Madeline. She let her thoughts roam freely, relishing every step and giving no thought to the additional price that would surely have to be paid.

When the doorbell rang, she got up to answer it, but was unprepared after all to receive the guest standing in front of her. "Madeline!" was all she mustered. Sherry couldn't recall her coming to the house in the past two decades, unless she was mad about something.

"Sherry." Madeline stepped inside the foyer before officially being asked in.

"What are you doing here?"

"Where's Dave?" Madeline asked, brushing against Sherry without acknowledgment.

"He's unavailable," Sherry said, bracing herself on the doorknob before deliberately entering the battle zone with a veteran warrior. "How can I help you?"

"Seems to me," Madeline said, sliding her sunglasses midway down her nose, "that you've already helped yourself to what belongs to me again. Why are you so determined to live out my life?"

There was no point arguing. Sherry preferred to let Madeline ramble. In the end, Dave's decision was the same.

"I have one child left and you won't get the chance to ruin his life like you did the lives of my other three," Madeline rattled.

Sherry didn't know how many more times she would get blamed for the series of horrific events, the ones she had no part in creating. Burying two children and being estranged from another one was surely difficult, but Sherry refused to take the blame. Madeline didn't have exclusive rights on grief and loss. Sherry wasn't going around blaming Madeline for the death of her first child. Goodness knows Madeline's relentless harassment throughout the pregnancy, and the resulting stress, hadn't been good for Sherry's baby. Yet there was no blame, just the sense of loss any mother would feel about the death of her baby, regardless of the circumstances surrounding the child's conception.

One day Madeline would have to take responsibility for the demise of her own children, someday, but clearly this wasn't the day. Sherry knew it. Today Madeline was squarely focused on her fourth and youngest child, Don, and was clearly prepared to battle on his behalf.

"Look, Madeline, I don't want to fight with you. If you can't tell me what you want, then I'm asking you to leave." Sherry aimed her words directly at the bull's-eye of her target, refusing this time to let the unexpected hurricane lay claim to her moment of victory, which was hanging by a frayed thread.

"I'm not going anywhere until I see Dave. Where is he?" Madeline insisted as she strolled up the stairs toward the bedroom section of the estate, pulling off her driving gloves one finger at a time.

"Wait, wait, wait," Sherry yelled, grabbing Madeline's arm as she hurried up the stairs. "Where are you going? He's not up there; we moved him into the guest suite months ago." Sherry savored a rare taste of satisfaction knowing something that Madeline didn't.

Madeline turned to come back down the stairs with her fitted tweed suit showing no signs of wear. "What's he doing in there? Just how sick is he? Oh, never mind," she said, waving off the question.

Making the decision to stay at home while pregnant with Joel had been easy for Sherry after losing her first child to sudden infant death syndrome. Her only regret was sacrificing the day-to-day interaction with Dave at DMI, a privilege Madeline never had to give up, thanks to the divorce settlement guaranteeing her a senior position in the ministry. The court hadn't forced Dave to keep Madeline on the board of directors. He had made that decision on his own. Unless the ministry was sold, which Dave would never let happen, Madeline would be at DMI until she died. There would be no peace.

Sherry found herself constantly battling the notion of Madeline having a stronger bond with Dave because of the professional interest they shared. Sometimes Sherry could reject the thoughts, but she knew the sad truth was that most times she couldn't. Going back to DMI as an administrative assistant had never been the answer for several reasons, two that she'd never forgotten. The corporate world didn't excite her, and she had zero desire to personally watch Dave and Madeline attend meeting after meeting together while she sat outside the closed doors taking notes and filing papers. She was certain that staying at home had been the right choice.

"You can't just barge in here and have your way in our house. My husband is not well."

Madeline yanked her arm away from Sherry's loose grip. "Our house? Your husband?" Madeline gasped, loudly enough to be heard outside. Her temples appeared to throb. "You can't be serious. Don't you know I designed every inch of this house, even the room where you lay your head every night—don't you forget that," she said, spitting her words while using the palm of her hand to brush down any stray hair that might have eased out of her tightly drawn French twist.

"I had the master bedroom remodeled fifteen years ago to suit me and my husband's taste," Sherry fired back, not willing to be pushed around so easily this time.

"Don't tell me about your husband. He was my husband long before you showed up," she ranted. "There's nothing you can tell me about Dave Mitchell that I don't already know. As far as this house goes, whatever Dave has, part of it belongs to the mother of his first four children, which would be me." Madeline fiddled with her gloves for a brief second before piercing Sherry with a staunch stare. "Face it, you, my dear, are a sideshow, and everybody knows the circus always comes back to center stage. Excuse me," she snipped, and pushed past Sherry on her way down the stairs.

"I'm not going to stand here and let you disrespect me. Regardless of what you say, this is my home. I've lived here for twenty-five years. You were only here for ten or twelve."

Madeline stopped. "Let's get this clear. The way I see

it, you might have a piece of the estate, but you'll never take my place in this house or anywhere else. No matter how many little women like you Dave gets, I will always be the first Mrs. Dave Mitchell," she said, striding down the hallway as if she still owned the place. "I didn't have to be ashamed when I got married. Can you say the same?"

No matter what cutting words came from Madeline's mouth, Sherry was determined to fight back, to hang on to today's win. She had to for Joel. He deserved more peace than she had experienced being a Mitchell. "After all these years, why can't you let me and Dave live our lives and you live yours."

Madeline stopped abruptly and spun around to face Sherry with a fiery look of contempt. "Don't you worry about me and my life," she spat. "You take care of your own. Just remember, what goes around comes around. You broke up my home. Don't you dare think I'm going to wish you well in your old age. It won't happen," Madeline said and turned away. The words didn't penetrate. Sherry wholeheartedly believed that the death of her child and the dissolution of Dave's devotion were her punishment. Nothing else could top those two. "You wanted Dave, well, you got him, along with every ounce of misery that you deserve," Madeline added.

Marrying Dave had come at a price. Sherry understood the reality, but at fifty-two she was no longer willing to keep paying the same price over and over. Her dignity and security were no longer currency. She had to fight for her rightful place in the family, unwilling to remain a victim. Sherry ran ahead and blocked the entrance to Dave's room. The door was closed, and Sherry's hand clasped the knob. Madeline never broke her stride as she approached the room.

"You better move. I'm going in there one way or another."

The wall of tension was mounting, but Sherry didn't let up verbally. She couldn't. Joel's security and validation depended on her ability to stand up—hers, too. "Who do you think you are running into this house and telling me what you aren't going to do?" Madeline didn't respond. "Did you hear me?" she blurted, keeping her eyes squinted and focused, looking away only once or twice. "I said my husband is not feeling well. If there is something you need to discuss with him, you can make an appointment with Abigail like everyone else."

"Humph. I'm not everybody else," Madeline snarled.

Sherry folded her arms tight across her chest. "That's only your opinion." No one could generate intensity and disdain in her like Madeline, but intimidation was not an option in this battle. Joel was the motivation Sherry needed to deal with the intruder.

Madeline took two steps closer to Sherry with arms folded and lips pursed. She reared back on one heel, with the other foot tapping.

Without warning, the door opened, causing Sherry to lose her balance.

"We thought we heard loud voices. What is going on out here?" Dave's assistant, Abigail, asked.

Madeline didn't wait for any more dialogue. She pushed past both ladies and entered the room, moving into Dave's line of view. "We need to talk."

Sherry pushed past Abigail, too, and stood between the armchair Dave was sitting in and the spot where Madeline was standing. "What is your problem, Madeline?"

"You."

"I've told you my husband isn't up for this. You need to come back when he's feeling better."

"And you need to step aside, because I've told you I'm not going anywhere until Dave and I talk, period."

"Fine, I'm calling the police. They'll get you out of here."

"Sherry, no, don't call them. Let me talk to her," Dave said, reaching for her hand.

"No, I want her gone," she hollered.

"Sherry, please, let me talk with her."

"Yes, Sherry, let me talk to him. Bye." Madeline added with a little wave.

Sherry was shocked by her own level of outrage. Her hands trembled uncontrollably. Watching Dave accede to Madeline's requests repeatedly didn't sit well. Perhaps his desire to please her was fueled by guilt or by loyalty. She desperately hoped it wasn't love. He had loved Madeline once, and could possibly fall in love with her again. Perhaps from a heavy dose of the same guilt, Sherry had let Madeline mercilessly shred her reputation year after year. Sherry wanted to wipe that smug look off Madeline's face. "I'm not leaving this room. Whatever you have to say will just have to be said in my presence," Sherry said, going to Dave's side. She had to protect him. No one else in the family, especially Madeline, knew how serious his illness was. That's the way he wanted it. Truth be told, Sherry savored another bittersweet taste of power in knowing about Dave's stomach cancer, knowledge Madeline didn't have. Sherry and Dave were battling the fight of his life, together, just the two of them. She took refuge and bolstered strength in what they shared.

"Sherry, sweetheart, it's okay. Why don't you and Abigail let me talk with Madeline for a few minutes."

Sherry didn't take a single step.

"It's okay," Dave said, caressing his wife's hand. "Really, it's okay. I was expecting this visit."

Sherry let her gaze roam up and down Madeline with one eye flickering. "I'll be right outside if you need me," she promised, and sealed the statement with a kiss to his forehead. She would protect her husband and her son from Madeline's wrath, regardless of the penalty.

Abigail kept quiet and exited with Sherry.

chapter

3

"Madeline, I've been expecting you," Dave said, prepared for her fury. Changing his mind about Joel's appointment wasn't an option. He'd heard from God and no force on earth would cause him to second-guess his decision. Hear from God, then act swiftly and without fear was his way, a way that had served him well with the Lord and with DMI.

"Oh, so you already know what you did today was foolish. What were you thinking, appointing a snot-nosed kid to run an organization I helped build? Don is the one you've been mentoring for the past ten years. You'd think his loyalty and hard work would count for something, but no, not with you. How can you put Joel in charge? He's a boy who's barely out of training pants and certainly doesn't know the first thing about running a billion-dollar company. Are you so sick and delusional that you've lost the ability to think rationally?"

"Madeline, my decision wasn't easy, and I know this is awkward for Don." His staunch disposition crumbled on hearing the fury mixed with disappointment in Madeline's voice. She was the mother of his children. She could get pretty rowdy, but at the end of each day, he called her a friend. He owed his friend a chance to speak her mind. "I made a mistake by not speaking with him first."

"You sure did make a mistake, a big one. That's why I'm here. Now we're getting somewhere."

"My only mistake was in letting Don hear my decision from someone other than having it come from me. I owe him an apology." Family was important to Dave. His heart was grieved. He didn't want to destroy his relationship with Don. Yet he knew being disobedient to the leading of the Lord was worse. He'd done that before, but never again.

"You owe him more than that, Dave, a whole lot more, and me too, but this is about our son. You've given Joel what rightfully belongs to Don. What possessed you to do such a thing? How do you think he feels? Do you really care so little about your own flesh and blood that you're comfortable treating him this way?"

"This wasn't a spontaneous decision. I've been thinking about my transition for some time, before I took ill. I've worked with both of my sons, and although Don seems like the most suitable candidate, I was led by God to choose Joel. I'm at peace with my decision."

"Oh, so it was God this time. Okay, let me get this straight. The last time you made the mistake of your life, you blamed it on love. Now you've run out of in-the-name-of-love excuses and you're going straight to God on this one. You know, you're a true piece of work. Sometimes I wonder what I ever saw in you," she said, turning away. "This isn't about some vision God gave you. This is about your weakness for that woman and her continued need to torment me. Admit it." He kept quiet. "She talked you into putting us out of the house after the divorce."

"Madeline, that's not true. You were angry at me and didn't want to stay there."

Madeline let her stance ease before stiffening again. "Well, it was still our house. If I didn't want to live there after the divorce, I certainly didn't want you living there with the other woman. But because Sherry wanted the house, you disregarded my feelings. I didn't understand why you did what you did then and I still don't. I just don't get it. What is it about the woman that makes a seventy-year-old man like you act so foolish? Honestly," she said, flicking her hand in the air, "I don't know, and I don't care. I just don't care what you do anymore. My only concern is Don and what you owe him." She drew closer to him. "You chose her over the welfare of your children many times before. I won't ever forget what you did. Dave, I supported you. When you asked me to adopt Andre after your friend died, I gladly embraced him as my own child. You know that." She was right. Dave nodded. "But you let Sherry lure you away from me and the children. They all needed you, but Andre needed you more. He'd already lost both of his parents and his grandfather. He needed you, and you weren't there. You were the second father who left him."

Dave listened. What she said rang with truth, but he refused to take on guilt. There was no peace in guilt, only hopelessness and despair. "The children knew that I loved them."

"But they needed you at home with them. That would have been love to them," she said, wringing her hands. "I don't know, maybe if Andre hadn't felt abandoned by you, maybe he wouldn't have done what he did to Tamara. Maybe Sam wouldn't have sought the ultimate revenge on his brother, ending both their lives. We could have spared their lives," she said, swiping her index finger across her eyelid. "If you hadn't left us for Sherry and her baby, all four of our babies would be alive and here with us."

He could have elected to live saddled with guilt and self-condemnation. The past was gone. "I've repented for the sins of my youth. God forgave me and I've asked for your forgiveness. There's nothing more I can do." He couldn't minimize his mistakes. They were too substantial. But the best part of his relationship with God was that the old was indeed old and each day was a new start, recognizing that not all consequences fell away as easily as his guilt. Madeline's relentless anger and Don's situation were evidence.

"You're so cavalier when it comes to moving on. Don't you understand what you did to your family? How do you expect me to forgive what you did?"

"Don't do it for me. Do it for your own peace."

"Easy for you to say. I'm not here for peace. I'm here to claim what belongs to the last son that I have. You'd think that shame or guilt would force you to do right by Don."

"I don't have any guilt."

"Of course you wouldn't. You're the mighty man of God, Dave Mitchell, who does what he pleases, no matter who gets hurt."

"I'm not going to wallow in the past. What's done is done. God has forgiven me, and I've forgiven myself."

"And that's supposed to be the end of it? You throw God at me," she said, raising her hands and shaking them in the air, "and hallelujah, the gates of heaven are supposed to open for me. Well, I'm not buying the religious antics. You can't do what you want to do, then go through a forgiveness exercise, which basically means you distance yourself from the consequences and leave the fallout for the rest of us. Forgiveness is all well and good, but there's a price to pay for your irresponsible and insensitive decisions, old man. The problem is that my family is the only one paying for your mistakes. What about Sherry? When is she going to suffer the same way that I've had to?"

"Sherry lost a child, too."

"Do you really think I lose sleep at night thinking about the death of Sherry's illegitimate child? All I have to say is that you created the situation that will affect so many people for many years to come."

"Look Madeline, I know you're upset, but in time you will see that I've done what was best for the ministry and for our family," he said, attempting to sit up in the armchair.

"Whose family? Certainly not mine; maybe yours, but not mine. Remember, I don't have much family left. You let Sherry see to that."

Dave knew where she was headed but didn't have the energy to curtail it. His words were worthless when Madeline tumbled into the abyss of her resentment. There was nothing more he could say to give her comfort. The best he could do was listen.

"Don is all I have left, and now the two of you are trying to destroy him."

The subject of the destruction of his children was painful and unspeakable. Rehashing it again and again with her wouldn't bring them back. Yet, Madeline wouldn't hear it. She needed to blame someone for the disaster in order to survive. "Come on now, Madeline, they're my children, too."

"I don't want to hear it." She stood firm, with piercing eyes. "I won't let you destroy him, Dave, not without a fight."

Wisdom suggested that Dave remain quiet and let the raging storm within her blow itself out, averting significant damage.

"Don was robbed of a position in the company that rightfully belongs to him. Forget about his MBA and boatload of experience; it's his birthright."

"I didn't overlook Don, and I'm fully aware of the value my son brings to the ministry. That's why I promoted him to senior vice president last year, reporting directly to me. I also gave him a seat on the board. He has full autonomy with the East Coast operations."

"Senior vice president?" she snarled.

"All right, I'll recommend that Joel make him executive vice president managing multiple divisions."

"Why should our son settle for a piddling little position when he should be running the entire company?"

"I don't deny he has what it takes to run the ministry."

"Why do you insist on calling this a ministry?"

"That's what it is. We develop leadership training programs for churches."

"But we're not a church. We're a business, Dave, a business. You threw the church notion away when you left your family for that woman. You're in no position to preach about a ministry when you haven't been able to keep peace in your own family. For goodness sake, at least be honest with yourself, and stop calling it a ministry. It just makes you sound like a hypocrite.

Her anger couldn't cause him to lose sight of God's directive. "God is my judge, Madeline, and I've done the work He called me to do. I will always follow His lead until I take my last breath, regardless of who agrees or disagrees."

"Please spare me the religious dissertation. What really happened today?" she said, with hand propped on her waist and toe pointed. "Oh, I get it. Ms. Sherry came groping over you and begging you to put her son at the top. Knowing how weak you are when it comes to her, I'm sure you caved in like a timid puppy. What's new?"

"Sherry is my wife."

"You think I don't know that? If no one else in this whole world knows what Sherry is to you, trust me when I tell you that I do," she said, poking her finger into her chest.

"Madeline, I don't want to hurt you any more than I already have."

"Then put Don back into the chief position. Do this favor for me, Dave." She came closer to him, close enough to touch his hand. "Do this for what we once meant to one another, once upon a time. I supported you when we were married. You owe me and Don at least this much."

Dave sat still, not pulling away from her touch. Finally he responded with, "I can't, Madeline. I just can't go against the leading of the Lord." He loved his children, each and every one of them, but his love and dedication to God came first. His love hadn't always been in that order. Dave's life had changed when God rescued him at a time in his younger years when his decisions weren't grounded and had him on a sure path to destruction. God preserved him, forgave him, and renewed his spirit. He was alive because of the Lord. For that reason, God's will took precedence over his own, even when it appeared to go against his wife's and his children's desires. Seeing Madeline express her hurt, which came across as anger, didn't make him feel good, but God's will was going to be done.

She snatched her hand back and shouted loud enough to be heard in the hallway. "I'm not letting you get away with this, not this time. You can believe me. You better pray that God is the voice speaking to you, because when I'm finished He's the only one who can save you."

Sherry pushed the door open with Abigail standing close by.

"You'll be hearing from my attorney, old man." Madeline smirked at Sherry. "You and your little afterthought of a son are not getting away with this," Madeline said before reaching the door. "Remember, the two of you started this war." She sliced between Abigail and Sherry right outside the doorway. "And you wonder why none of your family is religious, including her." Madeline stared at Sherry. "No need to—you have enough religion to choke all of us," she said loud enough for Dave to hear and left.

Time hadn't smoothed the rancid bitterness between Dave's wives. He didn't know what else could be done to douse the flame. Crafting million-dollar business deals was simple. Repairing his broken family was proving to be improbable. He could rely on the Lord for the healing, but in his heart he knew that there were times when God's wrath and inevitable consequences were interchangeable. His family's current predicament was one of those times.

chapter

4

---·---

It didn't make logical sense, but Sherry was probably the best hope Don had for correcting the injustice. There was no question about her having his father's attention, perhaps Joel's, too. For better or worse, he had wrestled with and subdued every reservation discouraging him from going to their house. Resistance was silent as he stood at the front door. He could turn around and drive away into the sunset of his despair, but the tugging at his heart kept him planted. He rang the bell, then rapped firmly on the door, praying for his strength and courage to hold out.

Sherry opened the door and offered minimal courtesies as he entered. "What do you want, Don? Are you coming to tell me how upset you are about not being appointed chief executive officer? If so, you can save your breath," she said, closing the door and turning to walk away. "Your mother already beat you here."

"Believe me, Sherry, I'm not here to cause a scene." He could only imagine where his mother's confrontation had registered on the Richter scale. The fact that the house was still standing and Sherry was mobile were good signs. "I accept my father's decision. I've already told Joel he has my support."

"Really," Sherry said, turning back toward him with eyebrows raised and eyes widening. She heaved a sigh. "Then why are you here?"

"I know you don't believe this, but I don't have any hard feelings toward you, even though I would be justified if I did."

Sherry maintained her footing, as her glee diminished.

Don knew the comment was powerful and could send any spiritually challenged individuals retreating into a place in their souls reserved for lingering guilt. He wasn't quite sure if this applied to Sherry. She was heartless—at least that's what he had believed growing up.

"There's nothing I can do about my father leaving us so many years ago for you. My mother took care of us in spite of what he did, and I'm okay," he said, pausing. "I have to be."

"So why are you here, if it's not to criticize me?"

"I came because Joel will listen to you." Don let his body relax and his pride sink. "He agreed to let me continue running my East Coast operation, but I'll need Abigail to work with me as a vice president, reporting directly to me." If he couldn't have the chief role, at least he would be able to breathe far away from Joel's day-to-day scrutiny, and to run a part of the organization he'd come to love. Yet business alone wasn't the sole motivation for his appeal to Sherry. The time hadn't been right yet to reveal his affection for Abigail. With his father's failing health in recent months, Abigail was consumed with expansion projects, hindering Don's ability to distract her with romance. The time would come when he and Abigail could build something special together, both professionally and personally—he believed it in his heart. All he needed was favor from Sherry, which equated to favor from Joel. Yesterday, he would have sought God for direction. Today he was on his own. "I have never asked you for anything, Sherry, until now. Having Abigail by my side would give me the management expertise I need to get me out of everyone's hair, to put some distance between us and reduce our tension. Please do this for me and for whatever remnants of a family we have," he said. Sherry didn't need to know his true motivation, and he definitely didn't want Joel to know.

He was conceding on every other front. Whatever appeal was necessary to get Abigail, short of selling his soul, Don was eager to use. Playing the "family card" would, he hoped, compel Sherry to a sense of atonement.

"I don't think it will be a problem. I'll talk to Joel and see what we can do."

"Good enough." Don felt a load of relief. If anyone could convince Joel to make his appeal a reality, it would be Sherry.

"Do you want to see your father while you're here? You could get his opinion on Abigail's move."

Don couldn't answer immediately. He used to count spending time with and getting business advice from his beloved father as a blessing that ranked one notch below talking directly to God. Any other time, seeing his father would have been automatic, but the rift between them was widening. He loved his father, and it hurt knowing he wasn't the chosen one. The years Don had spent working under his father's direction and vying for his admiration hadn't counted for much when it came to making the final decision about who would run the organization. Don reflected on what little effort Joel had to make when it came to impressing Dave Mitchell. Joel always ended up with the best their dad had to offer—his love, his car, his time, and now his company.

After a brief deliberation, he told Sherry, "No, I'm not quite ready to see him. Maybe another time."

It was hard to hide the disappointment and anguish resonating in his words and settling on his face. In spite of his circumstances, there was hope on the horizon. Sherry would convince Joel to let Abigail go. Visualizing time with her soothed his wounds. Looking forward to the future, he extended common courtesies and left his father's mansion feeling, for the first time, as if he'd finally gotten the best of what was being offered: Abigail, the target of his affection.

The Mitchell name was synonymous with money and lots of it. After an uneventful ride home, Don pushed number 34 in the elevator. Another five thousand dollars a month of his father's money would get him on the penthouse floor, five levels up, but he wasn't interested. Don skipped along, slipped the keycard into the slot, and entered his condo. His four-bedroom condo in the heart of downtown Detroit suited him fine. He draped his suit coat across the back of the sofa, loosened his tie, and went to the windows.

The floor-to-ceiling windows lining the condo gave him a crystal-clear view into Canada. The sky seemed endless. He drew in the view overlooking the river, hoping to be transported to another place, another time. He knew all the wishing in the universe couldn't change the frigid events of the day. But a flowing warmth melted a portion of his chilled soul. Abigail flooded his thoughts. She was the key to his future. Each breath he took was laced with her scent. He would gladly turn over the keys to his place, his share of the business, and any future earnings so long as he could have Abigail in his corner of the world—a small request in exchange for what should have rightfully been his.

The material things weren't important anyway, never were. Abigail was who he wanted, needed. Sherry had to convince Joel. A chill eased back over his soul. He was putting his faith in his mother's adversary. Joel had already gotten to God and won the prize along with favor from their father. Sherry was the only option left to get what he wanted done. She was the only one who could.

He stood at the window for what seemed like hours, contemplating calling Sherry countless times. In a fit of desperation and sheer anxiety, he grabbed the keys lying on the end table and dashed into the hallway. Don could have said that the years working under his father were a waste of time, but it wasn't true. Dave Mitchell wasn't the best father, but he sure knew how to run the business. He'd learned much and wasn't ready to walk away from DMI. Don felt the pinch of desperation. He couldn't let his entire future rest in Sherry's hands. Heck, she'd already had too much opportunity to recklessly paint the picture of his life and his mother's. If there was going to be a true defeat today, it would be based on his actions and not the result of being dangled from their ropes. He had a voice and he planned to use it, win or lose. Don pushed the elevator button several times in rapid succession, eager to get going and secure his plans.

chapter

5

Joel returned home with thoughts spinning. Stunned by the appointment, he sat in his car trying to figure out what to do next. Running a big company required lots of experience. Dad had his reasons, Joel was certain, but maybe Don should be temporarily in charge until he was more prepared to lead. Jumping in and out of prayer along the way home hadn't delivered the answers he wanted. The constant vibration of his cell phone didn't help his ability to concentrate. He slipped the phone out of his pocket, glanced at the name, and slipped it back. His new friend would have to wait until his mind was clear, just like the two women who had called earlier.

Joel had to see Dad to find out what he was supposed to do. He could only imagine how heavy traffic had been in and out of the estate. He finally got out of the car and went inside. His mother embraced him as he entered the foyer and hung on.

"Mom, you can let go now. I'm okay," he said, half joking and the rest of him sensing her need for an ally, someone who could see the situation from the same tiny Mitchell corner as she did.

"I know. It's just that this was a big day—a big day for our family," she said.

"Family, that's an interesting word when it comes to us. After today, I'm probably an only child." It didn't require years of business experience for Joel to recognize that his brother was feeling slighted and might be willing to stop at nothing to get even. He had to be prepared to defend his father's decision, whether Don liked it or not.

"We might be able to smooth the tension with Don. He stopped by an hour ago, after his mother left," Sherry said.

"Madeline came over here?" Joel tensed, fearing what his mother had endured while he was away. "Oh, boy, what did she do?"

"You don't want to know. Let's just say it wasn't pretty." Joel didn't bother to let his mind dance through the possibilities. There were too many, none of which were good. If only he could have been at the house to protect his mother. "I'm still trying to calm my nerves after she left. Ohhhh." She shuddered, nodding frantically. "I can't believe that after twenty-five years of marriage, she has me questioning my worth." She plopped down on the lower steps of the wide, winding staircase and ran her fingers through her hair. Joel's phone vibrated again, drawing his gaze away from his mother. "What's wrong?" she asked.

"Oh, nothing," he replied, pulling out the phone.

"Do you need to answer that call?"

"No," he said, recognizing the caller as an acquaintance who'd tried to reach him earlier, someone he saw infrequently. All of them had to wait until he could process the day.

"Anyway, I need to talk to you about Don."

"Let me see Dad first," he said, shutting off the phone.

Sherry nodded in agreement, resting on the steps. "Yes, you better go now, since it's getting close to his one o'clock lunchtime. We can talk afterward."

Joel kissed his mother on the forehead. "Everything's going to work out, Mom. Don't worry. This will settle down. You'll see. Don and Madeline will get over this; they have to." Exhibiting confidence to a mother who lived on the edge of vulnerability was his focus at this volatile juncture. His lack of confidence in the words spoken wasn't important.

When Joel got to his father's suite, he found Abigail in the adjoining office. They exchanged a few words before he went in to see his father. Joel sat near his hero, Dave Mitchell, the father who had taught him everything from how to ride a bike without training wheels to reading a stock market report. He was convinced a little illness couldn't keep his father down. "Dad, why did you make me CEO when Don is the one you've mentored?"

"I didn't, God did."

"Well, he's very angry." Joel could tolerate Don's insults to him, but not those to his mother. Don and Madeline had been cruel to his mother as far back as he could remember. Joel wasn't willing to watch her be picked on any longer. He was in a position to do something.

"In time Don will accept my decision."

"I'm not so sure, at least not right away. You should have seen him. He's really mad, and I don't know what to say to my brother." Joel vividly remembered Don's reaction when their father handed Joel the keys to his old Porsche as a twenty-first birthday gift. If Don was jealous of an old car, Joel couldn't guess the depths of his brother's outrage over losing control of the ministry.

"I trust God. This is His plan. Don will get over this. I don't know when, but he will."

"When he does I will still be left with a tough job. I don't know where to begin running a company this size. I'm too young. There is too much for me to learn overnight," Joel said, stammering.

"Joel, you have to step up, son. I was younger than you when I started the ministry."

"But you graduated from college when you were nineteen."

"Take courage and be a leader; none of this doubting and wavering. Boldness is what you need. When God calls you, He equips you. Everything you need will be provided. People will be drawn from all corners of the earth to work with you." Dad bounced his loosely balled fist on the back of Joel's hand, which was resting flat on the edge of the bed. "I've trained Abigail. She can help you. She's a loyal person to have on your team." Dad lay back, drew in a long slow breath, and released it equally slowly. "She can also serve as a mediator between you and your brother."

"After today I'm not sure Don will consider me his brother." He wasn't sure how he felt about Don. At times he could go either way. Sorrow filled him. Don was his last shot at having a brother in the Mitchell family.

"Joel, work this out with your brother, otherwise

you'll be distracted from the true enemies, ones that will constantly hound you and DMI."

"But that's nothing new. Far back as I can remember you've had to constantly fight off attacks on the company and you've come out on top each time."

"Sure, but look what it has cost me. For decades I've done nothing but fight war after war, retaining solvency in the ministry by the Hand of God, never losing one battle. God blessed me time and time again, but I'm tired now. I wish there was more I could do for the Lord, but my reign has ended." Dad's eyes watered, but the tissue he removed from the nightstand had already been used to blow his nose. "You have to fulfill the vision God has given about expanding into international markets. We have to share the word of God throughout the world. I'm passing not only the ministry, but the vision and the knowledge to you as well. Safeguard them both."

"I will do my best, Dad, in your honor."

"Do it to the glory of God, not for me." Dad tapped his fist again, softly. "I'm going to give you some very good advice. Whatever you do, stay faithful to the Lord. God rewards obedience." Dad shifted his body on the bed as if he was trying to find a comfortable position.

"Are you all right?" Joel asked, always concerned about his parents.

Dave waved off the question. "A little pain is nothing. Be tough," Dad said, grimacing, but Joel didn't ask his father about the pain again. "There will be times when you'll have to make the tough decisions no one else wants to make, can't make. Seek God and move forward. Learn to shake your fears and past mistakes off like dust on the bottom of your shoe."

"This is a big job for me." Thank goodness he had people like Uncle Frank, his father's brother, to help manage the finances. He didn't have much family, but at least there was one person he could trust in DMI. He felt inspired.

"And it's going to get bigger. Ministries are drowning in a sea of accusations, poor decisions, mismanagement, and scandals, which is why you have to fire Frank."

"Uncle Frank? Why?" Joel asked, struck with fear of losing his one ally.

"He embezzled funds from two churches we represent around the time I got sick. He invested the money and profited greatly. The ministry is vulnerable to a barrage of negative press if this goes public." Dad reached for the partially filled glass of water sitting on a nightstand near the bed. After taking a sip he handed the glass to Joel. "Always deal with mismanagement harshly, otherwise you jeopardize the integrity of the entire organization. Frank has to go. Son, don't let anyone cripple your ability to lead—family, friend, or foe."

Joel wasn't entirely sure what the CEO role entailed, but the first order of business was to get rid of Uncle Frank. Anybody Dad couldn't trust had to go. He hoped Don wasn't next.

"My season has passed. It's your turn to lead." Joel demanded the sting of sorrow stay at bay so as not to diminish his ability to digest the words of wisdom and fulfill his calling. Dad shook his hand with fervor as if to say the transition of power was now complete and the torch duly transferred to the new king. "There's only one other thing I ask of you, Joel."

"Anything, Dad, you know I'll do anything for you."

Joel drew in closer to preserve his father's waning energy, but Dad was determined to sit up and be heard.

"Don't let the ministry get sold or split," Dad commanded, with the same power he had in his voice before getting sick. "You have strength as a solid unit. Once you're broken into pieces, there's no recovery. I trust you to fulfill my request. Never let DMI get sold or split under any circumstances. I am holding you to this."

"I won't let you down. I promise."

"It's more important for you not to let God down. Don't lose sight of your calling. Stay true to His word and don't be distracted. Be the leader God has called you to be. If you don't, the wrath of God will surely fall on you, and failure will be your constant companion."

chapter

6

Sherry heard Joel trotting toward the kitchen as she struggled to pour a cup of tea without quivering. She tried desperately to put on a celebratory demeanor with the intention of hiding her concern from him. The less he had to shoulder the better.

"Mom, I'm all yours. What did you want to talk about?"

She took a few sips before responding. What she needed, only Joel could give her at this precise moment—undivided loyalty. "Would you like a cup?" she asked Joel, holding up the pot, allowing time to formulate her thoughts in a convincing way. This was the closest she'd come to having peace in the Mitchell household, and she clung to the notion.

They sat at the table. He declined a cup of tea as she

poured a little more into her cup, but he couldn't deny her request.

"Remember I told you Don came by earlier?" She sensed shakiness in her voice and perked up.

"Yes, but you didn't tell me what he wanted, or do I even need to ask?"

"Well," she said, turning away from him and concentrating on stirring the tea in front of her, "it seems like he wants to keep peace in the family. Unfortunately, I can't say the same for Madeline. She wasn't as pleasant."

"Mom, you have got to stop letting Madeline get to you."

"I don't care about Madeline. I'm more concerned about Don right now. He's accepting your father's decision. I believe he won't cause any problems so long as you let him continue running the East Coast operation."

"I won't interfere with him or the East Coast. Honestly, I'm relieved to have him running a major portion of the ministry. He can have the East Coast so long as he doesn't try to stab me in the back by doing something shady like Uncle Frank did to Dad."

Sherry had built up nerves and wasn't going to be derailed with a discussion about Frank. She'd blurt out her request and go from there. "How do you feel about Abigail working with Don? That's what he came over to ask me about earlier."

"Not possible."

"Why not, Joel? We've gotten the grand prize. Why not let Abigail be a peace offering to him? We can't completely destroy him." In her heart she had expected Madeline and Don to come after them like vicious animals, relentless, pounding and pounding until she and Joel were driven to the brink of insanity. Sherry peered into the cup filled with the dark liquid, stirring furiously.

"Mom, mom," Joel called out, prying her hand from the spoon.

"I'm sorry," she said, taking a long drink of tea. "What does it matter if Abigail goes to the East Coast with Don? You still have the entire staff of employees, the board of directors, and the consultants to support you. It will be better for all of us in the long run. We might not ever be a true family with Madeline and Don, but we can at least try to keep peace for the sake of your father. How about it?" she said, wrapping her hand around his tightly. "Please assign Abigail to the East Coast?"

"I can't say yes right now, and I won't say no," he said, lowering his gaze and sweeping his thumb across the table. "Not yet; I'll have to think about it."

"What's there to think about? We have to find a way to make peace with him, otherwise Madeline is coming after us."

"I'm not worried about Madeline."

"We have to be. She can be relentless," she said, resting her quivering hand on Joel's shoulder. "You don't know how cruel she can be when she feels violated." Sherry let her eyes falter. "I do."

Anything he could do to protect his mother from Don and Madeline, he was willing to do as long as it did not violate God and his father's request. "I can't make a major decision on a whim. I might not have experience, but if I've learned anything from Dad, it's how to seek God for guidance. But I have to tell you, Mom, letting Abigail go is a huge sacrifice."

"I'm sure, but she's the key to our future. Finally, I might be able to hold my head up and look Madeline and Don in the face," she said.

"Mom, Abigail has worked closely with Dad for five years. She knows the ins and outs of the ministry, maybe more than anyone else after Dad. Together she and Don could take over the ministry."

"You don't have to worry about Abigail plotting against the ministry with Don. She's always been loyal to your father."

"It's not her I'm worried about. Don's the one I don't trust. I think he might try to set me up if he's as mad about my appointment as I think he is. I have to be careful. That's what Dad said and that's what I'm doing."

"He's your brother, for goodness sake. Like it or not, that's the reality of the matter, and this is our chance to make matters better between us and them," she said, clutching his hand.

"We have the same last name and the same father, but Don has never really accepted me as his brother. We've never been a real family. We're not accepted as real people in this family, and pretending won't change that for us."

Joel had pried open the window of an issue she'd tried bolting shut countless times, but for some reason it kept flying open at will. "Is that what you really believe?" she let slip out.

He propped his arm on the table and let his face plop down into the cradle of his hand. "I don't know what I believe at the moment. Look, I need to meet with Abigail before she leaves for the afternoon." He embraced his mother and headed out. "I'll give this some thought, but I can't make any promises about Don. I'll have to call you later and let you know what I decide."

He wrapped his arms around her without saying a word. She believed everything was going to work out, and for once she'd gobble up a massive serving of contentment and family bliss within the walls of the Mitchell estate. She clutched Joel tighter, believing.

chapter

7

Sherry had to be avoided, and Joel, too. Don drove to the rear of the estate. The goal was to get in, meet with Abigail, and leave undetected. He hoped he could find her in the office alone. She was worth the risk. He picked at his keys until he discovered the right one. One forceful push and he was inside. "Don, you startled me coming through the side entrance," Abigail said.

"I'm surprised the key still works."

"That's right. I forgot that Dave gave you a key when he moved his office out here."

"It's one of the few things he's ever given me."

Abigail showed no reaction, which was just as well. The fewer people that forced him to rehash his defeat the better, especially the woman he most wanted to see him as strong and victorious, able to take care of them both.

"I didn't expect to see you this evening," she said, with a twinkle in her eyes that seemed to surface regardless of the situation. "I know your father will be glad to see you."

"I'm not here for my father," he said, letting his words flow without fear of rejection. "I'm here to see you." She stood stiff, without a response, and then turned to walk away. Don took a step toward her and gently touched her shoulder. "It's okay, really," he affirmed. "It's okay. You're okay," he said feeling her body relax. He nudged her around to face him. "You knew, didn't you?" Her gaze fell. "Of course you knew; my dad confides in you about every aspect of the business." He felt her tense again and pull from his touch. Unwilling to let her go, he placed his hand on her shoulder again. "Abigail, I mean it. You're okay with me. This wasn't your fault. I don't blame you." "I could never blame you" was what he wanted to say, but he held back, not wanting her to feel any more uncomfortable than she already did.

The warmth in her touch was soothing to his troubled heart. Maybe he should confess his love, right now, let her fall into his arms, and they could run away together, far from the clutches of the Mitchell dynasty, to build a real life, have a real family, a childhood dream that had yet to come true for him. He was on the verge of revealing his attraction, but opted at the last second to stay focused on DMI for now. Once he had Abigail working alongside him on the East Coast, there would be plenty of time to share his feelings.

"Are you sure you don't want to say hello to your father? He's been asking for you all day."

"I'm not here to ease his conscience."

"You have to understand his position. He did what he felt was best for the ministry and for your family."

"Not you, too. I know you don't believe that for a second," he said, withdrawing from her briefly. "He did what he's always done, taken every opportunity to give me and my mother the shaft in order to give his extra family the best of everything. I'm such a fool."

"No you're not. You're honest, and decent, with an incredible future."

He tried forcing his thoughts to move out of neutral and get past the day's events without much success. He could survive the shame and overwhelming sense of dejection if he could somehow fast-forward beyond today and whisk ahead ten years with Abigail.

"I honestly thought we were building a real father and son relationship. He sucked me in. I let my guard down and just like that, he pulls the company right out from under me. I could understand if he'd put you in charge because you've worked very closely with him, but instead my father puts his youngest child in the head spot. What an insult," he said, struggling to maintain control but not wanting to show his sincere hurt in front of the one who mattered. She was exactly the medicine he needed to recover from this fiasco. She didn't know it, but his life, his future depended on her faith in him. He had to go slow and not overwhelm her until the time was right.

"This isn't what you want to hear, but I know Dave loves you."

"My father is the last person on earth I want to talk about. He means nothing to me and it's obvious that I mean very little to him."

"He didn't base today's decision on his feelings for

you. That wouldn't be fair to you or to him. He did what he felt God told him to do."

Don didn't want to hear about God, not again. Every time Dave Mitchell got a revelation from God, Sherry and Joel were the ones who benefited. Each word could have driven him to the brink of anger, but anything coming from Abigail was palatable. He calmed. The battle with God and his father would keep until later. Before Abigail could continue, he jumped in and said, "Enough about my father, I'm here to see you."

"Me?"

"I want to make you an offer you can't refuse."

"I'm always up for a good deal."

"You've worked as my father's assistant for what, five years?"

"A little more than five years," she said.

"Don't you think it's time to take a lead role and step out on your own?"

"I have no interest in leaving this company. I love working for Dave. He sponsored me in the executive management program. I never would have gotten my MBA so quickly without his help and support. I owe him."

"I'm not asking you to leave the company, but if you stay in your current position as senior assistant, you won't be working for my father. You'll be working for Joel, who doesn't have a clue about what it takes to run this business and you know it."

"Don, you have to stop with the wisecracks."

"Okay," he repeated multiple times. "Come work for me," he blurted out. I have plans for the East Coast division that can only happen with you on my team. Together we make an unstoppable team," he said, reaching for her hand but pulling back at the first inkling of his emotions' being exposed prematurely.

"What would be my role?"

"Whatever you want it to be." He chuckled for the first time all day. "I'll make you vice president with the opportunity to run whatever part of the division you want."

chapter

8

———————◆———————

Joel approached his father's office not sure how to handle his mother's appeal. Maybe she was right—let Abigail go to the East Coast with Don and maybe, just maybe bring peace to the family for his mother's sake. He could do this for her. After all, he didn't feel good rubbing the situation in Don's face. Perhaps letting Abigail go was the first step toward getting what he longed to have, a family, a brother, or at least something close to one. He mulled over the request, eager to get his father's opinion. Joel reached the threshold of his father's office and heard the voices of Don and Abigail. He opted not to barge in. Giving Don his privacy wasn't much, but it was the only gesture Joel had in his power to give his brother. He waited outside the door.

"You have to say yes. This is your chance to establish

your own mark in the company. Let's face it, Joel doesn't have the maturity, or the integrity to lead this company."

"I'm not going there with you," Abigail said.

"Well, it's true and you know it. Joel is incapable of running DMI. He's not ready to lead this company and you know it, too."

"Your father wouldn't make a big mistake like that. We have to trust your father's decision. He wouldn't have made Joel CEO if he couldn't do the job."

"Forget about my father. This is about the two of us. If we play this right, the East Coast will be ours in less than a year, hopefully before little brother runs the rest of the company into bankruptcy. Nothing can stop the two of us," Don said, with a sting of overconfidence.

Joel had heard enough. "I can stop you," he said, barging into the room. Abigail stood speechless. Don, too.

"Joel," Abigail began to say, "it's not what you think."

"Don't worry, Abigail, you weren't doing the talking. My big brother was." He walked up to Don and stopped within a few inches of his brother. "Is there something you want to tell me?"

"Nothing at all," Don replied, holding his position. Joel could feel the heat from his brother's breath. "Everything that needed to be said was said earlier. As far as I'm concerned, I'll stay on the East Coast with Abigail, and you can have the rest of the world. I won't bother you and I hope you won't bother me."

"Well, big brother, I don't see this playing out that way," Joel said, also refusing to budge. "I want you out of this house."

"What?" He chuckled. "You have to be joking."

"I'm not."

Abigail tried to step between them but neither brother gave way.

"Who do you think you are, putting me out of this house? My mother built this house. Yours just moved in."

"You better leave her out of this. This is between me and you."

"Gentlemen, let's take a step back and get composed," Abigail said, stepping in.

"I don't need to get composed," Don bellowed, spitting his words like nails. "I don't care about this house. It means nothing to me, but the company is a different story. I'm not giving up the East Coast. That's mine and there's nothing you can do about it."

His father's words marched around Joel's thoughts. When it came to business, he guessed that family could be as foul as strangers, maybe worse. Joel couldn't knowingly let anyone set out to destroy his father's ministry. He was in charge and had to make tough decisions, beginning now. "Yes there is something that I can do."

"Oh, really, what?"

"You're fired."

"Right, fired," Don said, laughing openly. "Pulease."

Abigail tried to get a word in, but the tension and voices were raised too high for her to overcome.

"I mean it, you're fired."

Dad eased into the office, coming from his bedroom, amidst the fury. Joel wanted to stop the argument but the fury was too high.

"Who do you think you are, trying to fire me? I'm the one with the MBA and a legitimate right to this company. The gall of you, trying to fire me. Well, forget about it. I will be managing the East Coast division tomorrow morning like I have for the past seven years."

"Sons," Dad spoke. "Calm down. What's this business about getting fired?"

"You have some nerve, little boy," Don said, ignoring Dave's attempt to mediate.

"I'm out of here. Abigail, are you coming with me?"

"No, she's not," Joel answered.

"You can't speak for her," Don fired back.

"You're right, but I can speak for this ministry."

"Maybe, but you will never control me or my mother—never," Don said, and burst out of the room.

Dad called out for Don.

"Don, please, wait," Abigail cried out and ran after him.

Joel didn't budge.

"What happened?" Dad asked, clearly shaken by the outrage of his sons.

"Don was scheming to break up the ministry, so I fired him."

Dave stood on his cane, letting his gaze limp around the room.

"I didn't want to fire him, but what could I do? You've managed thousands of people. I trust your judgment. You told me to watch out for traitors, and not to be afraid to make tough decisions regardless of what other people think. I took your advice." He wasn't giving up anything to Don, not the house, not the company, and definitely not Abigail.

"He's your brother. Wasn't there any other way?" Dad said, barely loud enough to be heard.

"Dad, I know this isn't what you wanted to happen, but he had to go. If this ministry is going to succeed under my leadership, I have to cut out anything and anyone who is not here to support your vision," he said, hesitating, "and that includes family."

"Son, my heart is heavy with what I've witnessed between you and your brother. Don't give the enemy an opportunity to destroy our family or the ministry any further."

"Dad," Joel said, embracing his father, "I will make you proud, don't worry."

"I know you will," Dad said, turning to leave.

"Where are you going?"

"To see Don. I have to talk to him. He's heard from everyone but me. He's my son, and I have to explain to him why I did what I did."

"He's very angry. Shouldn't you wait until tomorrow?"

"Son, you will learn that it's better to meet tough conversations head-on. A strong leader is decisive today and accepts the consequences tomorrow."

"Do you think Don will listen to you?"

"I'm not going to see him as the former CEO of this ministry. I'm going to him as a father who loves his son and understands his pain. I'm not sure why God made this choice, but no matter what, Don is my son and I love him," Dad said, giving Joel a hug. Then he left.

Abigail came back into the room after Dad left. She was panting and her face was flushed. Joel knew the closeness Don and Abigail had developed from working together.

"I'm sorry that we put you in the middle of our argument. That was wrong, and I apologize," Joel said. The color in her face didn't go away.

"I wish there was something I could do to help Don. He feels awful, and I feel awful for him."

Joel was sensitive to her feelings and decided to let her talk, careful not to upset her more by adding his opinion. He needed her more than she knew if he was to have a smooth transition into the CEO role.

Back at home, Don stood in his living room staring out the window, looking but not seeing beyond his dilemma. He peered into the early evening autumn sky watching the sun dip behind the tiny clouds, appearing unable to maintain its rightful position in the forefront. Abigail was gone. She'd followed him in a gracious attempt to comfort him. Generally, her presence was sufficient to turn his cloudy days into sunny ones, but the blows he'd sustained from his father and Joel were too powerful even for Abigail's healing touch.

The sun rays finally succumbed to the resistance and faded behind the baby clouds, offering no warmth for his chilled heart. A little piece of the Mitchell dynasty would suffice, but he'd long ago given up wanting too much more from his father—then again, too much was a luxury he had never had. He fell against the drapes, letting himself sink into the fabric, hidden, obscure from the rest of the world. He imagined most windows on the thirty-fourth floor were exposed with no covering, open to the world. Not his; an air of decency and boundaries was his preference. The phone rang, drawing him back into the reality of his darkness. He didn't answer until the persistent caller rang two more times. The third time he answered, to find his mother on the other end.

"I was worried. I haven't heard from you all day," she said, garnering very little reaction from Don.

"I'm okay, Mother," he said, willfully lying to her. Why should she have to share in his pain? Hadn't she already borne enough of her own?

"Don, you're not all right. I can hear it in your voice. I'm coming over there right now and we're going to figure out a plan to straighten out this mess that your father, his prissy wife, and that illegitimate son of his have created. We may be down, son, but we're not out of the fight yet. As a matter of fact, I'm just getting started," she said.

"Mother, don't come over. I'm fine, really."

"Well, if you change your mind and want company, you know where to reach me."

"Mother," he shouted out right before she disconnected the call, "remember I love you, no matter what. I always have and always will, no matter what."

"Okay, now you're scaring me, I'm coming over there whether you want me to or not."

"Mother, don't bother, it will be too late," he said, uttering one more "I love you" and a good-bye.

chapter

9

Dave was as handsome today as he was the first time Sherry met him. His statuesque physique hadn't given in to his ailment. The man she met, became smitten with, and ultimately married was strong, honest, passionate, and loyal. Years of heartache, guilt, confusion, and loneliness couldn't erode the deep connection she felt to Dave Mitchell. There were moments of doubt, but all in all, sacrificing her dignity in exchange for being his wife was well worth it. Watching him approach, taking gingerly steps, she felt like nothing had changed. She rushed down the hallway to meet him. Joel was walking beside him.

"What are you doing out of bed?" she asked, latching on to his arm. "I didn't think today was such a good day for you." Many of his professional colleagues saw her

husband as a businessman who knew how to create success, but she knew the man, the heart behind the ministry—a person who felt, who loved, who cried, who lived
in a constant state of pleasing God. Everybody else came
second, even her, the one he'd committed to loving for a
lifetime. The joy of sleeping with her husband was no
more. She could have said it was due to his illness, that
he slept on the main floor to avoid the stairs. Truth was
she'd lost him to countless hours of nighttime prayer
and worshipping his beloved God long before the illness
claimed his strength. Daytime and nighttime belonged
to God, not her. She might have taken one percent of his
heart from Madeline but the reality was God owned 95
percent. Madeline and his children shared the other 4
percent. How could she have known coming in second
or third, behind God and Madeline in Dave's life, would
be more painful than living through an affair, or at least
she imagined that to be true. The closest she ever came
to experiencing infidelity was Madeline's constant intru-
sion. Either way, another woman or God—what was the
difference? Losing any of Dave's love and attention was
painful, regardless of who was on the other end. They
were her competition. That's why loving God and Dave's
first family was so difficult.

"Come and sit down," Sherry said.

"Oh, don't fuss over me. I'm fine, just fine."

"You don't look so good." Sherry encouraged him to
sit for a moment. His cancer, ironically, was restoring the
tattered bond she felt existed between them. Dave repeatedly tried to convince her that his love hadn't
changed, but the words never settled her churning soul.
Since the cancer, they'd become closer. She took solace
in bringing him a smidgen of comfort.

Dave leaned against the stainless Sub-Zero refrigerator, letting his slightly oversized golf shirt hang freely. Maybe he was a few pounds lighter, but he was still her beloved Dave.

For a split second, their eyes met and danced back to the beginning. Her soul warmed and galloped through her body, unbridled, resonating in her heart. Dave's legs buckled but he remained standing. Joel swooped in and allowed his dad to lean on his shoulder. At least one of the remaining Mitchell heirs cared about Dave. From an infant Joel had worshipped his dad and clung to his every step. She was the mother who carried him, but Joel was always his father's child, a reality Madeline seemed to take great joy in publicly and privately denouncing.

"Dad, why don't you take a seat?"

"Really, I'm fine. My legs just need a bit of exercise and stretching. A good run is what I need," he said, chuckling.

"Why don't we start with a nice short walk first?" Sherry said, leaning into his body.

"I need to see Don. He deserves to hear directly from me regarding Joel's appointment. I didn't want him to find out from anyone else."

"He'll be okay. He understands this was a business decision," Sherry said, feeling uneasy.

"But he's my son," Dave said, elevating his voice slightly. "He needs to hear from me."

The CEO decision was final, so visiting Don was no threat to Joel or to her. "I will drive you to meet him," she offered.

"No," he quickly responded. "I mean, why don't you stay here. You've had an emotional day, too. I've already called for the car. It should be here any minute."

She could have appealed. She could have demanded to drive him, to stay in his presence and not be cast aside in the sight of Madeline's son. Today of all days her anguish should have been contained, but it wasn't. What if Madeline was there with Don? What if she convinced Dave to change his mind and reinstate Don as head of the ministry? He was the eldest son. An even worse possibility snuck in. What if Madeline convinced him that she was his true love? Sherry pushed back the demons reminding her that she was a second-class wife, living in the shadow of Madeline. Twenty-five years of matrimony wasn't an automatic ticket to validation.

"Joel, please go with your dad. Make sure he gets there and back home safely."

"It's best that Joel not go. Most likely Don is angry, and Joel will be an easy target for his brother's misguided anger. I'm the one Don is mad at and I'm the one who has to face him," Dave said.

chapter

10

———————

Don let his 7 series BMW crawl out of the self-park garage and edge toward the exit as dusk whisked in. He stopped as the familiar chauffeur-driven car pulled into the valet, about a quarter of a block away. He watched his father get out at the front door of his building. Don took an extended look. His father was frail but no less the same Dave Mitchell that others revered and saw as a commanding leader from afar. From Don's vantage point, the view wasn't as appealing. Dave, Sherry, and Joel hadn't seen the last of him. If they wanted a fight for the company, that's what they would get. He had a few ideas about how to make them pay. Each one of them would one day feel what he and his mother had felt the moment Sherry met his father twenty-eight years ago—that was a promise. He whipped into traffic, leaving behind his condo and every other thing reminding him of the dismal past. Abigail and Mother weren't so easy to leave. He knew Madeline would worry and probably think the worst, since she'd already experienced suicide with his older brother Sam. Don wanted to spare her the agony but didn't have the strength to stay. One day, when he was established, he'd return prepared to reclaim what was rightfully his.

The convertible Bentley screeched into the valet. In a puff, Madeline was exiting the elevator, fumbling with a small platinum key box, the size of a business card holder. A couple of keys fell onto the floor without Madeline breaking her stride.

"What are you doing here?" she asked Dave, who was sitting in the hallway in a high-backed chair a few doors from Don's condo.

"I need to speak with Don."

Madeline continued fumbling, diverting minimal attention to Dave. Finally, she clutched the key she needed and shoved the box into her pocket. Missing the slot, the keys and the rest of the contents of the box spilled onto the floor.

"Let me get those for you," Dave said, picking the keys up and handing them to her, barely able to balance on his cane.

She hastily pushed and twisted the key. "Do you think I care about those keys? That's always been your problem. You're so easily distracted by the things that don't matter." The door popped open. "Don," Madeline called out, frantically going from room to room. She rushed to the bathroom but hesitated before entering, afraid of what she might find.

"Is he here?" Dave asked.

"Why are you asking me? I don't know."

Dave hobbled around calling out to his son.

The modest condo was spacious for a single man but no comparison to a mansion. There weren't many rooms to search, but Madeline refused to give up until there was a sign of Don somewhere. She peered into his closet. Nothing seemed to be missing, no huge glaring empty space. Where could he be? She ripped out of his bedroom and slammed into Dave. For a moment they stood face to face. Forty years of history flooded her thoughts, generating words sprinkled with compassion and equally doused with bitterness.

"Get out of my way. I have to find my son."

"He's not here, Madeline."

"Don't you think I can see that? I have to find him. I have to find my son," she said, resisting the swelling terror. "I can't bear losing another son. I can't do this." She was no longer able to hold back the flow of tears.

Dave pulled her into his embrace. She initially resisted, but gave in. She sobbed as they sat on the sofa.

"What have you done," she screamed, pulling away from Dave. She wanted to scream at the top of her lungs to purge the agonizing ache in her soul. She couldn't bear to think of her son injured, lying helpless somewhere without the benefit of knowing she was here for him, that she would never leave him or betray him. "What if he hurts himself?" She fell back into Dave's arms. "How can God continue to be so cruel?"

"The one element I know for certain is that God is not cruel. He's just."

"That's easy for you to say. You had two wives and two sets of children," she said, gaining strength. "But I lost my husband, my company, two sons, and my house."

"You didn't want the house."

"Whatever, I don't care about the house right now. I'm thinking about my family—the only thing that matters to me. Look at us. Our daughter doesn't have anything to do with any of us, because we didn't protect her. Now my last child is missing and possibly dead. How can you sit there and tell me that God is just? What kind of a just God would take everything away from me? I might have my own view on life, but I'm not such a bad person that I deserve all that's happened to me. Nobody does, not even your precious Sherry. Why should I have to suffer alone?"

"You're not suffering alone. I'm concerned about our son, too. That's why I'm here."

"Well, can't you do something? You and God always talk. He obviously likes you a whole lot better than He does me. So, can you get in touch with Him and ask Him to take care of Don? Personally, I really don't have much to say to God."

"All I can do is pray and ask God to protect our son."

"But you're the mighty Dave Mitchell. Don't you have more clout with God? You've always gotten everything you want. You're a special one, and right now, I don't care how or why you get so much favor from God. I'm asking you to use whatever favor you have to save our last son. Don is the last of our legacy together." Her anger wasn't far off, a constant load she carried, but right now her deep-seated affection for Dave wrestled her frustration to the ground and won out. "I need your help, Dave. I can't go through this alone. I will die."

"You're not alone, Madeline. You never have been," he said, drenched in gentleness.

"Don't get all soppy with me, old man. I'm not crazy. You're a married man and I'm long gone from your thoughts."

"I meant you and my children are important to me. I will always look out for you, but most important, God will always be with you."

She sprang to her feet. "You were doing fine until you brought Him into the discussion."

"Madeline, why are you so angry at God?"

"Why shouldn't I be? You left me and then if that wasn't enough torture, you gave our company away, the one I helped build, supposedly because God told you to." She extracted keys from her pocket. "You tell me, Dave, who should I blame, you or God?" She flew to the door. "I'll call you if and when I find our son."

"Madeline, wait," she heard Dave say as the door slammed. Waiting was exactly what she didn't plan to do.

chapter

11

—•—

Who was Dave's God? Surely she didn't have the same kind of relationship with Him as Dave did. What other reason could there be for yet again having her heart ripped out? Don was gone. She rolled from one side of the bed to the other. The clock, flanked by a land-line, cordless phone, cellular, and PDA, displayed one-forty-eight. Three nights and nothing, not a word from Don. She'd dialed his cellular and home phones so many times the message queues were full. Calling the police was too final. She couldn't make the fatal call. There had to be a shred of hope left. Her private detective had to find him. Don couldn't sever the last source of love she had flowing through her veins. Sam dead. Andre dead. Tamara estranged—same as dead. Don couldn't be dead, no way.

She desperately wanted to push past her anger and cry out to God, but couldn't budge the boulder sitting on top of her hurt and dejection. Madeline was convinced that God couldn't possibly care about her children. Where was God when sweet Tamara was violated? Where was God when Andre needed help or when Sam killed himself? She knew where Dave was. He was too busy playing house with Sherry. She didn't have an answer for God.

Heaviness would not let her find rest.

Two-fifty-five.

Three-thirty-eight.

Unable to manage the torment any longer, at five-ten Madeline decided to get dressed and go somewhere, do something, anything but continue chasing elusive sleep. She flung one foot onto the floor, followed by the other. The ringing tone had her dazed, not knowing which of the four phones to grab. She snatched up the cordless phone, sending the other phones crashing to the floor.

"Yes, hello," she said, out of breath, pulse racing, hands shaking, "Don, is that you?"

"It's me, Mother. I apologize for calling you so late."

"Oh, my goodness," she wailed, standing and sitting in rapid succession. "Where have you been? I've been out of my mind with worry. Are you safe?"

"I'm fine. I was confused and needed time to think, to clear my head."

"You had me worried sick. I thought you'd—" she said, and stopped before breathing life into her fears. "Well, it doesn't matter. Are you sure you're all right?"

"I am."

"Where are you, at home?"

"No, I hopped a flight to the Cape."

"As in Cape Town?"

"That's the one. I needed to get as far away as I could from Joel and my father."

"All the way to South Africa. Couldn't you go to Pennsylvania or Florida, somewhere on the East Coast?"

"The East Coast wasn't far enough away. I needed to put a few continents between us."

"When are you coming home? I want you here, near me, where I can see with my own eyes that you're all right. I refuse to lose you."

"Mother, you're not going to lose me. Besides, you have Tamara, too."

"I'm not talking about Tamara right now. The question is, When are you coming home?"

"Michigan isn't home anymore. I might come to the States in a few weeks to pack a few more things, then again maybe not."

"What are you going to do there that you can't do here?"

"Start my own business. I have a few ideas brewing, and I came here to tap a few investors."

"You don't have to start another company, not when you own one here. Don't worry, we're getting DMI back. Rest assured that I'm not letting this drop, not until your nameplate is on the CEO office of Dave Mitchell International. Come home, please, and we can fight Joel and the entire board of directors if we have to. Just come home," she pleaded, unashamed to let her emotions show with her son, the only person left whom she trusted.

"I love you, Mother, but I can't come back. There's no future for me with DMI. My father, God, and Joel have seen to it. So, the time has come for me to develop my own without my father's help or his money."

"The money is yours." Don's wealth was as much from her labor and sacrifice as it was from his father. That money belonged to him free and clear. "You're taking the money. I won't take no for an answer when it comes to your money."

"I'll call you in a few days, once I get settled and have more concrete plans."

"How can I reach you?"

"You can't," he said.

"Why not? What's wrong with your phone? I've called every number I have for you and couldn't get through on any of them."

"I left my phone in the car at the airport."

"Well, why did you do that?"

"I wanted a clean break, at least for now."

Silence hovered. She grappled with words. These were perhaps the most important words she had ever spoken in her life. Maybe she could convince him to come home, to not feel cast aside. She would fight his battle. But she couldn't form the words in time.

"Mother, don't worry about me. I love you and I'll be in touch. You're not getting rid of me quite so easily. I'll be fine, you'll see."

They exchanged good-byes and just like that, Madeline was alone, again. This time, she didn't have young children to raise, not like it was when Dave left to be with his mistress.

Her protective instinct overrode her frustration and grief. Don was coming home to claim his company. Determined to make Sherry suffer, Madeline decided to plot against Joel. Discrediting him was a good place to start, and she knew a few loyal workers who would be willing to help. By the time she was finished with him inside the walls of DMI, he wouldn't be able to run a newspaper route, let alone a billion-dollar organization. Madeline sashayed to her dressing room, invigorated by the smell of revenge.

Six-fifteen.

chapter

12

—————•—————

"Mandatory Staff Meeting—All Hands" flooded the interoffice internet, voice messages, bulletin boards, break rooms, and the old-fashioned employee mail slots. The big announcement was inevitable. Joel knew he had to stand before the people and inform them of his dad's decision. He also had to assure them that the ministry was stable—that their jobs weren't in jeopardy. The announcement was easy. Telling the organization Don had been fired by his own brother wasn't, especially since Don was well liked. Firing Uncle Frank this morning wasn't as difficult. According to Abigail, finance directors came and went when there was a change in the administration. His departure was easy to explain, especially with the rumors about his mismanaging funds. Dad kept saying God was supporting him in the

CEO position, which had to be true, otherwise Joel was in a boat taking on three gallons of water every second. Whether it would sink wasn't the question, only how fast.

Nearly five hundred employees squeezed into the special-event room—another five hundred dialed in by phone and internet. Chatter packed the room, sounding like a swarm of bees. His breathing was rapid, almost as rapid as his pulse. After Abigail gave a few introductions and a call to order, it was his turn. Joel slowly stepped toward the podium, organizing his words, comfortable in his polo shirt and khakis. He gripped the podium with sweaty palms. The words came almost as slowly as his steps, or at least that's how it felt.

"As some of you may have heard, Dave Mitchell has elected to step down from the CEO position and concentrate on his recovery." Pockets of chatter erupted. "I am the new CEO taking over for him." More chatter sprang up, like smoldering pockets of forest fires. The moment was slipping from his control. Madeline was right, he was too inexperienced. He had to step up and fill the role with boldness, had to. He was chosen to lead. Mustering a little confidence, he continued as Madeline bolted into the room, distracting attention from the podium. "As some of you may have heard, Don Mitchell has also stepped down from the East Coast operation."

Chatter turned into high-volume conversations. Joel was attempting to regain control when Madeline burst to the podium and began talking, loudly enough to be heard without the microphone. Joel eased away, letting her have control.

"Listen, everyone," she said, with conversations tapering, but not dying down completely, "may I have your attention." A gust of calm swept the room. "Please, I need your attention."

Joel stood helpless, behind Madeline.

"First of all, I know there is a great deal of rumor, questions, and confusion. I'm here to assure you that the company is not in jeopardy. There have been some changes in management that are difficult to understand," she said, cutting her glance at Joel long enough to slice right through him and then back to the audience. "I'm just as surprised as you probably are."

Concerned about how far Madeline would take her comments, Joel wanted to step forward and regain his position at the microphone.

"Nevertheless, we are a solid organization with steady growth. The East Coast operation is experiencing an expansion wave. Don lost his job, but so long as we all continue to perform at stellar levels, no one else is in jeopardy of being fired, I hope." She paused, with the last words hovering overhead. "I'll let your new leader answer your questions. I'm sure you have plenty for him—I do," she said, stepping from the podium amidst a flurry of laughter.

Joel stepped up, not sure how to react. Madeline was dangling him on a string, taking the podium and then tossing it back to him without warning.

Employees flooded the aisles waiting for their turns at the microphones placed around the room. Abigail came up front, which allowed him to breathe a sigh of relief. Madeline stood off to the side.

The first question came from the audience. "We understand that Frank Mitchell was fired today. Has a new finance director been appointed?" an employee asked.

Joel began to answer, but Madeline jumped in. "Typically, we don't release a person unless we've established a transition plan. I'm sure your newly appointed CEO is eager to share his plan with you," she said.

Joel was speechless. In his zealous effort to follow his father's instructions, he'd fired Uncle Frank without the slightest notion of who would be the new director. His shortsightedness was exposed. His mother was right. Madeline was a serious threat, not to be ignored.

Questions continued, rapid-fire, most of which he couldn't answer. It wasn't long before the employees began to present questions directly to Madeline and Abigail, rendering him ineffective. He retreated, out of the way, wondering if his father was right this time.

An hour and fifteen minutes later, the meeting was over, and not soon enough for Joel. "What a disaster," Joel whispered to Abigail, "a total disaster."

"Don't worry. You did fine for your first all-hands meeting."

"That's why I need you here with me." He could see why Don wanted her to work with him on the East Coast. There was a special quality about Abigail that was hard to describe. When it came to business, she knew how to talk with the people. That's what he needed, better people skills, and much more knowledge about the business. "I'm glad to have you on my team."

Today hadn't gone as well as Joel wanted. He couldn't exit the room without swarms of employees holding him captive. Random questions were still flying at him. He hoped Abigail would stay with him and divert as many questions as she could. She took her jacket off and laid it across the back of a chair. Joel breathed another sigh of relief. She was staying by his side.

*   *   *

Madeline stood near the door, personally greeting employees as they left. Despite her feelings for Joel, Sherry, and at times even Dave, she wasn't about to let forty years of sacrifice and investment in DMI be ruined. Madeline glided into the hallway. Stripping Joel would be easier than she had thought. She sailed along. The CEO position was theirs—hers and Don's. Once she reached her office, she packed up for the day and headed out. There was someone she desperately needed to see.

The last group of employees filed out of the room, leaving Abigail exhausted. "Shew, what a day," she said, collapsing into a chair near the back of the room. "What a tough crowd."

Joel sighed and took a seat, turning around to face Abigail. "I had no idea the questions would be so hard. I don't know if I can handle this job. I don't think I'm ready."

"That's not true."

"I don't mind admitting this is too much for me. Maybe Don should have been the one selected to be CEO."

Her focus drifted off. Butterflies danced on her insides as she wondered where Don was and how he was doing. She had cherished their friendship over the past five years. They'd spent countless hours developing the business plan for his East Coast expansion project. Many times she'd gotten his help with financial projections and explanations on various status reports. His cell phone number was on her speed dial. For the past few days, her attempts to contact him had failed, but he would be in her prayers until she was sure he was safe, wherever he was.

"Did you hear me?" Joel said.

"What?" she responded, shaken back into the conversation.

"Oh, no, you were daydreaming. Please don't tell me I bore you, too," Joel said, chuckling. "I can't believe it. The only friend I had the entire day, and I've managed to put you to sleep." He chuckled some more. "I have to give this job back to my dad."

"No you will not, Joel Mitchell," she said with a sort of force that startled her. "Don't give up so quickly. You can run this ministry. I know you can."

"How can you be sure?"

"Because your father knows his business. He is a good judge of character. If your father says you're the CEO, then by golly you're going to be CEO and I'm going to help you." Joel let his head dip down and rubbed the palms of his hands back and forth along his cheeks without responding. She grabbed his hand and said, "You can do this. I have total faith in you."

His gaze lifted to meet hers. "I'm probably crazy and may regret this later, but for some reason I'm thinking that maybe I can be CEO—that is, if you're with me." This time he caressed her hand.

"I'll be with you all the way," she said, feeling inspired by his touch, unexpected but welcome.

Joel took a quick glance at his watch. "Hey, why don't we grab a late lunch. I'm hungry and I could definitely use a break from this place."

Abigail said yes before the invitation was fully extended. Joel was young, three years younger, but there was a charisma, a characteristic about him that was difficult to describe but easy to feel. It was common knowledge that he made quite an impression on women.

Despite his budding reputation, she was alive in his presence, excited, inspired, and eager to take on the challenges of DMI. If his tenure was to be anything like his father's, then Joel was in for a lot of battles, but between the two of them, DMI was going to be in good hands. She was sure of it as they left the room together.

chapter

13

Madeline parked her car in the circular drive directly in front of the solid twelve-foot-tall double doors, the ones she had had flown in from Spain when the house was constructed. She could have driven around the rear of the estate and gone directly to Dave's office but chose not to bypass the likely amusement associated with going in the front door. She knocked, letting a smirk show. "Oh," Sherry said, releasing the doorknob and turning to walk away, "you. Can you please drive around back to his office from now on?"

"I'm not going through the back door. I'm not your servant. I'm here to see Dave. It's business."

"What kind of business?" Sherry asked, determined not to be disconnected because of her limited aptitude and interest in DMI.

"Nothing you or Joel would understand," Madeline said, as if she were the boss, and attempted to brush past. Sherry pushed back. Madeline froze. "What's your problem?"

"I'm not going to stand by and let you berate my son anymore, not the way I've let you treat me for so long."

"A bit juvenile, don't you think," Madeline said, and kept going.

Sherry ran ahead, forcing Madeline to halt. "Anybody who comes to see Dave about work is respectful and goes directly to his office entrance. Why did you insist on coming through this door?"

"Because I can," she said without blinking. "Now, may I please be excused so I can take care of DMI business?" Sherry stepped aside and let her pass. "Someone has to take control and keep the company out of bankruptcy."

"Nothing ever changes with you, always the same nasty, condescending attitude."

"Sherry, get your head out of the clouds. This is the real world. You expect me to be nice to you. Why? You tell me, how many women befriend their ex-husbands' mistresses? You got pregnant by my husband while we were still married, and don't give me that story about him not being happy. Whether he was happy or not, he was married to me when you met and seduced him. Don't expect me to be your friend. There are only two items we have in common. DMI is the first." Madeline approached Dave's office door.

"And what's the other one?" Sherry asked.

"You know," she said, giving one knock and opening the door in a single motion.

* * *

Inside, Dave sat behind the desk perusing what looked like the *Detroit Free Press* from Madeline's line of view. There were times when she valued Dave as her best ally, loyal and strong-willed. He could also be her worst opponent, relentless and tough, but she wasn't backing down, not when the stakes were as high as they were.

"Madeline, I wasn't expecting you. How did the employee meeting go?"

"Not very well, Sherry's son was a disaster. He fired Frank without a replacement."

"I should have gotten rid of Frank last year."

"The man has been on his way out for some time, but did today have to be the day? Why couldn't he wait a little longer? Reckless changes in management won't look good with the staff. Your son's timing wasn't wise, and you know it. I'm telling you he's a disaster. He couldn't answer questions, couldn't deliver a simple speech, and most certainly didn't boost morale. As a matter of fact, he caused more damage. He was simply out of his element right down to the polo shirt and pair of khakis."

"Clothes don't make the man," Dave said.

"Apparently not, because those clothes didn't help him much."

"Give him a little time. He'll be just fine. You'll see."

"Time is what we don't have. Revenue is up, but we have to implement an aggressive business plan next year in order to realize a return on our marketing and operations investments. We can't become slack now that the business is growing at a solid 10 percent each year."

"DMI isn't in jeopardy just because Joel is in charge."

"You're in denial. We need leadership, not a CEO in training. I won't stand by and watch the company I helped build fall apart. I'll have to take on a more active role. My first priority is to meet with Human Resources tomorrow and orchestrate a retention plan, which is going to cost us. We have to proactively attack the morale issue head-on. Otherwise we're at risk of half our staff walking out due to this feeling of uncertainty. Your stunt is going to cost us."

"I'm surprised. I thought you wanted to pull back."

"You give me no choice. Both of us can't quit at the same time. Who will be left to carry forth the vision, the one you had for the company in the beginning?"

"You worry too much," Dave said.

"If you saw him today, you'd be worried, too."

"I'm not worried at all about the ministry. My concern is with my son."

"Joel is so spoiled. Why worry about him? He always gets what he wants."

"Not Joel, I meant Don."

"Oh, you remembered your other son. Now there's a shock."

"Come on, Madeline, we're doing well today. Let's not deviate."

"Okay, okay, but it's a fair statement."

"I need to talk with Don. I've been grieved ever since he left without giving me an opportunity to tell him why I did what I did. I can't have my son believing devilish lies. He needs to know how much I love him, that I didn't rob him of the CEO position."

"Save your breath. He's not going to believe you. You mentored him for ten years and then gave the job away right under his nose. He's terribly hurt and feels betrayed."

"What else could I do? God comes first."

"That's your choice, but why do we always get left

out?" Madeline asked. "Think about that old Porsche of yours. Don knew how special that car was to you, which is why I think he wanted it. He wants anything that puts him closer to you, but instead of giving him the Porsche, you gave it to Joel. Joel kept the car for a few years and got rid of it, that's how little it meant to him."

"Come on, Madeline, I had no idea Don wanted the car. I would have gladly given the Porsche to him."

"Would you? What if both Joel and Don wanted the same car from you; who'd get left out?"

"You know, Madeline, I was once a young man and now I'm old, but I've never seen the righteous forsaken or the children of God begging for anything. I love both of my sons, and I've provided for both of them. I'm their father regardless of the many mistakes that I've made."

"You can say that again."

"By the grace of God, my conscience is clear in spite of my mountain of mistakes. His forgiveness has allowed me to live a full life. The only regret I have is not being able to do more for the Lord with this life that He has entrusted to me."

"If you're as wise as I think you are, you should be regretting your business decision by now."

"Why? I'm confident God will see DMI through the challenges under Joel's leadership, so long as he gets the kind of support he needs. As a vested owner in DMI I'm asking you to help Joel with the transition."

"Huh, don't think so. I'm not going to insult Don any further by training his rival."

"They're brothers, not rivals."

"Honestly, Dave, Sherry and I are rivals. You can't expect our sons to be friendly, let alone real brothers. Your expectation borders on delusional."

"If you can't help Joel, can you at least tell Don to

call me? It's urgent that I speak with him. I'm not feeling so great these days."

"Old man, nothing is seriously wrong with you. We expect you to live forever."

"I've been blessed with seventy full years. I could make eighty if my body holds out, but it doesn't look like it will."

"As much time as you spend praying, I know you have at least another hundred years to live. You're bound to outlive all of us."

"My time will come once I've fulfilled my purpose. I've gotten DMI up and running. We've assisted thousands of churches and ministries over the years. My labor was not in vain. Joel will have to carry out the rest of the vision for me by building a library in honor of the Lord and expanding internationally," he said as his voice dipped. "I've done my duty and now my responsibilities are over. Being a father is the last role I have to fulfill. Please tell me how I can contact Don."

"I can't. He's in South Africa. That's all I know."

"But you've been in contact with him."

"He called once."

"When?" Dave asked, with spunk and strength in his voice.

"Last night, but I'm hoping he'll call again soon."

"Madeline," Dave said, leaning against the desk. "You must have him call me. He must," he pleaded.

"There's no guarantee he'll want to speak with you."

"Madeline, as a favor to me, will you encourage him to call me, please."

She stood to leave. "I'll let him know you need to talk with him, but that's the best I can do. You can't expect me to mend your relationship in a ten-minute phone call. You've hurt him over and over. Every time Sherry and Joel win he loses. I can take whatever you throw at me, but he's your son. He never felt like he was until you began mentoring him. You have no idea how proud he was to work for you and to be trained by the man he considered to be the best. Then to be cast aside like a bag of garbage is more than he could bear. It's almost more than I can bear for him." She went to the door leading outside, this time not interested in needling Sherry on the way out. Once was plenty. No sense being greedy.

chapter

14

Madeline sat in her office contemplating ways to oust Joel. Nothing of interest had materialized, but in time she'd have a plan. The phone rang. The odd series of numbers on the display were similar to those on her phone the last time Don called. She grabbed the phone before the second ring completed. "Don," Madeline shouted, allowing her joy to rise and overtake her reservations hearing his voice on the other end. "I'm so glad you called. I've been jumping out of my seat every time the phone rings. I can't believe you've been gone over a week. When are you coming home?"

"Not sure, Mother. I'm not thinking long term, I'm taking a day at a time, and we'll see how it goes," Don told her.

"We need you. DMI needs you. I need you. This situation is very serious. Unless I keep taking charge, that child is going to run our business into the ground. A few weeks ago he was a junior analyst. His incompetence at meeting after meeting is confirmation that your father made a mistake."

"What happened?"

"I'm positive you don't have enough time to hear the gory details of Joel's inability to lead a Boy Scout troop, let alone a billion-dollar company. I actually think your father is senile. It's the only explanation for such craziness. But don't you worry. I will have DMI under your control in no time, and if Joel continues to perform as he has, they'll beg you to come back to save the company and restore employee morale."

"Is it that bad?"

"Worse. There are rumblings among the staff. I'm concerned about walk-outs. Profits are up for the year thanks to your East Coast expansion efforts, but we can't shoulder a massive exodus or pay out a slew of retention packages to keep the best employees on staff."

"At least they have you on board. You know what to do."

"Sure, but do I want to?" she said.

"Come on. You love DMI. You're never going to retire. That's why you've put up with so much for so long. I know your heart is there, and it's okay."

"Correction, my heart is with you and Tamara."

"Well, my vote is for you to stay with DMI, and don't worry about me."

"How can I not? You're halfway around the world and you tell me not to worry. Forget it, I'm your mother. I'm supposed to worry about you."

"I'm investigating a potential start-up opportunity. I'm meeting with an investor from London tomorrow.

I'll meet with the South African investor in a few days and with his colleague from Nigeria next week. If all goes well, I'll move somewhere between South Africa and the U.K. I could probably use some prayers from somebody since I'm not talking too much to God these days."

"I'm definitely not the best person to send up a prayer for you. Better get Abigail, because God and I haven't seen eye to eye since your sister left. Besides, I'm not asking God to move you across the Atlantic Ocean. Your place is in Detroit working with me to get our company back. Then, if you want to move to the other side of the earth, so be it. You can go with my blessings, but not before this mess is cleaned up and Sherry's son is out on his heinie."

"Mother, you have to move on. I have."

"I won't rest until Joel voluntarily resigns or I force him out. Honestly, how he leaves makes no difference to me, so long as he gets out without causing irreparable damage." She reared back in the chair. "I still believe your dad has lost his mind, I really do. He's made countless mistakes in his personal life, but when it comes to business, he's usually better than this. He doesn't make such mistakes, at least not until now."

"How is he doing?" Don asked.

"That old man is fine. Don't you worry about him, he's not going anywhere. He's as strong as an ox and as stubborn as one, too. You know how he can be once he makes a decision."

"The more reason for you to leave Joel alone."

"Never, and I want your father to be around when Joel gets kicked out on his heinie. Oh, that reminds me, your father wants you to call him. He's very eager to speak with you," she said, twiddling a few loose paper-clips on her desk.

"I'm not ready to talk to him."

"I understand, and he should, too. Is there a message you want me to give him?"

There was a pause and then he replied. "No, not yet, maybe in a few weeks or so I'll give him a call, but I can't make him any promises," he said, his voice fading out with every other word.

She was saddened not being able to help him. "I'll tell him. When will I hear from you again?"

"Not sure, but I'll be in touch."

"Call me any time, day or night. I mean it, any time," she told him.

Don was quiet for a moment and then he said, "How's Abigail?"

"Fine, as far as I know. Of course she's working her fingers off to help the new CEO figure out how to lead. You can imagine how swamped she is, poor thing," Madeline told Don, spinning around in her seat to look out the window.

"Tell Abigail I asked about her."

They exchanged "I love you" and ended the call. Madeline pressed the receiver as close to her heart as she could without cracking her ribs. Don was worth the fight.

chapter

15

Abigail found herself spending more and more time in Joel's office. She walked through the publicity plan for the third time. "I'm not as familiar with this as Don and Madeline are," she said, hesitating.

Joel must have picked up on the awkwardness. "It's okay if you talk about Don. I know he's a close friend."

She missed Don terribly.

"Have you spoken to him?" Joel asked.

"I haven't, but I'm hoping to hear from him soon. He's probably mad at all of us."

"You mean he's mad at me and Dad." Joel flipped through the publicity plan. "Maybe one day he will get over this."

"One can hope, but I wouldn't count on it any time soon," she said.

"Well, if you do speak with Don, let him know that I said hello." His gaze dipped. "Then again, you better not mention my name. There's no need for you to ruin your relationship with him because of me."

She prayed that one day Don and Joel could resolve their issues and at least become civil. Being sandwiched between the love of a dear friend and loyalty to her boss was miserable. She was sure a change would come in time.

Joel's cell phone buzzed on top of his desk, but he didn't move to get it. "Aren't you going to answer your phone?"

He shot a grin at her. "No I'm not. It's not important."

Joel often had personal calls coming in and she could tell by his tone that they were women, but she never inquired and he never volunteered information. This time she was curious and wanted to find out more. "How do you know?" she asked.

"It's probably the lady who helped me pick out a few new suits."

"You mean a personal shopper?"

He threw another suave cover-page smile at her and said, "Something like that."

She didn't know how to take his comment, not sure just how serious he was. "Your girlfriend might not like being ignored."

"That's why I don't have a girlfriend, just friends and acquaintances." She didn't go any further. Joel plopped the publicity document onto his conference table. "It's six-thirty. Should we grab dinner?" he asked.

Abigail was becoming accustomed to the two-week-old routine. She'd get into the office around seven to tackle her workload. The only other cars in the parking lot belonged to Joel and Madeline. By 3:00 P.M. she was in Joel's office, briefing him, reviewing documents, digging into reports, and helping him become familiar with the executive components of the organization. Between six and seven they'd go to dinner or have food delivered to the office. By ten-thirty she was home with no more than an hour of work to do. Weekdays and Saturday looked the same. Joel was committed to learning the business. His passion showed and sparked her enthusiasm, giving her energy at times when she should have been exhausted.

"We better eat in tonight," she said, laying her hands on top of the stack of reports. "We have the executive team meeting tomorrow, and there's much more to cover. I still have to fold the Southern division numbers into the consolidated report."

"We'll be all right. I want to get you out of here and get some fresh air," he told her.

"Don't worry about me. I'm okay," she said, unsuccessfully suppressing a yawn.

"See, that's what I'm talking about. I'm getting you out of here. You need a break. We can zip downtown and come right back. I'm willing to stay up all night if I have to, but you, Miss Abigail, are going home."

"Oh, no, I'm not," she said, clinging to the reports.

"No argument. After dinner you're going home. I'll have to be on my own." Before she could respond he said, "Decision made. We're out of here, especially you."

Abigail didn't feel comfortable leaving with so much preparation left to do. "Are you sure?" she said, staring at the stack of work.

"Positive. You need a break. Let's go," he said, getting to his feet and reaching for her hand. Against her better judgment she took his hand and left.

chapter

16

———— ◆ ————

The air was thick, the room frigid. Madeline refused to let her disposition warm. She tapped her Mont Blanc pen rapidly against the mahogany table. Poking pins under her fingernails seemed more tolerable than listening to Joel rant on and on about nothing. She looked around the room wondering who was going to step up and shut him down. She waited and waited, until she was unable to go a second longer. "Excuse me," she said, thumbing through the stack of papers. "We have a full agenda and cannot afford to linger on one topic. We need to move on."

"I only have a few comments regarding the upcoming publicity campaign," Joel interjected.

"You've had thirty minutes to talk about one item on the agenda. I have an entire division to run. I can't spend half the day sitting in a management meeting." She laid her reading glasses on the table.

"Madeline has a valid point," one of the other attendees said. "Can you sum up the key points surrounding the publicity campaign?"

Joel fumbled through his notes.

Madeline seized the opportunity, unwilling to let Joel fumble indefinitely. "We have to remember our core audience and hit the print, TV, and radio hard during the second quarter in order to promote the leadership conference. We have to generate the level of interest needed to sustain the projected participation," she interjected.

Joel sat quiet, still searching his notes.

"We'll need to work on the TV spots, but overall I think the proposed budget is solid," Madeline added.

"Any other thoughts or questions?" Abigail asked.

"Do you have anything else to add?" Madeline directed to Joel.

Joel resorted to scouring his notes, unable to offer any meaningful input, just as Madeline expected. She reveled in the image of his humiliation in meeting after meeting. With a few more performances like the one today, the staff would beg for Joel's resignation, leaving the door open for Don. Her disposition began to warm as she thought about Don returning home to DMI where he belonged.

"Let's move on to item number two on the agenda, an update on the East Coast operation," Madeline strongly suggested, sensing Joel's embarrassment without looking at him for confirmation. The mere possibility was sufficiently satisfying.

"Don Mitchell is up next," Abigail said. A blanket of silence covered the room. "Oh, my apologies, the agenda wasn't updated."

Seeing her son's name on the agenda with his seat empty chilled her all over again. The word "fired" played repeatedly in her mind, like an old, scratched 45 record stuck on the irritating part of a song. The past two weeks had been two of the longest in her life.

"Joel, I guess you'll need to give the update," Abigail said.

He hesitated and then said, "Give me a minute to read the status report."

"No need," Madeline asserted, "I've been running the East Coast operation. I can give the update."

"Joel, any objections?" Abigail asked.

He raised his glance to meet Madeline's and let it quickly drop back to the table.

Without taking a single peek at the stack of papers before her, Madeline rattled off the East Coast status report as if she'd run the division for years instead of being remotely involved for a few weeks. Becoming CEO wasn't supposed to be easy. Joel knew that much. He wasn't as experienced as his father, but today couldn't happen again, not if he was going to make his father and Abigail proud. Madeline continued with extreme confidence, drilling him further into the ground with each word. Not again. He would commit entirely to the CEO role, no more distractions. His female friends and acquaintances would be no more. His time and interests would be contained 100 percent within the walls of DMI, no exceptions. A fresh start would work. He made a mental note to change his cell and personal phone numbers. The only women getting his new numbers were his mother, Abigail, and his administrative assistant. Maybe he'd even get rid of his latest sports car. After all, that was a spark that seemed to ignite women's relentless pursuit of him.

Abigail slid a note across the table. Joel opened the full sheet of paper, which was folded into quarters, and read, "I apologize for not prepping you for this meeting. Let's meet later. I'll get you up to speed on the East Coast operations, no matter how long it takes. I'm yours for the entire evening. We can work as late as you need. Don't worry."

He slid the note into a pants pocket. She was a huge help, but Abigail couldn't carry him into every meeting. He had to find more. Dad's words resonated. "If God calls you to do a job, then rest assured that He'll equip you." He yearned for wisdom. Above all he needed knowledge to run this ministry, the kind that only God could provide. The meeting continued, but for Joel, praying silently to God for wisdom was his top priority.

chapter

17

Madeline wasn't opposed to seeing Dave, which was why she had agreed to his urgent request for a meeting, but he had to know she wasn't happy. The distance between them hadn't diminished her discontent. What could he possibly say that would extinguish the raging fire burning inside her? When her personal secretary entered, Madeline laid a stack of contracts on the desk and peered over the gold-trimmed glasses resting on her nose.

"Mr. Mitchell is here to see you."

"Let him in," Madeline said, without bothering to rise.

Dave entered, with Abigail following. Madeline resumed her review of the contracts with a brief pause to properly greet Abigail. Directing her glance back to the stack of papers, she said, "What do you want, Dave? I'm busy trying to keep an organization running that you've thrown to the wolves."

Dave and Abigail took seats facing the desk. "Have you heard from Don?"

"Of course I have," she said, letting each word force its way through her clenched teeth. "Who else is he going to call? He doesn't have anyone else."

"He has me," Abigail said.

"Of course, dear, I'm sorry. I didn't mean to exclude you from Don's tiny circle. You've been a good friend to him, and I'm grateful. He needs every ounce of support he can get from the two of us."

"I will always be his father," Dave said, with a ring of sincerity that Madeline didn't want to hear.

"I guess you will be. There's nothing the poor man can do about that," Madeline said, avoiding eye contact with Dave.

"Did you ask him to call me?" Dave asked.

"Sure did, but you can't expect me to beg my son to call the man who has humiliated him. Because you are his father, his pain is worse."

"Madeline, I'm not here to fight with you."

"Then why are you here, Dave?" she asked, dropping the papers and snatching off her reading glasses. She glanced toward Abigail and said, "I'm sorry, Abigail, Dave put you in the middle of this, so I apologize ahead of time if you hear some not-so-nice things. I'm giving fair warning."

"It's okay, Madeline. I'm here for one reason, to make sure Don is okay and to see how I can help ease his transition."

"Transition is a nice way to put it, but the bottom line is that he was fired two weeks ago from his own company, one he should be running," she spewed, letting her outrage flow.

"I didn't want Don fired. I'm very disappointed in the way this has turned out, and I need to talk with him," Dave said.

"Why? What do you have to tell him that's so important? Are you making him CEO?"

"Madeline, you know that's already settled."

"Okay then, are you at least giving him his job back, since your CEO fired him?"

Dave hesitated before answering. Madeline flung her pen onto the desk and moved to the edge of her seat. "Are you here to give him his division back—yes or no?"

"I can't give him the division back."

"Why not? It's your name on the company. Dave Mitchell International is DMI. You are DMI. What you say goes."

"Joel is the CEO now and I won't undercut his authority."

"Then we have nothing to discuss."

"Can you get Don on the phone? I want to let my son know how much I care about him."

"Well, I'm not betraying his confidence. Besides, he doesn't want to talk to you," she said, arching her eyebrows and fiddling with papers on the desk.

"I'm his father. I want to call him anyway."

"I can tell you that he's alive and trying to reconstruct his life yet again because of another one of your reckless decisions. Leave him alone and let him enjoy what small peace he's managed to find out of this mess. Leave him alone," she said.

"I'd like to hear from him, too," Abigail chimed in. "Let him know I'm concerned about him and want to help in whatever way I can. He's my friend."

"Honestly, I can't reach him myself," Madeline said, completely softening with Abigail. "When he calls me, hopefully in a few days, I'll let him know you both want to speak with him. If he wants to, he'll call you. Now, if you can excuse me, I have a staff meeting," she said, standing. "Abigail, I hope he does call you. Dave," she said walking toward the door, "I wouldn't hold my breath waiting on that call. Besides, what do you need from Don, you have Joel?" After they left her office, Madeline reflected on Don. She wasn't sure if he was beyond the point of tolerance, but she was. With the help of a few loyal workers, she would make sure that Dave Mitchell would regret the day he chose his youngest child to run the organization. She would make sure that the family's humiliation would be shared with Joel and Sherry.

chapter

18

Brisk air whisked in as Don stood near the cliff's edge overlooking the Atlantic, or was it the Indian Ocean? No one really knew where the oceans crossed. Many speculated and claimed to know, on the basis of water temperature, fish, and salt content, but in reality, no one knew the precise point. For the most part the vast bodies of water didn't coexist in the world, except for this one obscure place on earth that was shared. Was there a precise moment when Dave Mitchell had deemed him the lesser son? At what point did Joel become the chosen one? He could speculate and claim to know on the basis of when his father moved out or when he gave Joel the company, but really, he couldn't pinpoint an exact time. He meandered along the rock-lined path. Just like the oceans, he and Joel didn't need to coexist.

The small piece of DNA they shared would not cripple him for the rest of his life. Living was worthwhile, and he planned to do a great deal of it.

He strolled back to the Two Oceans Restaurant on the Cape, an hour early for his meeting with the Nigerian investor.

The waiter approached, and for the first time in over two weeks, Don was hungry, but there was a matter he had to tend to before eating. "Excuse me, sir, but do you have a phone I can use?"

"Sorry?" the waiter asked with a British accent.

"Do you have a pay phone I can use? I need to call the States." The perplexed look on the waiter's face was not the answer Don wanted. "Any phone; I'm willing to pay as much as you want," he said, laying his metallic black credit card on the table. Before the waiter could respond, Don flipped through his wallet, pulling out rand after rand, sprawling bills on the table. "Any phone," he said, trying not to seem overly excited.

"Sir, we have a tele' in the kitchen that you can use if this is an emergency."

"Yes, this is definitely an emergency. I have to share something very important with someone." Abigail had to know how he felt. There was no reason to wait any longer. There was never going to be a perfect time. The future wasn't definite.

"Go right over there, straightaway," the waiter said, pointing toward the rear of the restaurant.

Don plucked his credit card from the table but left the rands. Money wasn't important. He had grown up with lots of it and wasn't any happier. There was no replacement for true love. He hustled toward the kitchen, converting the 3:00 P.M. South African time to Michigan time. His adrenaline was charged, flowing, rushing so fast he couldn't convert the time, not really. It was somewhere around seven or eight in the morning back in Michigan—close enough. There was already an ocean between them; a few time zones weren't going to stop him now. He'd already allowed too much time to pass.

The door flung open, narrowly missing Don. He scooted around the waitress and made his way into the kitchen, bent on finding the phone, at any cost.

He placed one incomplete call after another, growing increasingly more anxious with each. Finally, after several attempts and with the help of at least three people over a twenty-minute period, the phone was ringing in rapid sequence. Exhilaration subsided after the third sequence. Not voice mail, not today, not now. He immediately began crafting a backup plan. He'd pick up a cell phone when he got back to Cape Town.

"Hello," he heard on the other end of the line, words of joy to his soul.

He wanted to burst through the phone and cry out with his love for her, but the words couldn't catch up with his intentions.

"Hello," Abigail said again, "is anyone there?"

"Hello, hello, I'm here. It's me, Don."

"Don, oh, my goodness, I'm so glad to hear from you," she screamed into his ear.

He could also hear rumbling in the background, but he wasn't deterred by the noise. A jackhammer pounding in the background wouldn't have lessened his enthusiasm. She was the focus of his desire.

"Where are you, when are you coming home?" she asked, tossing out question after question, not allowing him a chance to speak.

He could tell her excitement was as pure as his, another confirmation that she was the one for him. "Hang on with the questions," he said, squishing in close to the kitchen wall, trying, unsuccessfully most of the time, to stay out of the staff's way. "I'm in South Africa working on a start-up venture."

"Really. Why so far away?"

"We can talk about my reasons later. Listen," he said, drawing close to the receiver and plugging the other ear in an attempt to block out the kitchen noise, "I can't talk long, but there's something very important I want to tell you."

"Don, excuse me for one moment?"

Don could hear a muffled conversation and a ruffling sound in the phone. "Is everything all right?" he asked.

More ruffling was heard before Abigail said, "Perfectly fine." There was a pause and then she continued, "I'm a little tired. I was burning the midnight oil working with Joel last night." She paused again, probably not feeling as awkward as he did. He wanted to hear her melodious voice on the line and not a word about Joel but wouldn't tell her so. She continued talking and said, "Joel just picked me up and we're heading into the office—there's a lot more work to do. We miss you," she said. "Joel and I don't understand your division like you. Your mother does, thank goodness. She's been doing most of the work."

Don's hearty dose of hope oozed out, rendering him stiff against the kitchen wall. "Joel, huh," were the only words that formulated. He wanted to say more, probably should have said more, but couldn't speak. DMI was a loss he could live with quite comfortably, actually. Living without Abigail wasn't an option. He loved her and she had to know. The depth of his love was about to pour out, but the image of Joel sitting next to her as he confessed his feelings was like a punch to the gut.

"I'm so glad you called. I've been worried sick about you. Your mom told me you were fine but she didn't give any details."

"I asked her not to tell anyone where I was."

"Do you have a phone number, where can I reach you?" she said, with more ruffling in the phone followed by a muffled conversation.

"Are you still there?" he asked, starting to feel too awkward in the kitchen.

"I'm sorry. We have a management team update later this morning. Joel and I were prepping."

"Well, I see you're busy, plus I'm on a phone in the kitchen of a restaurant. I have to go, but I'll call again."

"Wait, do you have a phone number?" Her interest rekindled his reason for calling. He was about to give his hotel information when she interrupted. "Your father has been constantly asking about you. He'd love to give you a call."

His adrenaline rush slowed. Realizing that she was eager to get his telephone number for his father and not for herself slowed his adrenaline further, to a crawl. "I'm not settled, but I will be in touch. You can count on it," he said, extending his good-bye.

"Wait," she called out, "you said there was something important you wanted to tell me. What is it?"

Quite easily he'd walked away from DMI and left the keys to the building on the counter in his condo. Walking away from Abigail was unimaginable. "Oh, it can wait." Today wasn't the day after all to open up with Abigail, but the day would come soon.

"You sure?" she said, with Joel talking in the background.

"Positive." He gripped the phone and, for a brief second, felt as if Abigail was with him. "I'll be in touch. You take care of yourself," he said, letting the call disconnect while lingering in the kitchen. He was more inspired than ever. He would get the international leadership team up and running, then Abigail could join him and they could live out the rest of their lives in harmony. He left the hustle and bustle of the kitchen feeling like a new man with a new purpose. No one and nothing would distract him from winning the heart of his beloved.

He returned to his table and waited for the Nigerian investor to arrive. In the meantime, he beckoned the waiter, who came right over. Don scribbled out his name and Table Bay Hotel—Cape Town. Handing the business card to the waiter he said, "I'll leave money to cover the phone call. If I owe you more money when the phone bill comes in, please don't hesitate to call me. I'll take care of it."

chapter

19

Last night had been rough. Dave didn't complain, but according to the doctor he had to be suffering tremendously. Stomach cancer was slow and painful. Sherry poured a cup of chamomile tea, hoping to relax into a deep sleep at least one night this week. She'd given Dave's nurse the night off, desiring to spend more time with him, content knowing he truly needed her. Alone in the kitchen with her thoughts, Sherry felt an overwhelming sense of loneliness. The house was still, emptylike. The crackling sound of a floorboard coming from the hallway caught her attention, causing her to set the teapot down briefly. She continued after not hearing it again. She took a sip of the tea and stopped. She heard the floorboard again. This time she eased out of the kitchen and into the hallway with reluctance. Midway down the hallway, Dave was leaning against the wall, barely standing. "Dave," she called out, rushing to his side. "What are you doing out of bed?" she asked, wrapping his arm across her shoulder.

"I need to get in touch with Don and Tamara."

Where in the world did the notion of seeing Tamara come from, Sherry wondered? "Let's get you back to bed, then we can talk later."

"I don't have time later. My Lord is coming for me soon and I need to see my children before I leave."

Sherry struggled with each step. Carrying her weight and much of Dave's was turning out to be more than she could bear, but she refused to give up. This was their battle, just theirs to fight and to win. She was determined to stick with him all the way to the end of the hallway, and deal with the rest once he was safely tucked back into his bed.

"Sherry, my darling, I need your help."

She pulled as close to the bed as the chair would allow and stretched her body to cover the rest of the divide between him and her. "Anything my love, anything."

"Please call Madeline for me and tell her that I must speak with Don and Tamara. I don't have much time," he said, and then grimaced, struggling to get breaths of air.

Sherry tried to calm herself and think, but her thoughts, words, emotions, and actions were headed in different directions, none of which were in sync. She mumbled her words and jumbled her thoughts, finally able to eke out, "I'm calling the doctor. Joel, too."

Dave grimaced again, drawing his knees up and letting out a wail. Another clump of blood forced him to wipe his mouth.

"No, no, please don't bother with the doctor. There's nothing he can do. It's my time."

"Nonsense, I'm calling him. You're bent over with pain. I'm calling him this very second," she said, trying to pull her hand out of his grip.

"Sherry, go ahead, call the doctor if you must, but please," he said, drawing in a big breath of air and coughing up blood, "call Madeline first. I need her now."

Sherry wanted to frown at his words but stayed focused on getting him help. She wiped the blood from his mouth. She knew what was best for her husband, not Madeline. "Please take some of the medicine the doctor left for you," she begged, refusing to leave his side.

"Please call Madeline for me. I must see her tonight, I must," he said, growing increasingly anxious.

"Okay, let me call the doctor." Sherry grabbed the phone in Dave's adjoining office and called his personal physician. Call completed. He was on his way. She would call Joel later. Sherry felt a bit relieved. Dave would be better soon. Once the doctor arrived, everything would be okay. She believed he'd bounce back from his illness and be the same strong, commanding leader and loving man she'd known and loved for twenty-eight years. Adversity, thieves, business rivals, and even spies hadn't succeeded in bringing down Dave Mitchell. Nothing and no one could. His God loved him dearly and nothing, not even cancer, could shatter Dave's faith. Religion hadn't served her as well, but watching him become weaker and weaker drove her to a place of desperation. She was willing to have faith in whatever it was that could make him feel better. Right now her faith was in the doctor and his bag of medicine. She sighed, hoping for the best and returning to the bedroom suite to comfort Dave.

"Did you reach Madeline?" he asked, quite anxious.

"Dave, please lie back," she said, fluffing his pillow. "You have to calm down. This worrying isn't good for you."

"Sherry, please call Madeline for me. I have to see her. My time is near."

She refused to hear him speak in final terms, not ready to let him go. If he was gone, she'd have no one left. What would she do? What would become of her? The years had chipped away at their bond, but there was no man in the world she loved and cherished more than Dave Mitchell. He was the man who stole her heart then and had possession of it now, a possession she would let him carry to his grave thirty years from now—not tonight. Sherry wouldn't allow him to leave her now, she couldn't. Dave continued cringing without uttering a word. "I can tell you're in great pain," she said, rubbing his hand. "The doctor will be here soon, and he can give you something to help with the pain."

"My kind of pain the doctor can't help."

"What do you mean?"

"I feel the pain of my children. I have to make amends with them before I leave. My time is near. God is preparing me for my journey home."

"You can't worry about them right now. You have to concentrate on getting better, then you can talk to them yourself and work through your disagreements."

"Sherry, don't you understand, there isn't time later. Now is what I have. This is the day the Lord has made. I may have already seen my last tomorrow. I must reconcile with my children tonight."

"Why is it so urgent for you to do this now, right now, tonight?"

"Because I don't want to die and leave them with the

pain of not having the opportunity to forgive and to let God heal their hurting hearts."

"It's just as much their fault for choosing not to be in touch with you."

"That doesn't matter. I'm their father. They've done nothing wrong to me. Whatever I can say or do, short of denying my God, I will do to bring peace to my children."

There had always been a rift between her and the children he shared with Madeline. Maybe that's why Sherry had protested vehemently against letting Dave's oldest son, Andre, move in with them. He was having trouble in school, and Madeline had suggested he stay with his father for a while. Dave wanted to take his son in, but Sherry firmly said no. She couldn't run the risk of having three-year-old Joel mistreated by a half brother— or stepbrother. She was not quite sure how to label Andre. She recalled him getting into much more trouble after he was turned down. Sherry wasn't sure about Dave, but Madeline never forgave her for saying no. Even with hindsight, her answer would remain no, especially after Andre attacked his sister. He was dangerous. Sherry wasn't going to apologize for protecting her tiny family, not then, not now, which was why she wasn't willing to let Madeline's children kill her husband with their anger. Their bitterness and unwillingness to allow him into their lives was driving him to a crippling place of brokenheartedness. Cancer wasn't her greatest fear for Dave; rejection from his other children was. "What about Joel, he's your child, too."

"Joel is fine. He doesn't need from me what my other children need."

The front doorbell rang. "Must be the doctor, thank God," Sherry said. "I should have asked him to come back here, but that's okay," she said, leaping up. "I'll let him in and we'll be right back," she said, sailing out the door and down the hallway.

Dave didn't blame Sherry. It wasn't her fault. She didn't understand how important the call to Madeline was. Forgiveness would be the key for his family to move on beyond his death and be able to serve God willingly, as he'd done for most of his adult life. "Give me strength, Lord," Dave said, pulling himself into the office. He rested on the desk and dialed the phone. Calm poured over his body hearing the voice on the other end. "Madeline," he said, taking a break before uttering the next word.

"Dave, is that you?" she asked.

His energy was waning so the words didn't flow easily. "Madeline."

"Dave," she said, raising her voice, "it's almost eleven o'clock."

"I need to see you," he was able to push out past a clump of blood.

"I'm on my way," she said and hung up.

He rested first, before attempting to return to bed. He would do all that he could to foster reconciliation within his family until his final breath. Taking gingerly steps, he reflected on his choices. Living without guilt and regrets hadn't freed him of watching the people he loved most in the world struggle. Denying his love for Madeline would discount their bond with each other and with their children. Minimizing his love for Sherry would discount Joel's existence. He didn't wish to deny anyone. His life hadn't been sin-free. The path he'd taken was already sealed. After making a quick assessment of his life and his family, Dave braced himself on the cane. A surge of love washed over him. He was blessed in spite of the circumstances. His inevitable mortality was a reminder of his human frailty, his inability to fix everything. The unresolved matters in his family would have to be released to God, the only one with the power to change hearts and to heal deep-seated wounds and sins, regardless of how they had been created.

chapter

20

———•———

Sherry dashed to the front door. She instructed the doctor to come in and they both rushed to Dave. "Dave, where are you?" Sherry called out from the bedroom.

"I'm in here," he said, attempting to gain composure.

She dashed into the room with Dr. Constantine close behind. "What are you doing in here?" she asked, rushing to him. "Let's get you back to bed. Doctor, can you grab his other arm?" Help was in the house. She'd already filled the doctor in on Dave's condition. She knew he would be better now that the doctor was there.

Dave was back in bed, nice and snug. Her stress was beginning to vanish.

"Larry, I appreciate you coming out so late, but

there's nothing you can do," Dave said, clutching his teeth after every other word.

"Let me give you a shot for the pain. It will help you sleep."

"No," Dave said loudly.

"There's no reason to suffer when I can give you something to ease the pain."

"Please let him give you the shot," Sherry pleaded.

"I can't take anything. I have to stay awake in case I get a chance to speak with my children."

"Let's not worry about that right now. You need to relax, please," she begged. "Dr. Constantine, please tell him this worrying isn't good for his condition."

"She's right, you know. Stress isn't good for any condition," Dr. Constantine confirmed.

"I'm not stressed," he said, pressing on his stomach, "I'm a father. I don't want to rest until I hear from my children."

"Madeline's children don't want to speak with you. They've made it very clear. You need to rest now, please, Dave, don't do this to yourself, to us," she said, shedding tears.

"I have to try. Madeline will be here soon. She can help me."

"I'm here," Sherry blurted out, "what about me?"

There was a powerful rap on the office door.

"That should be Madeline," he said, with a rush of color to his cheeks, "please let her in."

"I'm not leaving you for one second," Sherry told them.

"I can open the door for you," Dr. Constantine said.

There was no way to avoid letting Madeline in, but this wasn't the right time. Sherry wanted this precious time to be with her husband. She wanted to block out the world and be alone with him. She desperately wanted to be his sole light, his rock of support, hers alone for once.

Madeline stepped across the office threshold into the bedroom, sending shivers down Sherry's spine.

"What's going on here?" she asked, going around the bedpost and plopping down on the other side of Dave.

Sherry maintained control, which required fighting with every fiber in her body. "What are you doing here, Madeline?"

"Dave called me," Madeline said, and turned her attention to Dave. "Are you all right?"

Before Dave could respond, Sherry jumped in. "No, he's not. He's extremely agitated and stressed about your children. He's determined to speak with Don and Tamara."

"Ah, Dave, don't get yourself worked up. You should take it easy," Madeline said.

"I have to see them, it's very important to me," he said, getting excited again, causing Sherry to feel desperately concerned. She was fully capable of taking care of her husband. Dave didn't need Madeline.

"Fine, I'll have my private investigator get a message to them, but it might take several days for him to make contact with them."

"That's what I keep telling him. Forget about them for now and concentrate on getting better. I want him to get well."

"He'll never be able to forget about them," Madeline said, making each word slice through Sherry.

"Worrying about them isn't doing him any good."

"Stress is definitely not helping the situation," Dr. Constantine agreed.

Dave winced in pain again.

"What, what?" Madeline asked. "What's wrong, Dave?"

"Let me speak to Madeline alone, please."

"Are you sure I can't give you a shot of morphine? It will ease the pain and let you sleep more comfortably."

"I'll be sleeping comfortably with my Lord for an eternity soon enough. Larry, go home and be with your family. You can't help me now. It's out of your hands."

"Morphine?" Madeline interrupted. "Why does he need morphine?" When neither the doctor nor Sherry responded, Madeline asked again, this time demanding an answer.

"My stomach cancer is in the final stages."

Madeline slumped but didn't pass out. "Dave, why didn't you tell me?" she said, reaching for his hand.

Dr. Constantine acquiesced. "If you change your mind about the shot, I'm only a phone call away."

"Larry," Dave said, extending his hand, "thank you."

"No thanks necessary. You didn't let me do anything."

"You've done what God has allowed you to do, and I'm grateful."

Dr. Constantine left but Sherry wasn't as willing. "I'm not leaving, no way."

"Please, Sherry, I beg of you, let me speak to Madeline. This is very important to me."

She didn't want to go, to leave her husband with Madeline, but chose not to cause him additional agitation. "Okay, but I won't go far."

chapter

21

I t's getting close to my time, that's why I want you to help me find our children. They have to hear from me."

"Deep down they know you love them," Madeline tried to reassure him while grappling with the news.

"But I want them to hear it from me. One day they will want to forgive me, and when I'm gone it will seem too late. Make sure they know it's not too late, that I love them unconditionally. Let them know I wanted their forgiveness, and I know they gave it to me in their hearts. Tell them not to let guilt consume them. They're free and delivered by the grace of God."

"They haven't fared as well as you have with God."

"God didn't create their anguish. I pray that someday they will turn to the only one who can help them. I want them to find peace, and you, too," he said, placing his hand on hers.

The warmth melted a section of the icy wall she'd created around him. Much of her wanted to hate him, to make him feel a small bit of what she'd felt, but the residual love continued melting the wall. The most she could muster was a dab of discontent. With a softened soul and words she said, "You better leave the God part out if you want a shot at winning them over." She inhaled a dose of air and let her neck wobble slightly. "This is getting too intense. Old man, you're talking like you're about to pass away any minute, when you and I both know you're too ornery to leave here without a fight."

"My fighting days are over. It's time for me to take my rest."

"And leave me here with that wife of yours? I don't think so," Madeline said, punctuating the words with a tinge of laughter. He couldn't go, not like this. The years of memories flooded her soul. Her life was so deeply intertwined with his, the ministry, the children, her livelihood. She wasn't ready to let him go, not twenty-seven years ago and definitely not now. She laid her hand across his and rested her chin on his head. Dave Mitchell was and always would be her only husband. She rubbed his head, not wanting to believe his time was so close. "You're all right with me," she told him, listening to his breathing become more erratic and strained.

"You, too," he said, letting his eyelids close.

"Dave," Madeline called out, praying for a response. She knew none would come but wasn't quite ready to give up. She shook him, but there was no reaction.

* * *

Agony gripped her body thinking about Madeline in the bedroom alone with Dave. That was it. She wasn't waiting outside any longer. Whatever had to be said would be said with her in the room.

"Sherry!" she heard Madeline scream.

Sherry ran into the room and saw Madeline kissing Dave. Rational thinking and reaction didn't have time to gel. She lunged at Madeline. "What are you doing kissing my husband? Get off him. Dave, how could you?"

Madeline turned sharply with tears streaming down her face. "Are you crazy? I'm not kissing him. I've been trying to give him CPR. He's not breathing," she said, climbing off the bed. "Call the doctor quickly."

Sherry saw Madeline's lips moving but couldn't process the words—jumbled, swirling. The room was spinning, faster and faster.

"Did you hear me? Call the doctor," Madeline said, and then pushed around Sherry. "Forget it, I'll call him."

She wanted to pull it together, had to. Madeline wasn't going to take charge and leave her standing there helpless, unable to take care of her husband. "I'll do it," Sherry said with as much fervor as her trembling body could muster.

"Doesn't matter now, we know he's gone," Madeline whispered, and sank her face into her hands.

Sherry rushed to his side and placed her head on his chest, sobbing inconsolably. Nothing made sense. "How do you know he's gone?"

"Because he said good-bye to me."

Sherry felt a hatchet chop through her chest wall and rip out her heart. "He said good-bye to you? I should have been here with him. It should have been me."

"I'm not going to fight with you, Sherry," Madeline

said. "Just be with your husband." She walked out of the room without saying another word.

Sherry wept openly on Dave's chest, curling up like a baby. She had spent day after day, hour after hour with him. The bags under her eyes were proof of her undying loyalty. He couldn't be gone. She didn't get a chance to say good-bye or to tell him one last time how much she loved him now and always would. The anguish of realizing his last seconds on earth were spent with Madeline was unbearable. Sherry was overcome with emotion. She'd stepped out of the room for only a few minutes. Rehearsing the image of Madeline holding his hand as he passed was almost as unbearable as his death. Sherry and Joel might have gotten DMI, but Madeline had received the greatest gift, a chance to say good-bye. The tears wouldn't stop. Without him, her life was forever changed.

chapter

22

Madeline couldn't get her thoughts together. She rubbed her temples, attempting to alleviate the throbbing surge in her head. She'd called Dr. Constantine, who was on his way. He wasn't far away, but it didn't matter. Dave was gone, that much she had to accept. She was in constant contact with her private investigator. Normally she was able to recite his phone number from memory. The surges in her head weren't allowing much to make sense. She scrolled frantically down the list in her PDA searching for his number and finally pressed the send button.

A few rings and he was on the line. "Ted, it's Madeline Mitchell. I have an urgent request for you. My husband has died and I need you to contact my children, both of them." She spoke softly while constantly rubbing her temples, with little result.

"My condolences, Madeline, I will get right on this."

"Ted," she said, wanting to convey the urgency, but unable to raise her voice, "you have to deliver the message this time regardless of what measures you have to take. Cost is not an issue. Just so you know, I authorize any expenses required to get my children home. Short of picking them up and forcing them on the plane, I want you to get them to Michigan. If you need a first-class ticket to South Africa or Antarctica or anywhere in between, do it."

"I'm on it. Don't worry, I'll make this happen for you, and again you have my condolences. I'll contact you within twenty-four hours."

"Ted, I'm counting on you to bring my babies home."

"You have my word. I will do everything in my power to make contact."

"Thank you," she said, controlling her emotions.

There was a line of people who had to be contacted, but they could wait. Dave had been like a father to Abigail. She deserved to hear about Dave before the media got to her. Madeline scrolled the PDA list again and dialed. Abigail answered. "I apologize for calling so late," she said, feeling another surge of pain and emotion meshing.

"I wasn't doing much, just catching the news and weather. Madeline, is everything all right?" Abigail asked.

"No, actually, it's not."

"Is it Don, did something happen to him?" Abigail asked, sounding more upset than Madeline would have expected. She knew they were friends, but Abigail was almost hysterical about Don, causing Madeline to hesitate before telling her about Dave. "Is it Don, is it?"

"No, no, I'm not calling about Don." The words were right there ready to sail into the air, but they were stuck and wouldn't release.

"Tell me, please," Abigail said in an alarmed tone. "What's wrong?"

"It's Dave, he's passed away."

"Oh, my God!" she screamed, forcing Madeline to hold the phone away from her ear. "When?"

"A short while ago. I was with him when he passed."

"Madeline, I'm so sorry," she said, struggling to choke out the words. "You have my deepest sympathy."

"And you have mine. You were more than an assistant to Dave. You were like a daughter to him. He truly cared a great deal about you."

"Thank you." Madeline heard the sobs and was about to tell Abigail good-bye and let her grieve privately. Abigail spoke, submerged in tears. "Is there anything I can do for you and Don?"

"Don hasn't been told yet. I have to find him first. Right now, I know he's in South Africa and that's about it. He never leaves a phone number, not even the name of the hotel where he's staying, but I have my private investigator looking for him. I pray that we find him in the next couple of days. I'm not letting the funeral happen until we get word to Don and Tamara."

"Have the arrangements been made already?"

"No, not yet." Sherry was his wife on paper, but Madeline wasn't going to let anyone forget that she was his business partner. No plans to bury Dave Mitchell would happen without input from her family. Sherry might as well sit back and get ready for a battle if she was planning otherwise. "I have to put my energy into locating our children."

"Now that I'm thinking about it, the last time Don called me, he was at a restaurant. I'm wondering if they might have some information we can use. Who knows, God might create a miracle for us. Don might be at the restaurant when we call. You never know what God is going to do," Abigail said, sounding clearer and less grief-stricken.

There was no question Dave's allegiance to God had rubbed off on Abigail. "I'll let you check with God and the restaurant while I keep my faith in the investigator. Hopefully between the two of us, we'll find him."

chapter

23

An entire month in Africa and his body hadn't adjusted to the time zone difference. The clock read 9:15 A.M., but his body said 2:00 A.M., Detroit time. Time was one of the many adjustments he had to make if South Africa was going to be his new home. The telephone rang in the hotel suite. He didn't rush to the phone, figuring the call was from the hotel staff. No one else, other than his investors, had his room number. It was only 7:00 A.M. in London and in Nigeria. Those investors weren't calling this early.

Don answered the phone, extending the basic greeting.

"Howzit, Mr. Mitchell, this is Arie Bleeker from the Two Oceans," the caller said.

"Who are you again?"

"Arie from the restaurant at the Cape of Good Hope?"

"Oh, right, okay, yes I remember you," Don said, taking a seat at the desk. "You let me use the phone to place a call to the States. I guess you've received the bill and need me to pay my balance. No problem. What's the amount?" he said, balancing the receiver between his shoulder and cheek while simultaneously rummaging through the desk drawer in search of his wallet. He must have taken it into the bedroom, he thought.

"No, Mr. Mitchell, I'm not calling about your bill. Your rands were quite sufficient."

"Really," Don said, stopping the search as his curiosity level increased.

"We received a call from a lady in the States who was most interested in reaching you."

He chuckled. Mother was persistent in her effort to bring him home. "Was it Madeline Mitchell?" he said with confidence.

"No sir, I believe it was Abigail Gerard."

Don sat up and paid attention to every word. "Are you sure it was Abigail Gerard?"

"Quite sure. She was most interested in reaching you straightaway."

He leaped to his feet and paced around the desk. "Did she leave a message?"

"She'd like for you to call her straightaway. It's most urgent. She left a number for you. I have it here."

"Yes, sure, give it to me," he said, ripping a sheet of paper from the hotel magazine. Abigail's going out of her way to find him was a miracle. Could it be? Did she feel the same connection? Eager to speak with Abigail, Don thanked the waiter and dialed her number as soon as the line was clear, the same one he'd dialed many times before when they were working together. Once the phone began to ring, it dawned on him that it was 2:00 A.M. in Michigan. He scurried to disconnect but was too late. She was already answering. Hearing her voice on the other end sent a burst of joy careening along his veins. He couldn't imagine being any happier. "Abigail," he greeted, not wanting to disrupt the flow of her melodious voice.

"Thank God you got my message. I wasn't sure if the restaurant would have any way of contacting you. I took a chance and thanks to the Lord, you got the message."

Her voice was a delight but didn't have the same heavy dose of enthusiasm as she had when they'd spoken a few weeks ago. He could sit and listen to her all day. What she talked about was irrelevant. Hearing her refer to God didn't send him into retreat either as it would have a month ago, thanks to a month of fresh air and the seclusion that South Africa had provided. Having her on the other end of the line made his day complete, and the day was only beginning. "I was quite surprised to hear from you. No one, not even my mother, knows how to contact me directly. I'm flattered you went to so much trouble to call me. Hearing from you means a lot to me," he said, bracing against the table and facing the window.

"I told your mother I'd try to reach you. I have news to tell you, Don," she muttered.

"What did you say? I couldn't hear your last words. Your voice was broken."

"I'm calling to tell you about your father."

"What about my father?"

"He passed away a little while ago," she said. Don froze. "Don, are you there? Did you hear me?" He wanted to speak but the sounds were held captive. "Don, say something, anything, let me know you're there."

"I'm here. I . . ." he stammered, "don't know what to say. My father is dead. How is that possible? He wasn't that sick when I left. What happened?"

"I'm not sure. From what I understand, your mother was with him when he passed. She has much more information than I do. You should call her right away. She wants to speak with you as soon as possible."

"Right, I'll call her as soon as I hang up with you." He was unable to process every thought. His words were on autopilot.

"Will you be able to come home?" she asked as her voice faded in and out.

"I'm heading to the airport right after I call Mother."

"Good, I look forward to seeing you."

"Same here," he said, drenched with a mixture of emotions about his father and her.

"Don't let me stand in the way. Get to that airport and I'll see you soon."

"You're never in my way. Hearing from you is comforting," he said, choking back his emotions.

"I miss you. Call me on my mobile phone as soon as you land. Most likely I'll be with Joel providing whatever support I can."

Joel, Joel, Joel, Don thought. Good thing there was nothing else to lose, otherwise he might be jealous. He finished the conversation with Abigail, reassured of her friendship, and proceeded to call his mother, a call he wasn't prepared to make, not now, not ever.

Two quick stops in Johannesburg and London couldn't be avoided. There wasn't a single nonstop flight going from Cape Town or Durban that could get Don to Detroit any faster, not at any price. The travel agent tried every scenario possible, including a private jet, but he didn't have time to wait for flight clearances and chartering a crew. He was glad to grab the last two first-class seats on a commercial flight headed to the States immediately after hearing the news yesterday. The one-way price of seventeen thousand rands per ticket didn't deter him from his goal to get home as soon as possible. He purchased the two one-way tickets for nearly five thousand dollars without flinching. Normally he wouldn't waste the money on first class when business class was just as good. But on this grief-laden journey home, he welcomed the extra plane space that allowed his thoughts to roam freely, unhindered by the intruding remarks of a neighbor.

"Ladies and gentleman, those of you on the right side of the plane can get a nice glimpse of the Statue of Liberty as we cross into New York airspace. We will fly through the state of New York and go over eastern Michigan, landing in Detroit around twelve-forty-five, a few minutes ahead of schedule. Relax and enjoy the rest of your flight," the pilot said.

Don stroked the stubble on his chin. He had done the best he could for a five-minute shave before going to the airport yesterday. A carry-on duffel bag, no clear plans, and soon he would be in Detroit with no way to say good-bye to his father.

The flight attendant brought meal after snack after meal. His stomach was too queasy for food. Once he landed and drove to his mother's, maybe he would grab a bite. He hoped his BMW was still parked at the airport. After a month there wasn't a guarantee. He reclined the seat, not quite to the full horizontal bed position that the first-class seat was capable of taking. He wanted to sleep, but for the past twenty-three hours of traveling, his restlessness had haunted him, refusing to release a peaceful moment. The past month had been like being on the run from his father. Each time he spoke with his mother she mentioned that his father wanted to talk. But the betrayal, rejection, and selfishness of his father had justified Don's ability to keep his distance. Maybe if Don had called his father once in the past four weeks, only one time, maybe, just maybe the grief wouldn't hurt so much. After all, he didn't hate his father. The love he had was irrevocably diminished by the CEO situation, but he didn't hate him. Many words waited to be said, none of which could make a difference now. It was too late. His father was gone again, leaving Don to nurse the wound.

He wondered if Joel had been with his father when he passed away. Then again, it didn't make a difference. So what if Joel was there; Don wasn't. His missed opportunity couldn't be recovered. There was consolation in being with Mother and Abigail. He needed them as much as they needed him. He stretched out on the seat and drifted to sleep for the hour and a half left until touchdown, hoping to embrace his father and have a few laughs and a good talk with him in his dreams.

chapter

24

Madeline gritted her teeth and clutched her coat, contemplating her decision. She was prepared to set aside her feelings about Sherry and Joel for the sake of the funeral. Dave better be very happy about this, she thought, stroking her hair. "You owe me," she mouthed, looking up toward the sky. She took a deep breath, braced her arm against the door, looked down at the ground, and released the air like a smoker taking a slow calming drag. She couldn't stand there forever; time to go in and face the circus. Madeline knocked on the door, not expecting that her gesture would be an easy one to make. Dave, oh, Dave, she thought, you really owe me for this one.

Sherry opened the door. Her face appeared dry and streaked. A dose of makeup would help to soften her puffy eyes, but perhaps playing the grieving widow was more to her taste. "Can I come in?" Madeline asked. Sherry beckoned for her to enter. Madeline tried to muster a grin, but the best she did was grimace at Sherry's halfhearted invitation to enter. Madeline was silently amused. Sherry wasn't likely to move out. At the very least she should hand over the Mitchell photos lining the hallway, the ones Madeline fondly remembered framing. Hearing Dave's voice, Madeline dropped her line of thinking for the moment, but Sherry had better not push her too far or the truce was off.

"You need help with the arrangements?" Madeline asked.

"No, Wiley & Associates are handling everything," Sherry said.

"Who are they? Dave and I have a relationship with Johnson & Sons Funeral Home in Southfield. They did an amazing job handling the burials of Sam and Andre. Why would you consider another funeral home?" Madeline asked. She wasn't going to let Sherry shut her out. She was and always would be the mother of Dave's oldest children, a significant member of his family. Dave would want them working together on the arrangements.

"I'm using the same funeral home that handled our baby's burial," Sherry practically whispered. Madeline didn't have any association with the funeral or the related details. Her only memory was of Sherry's pregnancy. "Joel and I decided to go back to the same place."

"You and Joel need to include me, and Don, too. We are just as much a part of Dave's family as you are. I don't want to be shut out of his burial."

"Who said you're going to be shut out? I didn't, Joel didn't. You, Don, and Tamara are welcome to come."

"Well, thank you, Ms. Sherry, for the invitation, but I'm planning to be there regardless," she told her.

"Do whatever you like, you will anyway, but as far as the funeral arrangements go, that's my duty to handle as his wife." Madeline clamped her lips together. Count to twenty, maybe thirty, Madeline thought. She wasn't thinking straight coming into the house under the guise of a truce. Madeline wanted to honor Dave's memory, but Sherry wasn't an easy person to accept, especially when she was savoring a taste of power. Sherry started walking away and stopped to say, "Look, I know we have our disagreements, but for Dave's sake, let's not quarrel. We need to work together for the next few days."

Sherry was right. "I'm sure Dave would be pleased if we could find a way to work together," Madeline said, remembering her promise to Dave. She took a seat in the living room. Sherry followed, without putting up resistance or offering feedback. "Let me know how I can help," Madeline said. Sherry took a seat on the other sofa and appeared to be mellowing.

Sherry was quiet; no response. She looked aloof, as if she was lost in space somewhere. Madeline was offering the once-in-a-lifetime olive branch. If Sherry was wise, she'd take the branch and get on with the arrangements.

"Fine," Sherry lashed out.

Madeline wasn't sure what was spurring the attitude and really didn't care. This was Dave's moment and he deserved to be buried with dignity. Letting Sherry believe she was running the show was one of the most challenging feats Madeline had attempted, but she was committed to keeping the hostility to a bare minimum. "Let me know what I need to do. If it will help, I can handle the obituary."

"No," Sherry immediately responded, "I'll definitely coordinate the obituary."

Madeline wasn't surprised, and she was willing to be quiet so long as Sherry didn't exclude her family. "Let me know if there's any information you need about me, my children, or DMI."

"Thank you," Sherry responded, fondling a used tissue.

The phones were ringing in every room. "Do you want to get that?" Madeline asked.

"Joel and Abigail are taking the calls. Reporters have been calling most of the morning. It's overwhelming."

"Why don't you let me handle the calls? I'll put out a press release followed by a press conference."

"I can't handle a crowd of people asking me about Dave and how he died." Sherry sucked in short breaths of air, not looking well. "I can't do it."

"You won't have to," Madeline said, grabbing her coat and standing. Sherry was sick about not being with Dave when he actually passed. And it was probably worse knowing the other wife had been there. Under any other circumstances, Madeline would use the situation against Sherry, but not in this case. Madeline was grateful to have been with Dave in his final moments. The privilege wasn't a badge of honor, merely reality. Besides, Sherry had had a relationship with the man. This much Madeline could acknowledge. "I'm going to Dave's office to get the media process underway. The press conference will be on our terms, short and sweet, no questions from the press," Madeline said.

"But they'll want to know how he died, when he died. They'll stir up the controversy between Joel and Don, even though it's been resolved," Sherry said.

Not hardly resolved, Madeline thought, but now

wasn't the time to address Sherry's delusion. She had to remind herself over and over that she was here to honor Dave if she was to stay sane in the mansion. Ironically, with Dave gone, Madeline had no interest in the place, not the same burning sense of entitlement she'd clung to for years—the sensation was faint.

"The reporters aren't calling the shots, we are. We tell them what we want them to know and shut it down when we're finished," Madeline said. There was no pleasure in knocking Sherry off her tiny spot of stability. Sherry seemed balanced, but Madeline was convinced that any harsh word or little blow of the wind would send her into a frantic, desperate meltdown. Had Dave been here to protect Sherry, Madeline would have found the tiff amusing. Without him to coddle Sherry, the adrenaline rush was pointless. Madeline was committed to keeping the tension down, but she had limits, ones she hoped Sherry wasn't planning to test.

Don didn't know how to feel. As he stood on the doorstep his thoughts were jumbled. His last visit to his father's estate had ended with a fight that catapulted him halfway around the world. The weaker part of him said to turn around and run. The part that he yielded to his mother kept him standing there but not ready to enter. He braced himself, calmed his racing thoughts, and rapped on the door. Sherry opened the door, much to his surprise. He had been expecting the housekeeper— or anyone else but Sherry.

"Don, I'm glad you're here," she said, trying to embrace him. He stood still, not wanting to engage in the sentiment but not bent on rejecting her either. She must have felt his lukewarm disposition, and she released her embrace.

Sprinting to the door was his mother. "Yes, you're here," she screamed, scooting around Sherry.

His natural reaction was to hug her tightly. He'd missed her more than he'd realized. She snatched him by the hand and led him through the maze of people doing this and that, until they reached the office. Seemed like too many people, but no one was asking his opinion, which was okay with him. He wanted to attend the funeral, see Abigail, hug his mom, and get on a plane back to South Africa. One out of four goals had been accomplished.

"Look who's here," she said with pride, bursting into the office. "Don is home, where he belongs."

Abigail heard the commotion and ran from Dad's bedroom suite into the office. She screamed, too, practically tackling him. Her embrace made his soul melt like ice cream on a hot day. He wrapped his arm around her waist and held on. He didn't want to move or breathe for fear of losing her touch. Joel eased out of the office and leaned on the door frame. Don saw him but didn't let his presence shatter the moment with Abigail.

"Don, it's good to see you."

"Joel," was the most Don could offer. Releasing Abigail, Don walked to Joel and extended his hand. He wasn't confused. Love and decency weren't the same. Joel had lost his father. Extending a kind hand at such a time was doable.

Madeline latched on to his arm. Abigail went to Joel's other side. Not a word spoken afterward registered with Don, except those coming from Abigail. A day-long flight was a small price to pay for the opportunity to be near her. He'd enjoy the time home and capitalize on every second in her presence. Detroit would always have a piece of him as long as she was there.

chapter

25

Dave Mitchell wasn't Abigail's father, but it sure felt as if he was as she stepped out of the limousine. Sherry had insisted that Madeline, Joel, and Don ride along with her in the same limousine, which was a miraculous gesture given the tension between the two women. Madeline had coerced Frank and his estranged wife to join the family in the limousine, too, which was an equally miraculous feat, given his anger toward Joel for firing him. Dave would have been pleased having his family in harmony for once. Too bad he hadn't lived to see this day, the single time when they were standing together without arguing, fighting, or lashing out at one another.

Abigail felt a tinge of joy remembering how much Dave had invested in her training. God was faithful. She hadn't been raised by her father, not really, but God had blessed her with Dave Mitchell. His fatherly presence in her life had helped to erode some of the devastation she'd endured growing up with alcoholic parents. Abigail wanted to believe that in some small way her presence in Dave's life had helped lessen the pain of Tamara's absence. She wasn't a replacement for Dave's daughter, merely another person who needed his sense of direction.

The mahogany casket, dark, distinctive, sat at the head of the family waiting to enter the church. Joel grabbed his mother's arm. Madeline clung to Don. Abigail was comfortable lining up behind Dave's two sons, wife, and ex-wife. Frank was behind her. She wasn't a blood relative but didn't feel slighted in the least bit. Just being there to pay tribute to her mentor was a substantial honor, certain that he was resting in heaven with God. If Dave Mitchell didn't get to heaven, the rest of them didn't have a chance.

"Abigail, come up here, please," Joel said, peering around Don.

She didn't move immediately, afraid of infringing upon Don and Madeline's rightful place in line. Don must have sensed her discomfort because he turned to her and said, "Go on, you're family." He'd been gone for a month but hadn't changed a bit. He was still the considerate, respectful friend she'd cared about for five years. She missed him and was hoping he'd come back home and help Joel run DMI for Dave's sake.

"Come on," Joel said again, this time reaching around Don and taking hold of Abigail, pulling her past his brother with his free arm. She brushed against Don in the process but didn't resist Joel's assertiveness. She found the gesture refreshing.

The funeral procession began as the casket was wheeled inside the five-thousand-seat cathedral. The choir stand was graced with what sounded like a hundred singers belting out hymns. There were so many flowers, flowers everywhere, too many to count, lining the front of the sanctuary. People filled the church, some she probably knew and most she didn't. Being on Joel's arm, safe from the onslaught of the world, made the crowd disappear. She tightened her grip on his arm and took refuge in his embrace. Challenges in life would come, but so long as love for Joel was in her heart and Don's friendship was close by, every good thing was possible.

chapter

26

Madeline didn't know what to expect. Dave had made a few questionable decisions in his last days. The certainty she once had about his business decisions had vanished with Joel's appointment as CEO. The two years of separation followed by twenty-five years of divorce hadn't diminished Dave's propensity to provide for her and their children. She had no reason to believe he would change his level of commitment to them in the will.

The attorney was seated at the head of the table. Madeline and Don were together on one side. Sherry, Joel, and Abigail were across the table.

"It's three-forty-five. I'm perfectly willing to wait for Miss Tamara Mitchell to arrive if that's your preference," said Dave's personal attorney, the executor of the estate.

Madeline had hoped and had even briefly considered saying a prayer that Tamara would come. Her daughter hadn't attended the funeral and it was highly unlikely she'd attend the reading of the will, but Madeline wasn't ready to give up yet.

"We've already waited forty-five minutes. I don't think she's coming. I think we should proceed," Sherry said.

"I want to wait," Madeline quickly retorted. "Another fifteen or twenty minutes isn't going to kill us. I say let's wait."

"Madeline, she didn't come to the funeral, for heaven's sake. Why should we expect her here?"

"I said I want to wait. Are there any objections? Let's take a vote." Madeline polled the room. Don didn't mind waiting, or Abigail. Joel either. Sherry was in the minority. "There you go," Madeline said to the attorney and to Sherry. "We'll wait until four o'clock. If we haven't heard from her by then, you can proceed. Thank you," she told everyone, crossing her legs and arms. Tamara's arrival had a very low probability, but Madeline refused to give up on her daughter. Wherever she was, Tamara was a Mitchell, and Madeline would ensure that the rights and privileges associated with being a child of Dave's would not be stolen. That was her duty as a mother and she took it seriously.

Fifteen minutes evaporated like her short-lived moratorium on battling Sherry. Their dueling match was resurrected as soon as the hearse pulled away from the cemetery. "You can go ahead. She may show up later but there's no sense making the rest of you wait any longer."

When the door opened, she was elated. Madeline leaped to her feet and plopped back down, dejected, when Frank entered. "Sorry I'm late. The traffic is nuts," he said and took the empty seat next to Don.

The attorney read the opening rhetoric, which took about ten minutes. Madeline wasn't interested in the generic aspects of the will. She wanted to nudge the attorney toward the details, the sections that stated who would get what. That's why she and everyone else in the room was there.

"Any questions on the disclaimers?" he asked. Silence filled the room, exactly what Madeline expected. "Now, we come to the distribution of assets," he said. "Let's begin with the real estate. The mansion located on Mayweather Lane and the contents therein go to Sherry Mitchell." Madeline kept her legs and arms crossed, listening to the attorney say, "With the exception of a Mitchell family photo collection and a detailed list of heirlooms found in section D, exhibit one, which shall be entrusted to Madeline Mitchell." She uncrossed her arms and sat tall in the chair. Perhaps Dave hadn't completely lost his mind in the last days.

"What does that mean?" Sherry interrupted.

"He has a list. Let him read the entire will and then we can raise questions at the end," Madeline said.

"I'm asking the attorney," Sherry fired in return.

Madeline looked away, letting her gaze bounce around the walls, sure her expression was displaying the agitation she felt.

"It is quite an extensive list. I do prefer to complete the section first and then entertain questions and exhibits at the conclusion if the approach is acceptable to each of you." There were no objections, so the attorney continued. "The vacation property in West Palm Beach now belongs to Don Mitchell. The property in Hilton Head goes to Joel Mitchell. The one in Kauai, Hawaii, goes to

Madeline. The townhouse in San Diego goes to Tamara. There is an exception clause written in for the property belonging to Tamara." Dave better not rob their daughter, Madeline thought, poised for battle. "In the event she doesn't take ownership of the property, provisions are made to cover the associated maintenance expenses indefinitely. The property will become a part of her estate in the event of her death. If a will does not exist at the time of her death, the property will be sold and proceeds distributed to a list of charities stated in section D, exhibit two, of this will." Madeline expected Sherry to comment but she didn't.

"I love Hilton Head," Joel said.

"He remembered how much I love Hawaii," Madeline said, drawing a heated stare from Sherry.

The attorney divided property and assets for the next hour before getting to the meat of the will. "The cash distribution and other liquid assets are as follows," he said, having Madeline's full attention. "Sherry Mitchell, thirty million; Joel, twenty million; Don, twenty million; Tamara, twenty million; Madeline, fifteen million; Abigail, one million; and Frank five hundred thousand dollars. The remaining $3.7 million will be distributed among a list of charities in section D, exhibit two, of this will."

Deep down Madeline had known he wouldn't forget her and their children.

"Are you sure I don't get more?" Frank asked.

"I'm reading the terms of the will as stated," the attorney affirmed, generating a look of disappointment from Frank, which Madeline didn't understand. He'd already stolen his share of the inheritance from DMI. He was lucky to get any money.

"That brings us to the distribution of Dave's stock

position in DMI," the attorney stated. Houses and cash were good but, she'd already received a generous cash settlement in the divorce. Percentage ownership of DMI was the only aspect of the will deserving Madeline's full attention. "Five percent of the DMI stock goes to Miss Abigail Gerard." There were tiny reactions but nothing major. Abigail's value to Dave and DMI was widely recognized. Five percent seemed fitting. The other 95 percent was her concern. The attorney continued. "Each child, Don Mitchell, Joel Mitchell, and Tamara Mitchell, receives an equal distribution of fifteen percent." Madeline was calculating furiously. Don and Tamara only accounted for 30 percent, not the majority amount needed to reclaim the company. She groaned softly, preparing for the ultimate defeat. Sherry had finally won. "The remaining fifty percent is to be split equally between Sherry Mitchell and Madeline Mitchell."

"What did you say?" Madeline asked, recalculating and repeatedly producing an answer of 55 percent with her and her children's stock. Was she in a dream?

"Twenty-five percent of the DMI stock reverts to you and the remaining twenty-five percent goes to Sherry Mitchell."

"Are you sure?" Madeline asked again.

"How could twenty-five percent be right?" Sherry chimed in.

"Sounds fair to me," Madeline said, relishing the victory.

"Tamara has made it very clear. She doesn't want to be involved with DMI. Shouldn't her stock be split among his other children?" Sherry asked.

"I don't care if Tamara never sets a foot in DMI again," Madeline said. "Her father left her fifteen percent and I can promise you that will be hers." Madeline made sure she punctuated the statement in a way that let Sherry know to drop the discussion.

"No stock for me?" Frank asked.

"None noted, sir."

"I guess I can take my five hundred thousand and get out of here. Doesn't look like my dear old brother is going to leave me anything else," he said. "Thirty years of loyal service. Five hundred thousand is less than seventeen thousand dollars a year, which is about eight bucks an hour," he sputtered, leaving the room. "Don't bother to get up, dear family, I know my way to the door, right, Joel?" he said, finally leaving and letting Madeline's blood pressure return to normal.

"I don't think this is fair," Sherry said.

"Why not? Seems fair to me," Madeline said, stroking her hair in case a strand had strayed. "I'm perfectly pleased with the distribution."

"Of course you would be. Your family has most of the stock, but Joel is CEO. His father chose him to run the company. In order to carry out his role, he needs controlling interest in the stock."

"What do you know about stock, Sherry? Wasn't your professional aptitude relegated to getting coffee and making sure the copier was stocked with paper?" Madeline said, rubbing the tips of her fingernails and avoiding eye contact with Sherry.

"Mother," Don intervened.

"Madeline, that wasn't called for," Joel jumped in, too. She didn't fault him for protecting his mother. Besides, some of his DNA, the portion she was willing to tolerate, today, came from Dave.

"Look, I didn't write the will. Dave divided the property and stock the way he wanted. I can't make a single change," Madeline said. "Not that I want to anyway."

Without warning, Sherry began a tirade. "This is wrong. You've taken everything from me," she said, yelling across the table in Madeline's direction. Madeline felt Don's hand pressed down on her shoulder, forcing her to remain seated. Sherry yelled on. "I spent an entire year taking care of my husband. I stepped out of the room a few minutes and what happened, he died in your arms," she said, with Abigail and Joel both trying to comfort her.

"You can't blame me. If you're going to be mad at anybody, it would have to be Dave. He's the one who asked you to leave the room, not me. So, don't get mad at me. That's between you and Dave." Madeline was rubbing her fingernail tips again, calm as ever.

"If it wasn't for you and your children driving him, pushing him, making him feel guilty and abandoned, he'd be here right now."

"Wait a minute," Don said, but didn't get to finish before Madeline took the reins.

"You can't possibly be implying what I think you're implying. I guarantee you that an argument about blame wouldn't go in your favor." Decorum was out the window when Sherry tossed accusations at her children.

"You wouldn't accept his decision. You tortured him for doing what he had to do. You never let him have one minute of peace after his decision. Dave wanted Joel to be in charge. Everyone in this room knows that's the truth." Slightly calmer, she spoke directly to the attorney at the head of the table. "Are you sure this is the most current version of the will? Dave appointed our son, Joel, to run the company in his last month due to his illness. He must have updated the will around then, too. You must not have the updated version," she said in a tone of desperation.

The attorney flipped to the signature page. "This is the latest version, I assure you," he said, pushing the signature page close enough for Sherry to see. "This last will and testament is dated two weeks ago."

Sherry shut up. The attorney read each exhibit in section D.

"This concludes the reading of the will," the attorney stated. "But before we leave, there's a note that Dave wanted me to read."

Madeline couldn't imagine what else was left to say. The division of property spoke loudly.

"To my beloved family, Sherry, Madeline, Joel, Don, Tamara, Frank, and Abigail, I leave these words of encouragement for you. I have lived a full life. I made many mistakes but by the grace of God I was forgiven. Living your life in honor of the Lord is a noble cause. I challenge each of you to forgive one another. Allow the past to be buried with me so that each of you can live the fullest lives God has purposed for you. I surely don't know all the answers and neither will you. Look to the Lord continuously for wisdom and direction. He will guide your path.

I have divided my material wealth among you to the best of my ability. I pray each of you will be good stewards of the gifts entrusted to you. I pray you will work together to take DMI to the next level in the ministry. By now you are aware of the stock distribution. The split was intentionally made with no clear winner. There's only two ways to gain control of DMI. You either have to set aside your differences and work as a single unit or you have to encourage Tamara to return to the family."

Madeline smirked, imagining Dave looking down on them from heaven. The old man was still trying to work his magic and make her and Sherry buddies. Why didn't he realize the friendship would never happen, not in this lifetime or in the next? She hoped he was in heaven with better things to do than pull her strings. "How does Dave plan to carry out this farce? No one can make Tamara come back to DMI. Most likely she'll choose to turn her stock over to one of us." Madeline hoped her daughter would turn the stock over to her. "She might never want to be associated with this company."

"Or the family," Sherry added.

"Well, Dave had me add a special clause, which states that the fifteen percent stock options owned by Tamara Mitchell can only be transferred within the physical DMI headquarters."

"Oh, come on, are you serious?" Madeline asked, bewildered that Dave would go so far.

"Those are Dave's wishes, and since the company is privately held, it's his decision to make."

"This is absurd," Madeline said.

"You can always appeal before a probate judge, but the likelihood of having the terms of this will overturned is small."

"I'm not talking about going to court, but you have to admit this is over the top, even for Dave."

The attorney shrugged his shoulders and continued reading Dave's message. "Let's see, where did I stop?" He quickly scrolled the page and then began, "My soul is overjoyed with the notion of uniting as a family to the glory of God. I'm equally thrilled about you restoring my only daughter's faith in our family. I give you this challenge. May the Lord watch over you and grace you with His presence. I leave you now to be with my Father. Be at peace knowing I am dancing in the presence of my God, my Savior and Lord. With everlasting love, your husband, friend, father, brother, and mentor, Dave Mitchell."

Madeline didn't always agree with the man, but hearing his note read aloud pushed her and the rest of Dave's family to tears.

Sherry was ready to leave immediately after the reading. Abigail heard Sherry ask Joel to take her home, sobbing. He'd driven both Abigail and his mother to the attorney's office.

"I'm going to take her home," Joel said, with Sherry clinging to his arm. "Are you ready to go?"

Don swooped in and said, "Excuse me, Abigail, can I speak with you for a minute?"

"My ride is about to leave."

"I can give you a ride home," Don told her.

She wasn't quite ready to leave and welcomed the offer. "Are you sure?" she asked Don.

"One hundred percent."

"Okay, then I guess I won't need a ride from you," she told Joel. "Go on without me." This would give her time to really sit down and talk with Don. The past days had been hectic and focused entirely on the funeral. She wanted to kick back and spend quality time with her friend, to find out what he was up to and how he was managing being so far away.

Joel hesitated. "I'll call you later," he told Abigail. He turned to Don and extended his hand. "You staying in town long, maybe we can grab dinner."

"I haven't firmed up my plans. Chances are I'll be leaving within a day or two."

"Well, I'm glad to see you. If I don't see you before you leave, take care of yourself."

Joel left. Madeline approached.

"All in all, today went well," Madeline said. "If you have a few minutes, I'd like to talk with you," she said to Don.

"I'm going to spend some time with Abigail. I will catch up with you a little later."

"Call me. We need to figure out our next step."

Don grinned but didn't respond to his mother. Abigail was thrilled to see the reading of the will end with very little discord. Sherry was upset, but it could have been much worse. She garnered hope from seeing Don and Joel talk. Today was a good day. She'd spend time with Don and let the rest of the day play out with Joel later.

The room emptied with only the attorney remaining. Don wrapped his arm around Abigail as they left the room.

"I can't wait to catch up. I'm sure you have lots to tell me about South Africa and maybe some young lady over there that you've fallen in love with."

Don chuckled as they meandered to the stairs. "I could say the same about you."

"Tell me yours and I'll tell you mine," she said as they descended the stairs chatting and chuckling.

chapter

27

Sherry sat at the bottom of the winding staircase. Back in the mansion, she felt empty. There was no more to lose. Her soul cried out but by the time her torment reached the surface it had transformed into tears, which streamed down her cheeks endlessly. Joel tried, but words couldn't remove her pain. The only one who could comfort her was buried and gone from her presence forever. The finality was too much to endure. "I just want to sleep."

"Rest is good for you, Mom," Joel said. "Why don't you go upstairs and I'll make some of that tea you like. Who knows, I might even drink some with you."

"No," she said, feeling too weak to hold her head up. "Thank you, dear, but I don't want any tea. My husband is what I want." She appreciated his attempt to comfort her, but honestly, she didn't want comfort. She wanted to feel every ounce of agony, distress, grief. At least she could feel something. Any emotion other than peace and happiness was welcomed. She had to carry the sting of her loss in order to legitimize her marriage to the love of her life. If she let go of the aches so quickly, no one would believe how much she truly loved Dave Mitchell. They wouldn't believe she had married him and stood by him for love instead of his money.

Joel wrapped his arms around her shoulders. "Mom, you're going to be all right. Dad loved us and we loved him. That won't change."

"I desperately want to believe your father loved me as much as I loved him, but I know he didn't. After God, DMI had his heart, and he split the small piece left equally between me, Madeline, and his children."

"You can't believe that, Mom. He left you more money."

"You think the money matters? He made sure Madeline was taken care of when they divorced and just to be sure, he left her more money. The way the money was split doesn't make me feel any better."

"But he was married to you."

"Joel, I have to face the truth. I wasn't his special wife. I was just one of his wives. He loved both of us. If I'd never come into his life he would have stayed with Madeline. Maybe that's why my marriage has been plagued with hurt after hurt. I've paid the price for falling in love with a married man." Joel tried comforting her, but his effort was fruitless. "My heart aches," she said, clutching her chest, "realizing Madeline has been right all along." She let her head rest on her son's chest. She craved sleep, not the short rest coming from a nap. She dreamed of a long rest, one where her worries, fears, and grief would melt away. "I have no reason to stay here."

"Why don't you come live with me? The mansion is awfully big for one person. I would feel much better having you close by so I can take care of you."

She sat up, took a breath of air, wanting to appear in control. Joel had endured too much already with running DMI. She didn't want to be added to his list of burdens. She wiped the tears from her cheeks and said, "Don't you worry about me. Your mother will survive." She patted his hand.

"Do you have an idea of what you want to do? Sitting around here won't be too much fun without Dad," he said, and stopped in midsentence.

She tried to assure him the mention of his father's name wouldn't make her crumble.

"You need to be around people who care about you."

"Well, that's a very short list. Are you trying to cheer me up or make me more depressed?" She wanted to laugh, but the effort was greater than anticipated. She wasn't ready for joyous moments. Breathing would be hard enough without Dave.

"It's true. You have many people in the office who've sent cards, flowers, and notes to you."

"Those tributes were for your father. He was the one they loved. I haven't accomplished anything spectacular in my life," she said, "except having you."

He stood. "I refuse to let you wallow in sorrow alone in this house." He gently lifted her arms and she let her body follow. "Dry your eyes and go get some clothes."

"Why, where are we going?"

"You're coming home with me, no questions asked," he told her. She was about to respond, but he didn't let her. "No, no, no, Mom, no excuses," he said, shaking his finger in the air. "You're coming with me and that's that." He engulfed her tiny frame with his hug. "I'm sure this is what Dad would have asked me to do."

She reciprocated the hug and said, "You are definitely your father's son, and I couldn't be any prouder of you than I am today. I thank God for you." She and God didn't have many conversations. His name rarely came out of her mouth. Dave was the one who had spent plenty of time with God, practically all his time. God had already taken most of what mattered, and finally, after twenty-eight years, he'd taken Dave, too. There just wasn't much to say to God, except thank you for giving her Joel. He was her only remaining love. Sherry rested in her son's embrace, feeling safe, loved, and needed.

"You'll stay with me for at least a few weeks until you decide what you'd like to do next."

"Then what? I don't have any skills or education. I'm hopeless."

"Remember," he said, wrapping his hands around her cheeks and lifting them up, "I'm CEO of a large organization. You can work for me."

She stepped back in order to have a full view of his face, looking for signs of fatigue. "What are you talking about? A job? I haven't worked in over twenty years. There's no job for me at DMI."

"Of course there is. Like I said, I'm CEO. I have the ability to create a job for you."

"Oh, that's just silly talk," she said, walking to the kitchen.

"It's not. Think about it. Madeline has been coming down hard on me. Abigail is always looking out for me, but I could use someone else in my corner, someone I trust," he told her.

She would gladly give her life for Joel, but what could she possibly do for him at the office? Her skills were limited to being an administrative assistant, and he already had one.

"You show up tomorrow and we'll find a role for you—not just any role, one that makes you happy. I'll talk with Abigail, she'll have a few ideas," he said, following her. "Don't you worry, we'll have you working at DMI before the week is over."

"I am going to have that cup of tea and you can join me," she said, excited like a kid before the first day of school. The thought of being productive made her suddenly felt lighter. A hundred pounds of loneliness was lifted. Tomorrow was a new beginning, thanks to her beloved son. He was Dave's single greatest gift to her and her alone, not to be shared with Madeline.

chapter

28

Madeline clutched the funeral program as if she could squeeze life into Dave. She relished the memories. No one had the ability to make her so angry and a few breaths later make her laugh and feel alive the way Dave Mitchell had. Forty years of connection. Divorce didn't destroy their bond. He was and forever would be her first and only. "I can't figure out if your father was smart or crazy."

"What do you mean?" Don asked, staring out his living room window.

"He made Joel CEO but didn't give him controlling interest. Dave had to know the stock split would strain the situation," she said. Don didn't seem engaged. Whatever was outside the window had stolen his focus. "Are you listening to me?" she asked, with no reaction from him. "Don Mitchell," she called, this time snatching his attention.

"What, Mother?" he said, appearing quite a distance away.

"Did you hear me? I said your father was crazy splitting the stock between the families. Goes to show you he never replaced me in his heart. The stock split was confirmation."

"I'm not following you, Mother."

"Don't you get it? This was his way of leaving us the company without blatantly kicking Joel and Sherry out on the street." Don looked confused. "If we take my twenty-five percent, your fifteen, that gives us forty. Tamara's fifteen percent gives us a total of fifty-five percent—controlling interest." She waved the program in the air like a music director, swaying from side to side, hearing soothing melodies that no one else could. "I can't believe we're so close to reclaiming our company. I told you we'd get your CEO position back," she sang, twirling around the room, feeling like dancing, the way Dave used to worship before his God. "Didn't I tell you, huh, didn't I tell you? With controlling interest, our first order of business will be to appoint a new CEO." She waltzed her way over to Don, who hadn't budged from his daydreaming spot in front of the window. "What in the world is so intriguing out this window that you can't talk to me?"

"Just thinking about what it was like when Sam and Andre and Tamara were at home with me, when we were growing up together in the mansion. So long ago, so long ago," he said, returning his gaze to the clouds pasted in the sky. "Nothing can bring those times back; they're gone, every one of them, including Tamara."

"At least she's still alive. My detective got the message to her about your father."

"She got several messages and she didn't come, doesn't that tell you something, Mother?"

"Tells me that she doesn't want to be crowded, but once I reestablish the company and create a position for her, I believe in my heart she'll come back to us. She needs us as much as we need her. She just needs a little more time, and we can give her the time. But we do need her stock to get our plan underway," she said, twirling around again.

"Your plan," Don said, slipping his hands into his suit pants and leaning completely against the drapes lining a section of the window.

"Not my plan, our plan. I'm getting DMI back for you and your sister. I want you to have what rightfully belongs to the two of you. I helped build this business and it rightfully belongs to you. I don't care if Sherry and Joel get a piece of the pie. There's more than enough left for us. Heck, I'll let her keep the mansion, too," Madeline said, dousing with laughter.

"The mansion is hers anyway, Mother. You heard the reading of the will."

"Sure, sure, but if I wanted to drag her behind into court for my half of the house I'm positive there's some overzealous attorney out there who's willing to take Sherry on."

"What a waste of money and time."

"I'm not saying I'm actually going to do it. I'm saying I could if I wanted to go that far. Luckily for her, I have bigger fish to fry. I have to take over my own company. Thanks to your father loving me more and giving me more children, I have the ammunition to win this time." She glided across the room to the sofa. "I'm so excited my head is hurting. Can you get me a glass of water, please?"

Don didn't hesitate. "Good thing you wanted water. There's nothing else in the kitchen."

"That's because you need to move back home and help me pull off my takeover."

"I don't want to be in the middle of this," he said, approaching her with the bottle of water and a goblet.

"You don't have a choice. We have no idea when your sister is going to show up. So, that leaves us. I can't do this without you."

"What about Abigail? Can she help you? She owns five percent of the stock."

"Even with our forty percent and her five we fall short. Besides, we can't count on Abigail, not the way Joel has claimed her. They're too tight. Consider her door closed," she said, sipping the water. She is ninety-five if not one hundred percent in Joel's corner." Don appeared agitated. "What's wrong with you?"

"Who, me?" he responded. "Nothing."

He wasn't convincing. There was something bothering him, but Madeline wouldn't push. She was content having her son on the same continent, within arm's reach. She wasn't about to drive him away.

chapter

29

Convincing Madeline was difficult. She was tuned in with his feelings most of the time, except when her reason was clouded by a heated disagreement with Sherry, like the one earlier in the day at the lawyer's office. Madeline meant well, and Don fully understood her desire to gain control of the ministry. He wanted to thank his father for giving his mother hope of regaining her rightful place in DMI. As for him, there was no place he wanted in the company.

"What's wrong? And don't tell me nothing," Madeline said.

"I'm thinking about my father and wishing I'd gotten a chance to see him before he died."

"He loved you, Don, he told me so. His last words

were spent on you and Tamara, sharing his love for you and apologizing for not being with you."

"I didn't get a chance to tell him how much I loved him and that I really don't hate him. He crushed me badly lots of times, but I can't find it in my heart to hate him. Trust me, I wanted to, but I don't hate him."

"Of course you don't, he's your father."

"But don't misunderstand. There are times when I'm very mad. I love him but I don't like him. Even with all that," he said, tightening his fists, "I wish I'd been here before he died. Maybe we could have worked out our issues. He tried and I said no. It's eating me alive inside."

Madeline beckoned for him to sit next to her on the sofa. "He knew," she said, staring into his eyes. "He told me the day would come after he died when you would feel guilty and sad about not reconciling with him. Your father was insistent upon your knowing that he accepted your apology, although he said none was needed from you. He truly did love you. I know it and in my heart you should, too. You can let go of your guilt," she said, tapping his forearm. "You can consider you and your father to be reconciled."

Hearing his father's words lifted a ton of the guilt but not all of it. He would let time deal with the rest.

"So," she said, taking a sip of water from the goblet, "when are you moving back into your condo? You're paying the mortgage. You might as well use the place."

"Good point. I'll have the realtor put this place on the market."

"No, no," she said, rushing the glass of water to the table. "I didn't mean for you to leave permanently. Keep the place. It will make me feel like a part of you is here."

"I can't afford this place here and one there, too, not

while I'm in the process of launching my company. My investors are on the light side, which means I have to use my capital to fund this project."

"You've inherited twenty million dollars. How much more seed money do you need?" Don glared at his mother without uttering a sound. "Oh, don't tell me that you don't want the money. I told you before, I helped build this company. That inheritance is yours." Don's glare was fixed. "Fine with me if you don't want to use the money in Africa. I don't want you to waste your money on a start-up anyway, not when you can assume leadership of an established business right here at home where you belong."

"Face it, Mother, I'm not staying in Michigan. My future isn't here."

"Your future isn't in Africa either."

"Maybe not, but it's definitely not here." A glimmer of interest from Abigail would keep him in North America. Without her, there was no reason to stay. He'd sign his stock over to his mother and she could easily wrestle the giants at DMI without his help.

"Is there any way I can convince you to stay?"

"Not this time." Her disappointment rang loudly. He didn't want to hurt her any further. "I'm flying out tomorrow but we have tonight. Let's grab a nice dinner at Coach Insignia."

"Ah, the seventy-second floor of the Renaissance sounds nice to me, as long as you're paying, since money doesn't matter to you," she said with a touch of humor.

He stood and brought his mother along. "Maybe we can take in a few dances, too," he said, twirling her around. He couldn't help but to think of Abigail. She was never far from his heart, even though he couldn't help but to acknowledge the connection between Abigail and baby brother. Whatever it was couldn't have become too serious in a month. Dueling with Joel over a car or a company was feasible; dueling over the affection of Abigail wasn't. The choice was hers alone, to be made without pressure.

"Well, I accept my defeat, at least for this round, but don't expect me to give up, not until you're home."

"I'd be disappointed if you did give up on me, Mother," he said, giving her one more twirl. "As a matter of fact, why don't you come for a visit? The vacation will do you good. This way you can check up on me and see for yourself that I have food, running water, and who knows what else you think I'm deprived of in Cape Town."

"Oh, I don't know about a visit."

"Why not? You're willing to do everything else for me."

He could tell that got her thinking seriously about the invitation. "We'll see."

"Good enough," he said, twirling her again, slowly this time.

"Who knows, one day you just might look up and see me at your front door."

"I hope so."

"You know," she said, "you are undoubtedly your father's son, with those smooth dance moves. Go on back to Africa with my blessing."

"What?"

"Go on back, have yourself a good time. Just don't fall in love with some beautiful woman over there and abandon us. Get this adventure out of your system. One day soon I expect you to help me run our company."

"Now that's the mother I know and love. You had me scared there for a moment. I thought you had changed and given in," he said, chuckling. "What's next, baking pies with Sherry?" he said, barely able to speak the words over his laughter.

She playfully pulled away. "The day I bake a pie with Sherry is the day you can consider Madeline Mitchell a bona fide nut case."

One Year Later

chapter

30

The library was a monstrosity, a complete waste of hard-earned dollars. The three-story building was practically the size of Neiman-Marcus, Nordstrom's, and Macy's combined. Even the interior was outrageous, a blend of Egyptian and Botticino marble, heated inlaid floors, twenty-four-karat-gold bathroom fixtures, meditation room, king-sized leather chairs throughout, Brazilian solid wood floors, and hand-painted stained-glass windows flown in from a small town in England. The place was absurd even for the high-spending Mitchells. Standing outside the Dave Mitchell Leadership Library, Madeline reflected on her childhood, trying to identify a time when she'd done something bad enough to warrant the endless torture she was experiencing as an adult. Joel's success was neverending. The more she tried to knock him down the more powerful he was becoming. The parking lot was jammed with cars and patrons, some of whom had waited outside overnight to claim a spot at the dedication ceremony.

Madeline and the other members of the DMI leadership team and board of directors stood in a line behind the podium as the mayor concluded his speech.

"As the mayor of Detroit, I extend a heartfelt thank-you to Mr. Joel Mitchell. Your contributions to the community and commitment to the great city of Detroit is what makes our city unique. By establishing an award-winning state-of-the-art library in Detroit, you're telling the world that this is a viable place to live, work, and gain knowledge. Mr. Mitchell, on behalf of the mayor's office and the city council, I present to you the key to our fair city. As you have demonstrated your loyalty to the city, we reciprocate with our loyalty to you. Thank you for believing in our great city," the mayor concluded.

Madeline couldn't spread her toes inside her stilettos, not sure which was the greater agony, her feet or her very presence at Joel's pompous event. At least pain in her toes was tolerable and worth the sacrifice. The same couldn't be said for anything related to Joel. There was a ray of hope. Maybe he would take the key and move into City Hall, leaving DMI to deserving people. She shifted her weight on the stilettos and glanced at her Rolex, wondering how much longer this farce could drag out.

Joel took the podium. Perhaps he'd forgotten. They were executives, not celebrities, she thought, crunching her toes. She couldn't waste an entire day at a flashy media event when there were matters to handle at the office, especially if DMI was ever going to be hers. "Thank you, Mayor. On behalf of DMI, I'm honored to present the Dave Mitchell Leadership Library. Many of you didn't know my father, but he was quite an extraordinary man. He dreamed of building this library for many years. When his health failed last year, I promised him I'd complete the library in his honor. Thanks to your generosity, we raised a staggering amount of money and completed the library seven months ahead of schedule. I'm grateful to the Lord for your support."

The crowd roared, irritating Madeline more. The people were fixated on him. Over the past year donors had tossed nearly $380 million at Joel to construct the library. His favor with strangers was ridiculous. She'd made several failed attempts over the past year to dethrone him and refused to give up. He had to be stopped. She would see to it, but first Madeline had to find the right kind of employees to implement a new strategy to save the company. The fastest route would seemingly be to convince Tamara to reunite with the family. After twelve years, five months, and nineteen days, the probability of her daughter's returning was too low to hang her takeover plans on. She had to create a surefire strategy, one that would destroy Joel's image in the process. Leaking rumors to the press, dwelling on his incompetence, hadn't worked. In the year since Dave's death, the menace had grown more powerful, professional, intelligent, wealthy, and self-righteous than her stomach could stand. He was on top, which meant he had farther to fall.

chapter

31

Followed by accolades from the crowd, Joel and Abigail proceeded to the limousine. Sherry was riding with them, too. Madeline had insisted on coming separately. Safely nestled in the vehicle, Joel asked, "What about grabbing dinner? The dedication was top-notch but the appetizers didn't cut it for me. I'm a growing man. I need food," he said, patting his flat stomach. His daily regimen of strength and endurance training was paying off. Little Joel was no more. DMI's leader was muscular and fit, looking like an athlete at the pinnacle of his game. The days of Joel's being pushed around, in or out of the boardroom, had passed.

"I'm tired," Sherry said. "You can take me home."

Sherry's melancholy tone wasn't surprising. Seeing Dave's dream of a library being erected a year after his death was probably overwhelming. The time Sherry had stayed with Joel seemed to help with her grief after Dave's death. Joel wanted her to stay longer, but Sherry was adamant about going home several months ago. He couldn't change her mind.

"Would you like for us to come to the estate with you and have dinner there?" Abigail asked, sensitive to Sherry's feelings.

"Good idea," Joel added.

"No, not at all. I prefer to be alone with my thoughts," she said, tapping both Abigail and Joel on the backs of their hands. "Drop me off and keep going. Enjoy your dinner, and don't spend a moment worrying about me." Joel didn't look convinced. "I mean it, son, go, don't worry about me. You made me very proud today. You've fulfilled your father's dream, one that he was never able to realize. You did it. So, yes, take me home. My day is complete."

"All right," Joel said, with a lingering sound of doubt. He picked up the phone in the limousine. Once the driver answered, Joel proceeded with his instruction. "John, please swing by the estate and then take us to the Chop House. Thanks," he said, pulling the receiver from his ear. "It's not too late to change your mind and come with us," he said, dangling the receiver. "John can swing around and jump on I-696. We'll be there in no time."

"Not changing my mind. Take me home, where I belong." Sherry's words were convincing this time. The air that she gave off said, "I know what I want." Joel accepted. He placed the receiver on the base and sat back looking as relaxed and in charge as usual—one of the many characteristics Abigail had grown to love about him over the past year.

chapter

32

Don plowed through the stack of contracts. The year had zipped by with his company consuming every waking hour. He didn't have time for anything else, including himself. He had more business than he could handle. Companies from Ireland to the Cape were eager to partake of his leadership-training program. He wasn't dealing with churches any longer, strictly with corporations that were considering expansion plans and needed leadership training. DMI didn't value him, but the rest of the world found worth in his abilities. There was no time to resurrect woes that were dead and buried. He had a chunk of work to complete. He tossed the pen into the air. He needed help.

Fond memories of working alongside Abigail and his father threatened to overwhelm him, but daydreaming was a luxury he hadn't been able to afford in at least nine months, not even those about Abigail. He was too focused on getting established to think about romance, but there were times when thoughts came uncontrollably. He carved his father out of the memory, unwilling to open the wound of grief, and zoomed in on Abigail. Twelve months hadn't driven her into his arms, but the future was yet to be written. In the meantime, he reflected on her zest for business. There were no limits on how large his venture could become with Abigail. He reached for the newspaper clippings containing a snapshot of his mother, Sherry, Joel, and Abigail in front of the new library. He ripped his mother's note from the page, full of not-so-nice comments about Joel's extravagant taste, a definite contrast to his.

The leased space was tight, situated in the heart of Cape Town's business district. Don had an office, a receptionist's desk out front, a small waiting area, a conference room, and two open areas that held his thirty employees. Most of them were trainers, with several customer service representatives, a marketer, an accountant, a receptionist, and a part-time attorney. He took in the bay view from his window. He didn't offer his employees much in the way of extravagant accomodations, but the view of Table Mountain from their desks carried some value. His company was overrunning the office space, but the views and location weren't easy to relinquish.

Leadership Training International (LTI) was growing rapidly, already booking over $3 million in revenue in less than seven months. His ideas surpassed his capital. He had a few investors but opted to hold off acquiring more. There was no interest in having too many external voices feeling empowered by their financial contribution to direct his company. He had amassed a decent amount of savings from the ten years of employment in DMI, which were the funds he used to get started. This was his company, built with his earned money, and it ran with his vision. Using his inheritance wasn't an option. Don was his own man, not his father's boy. He was determined not to let anyone lay claim to what was his. The cramped space would have to work for now.

The knock on the door startled him. With a rapid tap to his temple, he remembered the interview scheduled for 2:00 P.M. He took a quick glance at the résumé on his desk, searching for her name. He desperately needed an assistant, someone who could help him maintain order, sort of like an office manager. His receptionist brought the young lady in. Cape Town was drenched with a unique blend of African, Indian, and European culture, much like the candidate entering the room. The hue of her shaded skin and the texture of her hair didn't give him any indication of her nationality.

"Good day, Ms. Mophuti," he said, lowering his head slightly toward her, just short of a full bow. After many months, he still didn't know when it was appropriate to shake hands, bow, or do nothing. "Ms. Mophuti, please come in. Can I get you anything, water perhaps?" he asked, escorting her to one of the two chairs in front of his desk.

"No thank you, sir," she said with a dialect that he couldn't quite make out. Even her accent seemed blended.

"Please call me Don," he said, taking a seat after she sat.

"And you may please call me Naledi."

"Naledi, your accent, where are you from?"

"Here in Cape Town, but I studied in France."

"You speak French?"

"*Oui.* I've also worked in China and went to the States on an exchange program." Her accent was grabbing his attention each time she spoke.

"What other languages do you speak?"

"A bit of Mandarin. My English, French, and my four South African languages are stronger."

"What about experience?"

"Here's my document," she said, the words wrapped in her French-dipped South African accent. Naledi handed him a sheet of paper. He already had her résumé and was impressed. After meeting her, he was confident that Naledi was perfect for the job. He found himself gazing at her. There was an alluring aspect to Ms. Naledi Mophuti, not only her beauty, which was evident, but her confidence, her background, her willingness to take on the world. The office could use a boost of energy and local support.

"I've heard enough," he said, standing. "The job as my assistant is yours if you want it." Something about her gave him peace. Now his time at LTI could be spent doing what he did best—reaching out to people and growing the business, this time on his terms.

Don had moved out of the hotel and into a flat located near LTI several months ago—nothing elaborate. Money was tight. Raising close to a million dollars by selling the condo in Detroit was a viable option at times, but he wasn't ready, not really, to close the door on life back home. Madeline insisted on making the payments and wouldn't take no for an answer. He was glad, although she'd never know.

He plumped the pillows, antsy that his mother was

en route to his place. His mother and Abigail had an open invitation to Cape Town. Finally, after a year, Madeline was coming to the Cape. Don jetted around tidying. He'd picked up a few groceries, but knowing his mother, she was planning to eat out for each meal. The miserly side of life wasn't a place his mother cared to dwell. He didn't see her as a condescending kind of rich, but definitely a "let-me-enjoy-my-money" kind of person. He looked around the thousand-square-foot flat. His home would take some getting used to for her, but the main thing was that she was coming. He glanced at his watch and bopped downstairs to get a taxi to the airport.

A twenty-five-minute ride and he was there. The plane landed safely. They collected her luggage and talked nonstop from the gate to the taxi stand.

"Where's your car?" she asked.

"Detroit."

"Quit playing. You know I mean the one here," she said, holding on to his arm.

He beckoned for the next taxi to pull up. "Don't have one," he said, opening the car door for her before the driver came around to greet them.

"What do you mean? Never mind, I'm sure I don't want to know." She slid into the backseat still talking. "I'm glad I brought my checkbook. Looks like I have some purchases to make. I should have asked first, do they take foreign checks?"

He didn't bother responding. Having her on South African soil was good enough, his soul was quieted. It would have been nice for Abigail to come, too, but his mother was definitely not a consolation prize. She was the friendly face from home he needed to see. Don instructed the driver and watched as he loaded the suitcase, garment bag, and carry-on piece into the trunk. Losing one tiny piece of luggage would be enough for his mother to load him on the next plane to Detroit, fearing for his safety. Her exaggerated view of his world was harmless and, in a strange way, endearing. He climbed into the backseat and clutched her hand. "I'm glad you're here, really glad." No mother could have been more loving or kinder to him than Madeline. Every moment, as far back as he could remember, she'd taken care of him, sacrificed for him, loved him, encouraged him, protected him, and most of all believed in him at times when he wasn't sure of himself. His success was hers.

"I can't wait to see your place."

Don wasn't as eager for her to see his flat. He concocted a plan B. "I can't wait for you to see my office. Let's swing by there first."

"Don, I've been flying for twenty-three hours. I need to get refreshed before meeting your employees."

He hadn't factored that part in. "You look fantastic, Mother."

"Absolutely not," she said, running her palm over her hair. "I'm not going in there looking like I've been up all night."

"Okay, okay, we'll stop by my flat," he said, being left without options, "but I have to warn you."

"What?" she said, turning her body in his direction and then back to the window. She looked panicked.

"My place is tiny."

"How tiny?"

"About the size of your bedroom at home if you take out one of your closets and the bathroom."

He was caught off guard when she started roaring with laughter. "I love it. You'll be home sooner than I think. You might not be as extravagant as Joel, but you're not exactly the frugal type either."

"I'm making it work. Plus, LTI is growing so fast that money will be pouring in soon. I can ride out this little tight period."

"That's your choice because you know I can help any time. All you have to do is say the word."

"I appreciate the offer, but I don't want you to help. This is for me to do. I have to make LTI successful on my own."

"Well, you're doing a fantastic job, based on the reports that you sent me." She pulled a thick stack of papers from her briefcase.

"Mother, we're almost there, another five minutes."

"Oh," she said, stuffing the papers back inside, "we can talk at the office. I have some marketing ideas for you. I think there's more opportunity for you in Western Africa and Southern Europe. You know my expertise is with churches located in North America. General leadership in foreign markets is beyond me. So, I took the liberty of retaining a consulting group to do a quick country assessment on the key markets between South Africa and Europe. They're expressing the report to me at your office tomorrow. We have some work to do."

"I was hoping to get that marketing brain of yours working for me. I knew you couldn't resist an underdeveloped marketing plan."

"You won't let me do anything else to help. The least I can do is to spend the next two weeks working for you, since you won't take my money."

"Your expertise is priceless and is exactly what LTI needs."

"I never asked how you came up with the name LTI," she said.

"I started to use Mitchell Enterprises."

"Why didn't you? It is your name."

When he came to South Africa, his father and God were the last two he wanted to be connected with. The name he chose intentionally capitalized on pure training with no church or Dave Mitchell ties.

"LTI sounds better," he told his mother, and said no more. His mother didn't need to know the details behind the name. All he wanted her to see were the successes. The cornerstones were in place with his mother and Naledi running the office. The taxi came to a stop. The size of his flat wasn't an issue anymore. Madeline was in South Africa—his hero had arrived. He was sure the continent would never be the same.

chapter

33

Madeline had hatched idea after idea against Joel's reign with no mentionable success. A year since the library dedication and there was no progress on her end. She had gone to see Don twice. LTI was excelling, but Madeline wasn't giving up on the goal of bringing Joel down. She had a few new ideas, nothing concrete. Before she completed a plan of attack, she would make a few calls and rally the necessary support. Don wasn't interested in taking drastic measures to seize control, forcing her to take an alternative route. Who could she think of who would be as enthusiastic as she was about bringing Joel down to his rightful place? In the millisecond that it took for the idea to process in her brain, her fingers were already searching for the number and dialing.

A few rings and her ideal ally was on the other end of

the call. "Hello, Frank, it's been a few years. How's life treating you?" she said, using her pencil to pick at a short stack of papers on her desk. After the ice-breaking was completed she jumped right in; no need to drag out the call. She wanted an ally and she hoped Frank was her man. If not, she'd keep rolling until her plan was in place. "How would you like to work with me?"

"As chief financial officer at DMI?" he quickly responded.

"Not exactly," she said. Madeline was desperate to preserve her family's position in DMI, but she wasn't stupid. Dave should have fired Frank long before Joel got the chance. Firing him was the one correct decision Joel had made. She wanted an ally and would probably have to make a few promises that might or might not materialize, but her teeth wouldn't let the words "chief financial officer" squeak by. The lie would be too big for her to offer even in desperation.

"I don't know if I can work in the same place as that nephew of mine. He had the gall to fire me and damage my reputation."

Actually, stealing money from the company was what had discredited him. He managed to do that on his own without anyone's help, but who was she to save Joel. The more Frank despised Joel, the easier it would be for her to convince him to join her team. "I can't promise you a chief financial role, but I can make this proposition worth your while if you're interested. By the way, your nephew has nothing to do with this arrangement. This offer is strictly between the two of us. His nose doesn't need to be in our business. I will be your only point of contact."

"Now you're talking. I'm interested. Tell me more," Frank said.

"Not over the phone. I'll meet you at Dema in the Westin around 2:00 for a late lunch."

"Way out there by the airport?" he said.

"It's better this way. Don't worry. I will make the extra miles well worth the trip."

"I'm counting on it."

"I'm serious, and I suspect you are, too," Madeline said. It was about time the company got back on track and Frank was the ideal person to help her see to it. "I'll see you this afternoon," she said, and ended the call, releasing a load of anxiety. She was one step closer to fulfilling her dream of regaining control of DMI. Frank was a critical piece of the puzzle. She'd recruit the others next.

chapter

34

Today was the day—two years since Joel took over as CEO. Abigail zeroed in on the tiny picture in the upper righthand corner of the *Detroit Free Press*. She flipped past the other pages, not caring about the content, until she reached the cover page of the business section. She devoured each word in the headline: JOEL MITCHELL—THE NEW LEADERSHIP MINISTRY MOGUL. She fixed her eyes upon his bronze-toned skin, flawlessly displayed against the cream-colored tailor-made shirt and Armani suit. Her pulse sprinted and her palms moistened thinking about him. Relentlessly working out in the gym lifting weights had transformed his body into a solid twenty-five-year-old frame of steel. His five-foot-eleven body looked taller, more like Don's and Dave's. Standing with one hand in his pocket created an allure she had trouble categorizing. She stared a tad longer, letting her fingers trace his physique on the page, before shifting focus to the framed pictures on her desk, the one taken at the DMI Christmas party last year and the other taken last summer at the county fair. Abigail treasured the countless hours they spent together and his absolute commitment to being the best. Personal distractions had been eliminated, as he promised.

There was a rap on the door.

"Yes, come in," Abigail said, laying the newspaper on the desk.

Sherry entered with a cup in her hand. "I know you don't drink coffee. Would you like a cup of tea?"

"Why thank you, but I'll pass. Sherry, I keep telling you not to worry about me. You are Joel's assistant, not mine. Don't push yourself so much."

Sherry waved off the comment. "It's no bother. I'm happy to be useful."

Abigail picked up the newspaper. "Did you see the article yet?" Abigail shook the page in the air.

"Oh, I forgot, it is Wednesday," Sherry said, grabbing the paper, visibly excited.

Abigail relaxed in her chair. Thank goodness her pulse had slowed to a trot.

"Did you read this?" Sherry asked, with an expression difficult to interpret.

"Not yet," Abigail said, letting concern and excitement mix in her response. "Why, what does it say?"

Sherry folded the section in half and began reading. "This says Joel Mitchell, the youngest son of the late Dave Mitchell (founder of DMI), is in charge and living up to the . . ." she read, stumbling over several words. "Here," she said, handing the paper back to Abigail. "You read it. My reading glasses are in my desk."

"Are you sure?" Abigail asked as she accepted the paper and continued with the article. "Let's see, where were you?" She scrolled the article. "Okay, here it is," she murmured and then started reading at, " . . . Joel is in charge and living up to the well-publicized Mitchell legacy of success."

"Dave would be honored," Sherry interjected, with a faint crack in her voice.

Abigail paused until Sherry gave her the signal to continue. "But business isn't his only appeal these days. The twenty-five-year-old CEO is single, quite debonair, maintains a sharp spiritual edge, and seems to have a knack for adventure. You won't find this CEO vacationing in the Hamptons or on the golf courses of West Palm Beach. Oddly, we haven't found him cruising the Mediterranean coastline in the South of France with the company of other CEOs either. Perhaps we will soon see this eligible bachelor languishing in Monte Carlo with a sea of other rich, handsome men with lots of money, fashion models, power, style, and charisma."

"Did they really say charisma?" Sherry asked.

"Can you believe that?" Abigail responded. "He's going to laugh his head off."

"They make him sound like a playboy."

"I'm very glad he isn't," Abigail said, taking another look at their photos on her desk and briefly reflecting on his list of friends and acquaintances, as he called them. Abigail and Joel weren't officially committed, but for the past two years they had been inseparable. Like had gelled into love somewhere along the way as Joel went from novice trainee to commanding leader. Every moment she could have dedicated to relaxation was willingly given to him. She never doubted his ability to fulfill his calling and become a solid CEO. She poured her experience, knowledge, and hopes into helping him rise up the learning curve, but the jumbo dose of wisdom God had poured into him made the undeniable difference. She was there to help smooth out the rough spots and happily spent every minute with him, no matter what they were doing.

"Wow," Sherry said, standing, "you're in love with him?"

"How can you tell?" she asked Sherry, shocked that her emotions were so easily interpreted.

"By the look you have on your face when you talk about him. The same look I had when I met his father. Does he know?"

"I've never told him, exactly."

"Maybe you should."

"The time isn't right. He has to concentrate on DMI, I'd say, for another six months to a year. Once he has served as CEO for three years, he should be able to ease up and focus on other aspects of his life." She didn't believe pressuring and clinging to a man would push him into a commitment any faster. Besides, Abigail had her own timeline. She had another year and a half before turning thirty. By then they would have to be in a serious relationship or she'd have to accept his lack of interest as reality and move on. Thinking about the possibility of not being together was depressing. Keeping a positive attitude and the hope that Joel would eventually make his move drowned her unrest. "I can wait," Abigail said.

"I wouldn't," Sherry said, headed for the door.

"There's more in the article."

Sherry waved her hand, the one that wasn't holding her cup. "I heard what I needed to hear. Joel is safe. We always believed he was in the right job. Now the world knows he's more than capable of running DMI as his father wanted," Sherry said. She laid her hand over her heart and took a deep breath. "I'm so happy for Joel, and his father would be, too." She took a hard swallow. "I'm leaving your office now before I bawl over your entire rug," she said, appearing to force in a pinch of humor.

Once Sherry was gone and she was left alone, Abigail picked up the paper and read the rest of the article. The phrase "eligible bachelor" stood out. Little did they know that he was single but most certainly not eligible. He hadn't spoken the words, but the diamond necklace given to her last Christmas and the countless hours they had spent together were his way of telling her how special she was. Abigail was certain, reflecting on their time together, that the gift was nice but his devotion to her was immeasurable. He was well worth the wait.

chapter

35

"Lord, I give you the honor, the praise, and the glory, because you are the one true God. Let our mission in DMI bring glory to your name. Let us touch countless lives for your kingdom through the gift of salvation," Joel said. Madeline heard Joel praying as she entered the boardroom. Watching Joel rattle off prayers and hum hymns was irritating and bordering on the sacrilegious.

"Excuse me," she interrupted, having heard plenty, "I'm early."

"Nothing wrong with being on time, God always is," Joel said.

Madeline buried her comments in a binder of papers. If he rattled off another preachy "thus said the Lord" cliché, she was sure to scream until her lungs collapsed or she simply vomited, preferably on him instead of her Chanel suit. Madeline was relieved to see others entering the room. Next time she'd arrive five minutes late to avoid being caught in a room with the prodigal son of Moses, the one determined to preach from the mountaintops and the DMI boardroom.

Madeline saw him glance at the wall clock. "We have a full agenda; let's get started," Joel said, removing his suit coat and handing it to Sherry, which was appropriate. She called herself his executive assistant, but her presence was merely an attempt to keep her from dying of boredom alone in the mansion. Madeline dared not admit that having Sherry around DMI wasn't as nauseating as expected. She could respect a mother who reentered the workforce purely to protect and support her child's interest. Don and LTI popped into her mind. In a different life she and Sherry might have been friends, but as Dave's ex-wife and mistress, bonding wasn't feasible.

"I'm prepared to give an update on the East Coast operation," Madeline interjected, as she typically did, but her interest for the past three months had been set squarely on the Midwest, the center of her plan. She'd tried reuniting Tamara to the family, with no luck. With no other options left, she had taken creative measures. She was beginning to taste success, a morsel which had been elusive until now. Being this close to having control of DMI was exhilarating. Her toes tingled.

"We'll get to your update," Joel said, "because I'm very curious to see how we're doing with churches in the Philadelphia, Maryland, and D.C. areas. However, you'll notice that I've changed the order for today. Normally I'd have the division leaders present their reports first, then walk through the goals for next month, discuss issues, and conclude with senior-level promotions."

There was nothing wrong with the old format. Madeline was sick of him changing this and changing that. Joel had singlehandedly unraveled most of the procedures competent people had put in place under Dave's leadership.

"Any objections?" he asked the group.

She didn't expect this group to tell the CEO no. Madeline fidgeted in her seat, looking for a sign of support. Finding none, she stopped talking and started tapping her pen against her portfolio.

"Let me start by thanking each of you for your contributions. As a result of your dedication, make-it-happen attitude, and commitment to my father's vision, I'm pleased to announce we've booked record revenues this quarter."

Madeline was perplexed. "Based on what?" she asked, reaching for any kink in his report, hoping he was wrong. He consistently dominated meetings, but she wasn't about to let him hold the spotlight much longer. He had been incompetent before, and just as he'd learned how to run a meeting overnight, perhaps he would revert to incompetence just as quickly. If not, her backup plan would take care of the problem.

"This is such a monumental achievement, I wanted absolute certainty. George," Joel said to the chief financial officer. "Will you share the numbers for this quarter, please?"

"Gladly. Second-quarter revenues top off at $541 million. This time last year DMI booked $175 million in revenue, which was the highest second-quarter number we'd ever seen until now."

"Before we have a big celebration, are you sure those numbers are correct? I'd hate to publish the numbers and communicate this notion of a record growth only to find out we miscalculated. As a board member, I want to avoid bringing unnecessary embarrassment to the company," Madeline said.

"I understand, Madeline. I can assure you, my staff and I ran a fine-tooth comb through the numbers. The report is solid. DMI is on an unprecedented growth trend. Not only are revenues up, but costs are down, thanks to Joel's consolidation plan," George said.

"Are you saying that profits are up, too?" she asked.

"Yes, in fact, profits are also at a record high." The chief financial officer positioned his reading glasses and read more. "In the two years since I've been on board, we've realized a twenty-one percent profit margin, but this quarter we're at forty-eight percent," he said, pulling his glasses off. "The good news is that for the first time in the history of DMI, we're retaining forty-eight cents on every dollar generated, after expenses. That's unheard of in this industry."

"We have to give the praise to God. He has showered DMI with unprecedented favor," Joel said. "I'm convinced as we continue to dedicate ourselves to God's work, He will continually take this ministry to an unimaginable place of growth and success. This is only the beginning for DMI. There's more expansion to come. You haven't seen anything yet."

Madeline should have been happy for DMI. She owned 25 percent of the company, but her disgust at Joel didn't allow her to embrace the same level of enthusiasm as others in the room.

"Dave Mitchell obviously passed his business genes on to his son Joel," George said. "Congratulations on a record quarter," he continued, prompting a stir of casual acknowledgments from the room of managers.

So what if he had a decent quarter. The fight wasn't over. "Great news for DMI," Madeline said, rising to her feet. "Undoubtedly the tremendous growth is due to the tireless efforts of those around this table. On behalf of the DMI board of directors and management team, I say thank you. This would have been a proud day for Dave Mitchell, if I can speak for him."

"Actually, Madeline, I'd like to speak for him," Joel said, standing and forcing Madeline to sit. "My father committed most of his life to DMI. He strived to run the ministry with integrity and leadership. Many of us were fortunate to sit under his leadership and glean his management style, vision, and strategies. One person in particular had a tremendous opportunity to work closely with Dave Mitchell for five years."

Madeline knew he was referring to Abigail, but why was he wasting management time on the obvious? Dave's mentoring was old news.

"She was instrumental in handling the East Coast transition after Don Mitchell's role became vacant," he said.

Joel knew Madeline had taken over the East Coast the day after Don was fired and had run it ever since, practically singlehandedly. He wasn't giving her any credit. Madeline was mad and wanted to correct him, but wouldn't dream of exposing her hand with an outburst in front of a room of DMI leaders. She'd have to moan inside and bide her time. In a few weeks Joel would be sufficiently exposed.

"Abigail, since you're a key player in the livelihood of DMI, I'm promoting you to executive vice president providing oversight for all the division managers. In your new role you will officially report directly to me."

Cheers and greetings ensued for a brief time.

"I don't know what to say," Abigail responded, covering her mouth.

"There's no one here more suited for the position and no one I trust as much to get the job done," he said as Madeline watched Abigail blush like a schoolgirl. "Madeline will continue to run the East Coast. Barry will manage the Central Division, and Connie will keep the South." Barry and Connie nodded in agreement.

Madeline wasn't agreeing to any move made by Joel. Who was he to add a layer between her and the CEO position? She had to get Don, or herself, in position to save DMI and her sanity. Both, as far as she was concerned, were in jeopardy so long as Joel was in charge. The Midwest fiasco couldn't come soon enough.

"I'm appointing a new vice president to build the West Coast division. Abigail, I'll need your help filling the position. The good news is that you're totally in charge. The bad news is that you have to jump right into the role. I have three candidates lined up this afternoon for you," he said, generating laughter.

Madeline wasn't amused. This group laughed when Joel told them to, spoke when asked, and coughed on cue. They were no help. She needed people in the organization who could formulate their thoughts without assistance from the CEO and stand their ground when necessary. She hoped she'd found them in the small team enlisted for her confidential "project."

"Let's get to our division reports," Joel said. "At our next management update, Abigail will take the lead on this agenda item."

Madeline and Connie presented their updates and Barry went last. Madeline listened intently, careful not to attract attention during his report.

"Our Creative Concept Contest has garnered an overwhelming response with the churches, the media, and within the communities. Madeline, this was an excellent idea. Thanks for the recommendation."

She cleared her throat, not expecting and not wanting the recognition. Part of the plan was to stay undetected. She gave a nod and kept her mouth shut, letting Barry do the talking. She needed distance between her and the Chicago campaign.

"We're on track to announce the winner in less than two weeks," Barry said, to Madeline's satisfaction. This was the aspect of his update that she wanted to hear. "We haven't experienced a single glitch, which is great news because the spotlight is on DMI with this campaign."

"Has the winner been selected?" Abigail asked.

In due time, Madeline yearned to say, but wasn't about to leak the punch line, not this close to showtime.

"Not yet, but we've narrowed the entries to less than fifty, which is substantial, since we started with over seven hundred entrants," Barry answered.

Barry's update was water to a thirsting soul. Madeline fiddled with her pen, unconcerned about all seven hundred entrants; fifty was her limit. Two weeks and counting. The last component, the most vital, was in place, according to Frank. She was leery but had no option but to trust him.

When the takeover was final, Madeline would have Sherry pack and go home. She savored the thought.

chapter

36

"Thank you for clearing your schedules on short notice," Joel said, taking the last empty spot at the circular table in his office. He felt comfortable sitting at the head of the table. Continual prayer and the support of Abigail allowed him to lead. Having her seated close by felt right, especially after witnessing her effectively step up to the vice president role since her appointment last week. Her presence was critical. The other seats were filled by Barry, Connie, Madeline, and the new hire for the West Coast.

"As you know," Joel said, "we aggressively searched for a leader who could build our West Coast presence, and I'm pleased to announce that our choice is Brian Turnquist. He has an operations background and has led a team of fifty for the past eight years. What impressed us most about Brian is that he's a strategic thinker, which is exactly what we need in order to grow the ministry west of Oklahoma. With that said, Brian, I welcome you to the ministry."

"Thank you for the opportunity. I look forward to great achievements on the West Coast," Brian said.

"I'm on the board of directors as well as a member of the executive team," Madeline said, "and I'd like to know more about your strategy for the West Coast. As you can imagine, my role is to ensure that the management philosophy and principles of the company are preserved."

Just like Madeline, Joel thought. Before the new hire could get pulled into Madeline's web, Joel jumped in, to save him and to prevent the meeting from being derailed by her personal agenda. She was always trying to cause a disruption, but her comments no longer affected Joel. It was about as insignificant as twenty-five cents on a $3 billion finance report. She was no longer in control. "Brian, we were going to do introductions next, but this is Madeline Mitchell. She has part ownership in DMI. As she stated, she's a board member and is also overseeing the East Coast operation. She has a wealth of knowledge that you will find helpful as you implement the West Coast strategy."

Madeline let out a humph. She didn't need or want his endorsement. Her numbers spoke for themselves.

"We can talk after this meeting about your successes with the East Coast," Brian said to Madeline.

She nodded. "You may want to pull demographics on large ministries in the California, Nevada, and Washington markets in the meantime."

"Great suggestion, Madeline," Joel interrupted. "But God has given me a vision for the West Coast that requires us to start with the small churches, the ones in the neighborhoods that no one realizes exist. I believe we have to reach those deemed unreachable. Barry and I have already spoken about the strategy. You will hear more in a few weeks."

Madeline didn't look pleased, but Joel refused to let her continue disrupting. His vision would not be hindered. One day Madeline would have to get past her contempt and push DMI forward as a team, under his leadership. He'd offered kind words with no impact. She'd have to come to terms on her own, but the morale of DMI wouldn't suffer in the meantime.

"What a fantastic concept," Connie said.

"I agree," Barry added. "We've never looked at building a division from the ground up."

Madeline felt compelled to speak and set the record straight about DMI's history. "That's not completely true. How do you think Dave and I began this company? The so-called megachurches weren't as prevalent thirty years ago as they are now. We started by targeting the small neighborhood churches. It's the basis for the Chicago marketing campaign Barry is running." She tried to snatch the last statement back, but the words were airborne. Carelessly exposing her link to Chicago was dangerous. The building blocks were in place. Finally victory seemed attainable. She had to be cautious. Quiet and focused was the role she'd learned to play.

"Even more reason for us to use the small-church approach—we know it works, so let's capitalize on the proven model," Joel stated.

"We can do a few focus groups in the area to get ideas from the communities," Barry said.

"You can do our usual media blitz to boost awareness," Abigail added.

"I want to take a bolder approach," Joel said. "We'll layer our success stories and a regional marketing campaign around the expansion with a series of complimentary admissions to upcoming workshops."

"I thought you wanted to use the proven model. It's worked for us in the past. Why change now?" Madeline sniped.

"I want to improve the model by taking a few calculated risks."

Madeline could tell the team was mulling over the idea. "This company wasn't built on risky propositions. DMI has grown because of wise decisions rooted in sound judgment."

"I'm confident about the new approach. We can use several new interactive venues to get the word out, including the internet," Joel said.

"I think you have a great idea that we need to explore," Abigail said.

"It's edgy, creative," Connie asked. "I like the idea. Kudos to you."

"One hundred percent of the credit goes to God," Joel said, tapping his index finger.

Eighteen months ago Joel would have cowered, and she would have taken over the meeting. Now he spoke without showing the slightest sign of vulnerability or ignorance. If the suggestion had come from anyone else, Madeline would have considered it a stroke of genius. Coming from Joel, the strategy was a stroke all right, but on her nerves. Maybe there was merit in the idea of shaking off her animosity toward Joel, but the seeds of war were too deeply planted for her to walk away. Madeline glanced in Sherry's direction, only to be repelled by her smug look of pride and adoration.

During a brief lull in the conversation, Sherry slipped Joel a note.

"Okay, everyone, are there any other questions, comments, concerns?" No one spoke, including Madeline. The less they knew about her "project" the better. "All right," Joel continued. "Since there aren't any more questions, we can adjourn. Again, Brian, I want to welcome you to the team," he said, standing and extending his hand.

"I want to fill you in on the details of the campaign," Barry told Joel as the team greeted Brian before leaving the boardroom.

"I really have to run," Joel said, straightening his shirt sleeves and cuff links after putting on his suit jacket. "A TV crew is here to produce a story about DMI's recent success. When are you flying back to Chicago?"

"Tonight," Barry said.

"Have my administrative assistant carve out time on my calendar for us this afternoon."

"Good, because this is important."

"No problem, we'll definitely speak later," Madeline overheard Joel tell Barry as he left the room with Abigail and Sherry in tow. Madeline was left alone with Barry.

"How's the campaign?" Madeline asked, careful not to appear overly interested, but her hopes were riding on his division.

"Picking a winner is proving to be tougher than we expected," Barry said.

She wanted to sing songs of joy. "I'm sure Joel can help. He's the smart man with the answers," Madeline said.

"I'm sure we can figure this out if I can get a few minutes of his time," Barry said, not appearing to be suspicious about her interest.

"The media seem to take most of his time," Madeline said, intending to add fuel.

"That's the biggest challenge, getting on his calendar."

"Did he say a TV crew?" Madeline asked.

"I'm not sure if it was TV or some other medium. Nope, actually, now that I think about it, he did say TV crew. Yes, he did. Isn't that great news? Joel is really leading DMI to new heights. This is an exciting time to be on the leadership team," Barry said, practically skipping out of the office.

When would Joel's reign end? she wondered. Madeline could contain him within the walls of DMI, but with the media continually featuring him, her job of discrediting him was going to be rough. She almost had to believe he really was in cahoots with God. If he did have favor, she knew her plan was hopeless. She left the office, preferring to believe that Joel was a hypocritical young man playing at religion and that, like so many other lost ministers and religious leaders, he would find his secret sins exposed publicly, and there would be no one to blame but himself. Ah, the sweet taste of his impending defeat made her feet feel light as feathers. She floated into the hallway renewed, hopeful, determined, and eager to get to work. Keeping her East Coast revenues at record levels was important if she was to assume the CEO position; that was, of course, if Don declined the offer.

chapter

37

Abigail stood in the back of DMI's special events room, out of view. This was Joel's spotlight. The makeup person puffed a small dab of powder onto his face after initial resistance from him. She was perfectly content standing in his shadow, there to watch, admire, support.

"Testing one two three," the young reporter said, organizing a few index cards in her hands. "Are we ready?" she asked the cameraman, who gave a thumbs-up. "Mr. Mitchell, during the interview we won't mention the date or time of day. Without a time stamp, we can rerun the segment several times throughout the year. Is that acceptable to you?" she said, with a look of adoration that Abigail detected.

"You're the expert. I will take your lead," he said,

punctuating his statement with a grin that lit up Abigail's world.

"Hmmm, let's get started then." The cameraman counted down three fingers and pointed at her to go. "Welcome to another segment of the *Business Journal*. I'm your host, Samantha Tate. Today we have on our show the very popular Mr. Joel Mitchell. He is the chief executive officer of DMI, the fastest-growing company in the Detroit metropolitan area. Welcome to our show, Mr. Mitchell."

"Thank you for having me," Joel said. He was calm and well spoken. Abigail couldn't take her eyes off him in the dark blue suit lined with tiny pinstripes. His platinum cuffs stood out but didn't distract Ms. Tate from his commanding dialogue. His words sounded like poetry, with a hypnotic ring.

"You've become a regular face in the media thanks to your recent success at DMI and, of course, the construction of your half-a-billion-dollar library. To what do you attribute your rapid success?"

"Wisdom from God, my father's vision, and a dedicated team."

"You didn't hesitate answering such a tough question. Why is that?"

"Because I understand my role and my purpose. More important, I understand that God is without question the source of our success at DMI. He's the true CEO and our ultimate leader. He has imparted wisdom to me for the purpose of taking DMI forward. So long as I don't lose sight of God, we'll continue to thrive at DMI."

"You openly speak about God and His influence on your life and your company. I find your religious boldness quite rare in the corporate arena."

"I'm not ashamed to acknowledge God, not in any way."

"It's difficult to top that response," Ms. Tate said. "Let's talk a little bit about leadership. Dave Mitchell was the founder of DMI." Joel nodded. Ms. Tate glanced at her notes. "He won the Detroit businessman of the year award twelve times, the Michigan achiever award at least three times, a list of honorary degrees, and the list goes on and on."

"That's correct," Joel said, seeming totally composed and in control.

"But what is perhaps the most interesting element of DMI is your unique family-oriented management structure. Dave Mitchell was your father. Your uncle was the chief financial officer at one time."

Joel cut in. "My uncle is no longer with DMI. He stepped down from his position shortly after I became CEO two years ago."

"The buzz was that you fired him. Any truth to those rumors? Is Joel Mitchell really the iron-fisted leader who's not afraid to make the tough decisions even when there are personal ties involved?"

"Guilty as charged. Personal ties don't cloud my judgment when it comes to effectively running DMI. That's what I learned from my father."

"Continuing with our theme of personal ties, Madeline Mitchell, a leading Detroit executive in her own right, was your father's ex-wife and your stepmother."

"Correct again," Joel said.

"She's also a member of your board of directors as well as a line manager overseeing day-to-day operations for one of your divisions. How is that possible? Does her position constitute a conflict of interest?"

"No, I don't believe so," Joel said, maintaining his

calm. "We are a privately held company. We're not traded on the stock exchange, but we run a squeaky-clean organization. I challenge any governing body to audit our books. Although we operate with ethics and the utmost integrity, we have the flexibility to run the company in a way that capitalizes on our individual family contributions. Madeline is a classic example. She has been with the organization since my father opened it almost forty years ago. She possesses more knowledge about aspects of the ministry than others will ever be able to learn. Yes, she heads our East Coast operation and has for the past two years. Thanks to her efforts we have experienced double-digit growth."

"Clearly DMI has thrived under your tenure. Your success speaks for itself. So, I'd like us to switch to another topic," she said with a slight grin. "You're twenty-five years old, running a company, or a ministry as you called it." Joel nodded. "Either way, you've realized a goal most CEOs don't achieve until they're twice your age. With this much success early in your life, what's next for you? Marriage, children?"

He chuckled. Abigail didn't expect Joel to publicize his relationship in an open forum. He was much too reserved for such a move, but she was curious to see how he'd respond.

"Who knows what God has in store for me? I'm not looking too far ahead. Right now, I'm happy and enjoying the moment. No reason to get ahead of myself, or God, for that matter."

"Wonderful philosophy, but you are deemed one of the nation's most eligible bachelors."

"Ah, Samantha, you can't believe everything you hear or read," he said, with such a heavy dose of suaveness that Abigail blushed.

"Well, Mr. Mitchell, we'll leave it at that," she said, extending a handshake to Joel. He thanked her for the opportunity to appear on the show. Ms. Tate turned to face the camera. "This concludes another segment of the *Business Journal*. Tune in for our next episode. Until next time, stay tuned, stay informed, and stay grounded. This is Samantha Tate saying make this your best day ever. Good-bye."

When the camera light went out, Abigail rushed to Joel, who was engaged in a conversation with Ms. Tate.

"You interview very well," Ms. Tate told Joel.

"That's because you gave me easy questions."

"Somehow I don't believe that's true," she said, laughing along with Joel.

"You'll have to interview me again to see if it's true."

"You're an interesting man. What's your zodiac sign? With your personality, you have to be Leo the lion or Taurus the bull."

"I have no idea."

"Come on, you must know. When's your birthday?"

"I really don't know the zodiac signs. I've never followed the stars and the moon. God has always been my guide. He's the one I trust with my future."

Abigail stepped closer to Joel and said, "Hello, Ms. Tate, or can I call you Samantha?"

"Call me Samantha, please."

"Samantha, this is Abigail, my most trusted executive," Joel said. "She's the brains behind our operation," Joel said, in his teasing way.

Abigail and Samantha exchanged greetings.

"This was a very pleasant interview. You made my job easy. We'll get the footage edited over the next couple of days and hopefully be ready to air in our next segment. I'm eager to broadcast this one." Ms. Tate packed her belongings. The cameraman and assistant were ready to go. "Mr. Mitchell," she said.

Joel interrupted. "If I'm calling you Samantha, you're calling me Joel."

Abigail plastered a smile across her lips, but there was no sincerity in the gesture.

"Very well, Joel, I look forward to meeting you again, and perhaps I'll take you up on your offer."

"What offer is that?" he asked, with class oozing from his pores.

"Interviewing you again, but next time we'll change the venue. I'll pick the place."

"Works for me," he said, with his teeth as white as ivory keys on a piano contrasting against his coconut skin. Seeing Ms. Tate pull a business card from her briefcase and scribble on the other side reminded Abigail that she wasn't the only one in awe of his appeal.

"This is my direct line. Call me any time you want an interview, any time."

Abigail wanted to blurt out "back off," but why bother. She dwelled on the notion of being with him every minute. She hoped there would be a day when she wouldn't have to worry about the pushiness of other women. An engagement ring on her finger, or better yet, a wedding ring, was sure to ward off the undesired admirers.

Ms. Tate and her crew were gone. Abigail followed Joel to his office.

He pulled his tie off. "The interview went well, I thought."

"Very well," she said, "except when Ms. Tate showed her attraction to you."

"No she didn't," he said.

Abigail didn't speak. She merely raised an eyebrow and scowled.

"You really think so?" he asked.

Abigail couldn't tell if he was serious or not. "Definitely."

"It's amazing how easily people are distracted from the accomplishments of an organization and how quick they are to shine the spotlight on my personal business."

"You know you are the most eligible bachelor around," she said, feeling lighthearted.

"Not you, too? Maybe I should get married and put this bachelor frenzy to rest."

Abigail had a million responses but didn't share any that would expose her feelings. Instead she said, "Will you get married one day?"

"Probably, but that's a long ways off. I can't maintain a serious relationship right now." Abigail managed the blend of hope and disappointment internally, maintaining her attentiveness. "Do you feel too young to make a commitment?"

"No," he said without hesitating. "DMI is my mission and consumes my energy. I can't commit to any other venture." There wasn't much more to say. Abigail didn't have any basis to challenge his position. "That's why I value our friendship," he added. "Romantic distractions have never been a problem between us, and I'm glad to be honest. We're both driven to achieve. Work, work, work, that's what you and I do together, and quite well, I might add."

Each revelation was like a pin poking the balloon of her affection for him. Eventually he would want a seminormal life, one that, she dreamed would include her as more than a friend. Friendship wasn't a bad starting point.

"DMI is running smoothly. You should be able to pull back on the fifteen-hour days at some point."

"You're right. I figure another year and I can start to breathe easier. Who knows, maybe the two of us can take a well-earned vacation. You work just as hard as I do. Hey, I have an idea," he said, chuckling. "Maybe you and I should get married. No one else will tolerate our crazy hours," he said, amused more than she wanted to see.

She didn't want to take the conversation any further for fear of creating awkwardness.

"Seriously, if the media is hounding me now about my love interests, the rumors are sure to get worse once they find out that I'm planning to build a house."

"You are? I didn't know you were."

"Sure am, and I'm asking you to help me."

Her mind said breathe, short regular breaths. She didn't want to seem overly excited and misconstrue his words. She had to hear him clearly. "Me? How can I help?"

"I want you to design the house for me."

"Are you kidding me?"

"Not at all, I'm dead serious. I want you to have complete control over the design and the interior arrangement afterward."

"Why me?"

"There's no one else I trust to make it happen the way I trust you. Besides, I will be working on another project."

"What?" She was desperately anxious to find out.

"My father had two dreams, building the library and expanding the ministry into international territory. The library is complete. Now I can concentrate on the expansion."

"Your father would be pleased. The library was so important to him, and you did a fantastic job. He always wanted the documents, lessons, and tools available to the churches and small, growing ministries."

"I know, and I'm determined to have the same success with the international expansion for him. So many years he fought off attacks on his character, his ministry, and his health. He never had a free moment or a mass of excess capital to fulfill his vision, but I do. I will make this happen for him if it's the last thing I do. I'm that determined."

"I will definitely support you in whatever way I can."

"You can support me by handling the house construction. I will gladly pay you whatever price you set."

"No way, I'm insulted that you'd suggest paying me."

"I don't want to abuse your support. Having you in charge of my house construction frees me up to pursue the expansion at a time when DMI has the necessary discretionary funds to cover the project. I have this worked out. All I need is for you to say yes."

"I don't know what to say."

"Say yes and make me a happy man," he said.

"Yes," she repeated several times. Abigail was boiling over with enthusiasm and passion. A man didn't let a woman design his house unless he had plans for her to move in one day. She didn't have his hand in marriage— that would come next. Building his house was the assurance she needed, certain more was coming later.

chapter

38

Adjusting to the consistent seventy-eight-degree weather along the waterfront wasn't difficult. Being nestled among a diverse group of people with a wealth of culture reminded Don of San Francisco. Maybe the connection to the States was what allowed him to feel at home thousands of miles away from Michigan. Maybe it was living miles away from the constant reminder of his guilt. He wasn't sure why, but Cape Town was home.

In nineteen months he'd converted his leadership-training program into a $22 million business with 150 employees in three countries and an office five times the size of his original location. He was located right outside the metropolitan area where property was less expensive. Sticking to his strategy of staying away from churches and the religious sector was panning out quite nicely.

Don ripped open the oversized brown envelope and extracted the *Detroit Free Press*. After settling into his oceanfront flat over a year ago, he placed an order for the Sunday newspaper to be delivered indefinitely. The paper was a buck fifty, but the shipping cost was ridiculous, which wasn't a deterrent to Don. He was settled far away from Detroit but had a burning need to keep in tune with what was happening.

The mention of DMI on the cover page drew his immediate attention. He flipped to the pull-out magazine. Abigail and Joel were standing back to back with the DMI logo overhead. He studied the photo, thrilled for her success and for Joel. Begrudging his brother success didn't buy him happiness, but forgiving and letting go were huge bites to swallow too. He'd worked hard to diffuse his resentment for Joel and even Sherry, not wanting to carry the load of bitterness year after year like his mother, but wasn't quite ready to invite Joel to South Africa. Don wasn't confusing his tinge of compassion with brotherly love.

DMI was marching ahead in his father's absence, under the leadership of Joel. Don read the article, which focused on Abigail's promotion, Joel's effective leadership, and DMI's unprecedented growth and penetration into the church arena. The article was quite flattering to each. The paper was almost two weeks old, but Don couldn't help it. He wanted to congratulate Abigail on her success. Eight A.M. his time was one in the morning for her. He'd call later in the day, around two or three in the afternoon his time, after his workout and before she left for church. His thoughts rested on her image. She remained the rare gem in his eyes. Two years hadn't diminished his fondness for her, only the unrealistic hope of uniting in marriage in the near future. Don hadn't abandoned his desire entirely, but he wasn't sitting idle waiting for the magical day when Abigail confessed her love. He was working hard building LTI. She deserved stability and love, neither of which he planned to skimp on providing if he ever got the chance.

Don pulled out his Bible, the same one he'd started reading three months ago. He and God weren't buddies, but he was spending a little more time with Him, praying and reading the Bible. If his future was going to be the best that it could be, there were several relationships that had to be mended. The one with God was in progress.

Although Abigail spent most of her time at DMI, Sunday was more than a day she set aside to attend church. The day was set aside to worship, reserved completely for God. He was the one who had enabled her to survive the despair of her youth, to get a top-notch education, and to work for Dave Mitchell alongside his wife and two sons. She didn't have brothers. Having Don in her circle had filled a significant void. He was family, whether he was in Africa or America. Her friendship with him crossed the ocean every single night in her prayers. He was her brother, and she felt blessed. Thinking of Joel, Abigail was strengthened by the allure of love. Asking God for more would be greedy. Every good and special gift God had provided—a second set of parents, a brother, a fantastic job, and now maybe, just maybe, a potential mate.

The phone rang as she stared into the mirror and applied her lip gloss. She had a feeling the call was from Don—not sure how she knew, but there was a feeling. She tripped over a pair of shoes, absentmindedly rushing to the phone, and jerked the receiver from the base, collapsing onto the bed.

"Good deal. I was hoping to catch you before you left for church," Don said.

"Ah, it is you, I'm so glad to hear from you, Mr. South Africa," she said, recovering from the haphazard fall. "I've been thinking about you so much. How's everything over there?"

"My world is fantastic. I'm celebrating nineteen months of being in business," Don said.

"You're kidding. There's no way it's been nineteen months already. Are you serious?"

"I am."

"Well, congratulations. No one deserves the success more than you. I'm so thrilled for you," Abigail said.

"I understand that congratulations are in order for you, too. I read about your promotion to executive vice president. Great job, congratulations."

"I'm honored to have the position, but it's a huge responsibility."

"Nothing you can't handle. I have complete confidence in you."

"That's why I miss you terribly," she told him.

"We can fix that with a visit. The invitation is always open. I'm waiting on you."

"I know. I need to take the time to get my passport renewed."

"You're second in charge of a multibillion-dollar company. Hire a personal assistant to take care of those things for you, two if necessary. I have a little start-up business and I have one. I don't know what I'd do without her."

A certain ring in his tone piqued her curiosity. "Wow, sounds pretty special."

"She is," he said.

There was no explanation for the swirling sensation Abigail felt. Don had gone halfway around the world and found romance. She was rooted in Detroit, practically connected to Joel, and no closer to a relationship commitment than the explorers were to reaching the sun. "I'm happy for you," she said with sincere happiness for her friend, despite her own slow-moving romantic progress.

"Naledi is great, but Abigail Gerard is a tough act to follow. You're gutsy in the corporate arena." Her soul soaked in the flattery, savoring every word. "There's no replacement for you by my side, but Naledi is a godsend. She's made a real difference."

Abigail didn't want him to elaborate. She really was happy about his contentment and the lift in his spirit, but was equally saddened by the notion of sharing her devoted friend with someone else. She missed him tremendously. "When are you coming home?"

"I'm busy with the company. I haven't been able to squeeze in leisure travel."

"At least you have time for dating," she said, toying with Don.

"Who said anything about dating?"

"You and your assistant, I thought."

Don interrupted before she could finish. "She's a loyal assistant. We work well together but that's it, no romance. Who has time? What about you, any romantic prospects?"

Abigail felt giddy and was pleased being able to share her news with someone she trusted who wouldn't release her words to the media. She wasn't ready to be a public spectacle. "Joel and I have grown very close."

"Really," Don said. There was a temporary silence on the line before he spoke again. "Is it serious?"

"No, not yet, but guess what?" she said, barely able to contain her glee.

"What?"

"He's asked me to help him design his dream house. He wants me to have complete control over the floor plan and interior design once the house is built. Can you believe that?" she said. "I have a sneaking suspicion he's building this house for me, for us."

"He has you designing his house, but you're not sure the relationship is serious?"

"I know. It's backward, but who cares. I'm perfectly willing to go along with his method and wait on his timing. I'm not going anywhere, and I'm not worried one bit." She sat on the edge of the bed. "See, this is why I miss many of the old times. When your father was alive and running DMI, you and I had plenty of time to talk. You were my confidant."

"You can call me any time. I don't care what time of day or night, I'm here for you," he told her.

"I know, but it's different when you're two or three continents away."

"Not when it comes to our friendship. I'm only a phone call away, remember that, okay?"

"I'll remember."

"I'm very serious, Abigail. You have the numbers to my home, my office, my mobile, and the emergency number for my assistant. Day or night I'm here for you."

"That means a lot to me. Thank you." She took comfort in knowing their friendship was intact regardless of the distance and the past.

"Lots of love to you, my friend," he told her, and said his good-bye.

She finished getting dressed for church, reflecting on the magnitude of her blessings. Having God, Don, and Joel Mitchell in her corner was more than she could have dreamed possible. She closed the door to her house, thanking God for his many gifts.

chapter

39

Barry plopped down on the chair in front of Joel's desk. "What brings you to Detroit? Do we have a meeting scheduled?" Joel asked, scrolling through his itinerary for the day.

"I flew in this morning because our problem in Chicago has blown up," Barry said.

"What's going on?" Joel asked, as Abigail watched his every move. It was difficult to take her eyes off Joel. She tried to look away, but the force of his allure drew her gaze his way with every spoken word. She never grew tired of hearing him speak. The topics didn't matter; whatever he said brought solace. She scribbled a note on her portfolio, pretending to be productive, although only a few of Barry's words were registering.

"Let me start with the good news. The Creative Concept Contest has achieved the initial goal, which was to increase DMI penetration among new and smaller churches," Barry said, as Joel nodded. "The clear winner was a mustard-seed concept. The program is ideal for churches that don't have the financial resources or the membership base to support a major DMI effort and are apprehensive about locking in to our full program. With the mustard-seed approach, they can send one individual through an accelerated training program. The person can then go back and train others."

"I love the concept. It fits right in with what Brian wants to do with the West Coast."

"I love the concept too, and we were planning to announce the winner in two days, until we realized there was a major problem," Barry said.

Joel was distracted by the beep of his PDA on the desk. He rose to take the call. Mesmerized by his presence, Abigail had been struggling to stay focused, but her prowess kicked in at the mention of a DMI problem. As executive senior vice president, she was responsible.

"I'm not aware of a problem," Abigail said to Barry, wondering why he hadn't informed her first, since she was his new boss. She was semidistracted, watching as Joel scrolled the list of messages, probably searching for the number of the missed call.

"I tried to get on your schedule several times but you were out on personal business," Barry told her, "or at least that's what your administrative assistant said."

Abigail didn't respond. The truth was, she had been out quite a bit lately, interviewing potential architects and builders. Building Joel's house—their house—was tremendously important, but she didn't want to jeopardize the affairs of DMI during the process. Unsure what to say but compelled to respond, she said, "You're right.

I do have a full plate, but I'm never too busy to address DMI affairs." She gave thought to Don's suggestion. He always made good sense. Instead of sharing her administrative assistant with two other division leaders, perhaps she would get a dedicated resource to help manage her increasing workload. "Going forward, if there's a critical issue affecting your division, tell my assistant to either contact me immediately or force time onto my calendar. I'd like the opportunity to address the problem before loading Joel's plate with a list of division issues."

"No problem," Barry said. "It was an oversight. I'll make sure you're in the loop going forward."

Joel set the PDA down. "Don't worry, Abigail, I don't mind jumping in. Besides, I've unfairly loaded your schedule with a ton of both DMI's work and mine. I'm inundated with media interviews these days. I'll have to pull back on some of those and shift more attention to the office," Joel said.

"There's no need to modify your press schedule. I assure you I can handle everything," she said. "Besides, the more press you get, the more DMI benefits. I'd say that's a good problem for us to have."

"Then I'll count on you to let me know when you're feeling overloaded."

"Agreed. Barry, let's get back to the issue. What's going on?" she asked.

"We have two people in Chicago claiming the mustard-seed concept is their baby."

"You're saying two people have the same idea?" Abigail asked. "I guess having the same idea is possible, but it's not ideal for us."

"They have more than the same idea. Their submissions were identical, with the exact same wording," Barry clarified.

"So we're not talking about two winners. You're saying we have a thief on our hands," Joel said.

"At a minimum we're talking fraud."

"How did this happen?" Abigail asked.

"I have no idea. I realize this is not a good answer coming from the senior vice president of the division, but I honestly don't know."

"I'm surprised you didn't notice the problem earlier in the process," Abigail said.

"Probably because the names were kept anonymous during the selection process to ensure the final decision was one hundred percent objective and based solely on the merit of the concept. Since the submissions were identical we figured there was an extra copy in the packet. We didn't discover the problem until we made the final selection and tied the submission to the owner. Obviously the total campaign has been tainted."

"I see," was the extent of Joel's reaction.

"My staff has spent the past few days chasing down the source of the problem," Barry added. "We're trying to get answers, but with the clock ticking I decided to concentrate solely on establishing a clear winner. Our initial resolution was to drop the mustard-seed idea and go with the runner-up."

"Let's do it," Abigail eagerly endorsed.

"We can't. We've discovered all ten of the top ideas have two owners."

"What?" Abigail sputtered. "All ten have two owners?"

"Come on, you have to be kidding me," Joel said, with more passion this time.

"I wish I were," Barry responded, followed by a loud sigh. "Obviously the problem is more widespread than we thought."

"How can we have ten ideas submitted with duplicates? Did every entry have a duplicate or just the top ten? Not that I'm sure what difference it will make at this point."

"I owe both of you answers that honestly I just don't have at the moment."

"What about time stamps? Can we use them to determine who submitted first?" Abigail asked.

"There's another problem. Each submission had a coded time stamp, which was retained in our campaign database. Believe it or not, somehow the time-stamp field was erased from the file."

"Now this is going too far. How can someone or something have access to our databases?" asked Abigail.

"I want Ken involved on this. He's our chief information officer. We need his help," Joel stated.

"He's already on board and has come up short with answers, too."

"Okay, we can deal with the root cause of this problem later. I'm interested in our current options," Abigail said.

"As of this moment, we're up a creek unless we figure out how to resolve this issue. We've designed a huge publicity campaign around the program and the announcement of the winner. The press will have a field day with us. They're always anxious to reveal any unscrupulous activity associated with the church and the religious community," Barry said.

"We haven't done anything wrong yet," Abigail pointed out.

"I don't think they'll see it that way. We've tried everything and nothing has put us closer to selecting a final winner. Maybe we can get one of those fortune-tellers, a reputable one, not just anybody off the street?" Barry suggested.

"No, we're not seeking spirits to guide DMI," Joel spoke with the ring of authority. "This is God's ministry and we will not defile this place with alternative demonic practices. God has commanded us not to seek out the advice of soothsayers and fortunetellers."

"Once you open that door, it's like giving someone the key to your spiritual house," Abigail said. "They can come and go freely. It's the same with evil spirits once you let them in."

"And we're not about to unleash evil into DMI, not knowingly. Besides, there are no spirits, fortunetellers, card readers, or palm readers who know more about the future of DMI and this campaign than the Lord. Every spirit in heaven and hell has to bow to our God. So, why should we go to anyone or anything else but Him for direction?" Joel said.

"I'm sorry about the suggestion. I wasn't thinking. I guess the pressure of needing an answer in two days has me desperate. For a minute I was willing to try anything, but you're right. I apologize again. I meant no offense," Barry said.

"And none taken. Here's what we can do. Can you bring both of the contestants to Detroit? I need to see their faces when we discuss the problem," Joel said.

"I don't know if they'll come or not, but I'll try to get them here."

"Get them first-class tickets, with limousine service to and from the airport. Book a room for them at the MGM Grand or Ritz Carlton. Put them in separate hotels. We'll get to the bottom of this as soon as you get them here."

"I'll push," Barry said, practically bolting from his seat.

"There's no reason to push. I can't imagine the true

winner passing on the opportunity to come and plead his or her case."

"Me either," Barry said, "but you never know. This is already crazier than I expected."

"If they don't want to come here, I'll go to Chicago to meet them. Let it be their choice," Joel said. Abigail enjoyed watching him take charge and lead.

"Got it," Barry said. "I'll get on it right away."

Abigail remained after Barry left, gazing at Joel's handcrafted body while his confidence rang in her ears. She fantasized about being married and waking to him every morning.

"I owe you a huge apology," Joel told Abigail.

"For what?" she asked, unable to think of a single action he'd taken requiring an apology.

"I've shifted too much of my work on you—leading the division, building my house. What was I thinking?" he said, standing and coming around the desk to take a seat next to her. "Your DMI role is more than a full-time job. Don't worry about the house. Thank you for all the work you've done already, but I can't in good conscience ask you to handle both tasks."

"No way," she belted out before having a chance to fully formulate her thoughts. "I'm already into the design. There's no good reason for me to stop now. No way. I can handle both. I promise you I will not let you down."

"Are you sure?"

"More sure than I've been about anything in my life," she told him, desiring to convince him completely. Abigail felt at ease, but the reality was coming clear. She would have to sacrifice personal time, interests, and probably most of her sleep to effectively manage the executive vice president role as well as build Joel's house.

She had no intention of letting her failure fall on him. DMI and the little time she spent praying and reading her Bible were off limits. Forgoing a few church visits here and there couldn't hurt. She was totally aware of how much Joel relied on her in the two most significant areas of his life, home and work. There was no way she was going to let him down, none. The necessary sacrifices could be considered done.

chapter

40

Madeline was swamped, and under normal circumstances wouldn't have a free minute to spend trekking three hundred miles to Chicago for the announcement of a contest winner, but today no force on earth was going to keep her from witnessing Joel's humiliating moment exposed in the national spotlight. Realizing the fruits of her hard work and strategic thinking made Madeline practically whimsical. Her time had arrived.

The office was filled with chatter. Nothing was getting more attention within the walls of DMI. The first major campaign directed squarely at the public was about to blow up and she couldn't wait for the fireworks. Her calendar was instantly cleared. Meetings were canceled, shifted, and reassigned the second she heard Joel was heading to Chicago because one contestant couldn't make the trip to Detroit.

Once she received confirmation that the announcement ceremony was still on, Detroit was in her rearview mirror. She was glad to catch the flight without notice, but the truth was, she was getting there one way or another. If the plane or a private car hadn't worked, driving herself was the next option. If the Bentley couldn't roll she would resort to a scooter. A stretch of highway wasn't about to stand between her and the public annihilation. She'd worked too hard and too long for this day, with Frank's help and that of a few loyal employees in the Chicago office. Joel would finally be exposed.

Madeline squeezed past the room filled with media teams, microphones, and news cameras. She pranced into the conference room reserved by DMI for the contest discussion. Abigail, Barry, Joel, and Sherry were present along with a few others from DMI.

"Madeline, I didn't know you were coming. You could have taken the plane with us," Abigail said.

"That's okay, I took a commercial flight," Madeline responded, a bit winded, having literally run from the corner, where the limousine had dropped her off. She didn't want to waste five minutes while the driver maneuvered a maze of one-way streets in downtown Chicago. She hopped out at the traffic light, anxious not to miss a second of the impending spectacle. She felt a twinge of sadness thinking about the initial backlash on DMI. Dave had worked tirelessly to build a reputable organization. Because of a temporary lapse in judgment during his illness, he'd appointed someone incapable and unworthy of running DMI. She knew that from the beginning. Now the world was going to know, too.

"We don't have much time before the televised announcement, so let's get going," Joel said.

"Excuse me, I know this is your territory, Barry, but why didn't you cancel or at least postpone the announcement until the issue was resolved?" Madeline asked, determined to keep the flame of controversy blazing.

"Because we—" Barry and Joel said simultaneously. Barry deferred to Joel and he continued. "We're confident, I'm confident that we'll have a clear winner within twenty minutes," he said, glancing at his watch, "which will leave ten minutes before the press conference."

"How can you be so sure?" Madeline asked, savoring Joel's position.

"Because God said so."

Here he was with his God thing again. She cringed at having to admit he was undoubtedly the son of Dave Mitchell. How many times had she heard Dave recite the exact same line? Unfortunately, she'd be perceived as a foolish woman if she attempted to counter his response. She decided to sit back and watch the fireworks. Joel would fry, and the good news was that she didn't have to light the match publicly. He had his own blowtorch on the situation and was tossing kindling wood on the fire with each smug word.

"Here's the plan," Joel said with a cocky take-charge attitude. If he hadn't been Sherry's child Madeline would actually have thought him impressive, but he was, so he wasn't. "I'd like to ask each contestant a few questions. Based on their responses, I'll be able to declare a winner."

"Are you sure it's going to be that easy?" Barry asked. "We've interviewed each lady several times. We've gone as far as requesting background checks and character references and we still can't tell who is lying."

"Trust me, this will only take a few minutes. Please bring in the contestants," Joel said arrogantly. At his command, Sherry left the room to go get the two contestants.

There was no way he could pull this off. He wasn't that smart. It was virtually impossible for someone as young as him to have enough discernment and knowledge to slice through the character of two witnesses and determine who was credible and who wasn't. He wasn't a judge, and he definitely wasn't the chosen leader, as everyone would soon see. For reassurance Madeline had personally reviewed the profiles and handpicked several of the impostors that Frank had given her. Identifying people who were convincing and discreet was difficult to do from reading a sheet of paper, but she had made the best effort. The future of DMI rested on her gut instincts. Joel wasn't the only clever one in the office, as he would soon realize. She had a few brain cells, too, although he could never find out about her involvement. Her personal satisfaction was sufficient.

chapter

41

Madeline was eager for the show to get going. In a short while, Sherry returned to the room with two women.

"Thank you, Ms. Carthage and Ms. Donahue, for taking time out of your schedules to meet with us," Joel said, extending a handshake greeting. Both women were dressed conservatively, nothing flashy or suggestive. Nothing stood out about either woman. "I also want to thank each of you for submitting ideas to our Creative Concept Contest. Your interest, enthusiasm, and support are important to the continued growth of DMI and are greatly appreciated," Joel said.

Madeline uncharacteristically found herself fidgeting. Forget about the diplomatic speech and get on with the fireworks.

"As you are aware, we have one winning idea and two ladies who claim to be the owner. Unfortunately, there can only be one winner, only one person who receives the check for ten thousand dollars and a junior analyst position in the Chicago office managing the winning concept. Unfortunately, we don't know who our winner is. I'm sure you both realize how awkward this predicament is for DMI."

Ms. Carthage verbally acknowledged and the other lady nodded. Madeline couldn't help but notice the other lady keeping her head down and avoiding eye contact with Joel. This was easy. Madeline was filled with euphoria, anticipating the mockery of a press conference soon to transpire.

"We're in the business of helping churches reach their potential in leadership, stewardship, and integrity, which is why your idea was the clear winner. The person who proposed the mustard-seed concept understands the significance of local church bodies. The work we do is unto the Lord. So, I ask you, Ms. Carthage and Ms. Donahue, do either of you want to withdraw your claim? I assure you there will be no further consequences from DMI. You can leave here today with your conscience clear." Joel waited for a response but none came. "All right, Ms. Donahue, can you tell me your story."

"I've wanted to be in marketing for a very long time. I had to drop out of college to take care of my baby. The Lord blessed me with a chance to go back to college and finish my associate's degree last semester. God gave me this concept one night after I prayed to him about a way to help my church and other small churches like mine be able to grow. The idea just came to me," she said, stumbling over her words and speaking barely loudly enough to be heard.

Madeline couldn't have dreamed of a better contestant. The woman could barely speak, let alone be perceived as someone who could create a marketing campaign. The plan was a success. Madeline's pulse sprinted.

"Thank you, Ms. Donahue. Now we'd like to hear from you, Ms. Carthage."

"I have a marketing degree from Northwestern. I've created multiple marketing concepts during college and during my summer internships," she said, flipping through a binder of papers. "This idea is my baby," she said convincingly.

Joel didn't need to hear anymore. The winner was obvious, or at least Madeline hoped. Her thoughts were in "next step" mode. Much had to be done in the transition. She could fill in for Don while he took time to shut down his company or sell it. Her next action would be to convert Sherry's office into a conference room. She discreetly pulled her PDA out and worked on a list of emails. This sideshow was keeping Madeline from her real DMI work, but she wouldn't dream of missing his fiasco.

"Well, I find both of your stories to be plausible. Therefore, I've decided to honor the monetary terms of the contest, as we are legally obligated to do, but DMI will rescind the job offer and kill the small-church concept. We will opt not to implement the idea."

Madeline's ears perked up. Here we go, she thought. Joel was about to make a complete fool of himself. His loud posturing earlier and his confident gestures were doused as if a wet blanket had been thrown over a bonfire. With ashes smoldering, he would have to address the media. Madeline scanned the room for an alternative exit. He was on his own. She was filled with exhilaration. Her palms moistened. Finally, after two determined years, victory was hers.

"Wait," Ms. Donahue cried out. Madeline couldn't believe the woman was volunteering to speak. She wanted her to keep her mouth closed. Madeline could feel the kill. She was so close, and she didn't want Joel to gain insight on the real owner. Everyone else in the room was already fooled. "Please, Mr. Mitchell," she cried, "don't kill the project. It's my baby, but if she wants to claim it as hers, let her have it."

The tears were powerful but, Madeline hoped, not convincing.

Joel showed no reaction at first; then he spoke. "Ms. Donahue, I declare you the official winner. The mustard-seed concept is obviously your baby. The true creator of this concept clearly has a heart for small churches and our vision."

"But how did you know?" Ms. Donahue asked.

"Because you are willing to give up the job and money in exchange for keeping the project alive, I know you're the owner."

"What are you talking about?" Ms. Carthage blurted. "That's my analyst position. She's not cheating me out of my job. I worked too hard to take her idea."

"Excuse me?" Abigail asked.

"Oh, I mean, I worked too hard earning a degree to let somebody like her take my job and my ten thousand dollars. DMI owes me this job," Ms. Carthage said, getting loud.

Madeline was too stunned to move. She wished Ms. Carthage would stop talking and avoid possible legal charges. Madeline didn't want to take any chance of having the woman charged and spewing out names, especially hers. "I suggest you leave by the back way before we take legal action," Madeline said boldly, trying to throw off any bloodhounds who might remotely detect her involvement. She was certain no one did, but just in case she was keeping up the façade.

Ms. Carthage settled down and said, "I really do have great ideas, and I could do a great job for DMI. Just give me an opportunity."

"Ms. Carthage, you are free to leave. Ms. Donahue, we have a press conference to attend," Joel said, approaching the winner and giving her a hug.

"What about me?"

"What about you?" Barry belted. "What made you do this?"

"We should count our blessings," Madeline dived in, before Ms. Carthage could start rattling off names and accusations to save herself. Madeline's ship was sinking, and she was in rescue mode. "We have declared a winner. I suggest we proceed with the press conference and put this travesty behind DMI," she hastily recommended.

"I agree," Sherry said.

Sherry's endorsement was like an extra barrel of water dashed on her sinking boat, but Madeline couldn't concentrate on the other Mrs. Mitchell. There were greater concerns at hand. Madeline looked on, struggling to remember whether she'd deleted the email chains to and from Frank. She couldn't be tied to this debacle. Thank goodness she'd never met the impostors in person. The extent of her involvement had been reading profiles and selecting candidates. Frank had handled the rest. She wrestled internally for peace, acknowledging the lack of trust among coconspirators. She took a tiny shred of solace in the three million dollars Frank was getting—the price for his silence. There was no guarantee, but her options were limited, short of confessing her involvement, which would not happen. If she was going down, it wouldn't be at Joel's press conference. She gathered her few belongings.

"Am I getting arrested?" Ms. Carthage asked, still flapping her lips.

"Yes, you're getting arrested," Barry told her.

"No, we're not pursuing any legal action," Joel said.

"Why not?" Barry asked, clearly agitated.

Joel faced the impostor. "This you did unto the Lord. Therefore what happens now is between you and the Lord."

"Please forgive me," she said, practically groveling.

There was a knock on the door.

"They're letting us know the press conference is about to begin," Sherry said, collecting her papers.

Madeline turned away, disgusted.

"It's best for you to leave, Ms. Carthage, before the press conference begins," Abigail said.

Madeline couldn't decide if she was happy to avoid legal problems or sad that Joel had squeezed out of a tight situation, with gobs of accolades sure to come his way for being perceived as decisive, smart, and personable. How could this happen, again? She pushed away the taste of defeat. She wasn't giving up, not yet. Bringing him down was going to require more time, attention, and resources. After today, she was almost tempted to believe there really was something to his godly persona. Where else could he have acquired such a heavy dose of experience and confidence?

She had no intention of foolishly fighting God, but there was a chance, a desperate belief, that Joel wasn't operating under the heavy dose of anointing Dave

Mitchell had. There was the strong possibility that Joel had dumb luck and was within her reach to expose and destroy. The group followed Joel into the room where the press conference was being held. Madeline kept her seat. Her rational thoughts said let Joel go, move on, accept defeat, embrace her new life and be happy, but the other side of her thoughts didn't want to release Joel. She'd experienced so much loss and pain to his gain. To release him now would mean she had to find a new way of existing, a new focus, and a new mission. She headed out the rear exit, admitting she wasn't ready to reinvent her life. She wasn't ready to accept the reality of defeat. She couldn't save everyone, but if she could rescue DMI, then maybe, just maybe, she could also rescue her last two children. She exited the building, drawing in a lungful of air, and with eyes closed, let the sun warm her flesh. As long as there was breath in her body she would continue fighting for the return of what legitimately belonged to her.

chapter

42

Madeline tossed aside the crushing events of yester-day and went to work with a scarf draped around her head. A pair of deeply tinted sunglasses were tucked in her purse just in case, but today was a new day. Her vision was clear and she was in control. She slipped into the office intent on avoiding the DMI staff. The lobby was crammed with pockets of employees chatting. She briefly considered turning around and going home instead of enduring the "day after" torment.

Madeline stood behind a group of three young women chatting in the lobby while lining up behind other people waiting for the elevators. The women didn't notice Madeline and continued talking.

"What's taking the elevators so long? They must be broken," one woman said.

Madeline wouldn't dare walk up six flights of stairs with four-inch heels. She'd wait for the elevator until one showed up. Time wasn't a factor.

"Can you believe the woman in Chicago? What was she thinking?"

Madeline pulled the scarf tighter around her face and took a few steps back, wanting to be invisible. She plucked the sunglasses from her purse for backup.

"I'm surprised the crazy woman wasn't sent to jail."

Madeline reconsidered taking the stairs. She peered at her high heels again and abandoned the idea. Her mind could change depending on how much she had to hear about the botched job in Chicago.

"Mr. Mitchell figured out who was lying even though nobody else did. The newspaper said the results of a random poll pointed to the other woman."

"You mean the crook," one woman commented.

"Yes, Joel figured out who the crook was."

"So you call him Joel instead of Mr. Mitchell?" the third woman in the group said.

"You better believe I call that gorgeous man Joel."

An elevator came and a crowd got on. Madeline opted not to push forward and claim a front spot in the line. She'd wait in the rear, unnoticed.

"Oh, my gosh, he is too good looking and that body is tight."

"You and every single woman in the place are after him."

"Single and some married, too."

"Competition doesn't scare me. He's too good a catch for me not to try."

The three women laughed.

Forget the elevators. Madeline was tempted to take off her heels and hit the stairs, unwilling to hear anymore. The cackling women continued their infuriating conversation.

One lady said, "I'm not interested in him, but I sure do love the twenty percent bonuses we got this year. We've never gotten that much before. Mr. Joel Mitchell can be CEO for twenty-seven more years until I retire if he's going to keep putting extra money in my pocket."

The elevator came and the ladies got on. Madeline squeezed in the back undetected, with her scarf and sunglasses in place. She whisked into her office, closed the door, and forwarded calls directly to voice mail. She had a few loose ends to wrap up before the day was too far gone. The limousine ride home, instead of her flight, should have been the proper time to cover tracks, but Madeline couldn't breathe after the Chicago event. A five-hour ride home was the space she needed for rejuvenation.

She dialed Frank from her personal cellular phone, not the one issued by DMI. She wanted to have the conversation, destroy the evidence, and cut ties until the spotlight on Joel and DMI subsided. Frank answered.

"Yesterday didn't go quite as planned," he said.

"You think? Your plan failed miserably. I'm lucky not to be in jail," she drilled into the receiver.

"Don't be so dramatic. Your name was never mentioned," he said.

"Are you sure, because I can't lose my seat on the board or my leadership of the East Coast operation. I have to keep the division until Don comes home. Are you positive that Ms. Carthage doesn't know me?"

"I'm positive. My job is done. When do I get the rest of my three million dollars?"

"Why should I give you the entire amount when the plan didn't work? The campaign failed miserably."

"The most important reason to pay me is to keep my mouth shut."

"Are you blackmailing me?" Madeline asked.

"Not at all; I'm enforcing our agreement. I have expenses, too."

"Like what?"

"I need to pay my informants in information technology, marketing, and operations. Without their help, we couldn't have pulled off the plan," Frank rattled.

"We didn't pull it off," she said. "That's what I'm trying to tell you. This was a flop."

"Better luck next time. Please wire the money into my Cayman Islands account," he said, rattling off a string of numbers.

"Done," she said, unwilling to bicker any longer. "Frank, I have one last question. How can you guarantee that Ms. Carthage and the other twenty-five people won't talk?"

"Don't worry, they won't."

"How do you know for sure?"

"Madeline, trust me. You don't have to worry. Let's just say that I have business associates who are good at keeping people real quiet. You can consider this case closed."

"Better yet, let's make this case sealed and buried," Madeline told Frank. "I don't want to ever speak of this scheme again. As a matter of fact, we have to cut off future communication. There's no sense in raising suspicion and creating a bunch of trouble."

"You won't hear any complaints from me once I get a confirmation that the funds have cleared in my account."

Madeline couldn't believe she'd gotten caught in a spiderweb with Frank, a known crook. She could only hope he was being truthful. There was no guarantee. She'd move forward keeping one eye on his promise. The fiasco was over. She would stay in her office most of the day to avoid the Joel fan clubs. Tomorrow was a new day and the inspiration for a new plan.

chapter

43

Joel's administrative assistant stood in front of his desk with a long list of messages as she did every morning, particularly after he returned from a trip. Abigail came in behind her and took a seat. Maintaining professionalism was becoming increasingly difficult in his presence.

"Mr. Mitchell," the administrative assistant said, "there's a lady named Sheba Warden who's left several messages for you. She's interested in making a sizable contribution to the library."

"Let her know the library is already finished," Abigail said.

"I tried, but she wants to speak with Mr. Mitchell. She was very persistent."

"Why does she have to speak directly with you?" Abigail asked Joel.

"I have no idea," he said, reaching for the stack of messages. Lately too many determined callers were finding their way onto his message queue. Joel thumbed through the stack. "I'll take this one from Samantha Tate."

"Your schedule is full," Abigail said, reaching for the message. "Let me take her call."

"Thanks, but you're busy, too. I'll take this one from Samantha Tate," he said again, securing the note in his hand.

"What about the others?" the administrative assistant asked.

"Tell you what we're going to do. I'll handle Samantha Tate and Sheba Warden." He looked over the message. "I'm interested in anyone who's interested in contributing to my father's library. You can pass those to my mother," he said, giving the rest of the stack back to his assistant. "If you see my mother, please have her come in."

The administrative assistant left Abigail with Joel. She intended to capitalize on the time alone. There wasn't a particular topic of discussion she had in mind. Stealing a few moments of uninterrupted time with him in the middle of the day was the extent of her intentions. "I can't believe how many calls from reporters and magazines you're getting. It's overwhelming," Abigail said.

"You worry about me too much. I can handle the load. To tell the truth, I get an adrenaline rush from the interviews."

"Speaking of rushes, I have second interviews with two potential developers. The architect has completed his draft, and I'm very close to making a decision on the builder. Would you like to review the plans before I sign off?" she asked. Joel still held the note containing Samantha's message, which Abigail didn't like. "No, you go ahead and run with the development. I totally trust your judgment."

"I'm glad you trust me, but I'd feel better if you knew what was going on."

Joel put the note down and looked up. "You're right. The least I can do is let you fill me in on all that you're doing. I'm at your mercy," he said, leaning back in his seat. "Tell you what, let's grab dinner tonight. My last meeting ends around six-thirty. How does that sound?"

"Sure," Abigail acknowledged, and left his office.

After Abigail left, his mind immediately shifted to Samantha Tate. He looked forward to meeting her again. His daydreaming was interrupted when his mother stuck her head into the room. "Mom, I was looking for you earlier."

"I was busy doing my job," she said, with a smile bright enough to light up the building. He hadn't seen her so jovial in a very long time. Thinking about it, he couldn't remember her ever being too jovial. She was actually living and being useful. Encouraging her to take the job was one of the best recommendations he'd made. "We are showered with media requests. I have messages from the *Chicago Tribune*, *GQ* magazine, a show in Philadelphia called *Visions*, Tyra Banks, Ellen DeGeneres, and Larry King," she said, dropping a load of messages on his desk. "I was already digging my way out of a stack before your assistant dropped another pile on my desk."

"Did we hear from the Oprah show?"

"Not yet."

"Then let's not get too comfortable."

"Even without the Oprah show, this is amazing, Joel. Everyone wants to figure out how a twenty-five-year-old can run this company and realize the degree of success you've achieved. I'm so proud of you, son," she said, coming around the desk to give him a hug. "I don't care if it is inappropriate for an executive assistant to kiss her boss," she said, returning to her seat. "I'm your mom first and a working woman second." She laughed.

"I'm happy to see you this way."

"What way is that?" she asked.

"Alive."

"Thanks to you. Without your encouragement I would have never considered coming back to work after so many years. I was ready to ball up and vanish after your father died, but DMI has saved me. You have saved me. The most ironic part is that I finally feel useful."

"You're an independent woman making your own money, not that you need it. Dad made sure you were taken care of and would never want for money again."

"I don't need so much money. As long as I can pay the taxes on the estate, I'm fine."

"You can pay your taxes and practically everyone else's in the county. Do you realize how wealthy you are, Mom? DMI was worth $1.5 billion when Dad died. Since you own twenty-five percent you were worth $375 million two years ago, not counting your cash, investments, and other assets, such as the mansion. I'm talking about $375 million two years ago based purely on the value of DMI."

"And you've tripled the value of the company in only two years, which means my stock is worth," she said, calculating on paper, "$1.1 billion."

"When did you become the savvy businesswoman?" he said, with the satisfaction of seeing his mother exude confidence.

"Oh, quit, I'm hardly savvy, but I am pretty handy with a calculator and a stack of messages."

Pride gushed from her pores. She was valued and giggly, like a young coed. She had always been priceless to him, but he was content seeing her esteem lifted. "You're a billionaire. No question about it, you're a very rich lady. I bet you're the wealthiest woman in Detroit and probably in the top five around the country. The only women richer than you in the U.S. are Oprah Winfrey, the Wal-Mart women, and the lady who runs the mutual fund. I can't think of her name."

"Actually, there are over seventy women on the *Forbes* billionaires' list, not all in the U.S., though," she told him.

"How do you know? I bet you've been looking for your name on the list," he said, causing her to blush.

She scooted closer to the desk. "The money is not important. I have what I want, you and my independence. I walk down the halls of DMI with my head held high. I'm alive again. I can smell the roses again and appreciate the clouds floating in the sky. I have rediscovered me. As much as I loved your father, my spirit was dead in the mansion. His greatest love was God, and I was somewhere farther down his list."

"Mom, we've had this conversation before. Dad loved you."

"Yes, I know he did, but he also loved Madeline."

"But you were his wife."

"Yes, maybe, but none of that matters. I now accept the reality—your father loved two women. I don't blame him anymore for my years of loneliness or heartache. Believe it or not, I don't blame Madeline either. Truthfully, I've come to realize my jealousy."

"Of Madeline?"

"It's the truth. Madeline didn't ball up and die after your father left her and their children, not like I wanted to do. She is a fighter. As much as she drives me to the brink of insanity, there's a part of me that admires her drive, her determination to protect her children. With that said, I'm signing my stock over to you, my total twenty-five percent."

"What?" Joel blurted. "Why would you want me to have your stock? You can't give me your stock."

"Yes I can and I will. Don't bother arguing with me."

"Why?"

"My stock will give you forty percent of DMI. I realize you won't have the majority interest, but you'll be much closer. One day, who knows, maybe Abigail will officially give you her five percent, bringing your total to forty-five percent."

"You don't have to do this. I won't let you."

"You can't stop me. Please," she said, placing her arms across her chest and casting an endearing glance his way. "You literally saved my life. Let me have this opportunity to do something truly special for you in return. You're my only living child. When it comes to you, I guess I'm a lot like Madeline."

"How?" he asked, not coming up with any similarities between the two other than their last name.

"There's no limit to how far a mother will go to provide for and to protect her children," she said, reaching for his hand. "Now, you're the billionaire in the family."

"You know what this means," he said, sitting back in his chair. "You won't top Oprah or the Wal-Mart women on the *Forbes* list."

"That's okay. You can always give me a raise and let me earn my money back the old-fashioned way."

"We'll have to see about a raise," he said, chuckling along with her.

She gave a wink and gathered the messages scattered on the desk. "Let me get to work. How else can I make my billions?"

She neared the door and Joel said, "Mom, thanks." She did a finger wave and exited the room. Joel dropped his pen onto the desk and sat for a while. The word "billionaire" rolled around his thoughts. Billionaire; one of the wealthiest men in America. God was amazing. Joel didn't have to speculate. He knew his massive wealth and highly sought after advice came directly from the hand of God. He dropped to his knees at the desk, which wasn't unusual for him. "God, I thank you for your mercy and grace in my life. You are the same God of Abraham, Isaac, and Jacob, the same God of Dave Mitchell. I pray that my wisdom will endure and the wealth you've entrusted to me will be used to build your kingdom." His PDA buzzed, but Joel didn't interrupt his conversation with God. The caller could wait. "I pray DMI will continue to thrive and be a haven for your ministries. Thank you, God, for the responsibility you've bestowed on me. I shall follow my heart and your call."

He picked up the messages from Samantha Tate and Sheba Warden lying on his desk. He would get to Samantha, but something about Sheba was intriguing. Was it her name or her interest in the library? He honestly didn't know. Before he could establish a reason his fingers were dialing from his private office phone.

chapter

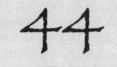

44

Abigail didn't know if the late-afternoon sunlight streaming into Joel's office was the source of her warm mood or if today was just a good day for no special reason. She glanced over a few handwritten notes while intermittently keying numbers into her laptop. Joel's conference room table was becoming her second office, third if I included hers at home. By four o'clock on most Saturdays, the office was empty, except for a few customer service representatives standing by to answer phones. Today wasn't any different. Joel pecked away at his laptop keyboard, updating the business plan. Together they made a powerful team.

Joel reared back in his seat, stretched his arms into the air, and locked fingers. "I'm getting hungry. Are you approaching a stopping point?"

She made one more entry into the spreadsheet before speaking, careful not to lose her train of thought. "I can stop if you want to grab something to eat. I have until Wednesday to get my comments back to George on the five-year projections."

"Then let's get out of here," Joel said, practically leaping to his feet. They hadn't gone to dinner as frequently lately. She suspected that Joel was starting to date again. She hadn't asked him directly; no need. The signs were visible, but she wasn't concerned, not yet. He'd put his charisma on pause for two years. Abigail wanted to believe she was okay with his hanging out so long as he wasn't getting serious, but she was bothered. "Sure you want to go out?" she asked.

"Positive, and I'll drive," he said, going to his coat closet. "Steak, Thai, or Italian?"

"We haven't been to the Chop House in a few weeks. Let's go there."

"Fine by me, the Chop House it is. I'll call from the car so they can have our table ready," Joel said.

"There was a time when we were eating at the Chop House so often that I'm surprised they didn't make us lease a table," Abigail said, lightening her brooding heaviness.

"Well, here are our choices. Either we eat out or we subject ourselves to my cooking."

"You have a very good point," she said.

"Pack up your laptop. I can drop you off at home on the way back from dinner if you don't mind a quick stop to see my mother."

"What about my car?"

"We can pick your car up after we leave church tomorrow," he said.

"Are you sure you'll want to come back out here?"

"Now, you know that's not a problem. Shoot, worst case, you can leave your car here until Monday. You're riding with me to church anyway. I can pick you up Monday morning, too."

"I don't know," she said, not wanting to be stranded without a car for the rest of the weekend. A few months ago no problem, but times were changing. He was changing.

"Why the hesitancy? I've given you plenty of rides to the office. Come on now. Don't give me a hard time on this. You need to take a break and get out of this office." She wasn't disagreeing. She could use the down time. "You said yourself, George doesn't need the documents until Wednesday."

"I'm willing to go, but I do plan to work later tonight."

"No," he said, reaching for her laptop. "No more work tonight. If you want, I will finish reviewing the five-year projections for you."

"What kind of sense does that make?" she said, propping one hand on the conference table. "I'm pulling the report together for you. What sense does it make for you to help with the draft if you're supposed to get the final report?"

"Whatever it takes to get you out of this office and to accept a night off, I'm willing to do."

"Okay, okay," she said, not really putting up much of a fight. The break and the free time with Joel weren't hard to sell. "I'm done until Monday morning, bright and early." She placed her laptop into the soft-sided Louis Vuitton briefcase that Joel had given her last year. "I promise not to work any more tonight."

"And you can't work tomorrow either. Pretty soon people will believe that I'm a slave driver around here because they don't know how driven you are without any influence from me."

"Ha, ha, most people don't know much about me, not like you do," she said, as they left the room, which was engulfed with persistent sunshine and warm air. "What am I going to do with free time—how about a movie?" The awkwardness in his gaze wasn't the answer Abigail wanted or was truly ready to handle. She didn't want to appear offended, especially since they'd never spoken about being together. Abigail refused to appear possessive. If Joel was to be hers, time would work out any concerns. She took refuge in hope.

chapter

45

Abigail could use thirty hours a day. Had her time not been partly filled with the construction of their house, she'd be fully submerged in DMI business. Madeline was her star pupil and didn't need or want managing. Barry, Connie, and Brian and their divisions were proving to be more challenging than rewarding, but Abigail was committed to fulfilling her role. She would rather sacrifice a hand and a few toes than to let Joel down.

She plopped onto the bed, partially dressed, unable to stop a gigantic yawn from having its way with her. She fell back on the bed and let her body sink into the softness of the twelve-hundred-count sheets, smoother than silk. Entering a nebulous dream state, while still able to hear the radio in the background, she forced her eyelids open and jerked to a sitting position. If she lay there one more second, sleep would claim her for the day. She popped to her feet and finished dressing in a whirlwind, determined to be ready when Joel arrived. The days were grueling and the week long, but neither DMI nor the house would crowd out her time on Sunday morning with the Lord. Attending the same church with Joel and having the special time together was a bonus, especially now that a few of his evenings weren't spent with her at DMI.

Completely dressed in a two-piece suit, she hustled down the stairs. In a dash she snatched a piece of fruit from the bowl. Eating a casual breakfast and getting a full night's sleep were luxuries she dreamed about on rare occasions. There was no time to waste on unrealistic wishing. With perfect timing, she locked the door behind her as the limousine pulled up in front. Her heart danced to the car as her body followed, anticipating being near Joel. Besides her faith, he was her reason for living. One day they would be a committed couple. She relished the thought and climbed inside, taking her rightful seat next to him. Abigail struggled to maintain composure. His teeth always sparkled against the deep, strong, manly skin that seemed to reach out to her and take her in an unbreakable embrace. His dark cashmere coat draped his body with a finesse equal to his charm. She struggled to keep her gaze moving around the car instead of shamelessly staring at him like a silly teen. She was content being in his space, tired, but content.

"I got a call late last night. I hope you don't mind, but we're taking a detour today," Joel said.

"I don't mind," she said, with no idea what he was talking about. Whatever he wanted to do, wherever he wanted to go, she was willing.

"Greater Faith Chapel has asked me to visit their church today. They want to make a donation to the library."

"Don't they know the library is finished?"

"I guess, but the donations continue to roll in, and I don't want to hinder the people's desire to give. If they feel led in their heart to give, we have to receive. The library can always sponsor events, provide endowments, and give out scholarships. There are plenty of good uses for the money. So long as we tell people upfront that the library is completed, it's up to them if they still want to contribute."

"I guess you're right," she said.

"Of course I'm right," he said, winking at her. She wanted to melt but held her emotions in check, undetected, as she'd learned to do to perfection. Dinner the other night had been no exception.

They arrived at Greater Faith Chapel early, which wasn't surprising, because Joel was a stickler about time.

"Aren't you the man who owns that big company in Detroit?" another early bird worshipper asked, approaching her and Joel as they went inside.

"Good morning, sir," Joel said, as cool as ever, shaking the elderly man's hand and placing a hand on his shoulder, too. This wasn't Joel's church, but he seemed right at home, as he did in most unfamiliar environments.

The lobby had sparse pockets of churchgoers, some boldly approaching Joel and others resorting to whispering and finger pointing. In the beginning, Abigail had been uncomfortable with the amount of attention Joel attracted, but she was growing accustomed to the fanfare. Dave had popularity, and as his supporter she was constantly exposed to his entourage, but never to this degree.

A short, elderly lady approached. Abigail envisioned Moses approaching, because the people lining the path between her and Joel parted like the Red Sea, letting her walk freely up to him.

"Good morning, young man," she said. "Welcome to Greater Faith Chapel. I'm sure hoping you're ready to praise the Lord, because that's what we do in Greater Faith," she said with a spirit you could sense was genuine.

"Why, yes, we are here to praise the Lord with you. There's nothing like a good Sunday morning worship service," Joel said.

"Excuse my manners. My name is Mrs. Emma Walker."

"Everybody calls her Big Mama," a lady standing close by said.

"What would you like for me to call you?" Joel asked.

"A child of the king," she said, punctuating the statement with a dash of laughter, causing Joel to laugh, too.

"That's the best answer," he said.

Mrs. Walker wrapped her hand around Joel's. "Son, I feel led to tell you that you are not here by accident today. The Lord has a mighty calling on you."

"Yes, I believe that, Mrs. Walker."

"No, I don't know that you do. See, the Lord . . ." she said, and then stopped in midsentence, took a breath and continued, "whew, you have a serious anointing on you, my child."

Before Abigail could figure out what was going on, the lobby of people swarmed around them like bees on a sunflower. She and Joel couldn't move an inch one way or the other. The crowd was praying in low tones while

Mrs. Walker talked. She wasn't the pastor, but anyone walking into the church at this moment wouldn't know. She had the complete attention of the audience, and as a result, she had Abigail's, too.

"You have been created by God and called for a mighty purpose."

Abigail believed in the gift of prophecy, the ability for someone to get a specific message from God for themselves or for someone else, but she'd never personally witnessed the act. Abigail couldn't tell the difference between the gift of prophecy and fortune-telling. She didn't feel any more confident with mediation being unable to distinguish the Holy Spirit from other bizarre spirits. To be safe, she stayed away from all of it. Good old-fashioned Bible reading and praying were her sources of communication with God.

The pastor entered the circle.

"Mr. Mitchell, good to have you with us today."

"My pleasure," Joel said, but Mrs. Walker wouldn't let his hand go, and it was obvious he was trying to get free.

"Don't worry about shaking my hand. Trust me, if Big Mama has your hand, then you're in good hands. We believe this woman sleeps at the door of heaven and talks with God every day all day."

"I'm giving him the word that I believe is from the Lord."

"Oh, let me get out of the way. I apologize for interrupting," the pastor said, and moved away from Joel. Whoever Mrs. Walker was, the crowd and the pastor had ultimate respect for her, and her words, causing Abigail's interest to elevate. Maybe Mrs. Walker could tell Joel to marry her. Now that would be a blessed Sunday morning.

"I believe the Lord is saying that you were created to fulfill the works of your father."

"I've completed the library my father started, which, of course, is one of the reasons I'm here today," Joel responded.

"No, your calling is bigger than the library. You're special," she said, peering up toward Joel, since he was nearly a foot taller than her. "You're a smart man, and I don't mean book smart. I'm talking about wisdom, the kind that comes from God. He has given you wisdom and favor beyond your years more than your father had."

Abigail shouldn't have been impressed, because Mrs. Walker hadn't said anything the press hadn't reported repeatedly. Everybody knew Joel was a well-known executive and that he'd taken over his father's affairs. There was nothing profound about what she said, it was how she said it that stood out and rang with a spirit of truth.

"You were chosen, hand-picked by God," Mrs. Walker said, pointing her finger up at Joel, "but the day will come when you will be tested."

"I love the Lord and I'm committed to doing his work."

"Yes, you are, but the day of trial will come. Hear me this day, young man. You must stay before the Lord, the one true God. Don't be deceived. Don't allow yourself to be courted by the enemy, to be lured away by the breast of evil, to be seduced with the lust of the world, to be mated with other gods, or I'm telling you this day, you will surely fall. Don't let your blessings and favor become your curse."

"Don't worry, Mrs. Walker. I'm committed to my Lord."

"You be mindful. Many will come from far and wide

but you gone have to watch yourself. Your life and your calling will depend on you staying in the presence of the Lord," she said, hugging Joel around his waist. "I'm praying for you, son, but this is going to have to be your walk."

"Thank you, Mrs. Walker. I will take your words to heart."

The crowd dispersed as Mrs. Walker went into the sanctuary.

"She's an interesting little lady with a firm grip," Joel said, massaging his hand.

Abigail wasn't sure how much Joel was accepting, but she was 100 percent on board with Mrs. Walker. There was an indescribable feeling being in her presence, and Abigail wasn't about to take her words lightly. She prayed Joel wouldn't either, particularly when it came to the flock of acquaintances desperately seeking to be in his circle. Abigail pulled a business card from her purse and jotted down the key points Mrs. Walker had mentioned so they wouldn't forget, especially Joel.

chapter

46

Joel was reviewing a corporate income statement when his administrative assistant poked her head in the doorway. "Ms. Sheba Warden is here to see you."

"Which line is she on?" he said, grabbing the phone, eager to jump on the call.

"She's in the waiting area."

"Here, in the building?" he said, plopping the receiver down. He straightened his tie and popped to his feet. "Send her in," he said. When his assistant's back was turned he checked his shirt to make sure it was tucked neatly into his pants. He twisted the square cufflinks around, making sure they were straight.

"Sheba Warden, please come in," he said, closing the gap between them and extending his hand. "It's a pleasure to finally meet you." He could maintain focus in a room of yelling executives tossing around ideas and egos, but standing here with Sheba Warden was more difficult. He shook her hand with a firm grip, tantalized by the softness of her hands. She was five-foot-five, with tender hot-chocolate-colored skin and a hint of cream covering her heavenly body.

"I apologize for barging in unannounced," she said, letting her savory words breeze across her delicate-looking lips. "I was returning to Chicago from Milan and couldn't resist the opportunity to land in Detroit and meet you in person," she said, flowing into the room with the grace of a gazelle.

"Did you have an entire plane diverted?" he asked, unable to restrain a grin that was destined to form.

"I did, but it's my plane. I can do that," she said, casting a smile back in return.

"I'm flattered."

"You should be." She spoke with a confidence he wasn't accustomed to seeing but found intriguing. "I don't drop by to see just any person."

"Really," he said, freely engaging in the playful banter. "Please, let me take your coat." As she handed him the full-length fur coat, he said, "You don't intend to get cold around here, do you?"

"I like to be prepared," she said, bypassing the chairs near his desk and taking a seat at his table instead. She crossed her legs, letting her stylish five-inch boots swing in a small circular motion.

His private line buzzed, but he wasn't willing to disrupt the flow of their conversation. He had an idea of who was calling, but she wasn't as captivating as Sheba was, the delightful woman standing right there in his presence. He would follow up with the other woman later. He turned a seat around to face her and sat with his chin resting on his partially closed fist. "What can I do for you?"

"I'm here bearing gifts," she said, extracting a check from her purse and handing it to him.

The check read $18 million. "Why are you giving me a check?"

"I was moved by your interview on WGN in Chicago, and I'd like to contribute to the construction of your library. The way you spoke so passionately about your father moved me, and I want to contribute."

"I'm grateful for your offer, but we completed construction of the library a year ago," he said, handing the check back.

"You've completed the building, but a library can use books, new equipment. I can think of a long list of uses for eighteen million dollars." She handed the check to him again. "There's something quite amazing about you, and I want to reward the man who is clearly already rewarded. Maybe you can speak a blessing over me."

"I don't know what to say."

"Say thank you and use the donation as you see fit."

"I really don't know what to say. Building the library in my father's honor was very important to me. Next to successfully running DMI, constructing the library was the second-most-important goal I had. I spared no expense. Nothing was too good for the library. On behalf of my father and myself, thank you. I promise you every penny will be used to expand the vision of the library." He toyed with the check, not quite overcome with emotion but definitely touched by her gesture. "Tell me, what can I do for you in return?"

"There are no strings attached to the check. It's yours," she said. Her words were full of melody, like a song to his ears.

There was a rap on the door. "Excuse me," he said, going to the door and wondering who could have such poor timing.

"Excuse me, Mr. Mitchell," his administrative assistant said as Joel stepped out of the office and pulled the door closed behind him. "I wouldn't have disturbed you except Barry insists on getting a few minutes with you to discuss a critical issue."

He pulled the door tighter. "I'm in a very important meeting. Let Abigail handle it."

"Barry can't get in touch with Abigail. She's at the construction site of the new house. I think there was a problem with the foundation or something."

He wasn't aware of a problem, but Abigail was in complete control of the construction and must have chosen not to bother him with the details. "I'm sorry, but this meeting can't wait. Barry has to track down Abigail for her input. She's his first point of contact."

"Will do; I'll tell him."

"Otherwise he'll have to wait until I'm free later this afternoon."

"Should I hold your calls?"

"Definitely, and I don't want to be disturbed until my meeting with Ms. Warden is over. No calls, no interruptions."

"I understand, Mr. Mitchell." He opened the door as his assistant asked how long the meeting was going to be. "It's not on your calendar."

"I'm not sure how long," he said, unconcerned about the potential conflict with other meetings. "Do me a favor, clear my entire schedule this afternoon."

"Everything?" she asked with a puzzled look.

"Everything for the entire afternoon—remember to hold all my calls, too. Thanks," he said, and swaggered into the office. "I apologize for the interruption."

"It's expected; you're the CEO, and it's not like I had an appointment."

He reclaimed his seat next to Sheba Warden, as intrigued as he had been when she entered the office. "Now, where were we? How can I help you?"

"I simply had to meet you. Now that I have, I'm convinced of your sincerity and authenticity. I followed the results of your marketing campaign in Chicago."

For the first time since she'd entered the room, he wanted to shift his glance from her alluring face. The issues behind the campaign hadn't been released to the public by DMI. Someone had leaked details about the two women both claiming to own the idea. DMI had come forward reluctantly and addressed the media.

"I have to tell you, I was quite impressed with the approach you took in resolving your issue, quite impressed. You're just what I need."

"How so?" he said. If he were ten shades lighter she would have seen the blood rushing to his face. He was safe.

"I have a chain of boutiques in Chicago. I'm ready to expand beyond the Midwest and I need a strong team to lead the charge within my organization."

"Are you offering me a job?" he asked, not able to read her interest or the direction of her conversation. He couldn't help but to be drawn into the mystery hovering around her.

"In a way, I guess I am offering you a job. I'd like for you to mentor me. There's something very rare about you. I've followed you in the media and done some other checking of my own. You are definitely special, gifted, young, and quite good-looking, I might add." She didn't touch him, but Joel felt as if she had.

She was pushing every "be professional at all costs" button, challenging his level of control. "How should I respond?"

"Say yes. I'm not going to leave until you do. I'm determined to be in your space. The gods must really like you, and the sun, moon, earth, and wind must be in harmony with you, too."

His grin crashed and his lips tightened. "Not many gods, just one God. There's only one true God for me, the God of Abraham, Isaac, and Jacob. He's the creator of heaven and earth and the sun and the moon, which bow at His feet daily." Her beauty was driving him into a stupor, but the mere notion of giving other gods glory over his Lord was instantly sobering.

"I'm sorry if I offended you. Clearly you have a very strong opinion on religion."

"My faith in God is more than an opinion. It's a way of life for me. I live for Him. I breathe for Him. I run DMI for Him, a belief I inherited from my father."

"Your passion is the reason I'm here. I want to understand the source of your success. I want to grow my boutiques, and the best way to gain knowledge is to be mentored by someone I consider to be knowledgeable. What do you say? Can I submit myself to your leadership? I will do whatever you ask for as long as it takes."

He clicked the check against the table. Anyone who possessed a fraction of the interest he did in constructing his father's library had automatic favor from him. "If you believe I can help you, then I'm yours."

She gave him a wink and retrieved her fur. "What hotel do you recommend in the area?"

"Depends on what you like?"

chapter

47

Today was a near disaster. The inspector had discovered a crack in the new house's foundation requiring attention. Abigail didn't have time to review the mid-quarter reports that were due in two days. Barry had loose ends to clean up from the contest fallout. Brian was getting up to speed with the West Coast but needed her daily involvement. Abigail checked her watch every five minutes. The assistant didn't know how long Joel would be in his meeting with Sheba Warden. Abigail racked her brain trying to recall Joel mentioning the meeting. Her mental database came up empty. Her search engine was frazzled. Long days and short nights. She needed sleep, but not tonight. She had dinner reservations with Joel. Abigail yawned and nodded off. Suddenly Joel's door opened. She watched as Joel and the woman, laughing and seeming too friendly, stood a few inches inside the doorway. Abigail approached.

"I like the best, and I can tell you do, too," the woman said, coming out of his office carrying a fur coat and wearing spike-heeled boots. "I don't know anyone in Detroit. How about having dinner with me?"

"Dinner it is."

Abigail was aghast. How could he forget their plans? She inserted herself into their path.

"Sheba Warden, I don't believe we've met. I'm Abigail Gerard, the executive vice president of DMI operations." Ms. Warden was courteous about the introduction but showed enthusiasm and interest only in Joel. "Joel, I need to speak with you about our dinner plans tonight," Abigail told him.

"Oh, I didn't realize we were meeting tonight."

"We sure are," Abigail said with boldness, rapidly shifting her eyes back and forth from Ms. Warden to Joel.

"I'm sorry," Ms. Warden interjected. "Joel, perhaps we can meet another time."

"Give me one minute," Joel told Abigail, appearing more comfortable than she felt. "I'd like to walk Sheba to the elevators."

Abigail's heart raced, as she dwelled on him at the elevator with a woman she didn't know. Madeline walked by reading from an open folder. "So, Abigail, you are here. Barry has been trying to contact you most of the day."

"I know. I was swamped today with the house and—" she was about to finish when Madeline cut in.

"That's Sheba Warden at the elevator with Joel."

"You know her?"

"Who doesn't? She owns a string of upscale boutiques in the Chicago area. What's she doing here?"

"Apparently she's interested in the library."

"The same library that was finished over a year ago," Madeline grunted, peering over her reading glasses with a bizarre look of satisfaction. "Humph, we know why she's here—two words, single and rich. Need I say more?"

Abigail's heart picked up pace. Her pulse was pounding. Who was this woman infiltrating her space? Stop worrying, Abigail thought. She was building their house. Abigail wasn't going to drown in a sea of speculation and jealously when the man of her dreams had entrusted her with two of the most important areas of his life, DMI and his home. She settled down, realizing the silliness of her concern. Joel was already committed. Sheba Warden had to find other plans for the evening.

Madeline flew to her office and dialed the phone so fast she felt lightheaded. "I couldn't wait to call you," she told Don.

"I'm sure this has something to do with Joel and these comical schemes of yours. What have you done now, my dear mother?"

"Nothing really. Didn't have to this time."

"When are you going to give up and accept the fact that Joel is CEO? He runs DMI. Give it up, Mother."

"I tried after the Chicago debacle. For a millisecond the wind was blowing across my face, and I was feeling nostalgic, and I have to admit I almost called it quits. But then I remembered our CEO is Sherry and Dave Mitchell's son. You know what that means."

"Nnnn-o."

"Means he has the infidelity gene."

"Oh, come on, that's ridiculous. There is no such thing as an infidelity gene. Where do you get this stuff?"

"He has the gene, I'm telling you the truth," Madeline said.

"I'm Dave Mitchell's son, too. Does that mean I have the gene?" Don was feeding his mother's unhealthy obsession with Joel, but humoring her on the call was the extent of his endorsement.

"Of course not, both of your parents have to be unfaithful in order to pass it on to you. Since I'm your mother, you're safe."

Don chuckled. "You make it sound like a communicable disease."

"It is," she said.

"I seriously hope you're joking and don't really mean any of this."

"Maybe not the gene part, at least not totally, but he has a weakness for women. I know that for sure."

"And how would you know, Mother?"

"I hear things, but today I could see with my own eyes. He had a visitor today and there's no doubt he was awestruck. I saw him sniffing behind Sheba Warden in the office today like a dog in heat. Poor Abigail stood around looking like a deer in headlights."

"I find it hard to believe that Joel would show interest in another woman right in front of Abigail." Don didn't want to believe what he was hearing. The decision to set aside his attraction for Abigail and allow her to explore her feelings for Joel hadn't come easily. He hoped he'd made the right decision in not telling her his true feelings before leaving Detroit. He felt content about avoiding any battle with Joel, particularly when there was an actual life involved. Love was easy and didn't require a duel, or so he chose to believe.

"I'm telling you he was interested in Sheba and Abigail looked pitiful. I really like the young lady but she needs to get a clue about Joel. Record my words, it's only a matter of time before he breaks her heart."

"Abigail is too smart to be duped by Joel. She has a fierce business mind."

"Business is business, love is love. Brains in one can look like sheer stupidity in the other. I can appreciate Abigail being a woman who knows what she wants, I get that part of the equation. But if Joel isn't interested, move on. Abigail's problem is that she's had so much success she doesn't know how to lose. Regardless of what anyone says, most likely she'll stick this out until the bitter end, which will hopefully be sooner rather than later for her."

Don couldn't dream of Abigail falling victim to heartache. He had had a taste of the pain firsthand and would go to great lengths to ensure she didn't have to suffer a drop of what he had. He'd call and check on her. If and when she needed him, Detroit was an airline seat away, no questions asked.

chapter

48

___

Joel waited in the Townsend Hotel lobby for Sheba to come downstairs. Quiet moments were rare. His schedule pulled him in different directions fifteen solid hours out of each day, with strategizing about the international expansion claiming a fair share of time. He glanced at the magazines on the oblong coffee table. Feet firmly planted in a pair of Ferragamo shoes, neck tilted back, he closed his eyes for a quick meditation.

"Excuse me, Mr. Mitchell, I'm the hotel manager. My staff informed me that you were in the lobby and I want to extend our courtesies to you," he said, handing Joel a business card. "Will you be staying with us this evening?"

"No, I'm here for dinner, but a friend of mine is staying in your hotel."

"Please tell me your friend's name and I'll make sure they're well cared for during their stay with us."

"Would that friend be me?" Sheba asked, easing into the conversation wearing a royal-blue dress fitted to her perfectly formed body.

Joel stood and took her hand. "This is my friend, Ms. Sheba Warden."

"It is Ms., right, or is it Mrs.?" Joel asked.

"I'm single. Ms. is fine," she responded.

"We're new friends," he told the hotel manager. Joel couldn't take his gaze off Sheba.

"I see," the manager responded, with what looked like a slight grin.

Joel could have explained who Sheba was and how they'd met but didn't feel the need to justify himself to the manager. Let him think what he wanted.

"Ms. Warden, if there's anything we can do to make your stay more enjoyable, please don't hesitate to call me on my direct line." He handed her a business card after circling a number. "Also, dinner for the two of you will be complimentary."

"That's not necessary," Joel said, putting his arm out for Sheba.

"This will be my pleasure, Mr. Mitchell."

Joel agreed and escorted Sheba into the restaurant. A special table was reserved in the front corner slightly off to itself. The waiter placed the thick linen napkin in Sheba's lap and left. Finally, a moment alone. The dim lighting and soft piano music was relaxing enough to put Joel to sleep. She'd donated $18 million to the library. The least he could do was stay awake and entertain his guest.

"Do you always get such favor?" she asked.

Joel nodded. "Ever since the media started hunting

me down like the paparazzi, I get more attention than I want."

"Am I the paparazzi?" she said, casting those brownish-green feline eyes at him.

He chuckled under his breath. "Not exactly."

"What am I?" she asked, in a luscious tone reminding him of the smell of fresh cookies pouring from a bakery vent, too tempting to pass by.

"You tell me. I'm curious to find out who you are and how I can help you."

"Like I said in your office earlier, I want to be near you, to be in your space. I want to learn from you. You have something unique going on, and I want to be in the company of success. Everybody talks about your gutsy business moves. You are described in the papers as a strategic thinker, and I want to soak up your knowledge. I want to get what you have." He grinned. "I mean professionally speaking, of course."

"Oh," he said, enjoying the relaxing flow between them.

"You know what I mean. I want to expand my boutiques into new markets like you've done with DMI."

"I have to be honest. My success with DMI is not based on my own efforts. I owe God and my father one hundred percent of the credit."

She gave a sigh and then spoke. "Interesting."

The conversation dipped in and out of seriousness, lightheartedness, and playful curiosity. Sleepiness had left the table two hours ago. Joel checked his watch. She was like a spider drawing him into the web, and he was going willingly.

"I saw you looking at your watch a few minutes ago.

We can call this an evening. I don't want to monopolize your time my first day in town."

"I'm in no hurry. Actually, I don't want our conversation to end. I don't get much free time to interact with peers anymore, not since I became CEO."

The waiter filled their partially empty water glasses, as he'd done several times before.

"I find that surprising. I expect you to have plenty of friends, especially female friends looking to have fun with you, like the lady at the office," she said, taking a sip of water.

"You mean Abigail."

"Yes, lovely Abigail. She looked awfully intense. Actually, I was surprised when you called to confirm dinner. I thought you and Abigail had plans."

"Apparently we did, which I can't believe I forgot. I don't know what happened there. In my defense, it wasn't on my schedule. Then again, we go to dinner several times a week and it's never on my schedule. I got my wires crossed, plain and simple."

"I hope I didn't cause a problem."

"No way," he said, taking a drink. "Abigail is one in a million. She's accustomed to my impromptu business meetings."

"Is this business or pleasure?" Sheba asked, running her finger around the rim of her glass.

"You tell me," he shot back. "Why don't we see how the evening goes and answer the question later?" he said, leaning back in his chair.

"That works for me," she said, letting her gaze traipse across his body. "Here's an easier question. The papers say you're single. Are you truly single and available or are you single and attached?"

"Definitely single but not available and not attached," he said, flushing. The term "attached" wasn't one he was ready to use with anyone. "Let's say that I'm enjoying life."

"No special lady on the horizon?"

"No, not yet."

Sheba gave a nod of approval. He tossed an adoring gaze back. One day he might consider settling down, but there was much more to be accomplished before a relationship took center stage.

"Then if you're not in a relationship, what does a twenty-five-year-old do for fun?"

"You know how old I am."

"Joel Mitchell, I know far more about you than simply your age. I've made it my mission to learn as much as I can about you. I know your age, your interests, and your hobbies."

"I'm at a disadvantage, because I don't know much about you."

"We can fix your tiny problem. I'm thirty-six years old, never been married, no children, my parents are deceased, and I'm an only child. My mother was a seamstress in Chicago for rich women on the upper north side. My parents saved their money, bought a tiny shop one day, and the rest is history."

"Sounds like we have a lot in common."

"Seriously, you'll have to let me know when you're ready to go, otherwise I could sit here and talk with you all night," she said.

"I'm not ready to go but I wouldn't mind getting out of this restaurant. The poor guy has filled our water glasses about fifteen times. Either my bladder has to leave or I do." Joel was spellbound by her delicate laugh, her refreshing enthusiasm.

"We can go to my suite, if you don't mind hotel living," she suggested.

"I don't mind at all," he said, assisting her from the table and letting her grip his arm. "How long are you planning to stay in Detroit?"

"Why, are you extending an invitation?"

"I guess I am. I think you should stay around for a few more days. You can come by the office and we can talk more about your expansion plans and mine," he told her, hoping she'd accept the offer.

"Are you sure you have time for a party crasher? You've told me how busy your schedule is."

"I'll make time for you. Don't you worry about that," he said, tapping the elevator button reserved for rooms on the executive floor.

chapter

49

Abigail sat in Joel's office and read her status report without emotion. The passion was drained from her tired body. Building the house and juggling her work schedule wasn't the problem. Those she could handle. Joel, she wasn't sure. She didn't ad-lib or interject as he spoke.

"You don't seem like yourself. What's going on?" he asked.

"Nothing really," she told him, too exhausted to get into a drawn-out emotional discussion.

"Abigail, how long have we been a team? Long enough for me to know there's something bothering you. What is it and how can I help?"

"If you really want to know, I'm upset with you."

"Me, what did I do?" he said, seeming dumbfounded. She felt worse because he didn't know why.

"We were supposed to have dinner at Chop House last night, remember."

He slumped in his chair and tossed his pen to the desk. "Abigail, you said it was okay to cancel," he said, coming around the desk to sit near her. "Sheba presented an eighteen million-dollar check to me for the library. Dinner was the least I could do. I didn't think you and I had any pressing DMI issues to deal with last night. Was I wrong?"

"Nothing pressing, I just needed a break."

"I had no idea you were this upset," Joel told her. She shouldn't have to spell it out for him. "I'm a total louse. Please forgive me," he said.

Forgiving him was as easy as scooping ice cream on a hot summer day. "Of course I forgive you, but don't blow any more of my meetings. That includes dinner and lunch, too," she said.

"Yes, Captain, or should I call you Mom?" he said jokingly.

She couldn't stay angry at him for very long.

"Seriously, I didn't have dinner on my calendar with you last night. I would have never made dinner plans with Sheba Warden if I already had plans with my buddy," he said, patting her shoulder.

"We don't usually have plans. We just go. That's what we do," she said, letting her arms rise and fall.

"Regardless, please accept my apology."

"Don't worry. You'll have plenty of opportunities to make up for last night."

"I bet I will," he said. "How many stacks of reports are you planning to plop on my desk from last night?" The unspoken connection between them resurfaced for Abigail as she listened to Joel. "Remind me to get you more help. I don't want you overloaded. What good are you then," he said, chuckling.

Her sense of calm had returned, only slightly bruised. "So how was dinner with Ms. Warden?"

"Flattering."

"What do you mean?"

"She wants to expand her Chicago market and wants me to be her mentor."

"You can't help her with boutiques and gowns. Your specialty is church leadership. She would be best served by partnering with someone in the clothing arena." Abigail wanted to say "anybody but you" but held her comments and decided instead to change subjects. "There's one way you can repay me."

"Tell me and it's done," he told her.

"Before the drywall goes up in your house, I have to complete a walk-through in the next couple of days. I have two inspectors scheduled to go with me, but I'd like you to be there, too."

"Might as well be your house; you've managed the entire construction process."

"But you're writing the checks, thank goodness." She warmed. He had ultimate grace in her heart. As long as Joel strived to fulfill the vision for DMI, he would have her vote of support.

"Put me down for the walk-through. I'll be there."

"Great," she said.

"Excuse me, Mr. Mitchell," his administrative assistant said, entering with a handful of messages. Abigail had forgotten to close the door when she came in. As a result, her private slice of time with Joel was about to end. "I hope I'm not interrupting."

"Come on in. I'm going to my office. I have a ton of emails and calls to make. I'll catch you later," Abigail told Joel.

"Hang on, don't go yet," he said.

"I'm sorry for interrupting."

"It's okay, what do you have?" Joel asked his assistant.

"Mr. Musar Bengali wants to speak with you later this morning about the international expansion."

"Good, I was expecting his call. Be sure to find me and interrupt me when he calls again. I don't want to miss it."

"I will, sir. Also, Ms. Samantha Tate has left several messages for you. She says it's urgent."

"Did she tell you what the urgency was?" Joel asked. Abigail had a few ideas about Samantha's so-called urgent matters.

"She just said it's important. I don't have any more information," the assistant said.

"I'll see you later," Abigail said, standing in his doorway. She turned toward the hallway and had a collision. "Oh, excuse me," Abigail said.

"Sheba," Joel said, springing to his feet like a jack-in-the-box. "You're here early. Come in." He beckoned her into his office.

Joel's administrative assistant slipped out. Abigail wasn't about to leave him alone with Sheba. She had mounds of work to complete, but it would have to wait.

"You truly inspired me last night. I jumped out of bed bright and early. I couldn't wait to get in and get started," Sheba said.

Abigail tried counting techniques in order to maintain her cool. Sheba Warden had no right bouncing into his office.

"You mean I didn't bore you to sleep?" he asked.

"Not a chance," she said, draping her fur over the chair. Joel leapt to take the coat for her.

"After our time together last night, I'm back for more."

"What exactly do you mean?" Abigail asked, trying not to let her uneasiness show.

"Oops, I didn't mean to sound sordid, but this young man is a force to deal with."

"Yes, I know," Abigail said, with brooding emotions festering. Sheba Warden had better watch out. Abigail had invested too much of her heart in Joel to let some starry-eyed woman squeeze into his life sucking up his free time. Forget the formalities. Joel was committed to the point where Sheba Warden should back off, and other women, too. She considered talking with Joel to find out where he was headed before she invested any more time and heart. On second thought, he had told her before that a serious relationship wasn't on his radar. She didn't know what to do.

chapter

50

Overwhelmed wasn't the right word. Don felt energized, submerged, rejuvenated. His enthusiasm and confidence were rekindled thanks to LTI, and in large part to his mother's endorsement. It wasn't what she said to him directly. It was what she did, coming to South Africa last year, helping him strengthen his marketing strategy, and having a marketing study done at her own expense. There wasn't a more supportive mother on earth, Don thought, scribbling a few notes.

Don anticipated the knock on his office door, since he'd called for Naledi earlier. "Come in, please," he said, standing as she entered. He reclaimed his seat once she was seated.

"You've been looking for me. I was out for a spot of

lunch. Is there a problem with my work?" she asked, sounding troubled.

"No, not at all," Don said, leaning back in his seat, bubbling with excitement. He slid a short stack of stapled papers across the desk to her. "Just the opposite, we got the Unilever deal." He could barely contain his excitement. "Can you believe it?" he said, jumping to his feet and coming around the desk to her side. "We did it. This is our largest international account so far."

"This is wonderful news," she said, standing and grabbing both his hands and shaking them fervently.

"Unilever touches all of our major markets. They're right here in South Africa."

"And in the U.K. and India," she added, with a spark of excitement. Naledi usually maintained a reserved demeanor, but when she was excited her eyebrows arched and she fidgeted, as she was doing now.

"And in the Middle East, Far East, and even in the U.S. They're all over the world. This is huge for us," he said, grabbing her in an impulsive embrace and yelling, "Yes." Don quickly released her, realizing how inappropriate his action was. He stepped back and rushed around the desk to his seat. The last thing he wanted to do was offend her. She was a godsend, a true lifesaver. She took a seat, which helped him feel a little more at ease. "You were an important factor in making this happen."

"I don't think so," she said, with the blended accent that was becoming more and more melodious to his ears. She gave him pointers on how to present the proposal to the South African division of Unilever. The deal had been in the works for six out of the fifteen months that she'd been with LTI. "I need your help again."

"Yes, please tell me what I can do."

"I need your help with France. Unilever wants us to do a plan for South Africa first and then France. We need to make a few changes for France. I can pull together the details. Before I get the attorney's input and the accountant on the numbers, I'd like you to review the plan and let me know if it's culturally correct."

"How do you mean?"

"Tell me if it has the right tone. If there are any phrases or terms that might be considered offensive. If you don't mind, I'd also like to get your assistance in translating the plan into French. Can you help me?" Don said, leaning on the desk.

"But of course, Don." Finally, she was no longer calling him Mr. Mitchell. No friend of his was calling him Mr. Mitchell. Naledi was definitely a solid assistant. More important, he also saw her becoming a solid friend. She was a refreshing colleague, smart, attractive, and attentive—a combination he hadn't seen in a woman since Abigail. He had to acknowledge God. How else could Naledi have shown up on his doorstep, exactly what he needed when he needed the support? God had abandoned him in the past, or so he believed. Looking around the office and at the stack of proposals and contracts on his desk, he didn't feel forgotten. His flow of success overshadowed old feelings of being orphaned by his father and by God. Sitting there in the moment of his accomplishment, the beginning of his future, the past hurts weren't as painful as they'd once been. He was feeling like his old self—actually better, moving on with life. The past was done. This was his new beginning. He was feeling like his own man. "How would you feel about joining me for lunch?"

"I've already had my lunch," she said, with a tone of disappointment, or at least that's what he thought he heard in her response. Maybe it was wishful thinking. Naledi was from a different culture. He didn't know what was appropriate in his requests with her. If she was willing to stay with him at LTI, he would take the time to find out more about her and her culture. He was interested in trying.

"That's right, you did say that," he said, giving a little laugh. "I should have said dinner. Would you be willing to join me for dinner? I'm so happy right now. I want to celebrate our hard work and our wonderful success."

"Yes," she said, giving a slight nod, "I would very much like to have dinner with you. That would be very lovely."

She'd said yes, which was what he wanted, but he found himself at a loss for words. He couldn't remember the last time he'd had dinner with a woman other than his mother. He was well overdue for an evening of relaxation and celebration. Naledi was the perfect companion for the evening. She understood LTI, the source of his passion. She was also very familiar with Cape Town, his refuge and newfound home.

chapter

51

Joel had a check in his spirit about Sheba's presence, a red flag, an uncomfortable notion. His spiritual guidance hadn't faltered in the past. Yet, he couldn't resist. Joel could contend that Sheba's entrepreneurial spirit was the element most compelling about her, but he'd be lying. He caught himself staring at her repeatedly, unable to shift his attention to another topic. She consumed his energy, his interest, his desire. "What can I get you, water, juice, you name it?" he said.

"I'm fine for now."

"I trust that your forty-minute ride wasn't too inconvenient. I intentionally recommended the hotel in Birmingham because it's out of the hustle and bustle of the city. The bonus is that your hotel is only twenty minutes away from my place in West Bloomfield."

Joel watched her lift one leg and cross it over the other, moving in slow motion. He scooted his chair close to hers, letting his elbows rest on his thighs and his shoulders slump, bringing his frame down closer to hers. "I don't need to tell you how much I enjoyed being with you last night. I'm exhausted but I have no regrets."

"I had no idea we'd spent half the night talking. If you hadn't told me it was two-thirty in the morning, I'd still be talking," she said. "I bet you have the same effect on every woman."

He let his laughter speak first. "I was serious last night. I don't actually get as many nights out on the town as you think, once a week or so that's not business-related."

"I find that hard to believe," she said.

"Seriously, since my father passed, my priority has been DMI. I don't have much time for dating. From the moment I took on the CEO role, my goal has been to keep DMI on track and to finish the library."

"Your dedication is obvious."

"If it wasn't for Abigail's friendship, I'd be eating alone most nights. She was my right and left hand at the beginning of my CEO appointment. I owe her more than I can ever pay."

"Abigail, huh?"

"Yes, she's the only one who can tolerate my working through dinner. We have the same work ethic—total dedication to the job."

"Are you sure the two of you aren't attached?"

He couldn't help but laugh. "Not that discussion again. As I said, I owe her big-time, but we're not in a relationship. Not the kind you mean, anyway. We're not attached."

"If you were looking for a serious relationship, would Abigail be on your short list?"

"Maybe you'll scoop me up and I'll never get to a so-called list, how about that?"

"Never know what the future holds," she replied in a sultry way.

"Are you sure I can't get you anything?" he asked.

"I'm sure," she said, switching the order of her crossed legs.

"Tell me, how did you end up here?" he said, touching her hand and drawing back instantly.

"The library was one reason, but honestly, I came to Detroit because I had to meet you in person. I had to see you with my own eyes."

"Well here I am, Joel Mitchell in the flesh." Joel's private line buzzed. He peered over the desk to see the number display but was too far away. He got up to check the number, expecting a call. "Excuse me, it's my assistant," he told Sheba. Joel answered the phone and was told Mr. Bengali was on hold. "I have to take this call. I've been trying to connect with him," he told Sheba.

"I'll go outside. Take your time."

"No, stay," he said.

"Are you sure? I don't want to distract you."

"If you're in the building you're going to be on my mind," he told her, "but you might be bored waiting for my meeting to end."

"I'm here to learn as much as I can from you. Take your call and don't worry about me. I'll sit here without making a peep. Consider me your eager-to-learn pupil."

Joel gave his assistant the okay to connect the call. "Mr. Bengali, finally we get a chance to talk. I received the materials about your company and I'm quite interested in exploring potential partnership opportunities. There are too many ideas to discuss over the phone. When can we meet in person?" Mr. Bengali extended Joel an invitation to his country. "I don't have any immediate plans to be in southern India. Will you be in the States anytime over the next two weeks?" Joel completed the call after instructing his administrative assistant to coordinate his schedule with Mr. Bengali for a face-to-face meeting within the next two weeks.

"Apparently the discussion went well, based on the look on your face."

Joel reclaimed his seat next to Sheba. "Very well, I'm finally getting traction with my international expansion. I can see DMI stretching from the northernmost territory in Canada to the tip of South Africa and from the Atlantic to the Pacific with everything in between. I will make this happen. Nothing will stand in my way."

"The passion burns in your eyes. The devotion you have for your faith makes you the man I want to get to know."

"We'll see if you feel the same after being subjected to my crazy schedule for a few days." Joel picked up her fur and stood near her. "Come with me. My assistant will get you set up in an office near mine."

Sheba strutted in front, tugging him along by her lightly scented trail of perfume. She smelled of fresh lilacs and lilies meshed together and drizzled over strips of sunshine.

"I want you to meet my mother, who also happens to be my personal assistant and handles my publicity engagements," he said, reaching for the door. "We'll get you settled in and you can stay as long as you like. Who knows, you might not want to leave," he said, whisking her into the hallway for official introductions. He hadn't given much thought to marriage or raising a family. Until she waltzed in, his purpose was fulfilling the vision for DMI. She was older, mature, engaging. He was drawn to her as to nectar. She had come to meet him, but, caught by her irresistible magnetism he wasn't certain who was getting the better deal.

chapter

52

Madeline tiptoed into the boardroom, not sure if Joel would be submerged in prayer as the old Joel used to be without fail. Based on his behavior the last couple of weeks, she wasn't sure what to expect. Instead of running DMI, he was hosting a coed sleepover, and no one seemed to know when it would end. He was on a different wavelength with Sheba around. Prayer appeared to be taking a backseat, at least before meetings. Madeline really didn't care about Joel's personal escapades. She had one concern: ousting him and claiming DMI. If Sheba could keep him distracted, away from the office and leaving DMI work to others, then as far as Madeline was concerned, Joel's playmate could hang around until he was seventy years old, or longer, if his flesh held out.

A few minutes passed and the room began to fill. Abigail entered, followed by Barry, Joel's administrative assistant, and a few others. Sherry wasn't in the room, fortunately.

"Hello, hello, everyone," Joel greeted, entering the room with Ms. Warden at his side. "Many of you have met Ms. Warden, but for those who haven't, this is Sheba Warden. She owns a chain of boutiques in the Chicago area. She's here to absorb our management style and may learn a thing or two from our practices at DMI."

Casual greetings were tossed at her as she took a seat slightly off to the side.

"What's the meeting about?" Madeline asked, wondering why Joel was sliding meetings onto her calendar without proper advance notice.

"I'll get to that," he said. "Is everyone here?"

"Everyone is here except for Connie and Brian. They're on the conference line," the administrative assistant said, pushing the volume button up and hearing them acknowledge.

"Thanks, everyone, for squeezing this meeting onto your calendars. Let's dive right in. As you know, I'm interested in expanding the ministry into international territory. I want to put international in the 'I' of DMI."

He didn't know about the vision Dave had when DMI was named. He wasn't there. Madeline looked around the room. No one else had been there in the beginning—just her. Joel's fancy talk was impressive for his guest, but sounded like more jibber jabber to Madeline, who didn't have time to waste on him showing off in front of his new girlfriend. She tapped her pen loudly, daring Joel to comment.

"I'm sorry. I should have asked if anyone objected to Sheba's sitting in on the meeting. I can assure you we're not discussing trade secrets. Also, remember, she's not in a competing industry. She's here to learn about us as we learn from her."

No one objected. Joel continued.

"I've been chasing down leads and potential opportunities for the international expansion. I've finally made contact with Mr. Bengali. He owns an organization in southern India, and he's interested in partnering with us to form an international presence. I haven't met with him yet, but before we get too far into the evaluation process I'd like to present my overall strategy and timing."

Abigail sat across from Madeline, lips drawn tight as a corset. Sheba appeared to be the most comfortable. Her lovestruck gaze didn't budge from Joel the entire time he spoke.

"The international arena isn't where our core competency lies," Abigail said, to Madeline's shock. Usually Abigail was the one coddling Joel and his suggestions. Today she was jumping on the attack wagon, a rarity. Madeline was amused. Perhaps she could convince Sheba to stay long enough for Abigail to join forces with her and Don. The look of disdain plastered across Abigail's face seemed to have her on the edge. A few more weeks with Sheba and Abigail would be over the edge, falling, and Madeline and Don could catch her.

"The West Coast is getting established. Do we want to split our energy across two major expansions going on at the same time?" Connie blared over the speakerphone.

Madeline was refreshed hearing others object instead of consistently being the only one to challenge Joel. Her job was getting easier, thanks in part to Sheba's being in the room.

"I agree. We don't want to spread ourselves too thin. We are experiencing the best financial time DMI has ever had. Why jeopardize our position by venturing into territories we have very little insight into?" Abigail added.

"Mr. Bengali—isn't his company the one that pushes the inclusion theory?" Brian said.

"What's that?" Barry asked.

"I don't know much about it, but I do know they're into Eastern religions and if I'm not mistaken they believe everyone is a god. All you have to do is tap into your own godlike energy for guidance and direction or something like that. I might not have the details exactly correct, but if this is the same company I've heard about, they push a heavy inclusion message. Basically, they believe everyone goes to a good place after they die and you have a god assigned to you for this life," Brian told the group.

"Kind of like a personal assistant," Madeline said. "Why would we consider partnering with a philosophy we know very little about?"

"Our company philosophy isn't built on fear of the unknown," Joel said in a brazen tone.

"But it is based on solid marketing research," Abigail said curtly.

"And good old common sense," Madeline added.

"Yes, but my decisions are based on the leading of God, first and foremost."

"Are you saying God told you to expand into India with a company that has anti-God practices?" Madeline asked, prepared for a debate.

"I haven't heard from God yet."

Madeline noticed Sheba squirming in her seat. "Excuse me, but does this make sense to anyone here?"

Madeline asked. "I'm definitely not claiming to be the hallelujah type. As a matter of fact, my time with God is limited to holidays. However, even I know we can't take a religious-based organization and expand with a company that doesn't believe in God. That would be foolish, and I'm no fool." Madeline spoke with authority, relishing the hole Joel was digging. She was surprised by his attitude. Normally he was in control and on target with good ideas, ones she resented. Not today. Perhaps having a woman zapping his energy was also searing his common sense. If Sheba was his kryptonite, Madeline would dedicate herself to keeping her around.

"One of the reasons I'm engaging the management team this early in the process is to get your support. I admit that expanding into India and other foreign lands and cultures will constitute one of our largest strategic undertakings. I need your support in order to make this happen."

"I can't say yes without much more information. If you had to have an answer today, mine would be no. We should stick with the current agenda for DMI, build out the West Coast, and then direct our resources to the next major project. Let's not spread ourselves too thin for the sake of immediate growth," Madeline said, with sounds of approval coming from the small group.

"The time to expand is now. Why wait?" Joel fired back.

"I can ask you the opposite question—what's your hurry? I vote to bypass the international expansion at this time and continue to concentrate on our strategic plan for this year, which is to penetrate all four regions in the U.S.," Madeline said.

"The Midwest is solid, thanks to the success of the Creative Concept Contest," Barry said. Madeline wanted to block out the contest and never recall the fiasco again.

"The West Coast is on track," Brian added.

"And the South is showing record growth," Connie said.

Madeline didn't bother to rehash the East Coast numbers. "My vote is no."

"Mine, too," Abigail said.

"I'm on the fence until I get more information," Barry said, "but if I had to make a decision right now the answer would be no."

"Connie, Brian, what about you, what do you think?" Madeline asked, sensing a majority in opposition to Joel's plan for the first time since he'd stolen the CEO position.

"I'm opting for one expansion at a time. Let's finish out the West Coast first," Connie suggested.

"Brian, what about you?" Madeline said, elated to be on top of an issue for once. Joel had picked the wrong meeting to showcase his girlfriend. Embarrassment would suit him well.

"I'm neutral."

"You can't be neutral. You're the senior vice president of a division. What's your recommendation?" Madeline asked Brian.

"I prefer to have more time to build out the West Coast without the extra pressure of having another major project drawing on the company resources."

"There you go," Madeline hurled at Joel, "four say no, one on the fence, and only one in the yes camp—that would be you. You're on your own. If the majority of your management team is saying no, you can bet the board of directors will shoot your expansion plans down, too."

"Perhaps, but I'm moving forward."

"Against the advice of your management team?" Madeline asked.

"I'm charged with making the final decision, and I'm moving forward," Joel told everyone.

"Do you think that's wise?" Abigail asked.

"DMI will expand into international markets. Unless God tells me to stop, I'm moving forward with immediate plans. Are there any more questions?"

"None that seem to matter with you," Madeline said.

chapter

53

The meeting adjourned and Madeline was pleased. Joel was beginning to show cracks in his armor, and she would find a way to capitalize on his vulnerability. In the meantime, she'd enjoy the moment.

"Ms. Warden, I'm glad to meet you. I'm Madeline Mitchell, one of the founders of DMI."

Joel stepped outside the room with Abigail.

"I'm pleased to meet you. Of course I know who you are. You've been a role model for me. Please call me Sheba."

"I'm flattered. I'm familiar with you, too, especially your boutiques. I've spent quite a few hours shopping on the Magnificent Mile, including your Oak Street store. I picked up a few Vera Wang gowns from your boutique. The complimentary hand and foot massage is a nice touch."

"Did you take advantage of the crystals we use?"

"No. Nothing personal, but I don't get into those new age products. I'm not into the wind and moon and stars or some obscure higher power telling me how to live my life," Madeline said.

"I hear you. I'm not the religious type either, at least I wasn't before meeting Joel. I came here not convinced that there was a God or any other heavenly being pulling the strings."

"Wait a minute, I can understand that you're not going crazy with religion, but you must know there is a God."

"Actually, I don't know how we came to be on this earth. I know we live, we die, and that's it—done. I don't know if there's really a heaven, or hell, or ghosts and goblins. I've been living in the present and not worried about the rest." Sheba told Madeline.

"You're an atheist?"

"I'm not necessarily into labels, but I'm not an atheist. I'm more of an agnostic, someone who is unsure about the concept of God and creation. An atheist flat-out doesn't believe in God, but I have to admit that gleaning from Joel has caused me to seriously rethink my belief *about* God. He definitely knows someone powerful up there," Sheba said, pointing upward.

"Excuse me for my ignorance, but I don't know the difference," Madeline said. "For me, either you believe in God or you don't." Sheba smiled as if she wasn't the least bit bothered. "How did Joel react to your religious belief?"

"The topic never came up. We talked about what he believes but not what I believe."

Madeline couldn't budge. She tried wrapping her rational thinking around Sheba's words but wasn't successful. "Interesting, but you do know this company is founded on religious principles?" Madeline was certain there had to be a hidden camera in the area, had to be. Sheba couldn't possibly be such a perfect distraction for Joel.

"You have the same faith as Joel?" Sheba asked Madeline.

"Oh, no," Madeline giggled, "Joel is one of a kind when it comes to faith and religion. I'm not in front of God's face every day like Joel professes to be. I do know God exists and I don't mess with Him, let me put it that way."

"I'm intrigued by Joel and his faith. I want to know more about why he believes what he does."

Madeline was slightly confused. She knew church was a fixed appointment in Joel's world. Anyone spending time with him would at least have to be willing to drop in. "Excuse me for asking, but how often does an agnostic go to church?"

"All the time, for weddings, memorial services, you name it. I live my life every day, fully, I might add. I don't worry about God and creation on a daily basis. That concept doesn't affect my life at all."

"Have you gone to a Sunday worship service with Joel yet?"

"No, but I'd be willing to go just about anywhere with Joel," she said, giving a wink and grin that were surely intended for Joel.

"I see. So, you'll be here over the weekend?" Madeline asked, curious to see what was coming next between Sheba and Joel.

"I plan to be."

Madeline nodded, taking in the depth of the conversation, savoring Joel's complex situation. She guessed that Abigail wasn't the intended woman and devoted confidante in his life after all. She couldn't wait to give Don the update.

"Well, I'm glad we met, Sheba. I have to run to another meeting. Feel free to drop by my office during your visit with us."

Madeline skipped out of the room, thrilled to be who she was, clever and in charge, scanning the area one last time expecting a hidden camera crew to jump out and start laughing.

chapter

54

Joel had asked Abigail to step out of the boardroom, out of earshot of the other managers. He'd spent the past ten minutes pleading with her. He couldn't let her walk away. "Abigail, I need your support. I can deal with the rest of the managers, but I must have you in my corner. We've never been at odds on an issue. What can I do to convince you that DMI needs to expand into international territory and that Mr. Bengali might be the route to go?"

"You can't convince me, Joel. Your father built this company by seeking the Lord for direction."

"That's what I've done since the moment I took over DMI. That's what I'm trying to do here, but I need you to trust me on this."

Sheba Warden and Madeline came from the boardroom. Madeline went the other way and Sheba Warden stood off to the side and didn't approach Joel, but she was within hearing distance. Having had her fill of Ms. Sheba, Abigail told Joel, "I can't misplace my trust. I can't go along with something I don't agree with. In my heart I don't believe the expansion is right for DMI."

"It is right. The goal all along has been to take our leadership program abroad."

"Yes, it was, but not by partnering with an antireligious organization. He would never have agreed."

"They are religious."

"You know what I mean," Abigail said, in a sharp tone he wasn't accustomed to hearing from her.

"I'm sorry you feel this way, but I'm moving forward. I hope you'll change your mind, because I need you with me."

"Why do you need me? Your dance card seems pretty full these days," Abigail said, and walked away, practically snarling at Ms. Warden.

Joel hustled to catch Abigail. They were definitely out of sync and he wanted to fix what was broken. Seeing her in this mood didn't feel good. "Abigail, come on, tell me what's going on."

"Joel, you have company, go on," she said without making eye contact.

"Talk to me," he said, determined to get her to open up. "Is your workload too heavy?" He slapped his palms together, thinking of the extra work she'd taken on for him. She was the one consistently spending long hours at work, while he managed to find moments of free time. He felt guilty relying on her so heavily. "I knew it, there's too much on your plate. Let me help clear your schedule.

Hire two or three analysts, assistants, junior managers, whatever you need."

"It's not my schedule that I want cleared," she snapped again and left.

Joel stood paralyzed, wondering what had just happened. He and Abigail had never disagreed about much. This was unsettling.

"Wow, she didn't seem very pleased with you or me," Sheba told Joel when the two of them were left standing in the hallway.

"Abigail is my greatest advocate. She's been my right hand and my left hand. I couldn't run this ministry without her support. She was loyal to my father, and she's been loyal to me. I have to believe she'll come around. She has to." He couldn't imagine his day-to-day existence in DMI without his trusted partner.

"Are you sure you're not getting loyalty mixed up with love?"

"How so?"

"I can only speak from the few encounters I've had with Ms. Gerard, but I think she has an eye for you."

"As I told you the other night, we're close, there's no question about our special bond." He hadn't grown up with a sister. Never had the pleasure; hadn't grown up with brothers either. The bond with Abigail was important, one he had no intention of ruining.

"Humph, Mr. Joel Mitchell, you're obviously a very sharp businessman. Does that intellect translate to romance?"

"We'll have to see, won't we?" he said. "My top priority today is rallying my team around the expansion concept and getting confirmation from God so we can boldly move forward. I will not bow to fear and resistance. If God tells me to expand, I'm expanding without hesitation, and I'll let Him part the waters and change the minds of those who doubt my purpose."

"You really do put a great deal of trust in your faith."

"My faith has gotten me this far. Quite honestly, it gives me the peace and confidence I need to run DMI."

"Intriguing," she said. "Before meeting you I didn't believe in God. I believed everybody lived their lives without any help. When you die, it's over, done, no heaven, no hell, nothing."

Her beliefs should have ended Joel's slightly romantic interest, but he couldn't pull away from her. It was as if she had a spell over him.

"I'm blown away by the amount of reliance you place on God." She placed her hand on his chest. Her simple touch was welcome, sending a surge through his body. "I'm willing to try your approach and take the faith route. Can't hurt—obviously, faith and God have served you well."

He chuckled, not taking her seriously.

"I told you from the beginning, I came here to learn from you, to gain insight into your business sense and to develop an expansion strategy for my boutiques. If faith in God is the route, then I'm on board."

"Whoa, you've caught me off guard. I don't know what to say."

"Tell me what I need to do."

"Are you sure? What you're asking requires a life-changing confession."

"I've never been surer. I want what you have."

"Okay, it's very simple. All you have to do is repent your past sins both known and unknown, acknowledge Jesus as the son of God and that he died for your sins, and then accept Him as your Savior. That's it, done, easy and you're instantly a child of the Most High God with a promise to spend eternity with Him in heaven."

She walked through the process, following it step by step with what appeared to be sincere conviction, and concluded by accepting her new spiritual place. He didn't need to know what she believed in her heart. His job was completed. As thrilled as he was for her, he couldn't take credit for her newfound spirituality. God was the only one who had the power to spark her curiosity about salvation. All Joel had to do was share the knowledge of God with her and let Him take care of the rest.

"Thank you," she said, wrapping her arms around him. "Joel, stay true to your heart and to your faith," she said, grabbing his hand after releasing him from her embrace. "You are an amazing man. If you feel strongly about your international expansion plans, I say go for it and don't let anyone deter you."

He detected the earnestness in her voice and couldn't resist sweeping Sheba off the floor with a gigantic hug, although unrest about Abigail was nipping at his peace. "See, that's why God has you here. You think you're here to get help from me, but I believe you're here to encourage me. I'm going to take your advice," he said, feeling uplifted. "What are you doing Sunday morning?"

"I don't have any specific plans."

"Good, keep your calendar free. You're coming to church with me. We're going to worship God together."

"Gladly. I'll go anywhere with you."

chapter

55

The weekend had given Abigail time to recover. Besides, Sheba would be gone soon and life would return to normal. Abigail finished dressing with a little haste. Joel was picking her up in less than ten minutes. Ten-fifteen Sunday morning was routine. Sometimes he arrived in his car and other times in the limousine, depending on what he had scheduled afterward. The thirty-minute ride to church was the rare occasion when they got to chat without an agenda or pressing deadlines looming. Abigail had to contain her enthusiasm. She wanted to be with him, alone, needed to be with him, to mend their disagreement. She grabbed her purse and jacket and was headed for the door when the doorbell rang. She took a quick glance at her watch. Ten-thirteen.

She wasn't expecting anyone except Joel, and he never got out of the car to ring her bell. Their timing was usually perfect, with her opening the door just as he was pulling up. Today she proceeded to the front door and pressed the intercom button. "Yes," she blared into the microphone.

"Abigail, it's me."

Hearing Joel's voice she immediately opened the door and greeted him. "You didn't have to get out," she said, gathering her jacket and purse again. "I'm ready."

"I should have called you ahead of time," he said as they left the house.

"Why, you knew I'd be ready. I always am," she said, walking toward the limousine. "Do we have an appointment after church?"

"No, but we do have an extra person joining us. Sheba's coming to church with us."

Abigail froze. Sheba was a name she had intended to block out of her vocabulary for the day. She'd had plenty of her all week at DMI. There was nothing to say. Abigail's time of refreshing was erased. She let her disposition do the talking.

"She accepted Christ on Friday and I asked her to join us today." Abigail remained standing in the same spot, more frustrated by Joel's excitement. Abigail hated being in this predicament. In her spirit she understood how important accepting Christ was for Sheba, both now and into eternity. Standing in Joel's presence, her spirit was dueling with her soul, her emotional engine. She didn't want that woman cutting into her time. "I hope you don't mind her riding with us."

Abigail still couldn't speak. Her legs moved toward

the limousine without any pep. Driving herself might be the dignified solution, but Abigail had no intention of leaving that woman in the car with Joel. She would put on a courteous face and endure the day. Tomorrow required a change. Somebody in Joel's space had to go, and she didn't intend on going anywhere.

chapter

56

Where was her Joel? Who was this man prancing a woman around the office and to church? The man entertaining other gods wasn't Joel Mitchell, the son of the renowned Dave Mitchell. Abigail crashed at her desk, resting her head in her hands, massaging her temples. Her plate was full. Division updates, projections for next quarter, and Joel's house. She picked up a snapshot of the nearly completed house. Four garages with side entries were attached in the front of the house, with five additional detached bays in the rear. Dual circular staircases in the front and two more sets in the back, coming down the right and left side of the house. One led into the smaller family room and the other into the atrium.

Where had she gone wrong? Abigail couldn't think clearly. Her plans, the house, Joel, and DMI were collapsing. She didn't know how to save them. She lifted the sticky note visibly displayed on her desk and dialed. Don would give her the encouragement she desperately needed. The phone rang several times. She was losing hope when she heard his voice.

"I'm glad you answered. You're just the person I needed today," she told Don.

"Well hello to you, too. What's going on, Ms. Gerard?"

"Everything and nothing," she said, not hiding her solemn emotions.

"What's going on?" Don asked, this time with a serious edge.

"I'm not sure. My life is crazy right now."

"Is DMI keeping you too busy?" he asked.

"I can handle DMI. What I can't handle is Joel and some of the choices he's making. I'm not sure who he is anymore," she said before thinking, wondering if she shouldn't tell too much. On second thought, this was Don, the one person with whom she could be totally honest. She continued letting her frustration pour out. "He moved this woman into the building and shows her around the office like she's his trophy. He had the nerve to bring her to church with us. How dare he let her invade my space."

"Joel?"

"Yes, Joel, can you believe it? He has a woman in this building for weeks and I'm supposed to believe it's strictly business?" she said, clearing her throat and apologizing.

"You don't believe him?"

"I'm not sure what to believe," she said, picking up a snapshot. "I honestly felt like we were progressing toward a future together. That's why random little women showing interest in Joel here and there didn't bother me, but this looks serious. This is different."

"Does he know how upset you are?"

"He's a smart man."

Don laughed.

"What's so funny?"

"You give us men more credit than we probably deserve when it comes to interpreting a woman's feelings. You should tell him what's on your mind."

Maybe Don was right. On the other hand, she didn't want to press Joel and come off as a desperate, whining woman. She wanted him to come to her ready to express his feelings and appeal for a commitment. She couldn't lose hope, not after waiting this long. She had to let Sheba pass like a brief summer breeze in Joel's world. "He claims their relationship is all about mentoring."

"Comes down to how much you trust him."

She wasn't sure, and praying to God about man troubles didn't seem right. She wanted to maintain trust in Joel. Abigail was enveloped with jealousy as she contemplated Joel's choosing to be with another woman. She quickly cast the notion aside, determined not to be derailed. He was what she wanted. "I do trust him, I guess, but I want more."

"Are the two of you committed to each other?"

"Not exactly. I mean, we never said the words, but it's been obvious to me. He asked me to build his house. He asked me to run DMI with him. He's trusted me with personal and professional matters. We are connected in every way except physically."

"You know Joel isn't my favorite person, I'm being honest, but you're not being fair to him. Again, I have to say that if you've never spoken about the relationship, then you can't assume he sees it the same way as you. You have to be direct with him. Let him know how you feel. Take it from me, if you're not direct in the beginning, you may regret it later."

"Why, who do you have regrets about?"

"Nobody you'd want to know. It's history anyway. I've recently begun to move on. Trust me, be direct."

"You may be right."

"I'm definitely right on this one," Don said, convincing her to take his advice. "Now that we've solved the worries of the world, what else is new with you?" he asked.

"Actually, Joel's other relationship isn't the only thing causing me to worry. I'm just as concerned about his obsession with expanding into the international arena regardless of the impact on DMI. He's at the point of entertaining other gods. We've tried to tell him this is wrong, but he's not listening to anyone. I'm not so sure he's listening to God at this point."

"Now that one I can't help you with. The concerns I have about DMI were left at the airport in Detroit when I hopped the plane to South Africa over two years ago. DMI is not my concern. My father didn't think I was the one to run the company and God didn't either. So, let Joel and his gods run the company into the ground if he wants, no skin off my back."

"I know you, and you don't mean what you're saying, not really. You love your father and you've always loved God."

"I do love my father. When I first left Detroit, I was angry and determined to get revenge for my father's decision."

"That was in the past."

"And I've had the time and distance to think about my situation."

"Have you gotten over your anger with Joel?"

"I wouldn't go that far, but who knows. I'm at least on speaking terms with God."

"But you still sound mad."

"I guess so. I go back and forth depending on the day. Really LTI keeps me so busy, that I'm not dwelling on too much negativity. We landed a huge deal with Unilever over here."

"Congratulations. That's fantastic, Don. I'm happy for you. You deserve this."

"Yes, well, thanks. Either way, I don't have time to wallow in the past. I have too much work to do."

"At least you're making progress," she said, not feeling as weighted down by her relationship woes. She wasn't really shocked by the change in Don. He had a love for the Lord, and in spite of his wounds she had always believed his faith would be renewed. Thousands of miles hadn't hindered her connection with him. She knew his kindness and forgiving nature would reemerge eventually. She was pleased for him.

"We'll have to see what happens with me and my baby brother Joel."

"You'll come around."

"I can't make any promises there. We'll see."

"He's asked for your number a few times, but I wanted to respect your privacy and said no."

"I appreciate that."

"But I do hope the two of you reconcile. Who knows, maybe one day you'll move back home."

"No, I'll pass on the move. I'm doing just fine here. South Africa is home. My business is growing, and I'm at peace away from the stress of DMI."

"I hate to think that you're over there alone."

"You sound like my mother. Both of you will be

pleased to know that I've had several dinner dates recently—at least I think they were dates, felt like it to me."

"Wow," she said, thrilled for him, but sad for herself. "Is it your assistant?" she asked, half joking.

"Yes, Naledi."

"I knew it," she shouted, laughing. "I could tell you liked her, the way you spoke about her the last time we talked, but isn't that awkward, dating and working together?"

"No more awkward than you and Joel."

"My heart is willing to deal with awkwardness. My head isn't so sure. We'll see what happens. As for you, be careful."

"Don't worry about me. I'm doing all right for myself, no complaints here. I'm enjoying the best season of my life. Joel is the one you have to worry about, not me."

chapter

57

Sheba tucked the last suit into her remaining Louis Vuitton suitcase and took a seat on the bed. "I can't remember the last time I packed my own suitcase."

"You don't have to leave. I'd love for you to stay longer. My place is too small and my new house isn't ready yet," Joel said, sliding closer to her, "but don't let that be a factor."

"You did mention a new house. How's it coming?"

"Nicely. Abigail is giving me a big hand with overseeing the construction, which has been a gigantic blessing. I decided to take the plunge and build a house not too far from my mother's estate in Novi."

"Must be a posh area if you're moving there."

He gave her a grin. "We have much in common," he said. "How can I keep you here? My mother has an entire mansion and you're welcome to grab a wing and stay as long as you'd like."

"I appreciate the offer, but I have to decline. I've already sent my personal assistants and the rest of my team home. Now it's time for me to go, too."

"You could have an entire wing in the house, with a separate entrance. She won't know you're there. Won't you consider staying?"

"Joel, I can't. I've worn out my welcome. Three weeks have flown by and I've enjoyed every minute of this time in Detroit with you, but there's at least one person who will be glad to see me go."

"Abigail?"

"You got it."

"She's very protective, but it's not what you think with her," he said.

"It's exactly what I think. She's committed to you, and my being here is an insult to her."

"You just won't believe me when I tell you we're not in a relationship. Our bond is different, deeper. We share the same God, the same loyalty to my father's vision, the same passion for knowledge. What can I say, we connect on every level, but we're not a couple."

"She's gorgeous. Aren't you attracted to her a little?" she asked, pressing her thumb and finger together and squinting.

"I didn't say I wasn't attracted to her. I'm a man who appreciates beautiful women, but that doesn't make us a couple. She's been my confidante, my friend, and my business partner. She's my sister in many ways. I need her in my life, but I'm definitely not ready for a lifetime commitment to anyone. My priority is fulfilling my father's vision. I've made my focus clear from the beginning, not only to Abigail, but to everyone. I have too much to accomplish. I don't have the capacity for a serious relationship."

"What about me?"

"What about you?"

"Come on now. We've played this flirtatious game since I arrived unannounced at your office. You have made time for me without resistance."

"Guilty as charged. What can I say," he said, waving his arms. "You have captured my attention. You're bold, full of interesting conversation, and flat-out sexy."

Sheba seemed amused. "Joel Mitchell, you can lead a company, but I'm not sure you understand matters of the heart. Abigail clearly has feelings for you beyond being platonic." She made quotation marks in the air with her fingers. "She probably loves you, which I can totally understand," she said, unaware of how she had him dangling on every word.

"I'm telling you, we're not in a relationship," Joel said, unsure what he could say that would be convincing.

"You might not be, but she sure is. Let me give you a word of advice. Call it romantic intellect," she said, taking his hand and a seat next to him on the bed. "The woman is most likely in love with you. Talk to her, find out where her heart is, and the two of you decide on what kind of relationship you have, otherwise you could end up losing a loyal friend." Sheba stood, ready to go. "Love can be complicated, especially when friendships are involved."

He nodded in acknowledgment.

"I've benefited immensely from being with you. You're an amazing man, Mr. Joel Mitchell. I'm grateful to you for introducing me to your God."

"He's not just my God. He's your God, too."

"Yes, you're right, my God, our God, the God of creation. It's hard for me to believe how much of an impact you've made on me in such a short time. Your zeal for God, quite frankly, is contagious. No one else has presented the concept of salvation in Christ to me as convincingly and as simply as you. I can't thank you enough for your warm welcome and for sharing your gift of business knowledge with me. You truly are special, and I have one last request before I go."

"Name it, anything," he said.

"I want you to sit on my board of directors. I want your favor to rub off on my business."

"I'd be honored," he said without hesitation. Any connection with her was welcome. "Are you sure you have to leave?"

"I do. I really do have a business in Chicago, which needs my attention, and you have other matters here that need yours."

"If you must go, at least take this as a token of our friendship and my belief in your expansion project," he said, handing her an envelope.

She ripped the envelope open. The check read $35 million. "What's this for?" she asked, with a look of total shock and vulnerability.

"You inspired me to go full blast with my international expansion plan. You're the only person who has supported my vision. I needed you here in Detroit. God sent you here for me. With this check I'd like to sow seeds into your expansion."

"How can I take your check? I came here to give you eighteen million dollars as a donation to your library. In return you're giving me nearly twice the amount I gave you."

"Take the money," he said, clamping his hands

around hers and the envelope. "This is my gift to you. Thank you for kindling my motivation."

"Thank you for introducing me to your faith. This journey was destined for me."

They embraced and said their good-byes.

"Don't forget, take good care of Abigail. She's a gem."

"I haven't forgotten what you said." They prepared to leave the suite. "Don't forget, you're only one state away. There's no excuse for us to lose touch," Joel said.

"Agreed. You'll tire of me long before my jet wears out. I'll be back for your wedding." She punctuated her words with a giggle.

"Are you prophesying?" They both roared with laughter.

The bellhop came for the complete sets of Gucci and Louis Vuitton luggage. Joel and Sheba followed. Their time together was too short. He'd drive her to the airport in an effort to get her to extend her stay. Once the Lamborghini hit I-94 West he might let it keep rolling to the great city of Chicago, with a limousine filled with luggage trailing behind. He'd found another friend who wasn't intended to be a replacement for Abigail. He could never replace her. Sheba appealed to a different part of him. She understood his untamed edge, the desire to succeed balanced with an unbridled appetite for taking risks, without fear. Abigail was steady, his anchor. Sheba was a storm that he hadn't been able to steer clear of for the past three weeks. The storm had passed for now.

chapter

58

Joel already told Abigail that he wasn't ready for a serious relationship. Waiting wasn't a problem if she was certain to be the woman on his arm when he was ready, but Abigail didn't have the assurance she wanted. Once Sheba was gone maybe life could return to normal. She sat outside Sherry's office at 7:10 A.M. prepared to wait the entire day if necessary. Around seven-thirty Madeline walked in.

"Abigail, what are you doing sitting alone so early in the morning? Do you have a meeting?"

"No, I'm clearing my head."

"You must have big-time problems if you have to sit here for peace of mind this early in the morning."

"It's Joel. I'm worried about him."

"What about him?" Madeline asked.

"You're not exactly his biggest supporter."

"That's an understatement, but I do like you. Tell me what's going on," Madeline said, beckoning Abigail into her office. Abigail followed and took a seat at Madeline's small round table lined with magazines.

"He's making bizarre decisions these days, probably because he's distracted by his girlfriend," Abigail said.

"You don't sound too happy about Sheba."

"It's not her. I'm sure she's nice, but how can Joel have a woman camped outside his office?"

"He 'had' a woman. I thought she went back to Chicago a few days ago?" Madeline said. Abigail was agitated that Joel hadn't bothered to tell her. Madeline continued. "For what it's worth, she doesn't believe in God. To me, she's an atheist, although she uses the term 'agnostic.' To tell the truth, I don't know the difference, but she's one of them. Either way, she's not Joel's type if she doesn't believe in God."

"Well, she does now." Abigail could barely discuss Sheba Warden clearly. "According to Joel, she accepted Christ. She went to church with us Sunday."

"You're kidding. Then you better be glad she's gone."

"There's more where she came from, plenty more," Abigail said, tapping on a stack of magazines.

"It's not my business, but unless the two of you are together," Madeline said, twiddling her fingers, "Sheba shouldn't bother you."

"Let's just say that I'm certainly not helping him build a new house to move another woman in. If he's not with me, I'm not thrilled about him being with anybody else. I'm patient, but not stupid."

"Like I said, this is none of my business, but if it were me, I'd tell him and eliminate any miscommunication.

Your choice could be much better, but if Joel is who you want, that's on you. You might want to tell him exactly how you're feeling and what you want."

"I shouldn't have to."

"Okay, continue letting him guess about your feelings, but don't be surprised if the next time Sheba Warden, or another one like her, stays longer."

Madeline was right. Don, too, but she wasn't ready to push an ultimatum on Joel and drive him away. It was easier to give him a little more space, finish up the house, and go from there. Joel hadn't intentionally let her down in the past. There was no reason to believe he would start now. She would squash the doubts and stay on course.

"Abigail, take this from a woman who knows. Don't give so much of your power to Joel or any man. You are who you are. If Joel or any other man can't accept you, move on. You have a great deal to offer someone who's willing to appreciate you for who you are. That's the best advice I can give you," Madeline said.

Abigail processed the advice. Her mother's loyalty to her father was the marital image plastered in Abigail's mind. She remembered how her mother stayed and endured the rough patches. She would do the same to get who she wanted. Sure, there were other men, but her feelings couldn't be satisfied with a substitute. She liked who she liked—Joel Mitchell.

chapter

59

Joel sat at a table in the Blue Pointe Restaurant, known for exquisite food at a hefty price. He was glad to have a minute out of the office but wasn't as relaxed as he could be. Once the interview was over he could pull off his tie and kick back for an evening. Sheba was gone but not without igniting a burning passion within him for romance and intrigue.

"Ms. Tate, I'm surprised you want to do another interview so soon. Twice in less than six months."

"I didn't invite you to dinner for an interview. This is personal," she said, letting her seductive words glide from her inviting lips. "You're a busy man, but even the great Joel Mitchell has to eat."

The wine steward interrupted, handing the wine list to him. "Would you like a bottle of wine for the table?"

Joel was going to pass, but Samantha said, "Yes, we would like a bottle of red wine."

"Any particular kind?" the steward asked.

Joel wasn't a drinker. He enjoyed having a fresh mind, clear-thinking at all times, but he was willing to entertain Samantha. Watching her cast an adoring look his way didn't hurt. "What do you recommend?" Joel asked. Though he was unfamiliar with wines, as in the rest of his life, he wanted only the best.

The steward pointed to four wines and gave a brief description of each. Joel closed the wine list and told the waiter, "Give me a bottle of your best red wine. I trust your recommendation."

"Yes, sir, right away, sir."

Samantha gazed at Joel as the wine steward left. Joel jockeyed for position in his seat, crossed his arms across his lap, and gazed at her in return. Samantha giggled.

"What's so funny?" Joel asked.

"I'm laughing because here you are, CEO of the most successful company in Detroit, and you're shy. Tauruses aren't usually shy, they're just the opposite."

Joel didn't have to publish his list of past female companions for validation. Samantha could get to know him and make her own assessment.

The wine steward brought the bottle, poured a few ounces into a glass, and handed it to Joel. "None for me," Joel said.

"Would you like to sample the wine and see if it's to your liking?"

"Come on, take a sip. God won't strike you down for taking a few sips of wine, Mr. Mitchell," she said.

As a gentleman, he would sample the wine for the lady. He took a sip and gave the okay, not sure if it was. The steward poured a glass for Samantha and placed the linen-napkin-covered bottle in a standing bucket of ice next to the table.

"Why don't you have a glass with me?"

"No, I'm fine."

Samantha poured a glass for him anyway. "One glass, one night, what can it hurt?" she said, unleashing an allure that seemed to yank him across the table and into her clutches.

One glass led to two, an innocent dinner led to an extended visit at his condo. The ritual continued for several weeks, a few nights at a time, until he met Cheyenne, the flight attendant assigned to his chartered Los Angeles flight. During the five-hour flight he found her to be engaging, leading to a conversation that extended beyond the runway and into a local restaurant. The jetlag from jumping time zones between Michigan and California didn't prevent him from making a stop in Chicago to see Sheba. Though his routine normally included winding down after a flight with a time of prayer and meditation, in the past few months he'd found himself too busy and too tired. There was no harm, he figured. He and God could communicate later. The impromptu interview with the *L.A. Times,* followed by one with Jay Leno on *The Tonight Show,* went better than he expected. The *L.A. Times* experience was more memorable than most. Paula's interviewing style and natural beauty kept him in Los Angeles an extra night.

chapter

60

———

Joel and Paula ate breakfast in their thick white robes, exchanging very few words in the living room suite of his hotel. He had about thirty minutes and then it was time to get dressed and travel to the airport. "Was I dreaming last night or were you singing after I fell asleep?"

"You probably heard me chanting over you," Paula said.

"Did you say chatting," he asked, eating a spoonful of the freshly made granola.

"Chanting."

"What's chanting?"

"You could say it's a form of religion. I use chanting to evoke the ancestral spirits to bring us blessings and peace."

"What kind of spirits are you talking about?" he

asked, clearing his throat and wiping the napkin roughly across his mouth.

"All kinds, I believe in everything, to each his own."

Joel began coughing heavily, covering his mouth with the napkin.

"Are you okay?" she asked.

His airway was clear but not his thoughts. His PDA buzzed on the round table near the front entryway, about three feet from where he was seated. "Excuse me," he said, going for the phone. He immediately recognized Abigail's number and answered.

"Finally," she said. "I've been trying to contact you for two days. Your assistant wasn't sure where you were. She said something about an interview but didn't have the details, and your mom has been impossible to catch up with, too. She's busy working with photographers and signing off on magazine covers. Where are you?"

"I'm in Los Angeles. I had an interview with the *L.A. Times* and a spot on *The Tonight Show*."

"Wow, those are huge. I'm surprised you didn't tell me."

"It was short notice."

"You're getting a tremendous amount of exposure," she said. He could hear the disappointment in her voice.

Joel took the phone into the hallway of the suite, leading to the two guest bedrooms. "I should have told you I was going out of town. I apologize. What's going on at DMI? Everything on track?"

"DMI is on track. I'm calling to give you the good news about the house. Finally, after weeks of dealing with the foundation issue and getting the wiring and plumbing contractors straightened out, the drywall is up and the place looks like a real house."

Her excitement was evident. She'd done a fantastic job with the house and with DMI. He couldn't imagine her not being in his circle. She was the ideal person to have by his side. If he ever got married it would be to someone like Abigail, the full package, beauty, brains, and a supportive attitude. "Thanks for making my life manageable. What would I do without you?"

"The good news for you is that you won't ever have to answer that question. When are you coming home?" she asked, sounding excited. "We have to complete another walk-through before the flooring goes in. By the way, did I tell you that the libraries in the guest suite and on the main floor will both have genuine herringbone leather floors? Tell me I don't know your taste," she said in an upbeat tone. "Anyway, the general contractor understands your crazy schedule and is willing to be totally flexible. He's offered to meet any time, day or night. I guess he would, since you're building a 15,000-square-foot home with a 2,500-square-foot guesthouse and another 2,000-square-foot place for the staff," she said, almost shouting with glee into his ear.

Joel could hear Paula moving around in the other room. He respected Abigail and didn't see the benefit in letting her know about his friendly encounters with women. Ever since Sheba had waltzed her way into DMI, Joel's craving for women wasn't easily controlled. His two year hiatus from openly "dating" was over. God was his strength and women his weakness. He preferred keeping his personal matters private and opted to end the conversation before Abigail overheard Paula. God was another story. Instead of hopelessly explaining his actions, Joel elected to limit his conversations with God to business.

"You know I trust you with the house. Don't schedule around me. Go ahead with the walk-through. I won't get in your way and slow the process down because of my intense schedule these days."

"Are you sure?" she asked, her disappointment choking the line. "This is your house and I don't want to make a mistake."

"I trust you completely. Treat the house like it's yours. Do what you think is best. I'm going to run," he said, hearing Paula approaching the hallway.

"One more thing before you go," Abigail squeezed in.

"What's that?" he asked.

"Can you drop by the Los Angeles office while you're there? Brian wants to boost enthusiasm among the new team members. He wants me to come out and speak to the group as a morale boost, but I'm swamped between the other divisions and the house," she told Joel.

"Do you want me to leave?" Paula asked, standing behind Joel.

He covered the mouthpiece on the PDA and shook his head no.

"Joel, were you talking to me?" Abigail asked.

"No, I wasn't."

"I thought I heard someone in the background."

Joel mouthed one minute and held up his index finger for Paula. She understood the code and gave him space to finish.

"Oh, well, anyway," Abigail continued, "can you stop by the L.A. office? They'd love an opportunity to meet with the CEO."

"Hmmm, I'd like to drop by, but I'm booked on the *Late Show* tonight with Letterman. I'm flying out on the charter in three hours in order to make the five-thirty taping in New York. I could possibly swing by for a few minutes, but the visit would be very short."

"Never mind, I'll find a way to get out there."

Abigail was working hard for him, and after a little thought, the answer was simple. "What am I thinking?" Joel said, "of course I'll go. I'll cancel the Letterman show or I'll reschedule, whichever one, but I'll go to the DMI office regardless."

"No way, you're not canceling. I'm not going to let you cancel," Abigail told him. "Hop on the charter and I'll see you in a few days."

"What about the L.A. office?"

"I'll do a turnaround flight tomorrow, in and out."

"Five hours each way isn't exactly in and out," he said.

"Don't you worry about me or DMI or the L.A. office or the house. I'm taking care of everything."

"Including you?"

"Including me," she said.

"Are you sure?" Joel said, as Paula entered the hallway again, fully clothed this time.

"I'm sure, now go and make us proud," she said with a good-bye.

Joel held the PDA as Paula nestled in for a hug. Abigail was amazing. He was blessed to have her in his life. God gave him strength and Abigail gave him grace. He couldn't live and thrive without either. He had to believe Sheba was wrong. He didn't intend on losing Abigail's support or God's favor either.

"Let me know when you want another interview," Paula said, "I'm yours any time." She gave him a peck on the cheek and left his suite, like many before her, and unless he could wrestle the urge away, many women afterward.

chapter

61

An overnight stay in New York, a stopover in Detroit for fresh clothes, and Joel was back at the hotel in Los Angeles. He wanted the perfect setting. This deal was important to the continued success of DMI. He had the concierge reserve a private room and lunch for the meeting with Bengali. The suite seemed too personal. Normally he would have Abigail sit in on a meeting of this magnitude, but with her mixed feelings about the international expansion, he thought it best to initiate the conversations with Mr. Bengali alone, confident he could sell his management team on the concept later. At one o'clock, a gentleman knocked on the door, right on time, accompanied by a lady half his age, wearing a scarf draped diagonally across her face, revealing her deep colored eyes, as deep a brown as her hair, and a prominent black dot on her forehead. Joel sprang to his feet.

"Mr. Mitchell, I'm Musar Bengali."

"We finally meet in person. It's a pleasure," Joel said, turning to the woman, unsure of the proper way to greet her.

"This is my daughter, Zarah Bengali. I hope you don't object to her joining our meeting. She's the sole heir to my company, and I'd like her to be involved."

"Absolutely, please have a seat," Joel said, pulling a chair out for Zarah and then taking one, too. "I'm glad you were able to arrange this meeting," he said, wishing Abigail could have joined them.

"The timing was ideal. We were scheduled to be in San Francisco anyway. Flying the extra hour to Los Angeles was not a problem," he said with clearly spoken English, except for a few words. "Have you had an opportunity to read the documents I sent you?" Mr. Bengali asked.

"I read the mission statement, your strategy, and your five-year plan. I was very impressed with the growth you've experienced in the past five years," Joel said.

"As I am with yours. We have an opportunity to unite people, faiths, religion, and spiritual forces throughout the world."

"I'm eager to see what we can do together," Joel said.

A hotel attendant interrupted with a cart holding a series of covered trays. "I took the liberty of ordering lunch. I wasn't sure what you ate so I ordered a little bit of every entrée they had on the lunch menu. I hope this is acceptable for you both."

"We have lamb, chicken, fish, filet mignon, and two

vegetarian dishes." The attendant took a few minutes to set up the food and beverages. "Is there anything else I can do for you?" the attendant asked as he finished.

"I don't think so, thank you," Joel told him.

Joel was temporarily distracted by Zarah's piercing eyes and by her hands, as dainty as a protected lily. "If you don't mind, I'd like to pray before we eat, to acknowledge God for my blessings."

"We'd prefer you not pray to a specific God," Musar said. "We pay homage to many gods, drawing on our internal energy as the source of our faith."

"God is an important aspect of the DMI ministry. I can't leave Him out."

"If you must include Him, please go ahead, but you will please forgive us for not joining in your personal appeal to your higher power."

Joel was thrown off balance. God was the one consistent thing in his life. He couldn't expand, grow, or move without God's presence. He was already shutting God out about his women. Excluding God from his business decisions wasn't an option. He had to figure out how to keep God in the room and Mr. Bengali, too. Joel had led Sheba to the Lord. He would lead Bengali, too. The international expansion was his mission, his newfound purpose. He would not fail at fulfilling the vision for DMI. Skipping a few prayers wouldn't diminish his faith. For this meeting, just this one time, he'd leave God outside the room, conduct the meeting, and reunite with the Lord afterward.

chapter

62

"I'll take those documents," Abigail told Joel's adminis-trative assistant, reaching for the folder marked SIGNA-TURE REQUIRED.

"He hasn't signed them yet."

"What do you mean? Did you forget to give them to him?" Abigail asked, unclear how the assistant had messed up such an important task.

"He was in the office for a few hours yesterday and then he left for California with a stop in Chicago."

"Chicago and California, again. Do you know why?" Abigail had done a turnaround trip to Los Angeles for him yesterday. She wondered why he would have her go if he was going back so soon, especially when she was so swamped.

"I believe it's another interview, but I'm not sure.

I've had a difficult time keeping his calendar up to date for the past four or five months, especially since his publicity schedule has required much more of his time. Mrs. Mitchell handles his press commitments.

"Who's handling his DMI schedule?"

"I am, when he's here."

Abigail wasn't going to grill the assistant. There was no point. She had little to no information on their boss's whereabouts, but there was someone who might. She went two doors down to the small office adjacent to Joel's and knocked on Sherry's door.

"Come in," Sherry said.

"Good, you're here," Abigail said.

"Of course, where else would I be?"

Abigail took a seat. "Hard to say these days. When we were a company in Michigan that the media didn't know much about, I could find everybody I needed most of the time."

"Isn't that true today?"

"I don't think so," Abigail said, not concerned about how much of her disappointment was visible. "Every time I turn around Joel has an interview or television appearance or an appointment with some company's board of directors. This is crazy."

"He is very busy these days."

"With publicity," she said, airing her frustration. Abigail didn't realize how starved she was. She couldn't handle his being gone twenty hours a day seven days a week. She yearned for more of his time.

"Publicity is good for Joel and for DMI."

"But do you have to cram his schedule so tight that he doesn't have time for anything else, including DMI?"

"Don't you really mean he doesn't have any time for

you?" Abigail didn't want to respond. "The answer is written on your face."

Abigail didn't speak in her own defense. She'd held back long enough. Why not let her feelings be publicly expressed. Joel was living in the public eye anyway.

"He doesn't know you're in love with him."

Abigail fumbled for words, not wanting to say too much, while at the same time not wanting to pass up an opportunity. "What am I supposed to do? I can't force Joel into a timetable."

Sherry laughed. "You remind me so much of myself thirty years ago when I met Dave. I was young, full of dreams and hopes for the future. After I fell in love with him, my goal in life was to please him and to just be near him. Dave Mitchell could have told me to jump off a bridge and I would have gladly jumped without hesitation. Did you know I was engaged to another man when I met Dave?"

"No, I had no idea," Abigail responded, shocked that she'd never heard about more of Sherry's past.

"I sure was, engaged and ready to get married until my fiancé lost his job. We struggled." Sherry had Abigail's full attention. "When Dave found out, he got my fiancé a job working out of town. I was brokenhearted."

"Why didn't you go with him?"

"I don't know. He died unexpectedly, not long after he left. Dave was very kind to me during that time. Dave became my world, my source of joy, my reason for being. Every breath I took was for Dave Mitchell. You have the same look."

Abigail wasn't sure exactly what Sherry meant. She was in love with Joel. He was the one in her dreams, but the source of her joy and her reason for being was still the Lord.

"Don't keep waiting," Sherry said, organizing a deck of press kits.

"Why, did he tell you about Sheba Warden?"

"No he hasn't, but I'm telling you not to wait. Don't waste years like I did waiting for life to embrace you. Life doesn't wait. Time will keep moving, and if you let it, you'll be left behind holding a handful of empty promises that will follow you to your grave," Sherry said, and returned to combing over press kit material for Joel.

Abigail wandered into the hallway. She'd committed to Joel in ways that counted. Spelling out the words wasn't going to add any more passion than her heart had already relinquished. She'd nursed their love for almost three years. Begging him wasn't her way. If he valued her, he'd have to come forward. The next step was his.

chapter

63

Madeline was seated in the boardroom working on her laptop as the management team filed in. Sheba Warden hadn't worked out, but there were more women to play the starring role in Joel's downfall. Madeline was bursting with glee reading the headline in *People* magazine. JOEL MITCHELL MASTERS THE BOARDROOM AND BEDROOM. She liked the *Post* article, too. WISDOM, WEALTH, AND WOMEN—THE JOEL MITCHELL STORY. She could taste victory. According to the *People* article, he didn't have to look too far for women willing to nestle up to the great Joel Mitchell. They were lining up, and according to the article he was doing his best to accommodate. She couldn't get ahead of herself this time. Her plot would work, had to. She was growing tired of spending energy with no results. Joel had escaped her for far too long. She had always known that eventually her time would come. She was certain the time was now.

Madeline read further into the article. "The twenty-six-year-old mogul has tripled the value of his family business in less than three years at the helm of DMI. He's gained notoriety with ingenious marketing campaigns and a quick wit. He is often described in the corporate world as a gutsy strategic powerhouse. Where did Mr. Mitchell garner such business knowledge? He doesn't hold an MBA from Wharton or an executive management degree from Harvard or a marketing degree from Northwestern. No top-notch degrees or management programs can explain his aptitude in business. According to Mr. Mitchell, his source is God. Unusually mature for a man in his midtwenties, Mr. Mitchell is described as a lion in the boardroom, able to fearlessly make the tough decisions that yield results. He's also characterized as a stallion in the bedroom, with charm that should be bottled and sold." Madeline couldn't contain her euphoria. This was the part she couldn't wait to finish reading. "Mr. Mitchell's love for making deals is trumped by his love for women." She didn't have to read any further.

"Let's go ahead and get started with the status meeting. I guess Joel isn't coming," Abigail said.

"It's hard to catch up with him these days," Barry said.

"I hear he's been in L.A. quite a bit lately, but he hasn't been to the DMI office," Brian added.

He hadn't come to the East Coast, unless Madeline counted his frequent publicity trips to New York. She was glad to have him stay out of her territory. Less of him was better. "Where is he anyway?" Madeline asked, not sincerely caring, but wanting to increase the tension she detected among the group.

"He's in L.A.," Sherry said.

"Brian's here. So what could Joel possibly be doing in California? Was this meeting canceled and I didn't get the memo?" Madeline asked.

"He had a publicity trip," Sherry said.

"More publicity. Good grief, he gets more air time than Oprah. Is he selling himself or leadership programs for DMI? Somebody please tell me something," Madeline said, fueling a forest fire with Sherry. The two years of working with Sherry had been tolerable, but Madeline enjoyed the random acts of torture—they reminded her of the good old days when Dave was alive and Sherry was vulnerable.

"How dare you make such an inappropriate comment. He's not selling himself, as you put it. Joel is running DMI better than ever and you're jealous because of the popularity he's getting as a result of his hard work," Sherry responded.

"Hard work is relative," Madeline said, thumbing through the article, searching for the section that talked about his sexual escapades. "According to this article he's busy all right, with one woman after another. He has plenty of women and plenty of gods these days."

"Madeline," Abigail said, with a firmness she hadn't seen, "this is a management meeting. Let's stick to the agenda and leave personal issues outside. Let's get started with the status reports."

"Good point. This is a senior management meeting," Madeline said. "Sherry, I don't believe we'll need you here."

Sherry flushed. "I'm here because the CEO wants me here."

"Yes, but the CEO is not here."

"Madeline is right, Sherry, this is only for the senior team," Abigail affirmed.

Sherry took a few seconds to process the request before leaving, appearing stunned. Abigail's sharp-edged tone left Madeline shocked, too. If Abigail had used the same tone with Joel, they would probably be married with a few children by now.

After Sherry left, Abigail was curt with each report. Her passive anger didn't seem to subside until three out of four reports had been presented. Abigail was a nice girl, Madeline thought, but if she wasn't willing to recognize the reality of Joel's playboy lifestyle then she was undoubtedly headed for heartache. Any child birthed by Sherry was bound to be unfaithful; it was genetic. Don didn't believe her but it was true. She was counting on his uncontrollable passion for women and his egotistical desire to achieve new heights in DMI. Her granddaddy of all plots was riding on his weaknesses, women and wealth.

The meeting adjourned after an hour and a half with no sign of Joel. He'd become a phantom within the DMI headquarters. Joel was going down, but Madeline saw no reason for Abigail to go with him. She couldn't tip her plan to Abigail and spoil her last shot at knocking him off the DMI throne and snatching the reins for her family, but Madeline was willing to give Abigail a subtle warning.

"Listen, Abigail, you are a sharp young lady. You have education and class. You were mentored well. You're the executive vice president of the fastest-growing company in Michigan. Be smart about your choices," Madeline said, handing her the article.

"I've read the article."

"And?" Madeline asked.

"And you can't believe everything you read," Abigail responded.

"Don't be stupid. Don't settle," Madeline told her, letting go of the magazine and walking away. Maybe Don could convince Abigail to put distance between her and Joel. He was going down in flames, and anyone close to the fire would most likely get burned.

chapter

64

Madeline returned to her office and immediately dialed Don in South Africa. Ten in the morning her time was five in the afternoon for him. Don answered after a few long rings. Standard greetings concluded, and Madeline jumped into the meat of the conversation, eager to share the publicly displayed crack in Joel's armor. "You should know that Joel is getting quite a reputation here in the States."

"I'm not surprised. DMI has tripled in value in only a few years. Hats off to him."

"His soaring reputation isn't about tripled growth. Abigail and I are running the company, but we'll save that conversation for another time. Joel has built quite a reputation for chasing women."

"No way."

"I'm telling you, he's characterized as a lady's man. Do you get *People* magazine or the *Washington Post* over there?"

"Yes, Mother, I can get the same magazines and newspapers that you get and more. Cape Town is just like San Francisco. I didn't fall off the face of the earth, you know."

"I have no idea how you're living over there."

"Yes you do. You've been here. You know I'm doing okay."

She was filled with pride. Don was recovering from the DMI devastation. He had her unconditional support, but having him home was always going to be her preference. "You still need to come home and help me get our company back."

"Oh, pu-lease don't start down the same old road, Mother dear, please don't. I'm doing well with LTI, my feelings about my father, and my relationship with God. You're the one I'm worried about. When are you going to give this foolishness up and accept the fact that God and my dad wanted Joel to run DMI? He was appointed CEO and he's done a fantastic job, a better job than I could have done."

"That's not true. You would have done at least as well as he has. Half of the initial increase came strictly from the East Coast revenue that you generated. Joel isn't growing this company by himself. We are here day in and day out working our behinds off while he gallivants around the country like a movie star. He's out of the office ninety percent of the time. You tell me, how can he be a CEO if he never shows up?"

"How's Abigail handling the pressure?"

"She's cross-eyed in love and clueless to what he's doing. You should talk to her and get her to see the truth about Joel. Everybody can't be lying about him and his thing for women. I believe the articles because I was married to his father. I know what Joel's capable of doing."

"Poor Abigail, she deserves to be happy."

"Won't happen with Joel Mitchell. She better look for happiness elsewhere. Anyway, enough with Abigail, I need your help," she said.

"What?"

"I need you to help me pull together the final pieces of my plan."

"Oh, come on, Mother, the answer is no. I'm not getting involved with your pitiful attempts to discredit Joel. You're only frustrating yourself. The schemes never work."

"You're right, but I prefer the term 'plan,' and it will work this time."

"How can you be so sure?"

"Because I'm using his two greatest loves, women and DMI, as the bait."

"God's on his list, too, which is why you'd better leave him alone."

"Not anymore. Between the press and panties, he doesn't have time for God or church. I'm telling you, he's out of town most of the time. I wouldn't be surprised if he resorts to crystal balls and reading tea leaves for direction on how to run DMI. Or maybe he's using the good old magic eight ball," Madeline said, amused. "Heaven knows he isn't seeking God for direction."

"Mother, are you exaggerating?"

"No, I'm telling the truth, as bizarre as it may sound."

"I didn't realize the situation was so serious."

"That's what I'm trying to tell you. We need to get

him out of the CEO position before this company comes crashing down around us. We have to save DMI. I'm not willing to give up. I helped start this company. DMI is as much mine as it was Dave's. I will not stop fighting for our company. It's our legacy. Are you going to help me?"

Don held his response, sparking a shimmer of hope in Madeline, until he said, "I'm not going after Joel. My father believed in him and so far he's doing well."

"Your father was senile in the last months of his life. You have to overlook his mistake and work to fix it for him."

"Father said God called Joel to run the company, too."

"I'm not convinced Dave was hearing correctly when he made his ridiculous decision, and we're seeing the results. Joel was and will again be unfit to run DMI."

"Mother, leave him alone."

"This is no time to ease up. His glow is definitely wearing off, one woman at a time."

"What he does is between him and God. Don't get caught in the middle," Don told her.

"When did you become so reasonable?"

"When I decided to let go of the past. I'm not completely there yet, but I'm working on it. You should, too."

She was amused at her son's crazy notion. Most of her adult life had been spent fighting to reclaim her place in DMI and probably Dave's life. Discarding her sense of entitlement, her motivation for getting up every day for the past twenty-nine years, wasn't an option. Letting go would leave her with no purpose.

"Doesn't matter what I say. You're not going to listen, are you?" he told her.

"No, but I love you."

Don snickered. "You know how to reach me when your doomed plan goes badly, as I'm sure it will. I'm here for you," he said. "Give me a call. If you can't reach me, Naledi will know how to find me."

"How's Naledi?"

"Perfect."

"For you or for LTI?"

"Maybe both. I have to run, Mother." He gave her his love and ended the call.

A film of peace covered her. Don was thousands of miles away, safe, stable, and succeeding. She could concentrate on Joel without having to worry about Don. Her joy was nearly complete.

chapter

65

Madeline hadn't changed her mind. The international expansion was not a favorable venture for DMI. Joel was determined to push the issue. Today's presentation was sure to be a waste of time. Connie, Brian, and Barry didn't bother to fly out for the meeting. They were joining by conference call. If Joel had given more notice, she could have escaped to the East Coast and tucked away on the conference call like the rest of the management team. The speakerphone was on and everyone joining was on the line. Abigail came in. Joel came in a few minutes later, followed by a short man and a young woman with a scarf covering half her face.

"Mr. Musar Bengali and his daughter Zarah Bengali are joining us from southern India. They're the owners of Harmonious Energy. I'm very pleased to introduce you to our DMI management team," Joel said. "We have four divisions spread out across the U.S. The senior vice presidents running those groups are present today." Greetings ensued, including those on the line. "After weeks of coordinating schedules, we're very pleased to have you here."

Joel's administrative assistant passed glossy folders to each attendee. "As you know, the international expansion is vital to the long-term growth of DMI. Mr. Bengali and I have considered various scenarios, and we have created a strategy that seems to work for both organizations. Please open your folders and we'll walk you through the proposal. I'll let Mr. Bengali open with the objectives and mission statement."

"Thank you," he said, with a lightly seasoned accent. "You can follow along with me on page two of the handout. Our objective is to partner with a company that can spread spirituality throughout the world."

Madeline couldn't believe Joel had searched around the world until he found another religious fanatic. She wanted to take the projector button from Joel's assistant and zip to the last slide. Mr. Bengali and his daughter should have saved the cost of airfare from India to Detroit. A glossy presentation wasn't going to change her mind. Her answer was no before and it would be no now. Madeline scrolled the email box on her PDA while Mr. Bengali gave his spiel. She kept busy for a while and then grew tired. Since she couldn't get her hands on the projector remote, Madeline took another route to speed up the presentation. "Excuse me, Mr. Bengali. DMI is founded on Christian principles." She wasn't exactly the ideal representative of exceptional godlike behavior, but Mr. Bengali didn't know where she stood spirituality. "What do you believe in?"

Joel popped up like a bouncing ball. "We should focus on the goals, the strategy, and the recommendation before we get into religious philosophy."

"We can hear the strategy and other stuff after Mr. Bengali tells me what or who he believes in."

"But I don't want the discussion derailed."

"And I want Mr. Bengali to answer a simple question. Is there a problem with his answering the question?" Madeline asked.

"None at all," Joel said, taking his seat without exhibiting his usual confidence.

"What are your company's guiding principles?"

"We worship many gods, drawing on our internal energy as the source of our faith."

"You believe in what?" Madeline asked, certain her hearing was slipping.

"I understand your commitment to a higher power in the form of a single God, and we applaud your religious quest. Together, Harmonious Energy and DMI will be a company predicated on catering to all religions and beliefs. We will be known as the center of spiritual inclusion."

"What do you mean by inclusion?" Abigail asked.

"We believe every living being is going to a place of goodness and contentment after they complete this phase of their spiritual journey."

"Joel, what kind of crazy mess is he talking about?" Madeline burst out. "Is this a joke?" They had to be on one of those hidden videos. The conversation with Sheba regarding religion popped into her thoughts.

"I assure you our spirituality is not a joke," Mr. Bengali said, which Madeline wasn't expecting. The daughter was awfully quiet, too quiet for Madeline's comfort.

Madeline closed her glossy folder. She'd heard

plenty, and she was beginning to suspect Joel had lost his mind. The rest of the meeting could skate by. She had zero interest.

Forty-five minutes into the proposal, Joel was feeling merciful and gave his concluding statement. "The merger will expand DMI territory into twenty-five countries, and that's only the beginning."

Madeline had plotted and planned for nearly three years, every day, most of the day, and she had been unable to bring Joel down. Sitting in this meeting, she was overjoyed at watching him crumble without her intervention. She had to be dreaming.

The presentation ended. Joel escorted Mr. Bengali and his daughter from the room, which was the opening Madeline wanted.

"What just happened in here? I'm sorry, but has Joel lost his mind?" Joel returned as she was speaking. "Dave Mitchell founded DMI based on Christian principles. We don't believe in somebody's higher power or talking moons and stars and this and that. We're not about to chase a bunch of little gods and balls of energy around Europe and Africa and Asia. We can't expand into international markets at the expense of this company's reputation."

"Don't jump to any conclusions," Joel said. "We have to consider the possibilities. By merging with Harmonious Energy, we can expose them to God and possibly introduce salvation to the Bengalis and millions of others."

"This sounds risky," Brian said.

Madeline had almost forgotten that others were on the line. Everyone had been quiet from the beginning of the meeting until now. They were probably as dumbfounded about the presentation as she was.

"I'm no saint. I'll admit my shortcomings, but even I know not to play with God. You're asking for trouble trying to merge two companies with totally different philosophies."

"We're not so different," Joel said.

"Are you serious?" Abigail said. "They believe in going to a happy place after you die."

"It's like our heaven."

"But to get to our heaven, there's only one route, through the acceptance of Christ Jesus as our Savior," Abigail said.

"With Harmonious Energy you rub a few rocks together and toss sticks in the air and, according to Mr. Bengali, poof, you're in the happy place."

"That's absurd," Joel responded.

"You're absolutely right," Madeline said, snickering briefly, "this entire meeting was absurd. You could have taken the vote five minutes into the meeting and gotten the same answer from us that you're going to get now."

"This is good for DMI. There are a few concerns with Harmonious Energy, but this is our opportunity to expand. This is what my father wanted."

"He didn't want you to sell your soul to get a few other countries on our roster. That's not Dave talking, that's you," Madeline responded.

"Let's talk about the issues so we can move forward," Joel said.

"Let's not move forward." No one else was talking. Madeline prayed they were quiet because the decision was obvious. Mr. Bengali had said plenty. She'd take her chance. "Let's take a poll to see where we stand." Before Joel could respond she was calling out names. "Abigail, what are your thoughts?"

"I say this is a bad idea. We can't partner with a company that doesn't acknowledge God, period."

Joel tried to regain the reins, but Madeline held on tightly. "Connie, Barry, Brian, what do you think?" No one spoke. "Don't all speak at once; what do you think?" she asked again.

"I say no," Barry said.

"Definitely no for me," Connie said, "based on DMI's founding principles."

"It's a no for me, too," Brian said.

"There you are. Your senior management team votes no. Now what are you going to do?"

"I'm going to do what's best for the company."

"Humph. I'm surprised you referred to DMI as a company. You know I've never held a religious perspective with DMI. Since Dave and I divorced, I've always seen this as a company, but that's me. When you were hearing from God, this was a ministry to you. After Mr. Bengali's influence, all of a sudden DMI has become just a company to you. Doesn't the change tell you anything?"

"Tells me we have to be more strategic if we're ever going to realize the full potential of this ministry."

"I think the excess publicity and spotlights have fried your brain cells. You're not making any sense. We'll see what the board of directors has to say."

"They can't stop what God has called me to do. Thank you, everyone, for your input, but as CEO, I will make the final decision."

"Meaning you're not going to listen to us?" Madeline said.

"I will seek God as I always have and make the decision I'm led to make."

"With the boatload of different gods hovering around you and Mr. Bengali, how do you know which god is speaking to you? Can you be certain the voice you're hearing is the voice of our God?" Madeline asked, pointing to herself and Abigail. Joel didn't respond. "I didn't think so."

chapter

66

Madeline harnessed her thoughts, which were flying about. Joel truly had lost his mind. She had to think quickly. Her other plans had failed and failed miserably but today was a new day. She was fired up and ready to jump into the boxing ring with Joel, and Sherry, too, if need be. The heavyweight match was on and she wasn't coming out of the ring without a knockout. Madeline dashed into her office. Joel was going down. His handful of rocks and stones and pebbles and crystals and toy gods couldn't save him. She wasn't crazy enough to test the one true God, but these other little ones didn't stand a chance.

Don's number was on speed dial. Please, please be there, she recited silently. His receptionist answered and said he was out of the office. Madeline tried his cell phone next, ready to try his home, Naledi, and every restaurant, gym, and local gathering place in Cape Town if she had to in order to reach him. When he answered she waived the standard greetings and jumped in to the meat of the matter. "You should listen to your mother more often."

"Hello to you, too, Mother," Don said. "What's going on now?"

"Didn't I tell you Joel was losing his grip? He's been running around with a string of women, and that's not the only thing he's been chasing. He's hooked up with this guy named Musar Bengali who owns a spiritual healing kind of company based in India."

"And what's wrong with the spiritual healing company?"

"Mr. Bengali doesn't believe in God."

"What?"

"I just left a meeting where Joel, Mr. Bengali, and his daughter were trying to sell the management team on their partnership. The man was talking about higher powers and using the energy in your body to take you to a happy place after you die."

"Are you serious?"

"I'm telling you it was like a joke. I couldn't believe my ears, not coming from the almighty Joel Mitchell, the one who was touched by God and chosen to run DMI. Your father would be turning over in his grave if he heard his son today. The meeting was awful. Remember, I told you he's been turning away from God and reading tea leaves and crystal balls."

"Mother, you're exaggerating again."

"Maybe a little, but trust me, I'm not too far from the truth. He has lost it. That reminds me. I never told you that Sheba Warden was an atheist. It's hard to believe that he went crazy over a woman who didn't believe in God at all." She left out the part about Sheba accepting Christ, not wanting to minimize the drama until Don realized how dire the situation of DMI was with Joel running the place.

"I can't believe what's going on there."

Madeline was hoping, dreaming that Don's passion for DMI and the thrill of growing a business would surface and catapult him to Detroit. "I told you, he's lost it."

"What happened to him?"

"Panties."

"Oh, Mother," Don said with a sigh.

"For real, I think he got caught up with an obsession for women and he let them influence his beliefs. It's either the women or maybe his ego got too big with the constant media attention. Who knows, maybe he thinks he's a little god now. I wouldn't put it past his arrogance. If it wasn't against every fiber in my body, I'd almost feel sorry for him. What a waste."

"Wow, what's Abigail saying about Joel's change?"

"I haven't had a chance to talk with her privately but she was as outraged as I was in the meeting. He didn't get support from anyone on the management team. We tried to tell him partnering with a company that doesn't believe in God is a mistake. He wasn't listening to any of us."

"Maybe he'll listen to Abigail."

"I hope he doesn't. This is a good opportunity for him to get out of the CEO position. This is the best shot I will have to get him out. I'm going to the board of directors. He won't listen to anyone else. I honestly don't believe he's listening to God. He's doing what Joel wants to do and doesn't give two hoots about anyone who objects, but don't worry. Baby boy has something coming.

His cocky attitude is going to be his downfall yet. Now you see why I need you here."

"Me? What do you need me for? I'm sure you have the situation under control."

"I can get the company back. I will get the company back, but I need you to run it. Don't get me wrong, I enjoy running the East Coast division. You know how much I love my monthly trips to New York and D.C.—love them. When you take over, I promise to keep the East Coast going for you, but as far as running the rest of the company, that's not for me. It's your job, you should be CEO."

"You're the only one who thinks so."

"Weren't you the one who told me to forget about the past? This company can't survive with Joel. He's tossing us into a den of wolves with these crazy gods and higher energies. I'm in no position to be running the company," she said, twitching her toes inside a pair of her standard four-inch heels. "We need you. I need you to save our legacy."

"I can't, Mother. I won't come back to Detroit and set myself up for heartache again. I have a nice company here. I'm settled and beginning to build a nice life here. I'm at peace."

"Are you, are you really at peace? You're still angry at your father, and he's been dead going on three years. You're mad at God, too, I can tell."

"I told you, I'm not mad at my father. God either."

"Look, you know your mother isn't exactly a Bible-toting kind of person, but I've seen what happens to people when they lose sight of God. I saw it this morning in the meeting with Joel. You have the right to be upset, but you need to come home and handle our company business."

"My business is here. I can't walk away from LTI."

"Sell it."

"I built this company on my own without my father's help or approval. I did this myself, and I'm not throwing my accomplishment away just to run back to Detroit to save DMI. I'm staying with my company and my new life."

"I'm proud of what you've accomplished, and you're right, you shouldn't have to walk away from the company you built singlehandedly, you're absolutely correct. I apologize for the way that came out. Here's an idea. Bring the company with you."

"What do you mean?"

"We're looking to expand into the international arena. LTI will be perfect. Your company has a leadership development thrust. Maybe that's why God let all this happen to us, so we'd be prepared to take over. There's no other explanation for the suffering we've endured. There has to be something good at the end of this long, dark road that we've traveled for so many years. Your company is the perfect segue into the international market, so long as you're not over there letting Naledi talk you into praying to fig trees or letting the wind be your spiritual guide. I don't know if there are fig trees in South Africa, but whatever trees they have, I hope you're not praying to any of them."

"You know me better than that."

"I believe I do."

chapter

67

Abigail struggled to make sense of the meeting. She hated siding with Madeline against Joel, but Madeline was right this time. Abigail poked her head into Sherry's office and was relieved to find her. Winded and hustling from the meeting, Abigail drew in a deep breath, leaning against the corner of Sherry's desk.

"You all right?" Sherry asked, peering over her reading glasses.

"No, I'm not all right. Joel isn't either."

"What's wrong with Joel?" Sherry asked, dropping the papers in her hand.

"He's not thinking clearly. A few minutes ago we had a meeting with a potential partner from Harmonious Energy. The owner of the company doesn't believe in God. He worships other gods and some other stuff, which I can't remember, but it's definitely not God."

Sherry's eyes widened but she didn't speak against Joel. Abigail respected the loyalty, but she had to convince Sherry that what Joel was doing wasn't best for DMI. If Sherry could speak with him and get Joel to change his mind the ministry could get back to normal and Madeline could cool down.

"Joel is very smart with business, much better than I am. He makes great decisions. Everybody says so," Sherry said, lifting a stack of magazines and letting them drift back to the desk.

"Yes, I agree with you, until today. The person in the boardroom today wasn't Joel. He wasn't reasonable. Despite opposition from the entire management team he still wants to move forward with the international expansion."

"He's doing the expansion in honor of his father."

"Fine, I'll support him with the expansion as I've done with every other endeavor he's undertaken." It must have been her tone that caused Sherry to look up and lock in on Abigail's words. "But this is the wrong partnership. I'm terrified about what will happen to him and DMI if this deal goes through. God only knows what damage will be done."

"I'm sorry, but I don't believe Joel would be as reckless in his decisions as you're describing."

"I didn't want to believe it either, but I was there. I heard the plan with my own ears."

"I bet Madeline has something to do with this. She's never accepted Joel as CEO or as Dave's son. I could see her doing something devious or spreading vicious rumors."

"Sherry, don't you understand, I was in the room.

This isn't Madeline's idea. This is Joel's. He's the one who found Mr. Bengali. Even if Madeline was involved, she can't push Joel to partner with Harmonious Energy. No, this is definitely Joel's decision and there's something very wrong."

"Why are you telling me this?"

"You're the only one on earth he'll listen to," Abigail said, drawing close to Sherry. "He has to listen to someone. I'm terrified about the consequences if he doesn't."

"I'm his mother, not his boss. I respect my son's leadership. He has done an incredible job leading DMI. I'm proud of him and I trust him to make the right decisions."

"Sherry, please, I'm pleading with you, don't let Joel make this mistake. I worked closely with Dave for almost five years and this is not what he'd want. Don't let Joel do this."

Sherry returned her gaze to the papers on her desk. "Abigail, I'm so sorry, but I can't help you. I trust my son more than anyone in this world. If he says Harmonious Energy is the partner for DMI, then I will stand behind him. I hope you understand my position as his mother. I have to support him when no one else will. You know how much I respect you, so please forgive me."

"Fine, so long as you're willing to stand by him when his decision fails," Abigail said, and darted out the office feeling more lost and confused than she had before speaking with Sherry. She needed to have two more conversations, one with God and then one with Don. God was for direction and intervention. Don was a haven, a friendly ear, the kind voice she greatly sought. Naledi would have to understand.

chapter

68

The meeting hadn't gone as smoothly as he'd liked. Joel had proven his ability for ten straight quarters. The company had grown beyond expectations. By every account, he'd succeeded and taken the company to heights his father hadn't realized. Why didn't they trust him this time? He was the same man today as he was six months ago, the legitimate heir and cherished son of Dave Mitchell. His success was the validation his mother longed to have. By running DMI, he'd honored his father's dream and orchestrated his mother's path to validation and positive worth. The world expected him to fail, but he'd show them. The expansion would happen and the doubters would marvel at his accomplishment. The amount of publicity he was receiving now would be equivalent to a pimple on the back of an elephant once he showed them what he could really do with the company and garnered monstrous exposure. He was charged and ready to get on with the partnership.

Musar and his daughter had stepped out to make a few calls and to make use of the facilities. As they entered the office escorted by his administrative assistant, Joel extended courtesies as they took seats at the conference table.

"Excuse me," Joel's assistant whispered to him. "Sheba Warden is trying to reach you." He warmed hearing the message. Sheba's charm hadn't lost any luster in the months that he'd known her. He instructed the assistant to tell Sheba he would call back later.

Important DMI business had to be addressed first. Joel was stretching the company into foreign territory, but his strategy had successfully carried DMI in the past. This venture was no different. He would continue rehearsing the concept in his mind until the nagging unrest subsided. He prayed to God sporadically but hadn't received an answer. He'd keep trying, although he was often distracted by his romantic thirst. He needed to repent but hadn't bothered. Until he was ready to cut off women, he felt repenting was hypocritical. In the meantime there was a deal to be made.

"Again, thank you for making the long trip from India," Joel told Mr. Bengali.

"It is my honor to be here," Musar said, practically bowing from his seat.

Joel didn't want to be rude and exclude Zarah Bengali from the conversation, but she rarely joined in anyway. This was their third meeting in person and Joel didn't recall her saying more than a dozen words. She consistently walked about a foot behind her father. Joel didn't fully understand the dynamics, but she wasn't his concern so long as the required signatures from Harmonious Energy were on the contract.

"I have to apologize for the reaction of my staff. They are very conservative and want to make sure the company is moving in the right direction."

"Will this partnership present a problem for you?" Musar asked.

"No, no, not at all, as they become more familiar with the benefits of our union, they will support the concept."

"What if they don't?"

"As CEO, the final decision is mine. My father entrusted the leadership of this company to me and I will run DMI as I see fit."

"Good, I'm glad to hear the certainty in your decision, because this union is most important to me. I want to partner with a strong leader, a man who can stand up to opposition," Musar said. The majority of his words were very clear. The ones doused with accent were easily translated. "This is more than a business deal for me. You see, I'm not expected to live long, according to those who practice Western medicine in my country."

Joel's attention zoomed in on Musar. "Are you sure?" Joel said, not sure what else to say.

"Quite sure."

"You have my prayers, well, I mean my condolences, since you don't believe in prayer."

"I embrace the next step in my spiritual journey. I have less than a year to live, which makes the timing of this deal vitally important."

Joel wasn't following. Merging seemed futile if he was dying and wouldn't be around to realize the benefits of the partnership.

"You weren't randomly selected. I did extensive research before determining you to be the most viable partner for Harmonious Energy. You're good for business, very smart, and you've not yet taken a wife. You're the one I've chosen to run my company and to marry my daughter."

Joel's neck stiffened and he cringed. "What did you say?"

"I want you to take over my company in a full merger. You'd have total ownership. In return I have two requests. I would like you to take my daughter's hand in marriage. She's the sole heir to my company. I want to make sure she's provided for." A flush filled his daughter's face, accented by the sheer red scarf, but she didn't utter a word.

"And you want me to marry your daughter?" Joel was stunned and hindered in his ability to respond openly with Zarah in the room. His mind couldn't tackle the enormity of Musar's request. "You said there were two requests. What's the other one?" Joel asked, leery of the response.

"In good faith I'd like for you to give me a portion of your company."

"What do you mean?"

"A division will be most suitable. I will give you full ownership of my company in exchange for one of your divisions, any one you choose I'll accept."

"Oh, I could never sell off a piece of the company," he said, hearing the ringing sound of his father's words, "Don't split or sell the company." "Splitting the company isn't an option."

"I'm not talking about splitting the company forever. You can title the division to me. You can leave your current team in place to run the division."

"In that case, what do you get out of the deal?"

"Security for my daughter and a small measure of sacrifice from you. Once I die, the division would revert to my daughter through a transfer clause."

"Why?"

"You want your company to remain whole, of this I'm most certain. If she owns the division, I'm guaranteed you'd never leave her. As long as she owns a portion of DMI you will keep her as your bride." For the only time Joel could remember in their meetings, Musar shifted his gaze toward his daughter as he spoke. "This is the duty of a father, to provide for his daughter both in this phase of my journey and in the next."

This was a test, had to be. Joel's thoughts were bubbling like a pot of soup, mixing words from Musar, Dad, the church mother, and Abigail. The church mother implored him to be watchful and not to entertain other gods. On the other hand, people were constantly trying to trick him into doubting his faith and God-given wisdom. He hadn't heard clearly from God on the expansion, but then he hadn't consistently asked Him for help. The plan had seemed pretty simple until today. He needed direction. A quick trip to see Sheba would have been his choice, but business and pleasure were bound to get twisted. Resolving the issues surrounding the merger required his undivided attention, an impossible goal in the presence of Sheba. With nowhere to turn, he hoped the church mother could help.

chapter

69

Abigail's emotions were like a tangled ball of yarn. She could see the beginning but had no idea where the end was. The hour she spent in the ladies' lounge right after leaving Sherry's office didn't help untangle her messy situation. She was holding the snapshot of the house in her hand and letting the words of the church mother reel through her mind when Joel entered her office.

"I've been looking for you since Musar and his daughter left," he told her.

Her thoughts were plentiful. Her words were few.

"We have to talk," he said, closing her door and approaching her desk. He didn't sit. "Abigail, I need you to talk to me. Tell me what's going on between us. You're the one who keeps this company going. You keep me going. Why can't I have your support?"

"How can you ask me that? Support for what?" she said, laying the photo on her desk and sliding it toward him. "You asked me to build your house, and I have," she said, her voice rising with each word. "You asked me to take on a leadership role in DMI, and I have. Now you're asking me to support you in a bad decision? I can't."

"You and I have talked about expanding into international territory. You know better than anyone about my father's dream to expand. I'm fulfilling his dream. What's wrong with honoring my father's wishes? You supported me with the library. What's the difference?" he said, taking a seat on the other side of her desk.

"What you proposed today is nothing like the library. God was in your decision to build the library. God isn't in this decision. This is your doing."

"How can you say God's not in this?"

"It's obvious, Joel, and that's what frightens me. You don't see the problem here. You want to merge DMI, a God-centered ministry, with a company that doesn't believe in God. What sense does your decision make? Merging these two companies is the same as two people getting married while practicing different religions. This marriage between the two companies won't work. It's not equally yoked. The beliefs are drastically different. Don't you see this?" she asked, desperate to reach him and save them all.

"Abigail, where is this coming from? Sounds like Madeline, not you."

"This has nothing to do with Madeline. I'm telling you as a friend and as your executive director, the decision to merge with Harmonious Energy is a bad one, and I can't support you if you move forward. To be honest, I've had to question your judgment ever since you got involved months ago with Sheba and her strange spiritual beliefs. You've been different ever since."

"Has our relationship come to this?"

"What relationship?" she said, tossing the photo across the desk to him. "Do we have a relationship? I've waited and waited and waited for you to speak up for us. I've been faithful to you. Every breath God has allowed me to take since you became CEO was spent on supporting you and meeting your needs."

"And I'm grateful."

"I don't want gratitude. I want a relationship, a commitment, can you give me that?" Joel didn't respond. "I've earned my place with you."

Joel's gaze fell to the floor. "Abigail, love isn't earned in a relationship. It's given freely."

"Stop calling it a relationship," Abigail yelled, and took a time-out before speaking again. "We don't have a relationship. Don't you get that?"

Joel moved the chair closer to the desk and reached for her hand, but she pulled away.

"I've always been honest with you about where I am with commitments."

"So what, I don't want to hear that," she blurted, refusing to be consoled with his touch.

"I've hurt you and I'm sorry."

"This isn't about me anymore. I'll get beyond our 'so-called' relationship, but you're going to fall flat on your face if you don't stop the expansion with Mr. Bengali. You are making the biggest mistake of your life."

"Abigail, I have to do this merger."

"Why?"

"Because failure is not an option. I'm my father's son, finally." Abigail didn't try to act as if she understood what he meant. "I've lived my entire life being the other child. My last name was Mitchell but my mother and I weren't recognized as members of this family until I became the successful CEO. We're not outsiders anymore. My father made me legitimate when he handed DMI to me. The promises I made to him I will keep. Failure is not an option."

"What about the promises you made to God, to love Him and to put Him before other gods? Do you remember what the mother at Greater Faith Chapel told you? She said you would be tested." Abigail searched in her purse, which was tucked inside her lower desk drawer, and found the business card with her notes from church. Quickly scanning the card, she began paraphrasing. "She said you have to stay before the Lord, the one true God. Don't be deceived. Don't be lured away and mated with other gods. She warned you not to let your favor become your curse. Do you remember any of this?" she said, tossing the card in his direction.

"I do, but we're safe. This is purely a business deal, nothing more, nothing less."

"Something is wrong, don't you see, Joel? She warned you that people would come from everywhere to bring you down. She told you to watch yourself and I believe that old lady knew what she was talking about. You are allowing yourself to be deceived by God only knows what."

"I haven't replaced God in my life. I'm just making room for other beliefs in the building. Harmonious Energy promotes inclusion and harmony. Aren't those qualities we embrace in DMI?"

"If the harmony doesn't come from God, I don't want it."

"You're being close-minded. This isn't like you. This is Madeline talking."

"Maybe so, but when you choose to serve God, some actions are no longer an option. You can't have it both ways," she said, reaching into her purse again. She extracted a ring of keys and handed them to Joel.

"What's this?"

"The keys to your house."

He propped his elbow on the arm of the chair and let his temple rest on his index finger. She dangled the ring of keys at him but he wouldn't take it.

"Are you this upset?"

Dropping the keys near the edge of the desk, she said, "I'm not abandoning you, Joel. Like I said, you can't have it both ways. I can only serve one God and support one mate. You have many of each, and I can't look the other way, not any longer. Playing house with you and waiting for your proposal was a fantasy. Time for me to wake up. You've forced me to wake up," she said, sliding the keys to the very edge and slipping the photo underneath.

Joel didn't move, didn't speak, didn't blink. Her heart was shattering. Abigail wanted him to wrap his arms around her and save them, but she knew he couldn't. His empty stare said he was too far gone. How, why, and when his transformation had occurred, she wasn't quite sure. Maybe if she'd been bolder in the beginning and confessed her feelings there might have been a shot at love. She could second-guess for days, but at this moment her pain was too raw for comfort. She refused to shed a tear while he was in her office. She'd kept her feelings for him to herself and would do the same with her heartache.

"Is there anything I can say to change your mind?"

She shook her head no. Speaking was too risky.

chapter

70

The perks of stardom helped at critical times, such as tonight. Pastor Clyde Daniels probably wasn't in the habit of sharing church members' information with other people. Joel appreciated the favor. The Lamborghini cruised along Outer Drive, as he looked for Eight Mile. Mrs. Emma Walker had agreed to meet with him and he was in a hurry to get to her house. He hadn't heard clearly from God in a while. Mrs. Walker had had a connection the last time they met. He was pretty certain Harmonious Energy was a merger he should make. The marriage and spinning off one of the divisions were twists he didn't quite know how to handle. There had to be ways around those components of the deal.

A few more blocks and the house numbers were in the right range. He slowed, peering at each house as he approached hers. He pulled to the curb, double-checking the number. This was the house. He whizzed to the door and she opened as he approached.

"Mrs. Emma Walker?"

"I have to hear my name two or three times before I know you're talking to me. Most people call me Big Mama at the church."

"Which name do you prefer?"

"I answer to them both."

"Mrs. Walker, thanks for seeing me."

"I'm glad you called me. You've been on my mind a heap. Where are my manners—come on in this house and rest yourself."

"Can I leave my car there?" he asked.

"Your car will be fine right there. It's an awfully fancy one, isn't it," she commented. "Come on in and make yourself at home."

"Thank you, but I don't plan to stay very long. I'm barging in as it is. I wouldn't dream of imposing beyond a few minutes," he said, flexing his fingers.

"Nonsense, anyone who wants to talk about the Lord is welcome in my house any time of day or night."

Joel wanted to ask his question, get confirmation, and get out of her house in five to ten minutes, but he couldn't be rude and rush her.

"What brings you over here to see me?"

"I need your help. Actually, I need confirmation on a business deal I'm considering."

"I'm not much for business."

"But you know how to hear from God."

"Now, that I do know how to do, but so do you. I've heard and read some of the stories about you. You can solve problems where other people can't. God has given you the gift of knowledge and wisdom, so why do you need me to help you answer a business question when you're already equipped with answers?"

"Six months ago I could answer the question without needing confirmation. Today I'm second-guessing myself. Something has changed."

"Well, we know God doesn't change."

Joel was prepared for a lecture, a small price to pay for a confirmation, but none came.

"Let me pray with you," she said, jumping right in, getting him fired up by the way she combined prayer and worship. Her prayer sang like a song, personal, with authority, the way he used to pray before his schedule and his days became too packed, not leaving nearly as much time for God as he once had.

When she concluded the prayer and closed with amen, Joel was rejuvenated. The presence of God felt thick around Mrs. Walker. He was convinced she'd be able to confirm his expansion plan and shut down his management team, who were drenched with doubt.

"Well, son, I will keep you in my prayers and I'm awfully glad you came by."

"Wait, that's it?" He needed an answer. "I came for a word of prophecy about my business deal."

"The gift of prophecy doesn't work that way. You can't put in orders like at the restaurant. You have to take what God gives you when he gives it to you, but like I said, I will keep you in my prayers, because I sense a heap of trouble coming your way. You best be watchful. Those are the words I hear repeated over and over in my head. I believe those words are for you."

He wasn't supposed to get specific, but he was desperate for an answer, for a confirmation he could use to sway the rest of the management team, especially the board of directors. "Do you hear anything about me merging with Harmonious Energy? I have to find out if I'm making the correct decision."

"I'm sorry I can't help you, son. I can only take what God gives me for you. Make no mistake about me, I'm not a fortune-teller. I'm a servant of the Most High God. I ain't going to tell you what you want to hear. I'm going to tell you what the Lord says."

Joel was at a loss. He needed answers, and his sure shot wasn't being any help. He thanked Mrs. Walker and approached the door. She caught his hand and said, "You know the Lord. Why aren't you seeking Him for yourself?"

"I have, and for the first time since I was named CEO, I can't hear His voice."

"Maybe it's because He's already spoken."

"How do you mean?"

"Do you have children, Mr. Mitchell?"

"No, I'm not married yet."

"Well, I have one daughter who passed away in a car accident many years ago. I raised my granddaughter, Rachel. She lives in that big Chicago. I remember times when I would tell her to do something. She'd mess around and not do what I told her to do. A time later she'd come back and ask me the same question over and over, 'What did you tell me to do?' I stopped answering because she already had the answer. Come to find out Rachel asked me the same question a heap of times whenever she didn't like the answer. I guess she figured the more she asked the more the answer was going to change. You know, Mr. Mitchell, God's word never changes. His answer and promise is the same today as what He promised you when you took your big job. Don't be fooled or led away from our Father in heaven. If you do, I fear you'll be lost."

Joel wasn't leaving with the clarity he wanted. More questions, no answers.

"Why don't you stay for a bite of supper?"

"No, but thanks for the offer. My job keeps me on the go. I have to run."

"Well if you're ever in my neighborhood, please stop by. You don't need an invitation. If you catch me just right I might have a fresh pie cooling on the windowsill," she said, as humble as ever.

She didn't have the answers but he was glad he had come. There was a certain glow in her disposition when she talked about God, a familiar feeling he remembered having not very long ago. He left the house and drove the Lamborghini into the downtown area, combing the streets slowly. He had tried reasoning with the management team with no luck. He had said a few lines of prayer with no response. He'd spoken with Mrs. Walker and nothing. His options were limited, and Musar was expecting an answer. He kept driving until he saw a sign. The lights were on in the shop. He'd never been to a place like this, but one visit couldn't hurt. He wanted answers. He parked down the block in case someone recognized him and walked into the shop with the front entrance lit by the words PSYCHIC—TAROT CARDS—PALM READING. A cold rush flashed across his soul. He stopped and reconsidered before going inside. There were no more options. He needed a spiritual confirmation. Going to a fortune-teller was like getting a word of prophecy from Mrs. Walker. He went in and concentrated on getting out quickly for the sake of his peace and for his car.

chapter

71

Joel wrestled with the nagging voice that had tormented him most of the night, except for the two hours of sleep he claimed right before dawn. One moment the answer was a definite yes and at other moments he wasn't sure. Standing at Abigail's office door, his father's words rang out: "A leader has to make the tough decisions and stand by the consequences." He'd waffled too long; the decision was done. The impromptu management meeting was in an hour but he had to speak with Abigail first. He could live without the endorsement of the rest of the group, but Abigail was special. Her opinion mattered. He entered her office and closed the door.

"What's this meeting about at eleven?" she asked him, peering into her laptop and tossing a few glances at him. They hadn't spoken much since she gave him back the keys to his house.

"I called the meeting to talk about Harmonious Energy."

"Joel, I pray you've changed your mind. Please say you've changed your mind."

"I'm firm in my decision to move forward."

"Then what else do we have to talk about?"

"I want to tell you about the terms of the deal and why I'm doing what I'm doing."

"You've already told me more than I want to know about Harmonious Energy."

He took a seat in front of her desk. He wanted to get closer but wasn't going to crowd her. "The deal requires me to split off one of our divisions and transition ownership to Musar Bengali. I've selected the West Coast division to go."

"Come on, you have to be kidding me. You're not seriously considering splitting the ministry? Your father was adamant about not selling or splitting DMI."

"And you don't think those words are bouncing around in my head? He also told me to expand into international territories and to make tough decisions today, not tomorrow."

"But this makes no sense, Joel," she said, plopping her elbow on the desk and burying her forehead in the palm of her hand.

"I'm wise enough to figure out how to keep DMI intact while fulfilling Mr. Bengali's wishes at the same time. This is another one of the many tests I've had to handle as CEO, just like my father had to do when he was in charge. You haven't doubted me before, please don't start now. I need you."

"I will never agree to spin off a piece of the ministry. I can't."

He didn't want to tell her the worst of the deal, but time was running out before the group meeting. She deserved to know. "There's one more piece of the deal that I have to tell you."

"You mean there's more? What could possibly be left to do or sell?" she said, half laughing but not in a funny ha-ha way.

"I haven't told you about the marriage."

"What marriage are you talking about?" The intensity in her eyes made him wish there was another way to break the news. Abigail was one of two people on earth he absolutely didn't want to hurt, but his purpose didn't leave him a choice.

"In Musar's original proposal, he wants me to marry his daughter to guarantee a long-term merger between DMI and Harmonious Energy."

Abigail thrust back in her chair and tossed the pen in her hand into the air. "This gets worse with every word, and you honestly can't see the mistake in what you're doing? You used to be smarter than this."

"I've worked out a deal that allows me to regain control of the West Coast division in six months, and Musar and I are reworking the deal. DMI will agree to pay a negotiated price for Harmonious Energy."

"Where are we getting the capital? Most of DMI's worth is in stock value."

"Some from retained earnings and the rest from secured debt."

"What are you talking about?

"We can use the library as collateral." Abigail didn't say a word, but her troubled expression spoke loudly. He didn't linger on the financial discussion. Money wasn't a concern. "Musar will have ownership of the West Coast for six months. During the six months I will get to know his daughter. If I decide to proceed with a marriage, the West Coast reverts to me. If I don't, then he keeps the West Coast, but he will be willing to sell the division back to DMI at his set price."

"What can I say?" she said, with dejection in her voice. "You're taking a huge risk. What if the price is too high to buy back the West Coast? What if Musar doesn't agree with your proposed changes and requires you to marry his daughter? That can't be what you want."

"I've never operated under fear, and we've booked record sales under my leadership. I'm not going to shy away from the biggest deal in the company's history." He had expected her to be outraged by the marriage announcement. If she was upset, it didn't show. He was relieved.

"Your father wouldn't have risked the stability of the ministry like this."

"And my father was never able to see his international expansion dream come to fruition either. I will."

chapter

72

Madeline scoured her sales report. Close to three years of record sales in the East Coast division under her management and seven years with Don. If Joel continued down his path of recklessness, the sales and their stability would crumble. She was too heated for words. Fifteen messages from Maryland, Pennsylvania, and D.C. alone. Six of her largest churches wanted to hear from DMI. She couldn't tell them the bad news was true—that DMI was partnering with other gods. She wasn't in a position to denounce rumors in the media. Madeline buried her head in the palm of her hand. She'd fought, scrapped, and plotted to protect DMI from the moment Joel was named CEO. He was inexperienced and dangerous from the beginning, but she had never dreamed he'd be this reckless. She was tired of plotting and planning. Begging was the only option left. She grabbed her stack of messages and hit the hallway, not stopping until she was in Sherry's office with the door slamming behind her.

"How can I help you?"

"Well, he's finally done it."

"Done what, Madeline?" Sherry asked, without shifting her interest from the papers on the desk.

"In less than three years your son has managed to ruin the stability of a forty-year-old company."

Sherry didn't shift her interest toward Madeline.

"Look at me," Madeline said, elevating her voice and shaking the stack of messages in Sherry's direction. "These are messages from our top clients. Do you have any idea why they're calling me? Do you? Do you? No, you don't," Madeline said, without giving Sherry a chance to speak. "Your son has to go. This is the final straw. I've put up with his arrogant holier-than-thou attitude and I'm sick and tired of playing his game. This ends now. I'm calling a board meeting immediately to get his behind kicked out on the street. I'm tired of playing around. I'm not letting him destroy the company my husband and I built."

"Madeline, we're not having a conversation about Dave. You have pushed me . . ." Sherry said, rising to her feet, speaking in a firm but controlled tone, her eyes fixed on Madeline. "You've insulted me and tried to make me feel like nothing, but your reign of terror is over in my life. I have work to do," she said, taking her seat and returning her attention to the papers on her desk. "Please leave."

On her way out of the office, Madeline said, "I'll leave all right, and Joel will, too." She was almost out the door, but she turned to say, "You know what's ironic about Joel? When his father was young, women were his weakness, but of course you already know that."

"I'm not going to listen to this," Sherry said. "If you won't leave, I will."

Madeline blocked the doorway. "You're going to hear me out. Dave's weakness destroyed our marriage, our family, and our children's lives. Thank goodness there's justice. Your son's weakness for women is turning out to be his downfall, too."

Sherry approached the door, but quickly retreated. Madeline wasn't finished, which meant no one was leaving the room until she was. "I'm giving you fair warning. I'm not going to sit back quietly and let your son destroy my company. If he wants to worship other gods, let him go right ahead, but it won't be at the price of my company, not the one I helped build."

"Joel is a grown man, and he's the CEO of your company. When are you going to deal with it?" Sherry said, reaching around Madeline and pulling the door open.

"You might as well pack up your office and be ready to leave when I kick both of you out," she yelled as Sherry strolled away. Sherry's newfound smugness infuriated Madeline, fueling her passion to dethrone them both.

Taking over the ministry was no longer about Dave. This was about saving her legacy, her vision, her dignity. Madeline put on a brave front. Watching Sherry prance around the hallways of DMI as if she completely owned the place was the backbreaker. Madeline was resolute. She'd get her two children to understand how critical the takeover was. Her one request in life was for the three of them to reunite and rise above the adversity inflicted on them by Sherry and Joel. For three decades she'd taken a backseat to the other woman, but Madeline could feel the wind shifting and blowing Sherry and her offspring into the path of oncoming traffic. Madeline felt slightly guilty for the thought. Nobody had to get hurt, just out of Madeline's way and preferably her sight.

She hurried to her office with rekindled determination. Calls had to be made to Don and the private investigator. Madeline didn't bother including Frank. They hadn't spoken since the Chicago ordeal, and she was intent on keeping it that way. Getting kicked out of DMI before Joel got ousted wasn't an option.

chapter

73

Abigail was in her office reflecting on the recent disagreements with Joel when Madeline came in. "What are we going to do? I've asked Don to come home and help me work out a strategy."

"You don't have much time," Abigail said, pointing to the computer screen. "According to the email Joel sent yesterday, the contract should be ready for signatures after the legal review is finished."

"That only gives us about two weeks. Since this is an international deal, we might get an extra week or two at the most," Madeline said. "I can call a board meeting. We can get Joel out, but we'll need the majority ownership to make it stick."

"You can have my five percent, for what it's worth."

"Thanks, but your five percent, my twenty-five percent, and Don's fifteen only gives us forty-five. We need fifty-one percent to control the decision and to make this stick. We need Tamara's stock, but I haven't been able to reach her."

"Do you know where she is?"

"I do, but she's not going to talk to me. The only person she's maintained any kind of contact with is Don. He doesn't think I know but I do. He calls her on holidays and every birthday. Apparently she talks with him for a minute, literally like a minute, and that's the extent of her connection to the family."

"How do you know this?"

"I have my ways. Anyway, I can't get through to her. Don might be able to, but I'd never be able to convince him to lift a finger for DMI. He hasn't admitted it to me, but I think he's still hurt about his father's decision to make Joel CEO, especially now that he sees Joel making a mess of the ministry. I have to come up with a plan, and quickly."

"I can give you my stock but I'm not willing to go any further." The ache of losing her confidant, her partner, her love interest was crippling. Abigail's thoughts were choppy and incoherent. Her heart wanted to believe the best of Joel unconditionally, which was why she didn't tell Madeline about Joel's plans to take on debt. She still felt compelled to protect him, but her mind taunted her to accept the reality and minimize the damage Joel was doing to DMI. Her gaze fell.

"Are you okay?" Madeline asked.

"I guess. I'm thinking about Dave. I remember how much he loved this ministry and how much he loved his family."

"He would be distraught watching his ministry be sold to someone who doesn't believe in God. Abigail, you have to take a stand. Either you're with Joel in his decision to merge with Harmonious Energy or you're not. You can't straddle the fence. You have to land on one side or the other. I'm not trying to pressure you, but you know what Dave would want and what he wouldn't. He never wanted the ministry sold or split, and he definitely would never want to partner with anyone who didn't at least acknowledge God."

"You're right."

"So can I count on you to help me do whatever it takes to save this company?" Madeline asked, with a conviction and a controlled passion Abigail hadn't witnessed before from her.

"I'm not sure what I can do."

"You'll be shocked to hear me say this, but you can pray. Seriously pray for us to save this ministry. Dave Mitchell knew how to pray and he always got results. His results didn't benefit me but they seemed to work well for him."

"What about you? I'm sorry, but I can't picture you on your knees praying."

"No, prayer isn't exactly my favorite approach. Let's face it, since Dave and I divorced, God and I haven't spoken much. That wasn't always the case, not in my younger days when Dave and I were starting out. However, I'm no fool. I'm not Sheba Warden. I've never been confused about who God is. I know He has ultimate control over my life and this place. I just don't ask Him for help or for much of anything, but this one, I can't fix on my own. I refuse to let DMI fail. I'm willing to do whatever I have to. If that means praying, I'll pray, but you have more practice. I'm very rusty on the prayer end, which is why I'll stick to what I'm good at doing."

"What would that be?"

"You don't want to know," Madeline said, with a cunning grin.

"Madeline, what are we going to do with you?"

"I have no idea, but at this point, I'm too old to change," she said, and sauntered out of the room looking as jovial as a child on Christmas.

Agree with her or not, Madeline was consistently the same. When she believed in something she took a stand, and she was relentless in her pursuits. Abigail admired Madeline's tenacity and commitment to her beliefs in spite of opposition. Abigail reflected on the ministry's vision. She scrolled her phone directory and stopped at Don Mitchell.

Five rings and Don was on the line.

"Don, I need you," Abigail said, layering a chill across his body. "DMI is in trouble and we need you to help us gain control."

"I'm surprised to see you side with my mother against Joel."

"I don't see this as going against Joel. I see this as standing for what's right."

"What about your feelings for him?"

"Feelings are what they are, uncontrollable, unexpected, and in this relationship unreciprocated."

"I can hear the hurt in your voice, and I'm sorry."

"There's no reason for you to be sorry. You're the last person to apologize to me. You've done nothing but support me and encourage me. I'm grateful for you."

"Our friendship hasn't changed. You can always count on me."

"Even when it comes to saving DMI from Joel's misguided decisions?"

"That's asking a lot. DMI is not a problem I care to take on."

"But I do. I care about DMI, and me and your mother need your help to keep this ministry on track. I don't want to see DMI fail after your father and mother spent so many years building this business. You know your dad was like a father to me, one that I didn't have growing up."

"I didn't either."

"I know, and I'm not trying to cause you any pain or make you feel guilty, but at least your father loved you."

"He had a weird way of showing his love for me and my brothers and sister. We were never made to feel like Dave Mitchell's special children."

"You're not going to like this, but Joel felt the same way about his childhood. He told me several years ago that he felt like an outsider in the Mitchell family, like he didn't belong."

"My mother called earlier, and there's nothing I can do to help. I will gladly sign over my stock but you'll still have the same problem."

"What about your sister, Tamara? You're the only one who talks to her. Maybe you can convince her to work with your mother." Don laughed openly. "What's so funny, this is very serious," Abigail said.

"You don't know my sister very well. She has even less interest in saving DMI than I do, if that's possible to imagine."

"What happened to your sister to make her so distant?"

"That's a long story for another time. Suffice to say, my sister and brothers paid the price for the happiness of my dad's other family."

"From what I've seen, life wasn't perfect for Sherry and Joel either. Seems like everyone suffered to some extent."

"Except my father. He enjoyed the best of both

worlds with two women who loved him. I should be so lucky. Dave Mitchell was the clear winner, but the truth is that he's still my father and I love him. I haven't always liked him, but he's gone now and the past is dead. I've accepted my reality and moved on with my life. I'm finally savoring a bite of contentment, which you shouldn't ask me to surrender. It's taken me a lifetime to get here. I'm actually finding peace with my father again, and I'm not willing to sacrifice my progress to save DMI. In order for me to love my father, I have to disassociate with the company."

"I understand how you feel."

"You don't. No one can. I spent ten years being mentored by him, and when the opportunity came to reward me, my father slapped me in the face. Isn't it funny—my father made a boatload of mistakes, starting with his adultery. He ruined our lives, but he never suffered. I've resented him for longer than I want to admit, and I don't want to carry the burden of my bitterness any longer."

"I truly believe he was sad about the distance between him and his children."

"I'm sure he was, at least at the end." Don succumbed to nostalgia, and suddenly the eight thousand miles between Cape Town and Detroit was too short. There was a gentle nudging in his spirit. He was actually close to entertaining the proposition, but the nagging residual effects of rejection and pride kept him at bay. His father's vision for DMI was honorable, that he couldn't deny. His thoughts were tossed back and forth, finally landing on the side of no. "I don't think fulfilling my father's vision is enough to get me home."

"What about me, is my friendship and your mother's dedication enough for you?"

chapter

74

Don had promised Abigail he would come if and when she called for his help, no questions asked. Close to three years had passed and she hadn't asked for anything. Now she had finally asked. He didn't want to disappoint her, but he couldn't commit to tossing himself onto shaky Mitchell turf, not when he was solid right where he was. Torn between undying devotion and self-preservation, Don found himself on the ferry to Robben Island. The open sky and endless sea ushered him into a place of escape far from the turmoil in Detroit and in his soul. The forty-five-minute ride to the island chipped away at his unrest. The rush of people didn't hurry him off the ship. He stepped onto the concrete platform and was captivated by the mural of men who had once been incarcerated on the island. He was humbled, acknowledging that many had been tormented by what he longed to possess, solitude. Maybe he could lose himself in the block of cells and not surface until Abigail and Mother changed their minds about wanting his help.

He took the bus tour half listening to the short, black South African woman who made clucking sounds in between words, letting him know she was from the Zulu tribe. Take away her accent and she looked like any woman on the streets of Michigan. A sinking feeling tackled him. He missed Detroit but couldn't go home. This was home. Cape Town was his haven. Peace and love warred internally.

"This is the limestone quarry where Nelson Mandela spent years breaking big rocks into little rocks under the blistering sun. The sun was very harsh to Papa Mandela and his eyes became very bad. To this day when photos are taken of Papa Mandela, he can't look at the flash," the short woman said.

Compassion for the former political prisoners consumed him. Don had suffered at the hands of either his father or fate or God. He wasn't quite sure who the conductor was, but he'd suffered. Mr. Mandela was one of the few people who could understand his pain.

"During the years in the quarry, Papa Mandela taught the young rebellious prisoners about the meaning of freedom and how to survive in the prison. He taught them in there," she said, pointing to what looked like a cubbyhole in the rocks.

Don was perplexed. Mandela had the right to be bitter and self-consumed during his prison stay. Don couldn't imagine being wrongly imprisoned and then having the kind of conviction that would allow Mandela to teach others. Don had been fired and had no intention of teaching anyone anything at DMI.

The tour bus bumped along the partially paved road as the Zulu woman pointed out landmarks and one horrific story of torture after another concerning Mandela and countless other South African men like him who had been wrongly incarcerated and treated inhumanely. After forty-five minutes on the bus Don was deposited at the row of cell blocks.

The guide pointed out the bus window. "This is where Papa Mandela spent his time on the island. You may exit the bus and walk the remainder of the tour. We thank you for coming on our tour today. *Hamba Kahle,*" she said, bowing quickly, "which means good-bye and go well."

The group on the bus was met by another tour guide, who introduced himself as a former prisoner. He said his name two times but Don couldn't repeat it. The guide led them through building after building, cell after cell, telling stories far more horrific than those told on the bus. Don was sobered, walking into each of the cells, which displayed photos of the former occupants. Samples of their personal items and letters about their experiences while incarcerated could be found throughout the prison. The trip was intended to be an escape, but the guide had given Don a lesson in perseverance—the sheer will to live and fulfill a purpose in spite of the most adverse conditions. Don had lived in the presidential suite at Table Mountain Hotel, overlooking the ocean, for a few weeks before downgrading to the executive suite when he arrived in Cape Town. The accommodations didn't bear a shred of commonality with those the inmates had endured. His mind couldn't wrap around the notion of Mandela sleeping on the concrete floor with a thin mattress. One blanket against the damp, cold night wasn't fathomable. Don thought about the countless days and nights the men had spent away from their families, never knowing if they'd return home alive. He was away from his family, willfully.

Don hung around waiting for the small group of tourists to leave. After they were gone, he approached the narrator and asked him, "How could you forgive people who treated you the way they did?" He couldn't help but think about Joel and his father and how they'd treated him.

"It was Nelson Mandela who saved my life. After we were released from prison, I was angry, very angry. I wanted to kill those guards with my bare hands. I wanted to get revenge. I was ready to fight, but Nelson Mandela told me that in order to see hope in the future I had to let go of the past."

"That's really tough."

"Mandela was able to forgive, and he taught me how to forgive," the guide said with a singing flow in his accent. "To this day I am friends with many of the guards. We live here on the island together."

"Together," Don said, feeling his eyelids expand, "on Robben Island? You're kidding me, man." He had no words, completely overcome by the gravity of what the former prisoner was implying.

"The very island that was once my prison and personal hell has become my home."

"It's hard to believe that a person could be so forgiving after suffering so much."

"I believe it was a part of his destiny, and Papa Mandela has always understood his destiny. He did not run away."

Don stared into the guide's eyes for what seemed like a long time searching for any sign of dishonesty and found none. He let his gaze drop to the ground, unable to lift his head, almost in shame. His father had dealt him several heavy blows in his life, beginning with leaving their family when he was a child. Handing Joel the reins to DMI was another jab to his gut, with the final knockout coming when his father died before Don got a chance to say good-bye. Don's life had struggles, many, but his battle wasn't like those of the men unjustly incarcerated on an island in the middle of the ocean, tortured and treated worse than an animal with rabies. Burdens from his youth seemed to lighten.

"Are you all right, sir?"

"Oh, yes," Don responded, "I'm better than I've been in quite a while. Thank you," he told the guide, and slipped him five hundred rand. He was reluctant to take the money, but Don shoved it into his palms and closed his fingers tightly around the bill. He didn't owe money at the end of the tour and the guide certainly didn't ask, but he felt compelled to do something to help right the wrongs of the past even if they weren't from his deeds.

He strolled to the dock, not in a hurry to get on the ferry. His mind was clear. His thoughts were pure. For the first time in nearly three years he spoke to God openly, without the taste of diluted bitterness. "I don't know what your purpose is for me, but I'm willing to listen to you. Please give me direction," he said, walking slowly and taking in the solace of the island. He wanted to help his mother, but not for her reasons, not for revenge. She'd made countless sacrifices for him and his siblings. DMI was as much hers as it was anyone's. This was a time when he could give her back a small pinch of the unconditional love and support she'd showered on him since birth. Don wasn't sure what he could do in Detroit, but he was willing to find out. As soon as he got back to shore he'd surprise Tamara with a call, right after his call to Abigail. A lengthy talk with his sister was long overdue. Forgiveness and restoration was an uphill climb, one he was willing to make.

chapter

75

A surge of media coverage, women, and record sales hadn't clouded his judgment. If anything, Joel was wiser, stronger, better at following his passions. The management team and anyone else who didn't function at his level needed to deal with his success and get over the personal attacks and waves of jealous antics. Leaders lead, others follow. He was confident with the decision and refused to hear a pack of naysayers attempt to steer him in another direction. He'd proven to be a solid leader for the management team. God hadn't told him no, so who were they to say no. Then again, God hadn't spoken to him at all, but he didn't need God to make this decision. He remembered his father telling him to wait on direction from God, but that was another time. In the beginning of his CEO role he had needed help from God and had sought Him on every decision. That was almost three years ago. He wasn't a rookie CEO anymore. He was equipped with experience, charisma, and success. He could make his own decision and didn't need validation from anyone.

Joel entered his mother's office and found her sitting at the desk working on a laptop with reading glasses perched on the bridge of her nose. "Were you looking for me?" he asked.

"I was. I wanted to check on you and see how you're doing with the expansion," she said.

"I'm fine with the expansion." He leaned against the window and stared into the distance with one hand in his pants pocket. "It's the rest of the team who has a problem, but what do they know? I'm the one who knows what's best for DMI."

"Joel, I trust your judgment. Are you absolutely sure merging with Harmonious Energy is best?"

"Mom, I'm not a hundred percent sure, but I'm willing to live with the consequences."

"You are so much like your father," she said, casting an adoring gaze at him. He could feel the drenching unconditional love and welcomed it. "You have my support."

"I wish I had Abigail's support, too. She matters to me."

"Don't worry, she'll come around. You'll see."

"I'm not so sure. Madeline is influencing her opinions." He jingled the keys in his pocket, remembering how upset she was about every aspect of the merger and their relationship. "But I can't be worried about what people think. I'm CEO of this company and I will make the tough decisions. I will lead as I see fit and will follow my plans regardless of the opposition."

"We finally get a chance to have a say in the running of this ministry. I'm proud of what you've done. Madeline can try as hard as she likes to destroy us, but so long as we stick together she can't touch us," his mother said.

"You really have changed, haven't you? You don't seem as intimidated by Madeline. I'm glad to see you have more confidence when it comes to her."

"I have changed because I discovered the key to my depression wasn't your father's commitment to Madeline or to his other children, it was my lack of commitment to me and to my hopes and dreams. I gave my power to Madeline every time I let her waltz into the mansion and treat me like hired help. For years I blamed your father for not protecting me, for not showing his undying loyalty to me and to me alone."

"So what changed?"

"No matter what happened with your father, he understood the concept of total devotion and commitment. He understood what it meant to love beyond life. I experienced it firsthand with him."

"So you do know how much he loved you?"

"Ah, maybe, but the love I'm talking about is the one he had for God. Nothing and nobody on earth took the spot in his life that he'd reserved for God, no one, not me, not Madeline, not you, not Don, not his other children, and not DMI, no one. Your father was successful because he never lost sight of his greatest love. He never allowed his relationship to be destroyed. That's the advice I give to you: Stay true to your greatest love. Never lose sight. Your father never lost sight of God. I'm convinced that was the reason he lived with so many battles yet had so much peace and success." She took Joel's hands. "I'm glad you are your father's son and mine, too."

The words splashed into Joel's spirit. His father wasn't as wise and had to rely on God. Joel didn't feel as dependent. That was the purpose of wisdom. He felt confident and didn't need anyone telling him what to do. A shot of Sheba's zeal wouldn't hurt though. She offered him what he no longer seemed to have from Abigail, nonjudgmental acceptance. Joel went back to his office. As soon as the meeting ended, he was set to spend a worry-free night in whatever town Sheba was in, didn't matter where. He needed her comforting support desperately.

chapter

76

Adrenaline charged through his veins, threatening an explosion. Standing in the lobby of DMI made him woozy. When he landed in South Africa for the first time, he was determined never to step foot in DMI again. The twenty-two-hour flight with a brief stop in France hadn't settled his nerves. He was humbled, reflecting on the conversation with the former prisoner on Robben Island. Purpose, forgiveness, destiny, and unconditional love brewed a powerful concoction. Against the impulse of every fiber in his body, he was standing in the lobby of his father's company.

"Are you sure you're ready to do this?" he asked her.

"I'm not sure, but I'm willing to do this for you," she said, "so long as I don't have to see Mother. I'm definitely not ready for a family reunion."

"She'd love to see you."

"Maybe one day, but not today. If it's okay with you, I'd like to sign the papers and hop the first flight back to Monaco. I want to be home tomorrow morning."

Don shook his head in affirmation but refused to accept a response of no to his hug. They embraced, regrouped and approached the security desk. "Don Mitchell and Tamara Mitchell are here to see Attorney Ryan."

"Of course, Mr. Mitchell, it's good to see you. Feel free to go right up. You don't have to sign in with us," the guard said.

"I don't want to go upstairs," Tamara said, frantically waving her hands, "I don't want to run into Mother. I can't."

"Okay, okay, it's all right. Can you please call Attorney Ryan and ask him to meet us in the lobby?" Don asked the guard.

"I'll let him know you're here."

"This is your last chance. You can take your stock and run back to Europe and Mother won't ever know you were here."

"I'm tempted, believe me, I'm very tempted." Tamara initiated the hug this time, not as shaken as she had been a minute ago.

"Excuse me, Mr. Mitchell, Attorney Ryan will be right down," the guard told them.

"Thanks."

Don spun around the lobby in slow motion. "It's hard to believe I'm here. I never thought I'd set foot in this place again, I honestly didn't, but God had another plan."

"And to think, you may be appointed CEO before the day is over," Tamara said.

"As soon as the board meeting is over, we'll see, which is in about three hours," Don said, peering at his watch. "Thank you for signing your stock over to me. I couldn't do this without you." Having his sister within arm's reach was the best gift.

"The stock will have much more value for you than it does for me."

"Mother is going to burst a blood vessel when she finds out you're home."

"I'm not home," Tamara said, shaking her index finger at him, "Monaco is home."

"Un-huh, I said the exact same thing when I moved to South Africa, and look where I am," he said, stretching his arms wide. "I'm not sure where my heart is," he said, dancing DMI, Naledi, LTI, and Abigail around his thoughts, "but this is where God has me for now."

Reader's Group Guide

───────── ◆ ─────────

ABOUT THIS GUIDE

The questions and discussion topics that follow are intended to enhance your reading of *Chosen* by Patricia Haley. We hope you found the novel enjoyable.

Reader's Group Guide

THOUGHT-PROVOKING QUESTIONS
FOR DISCUSSION

Now that you have read *Chosen*, let's talk. Grab your reading friends and book club members and have fun.

1. Joel had God's favor, wealth, unprecedented wisdom, purpose, and tremendous appeal, but he lost his edge. Where did he go wrong? Compare to the lifestyle of King Solomon (1 Kings, chapter 11).

2. After twenty-five to thirty years, why is Madeline still angry and Sherry insecure? What could or should Dave have done to resolve the conflict between his "wives"?

3. If Joel splits up the ministry, did Dave make the right decision in appointing him as CEO? How does God's plan change when we fail?

4. Abigail is torn between love and loyalty. Did Joel mislead her romantically? Was Abigail right in waiting for Joel to initiate the relationship or should she have taken the first step and approached him?

5. How can Dave have such a strong relationship with the Lord while the rest of his family is either struggling with or flat-out rejecting religion?

6. King Solomon was chosen by God to rule after his father (King David). How does an older child handle being overshadowed by a younger sibling?

7. Should or shouldn't Tamara return to the family?

8. King David was a mighty warrior who defeated the giant (Goliath) as a young boy. He was honorable but also a man plagued with horrific challenges and sin that fell upon his family. Yet David is not remembered for his shortcomings. He's revered as "the man after God's own heart." Why isn't he framed by his mistakes? Does forgiveness always, sometimes, or never erase consequences?

9. Should Don stay in South Africa and continue building LTI or return home to run DMI?

10. What was Big Mama's warning to Joel?

11. Abigail didn't seem attracted to Don, yet he was clearly smitten with her. Should he have told her about his feelings upfront? Why didn't he?

12. Describe the connection between Sheba and Joel. For extra drama, check out the Queen of Sheba's visit to see King Solomon (1 Kings, chapter 10).

13. Madeline was with Dave when he passed. What do you think about that? Are you glad or sad for Sherry? Do you see Sherry as a victim or a villain?

14. Describe Don's feeling toward his father (love, indifference, resentment). What's worse: Don feeling rejected while his father was alive, or guilty for not resolving their issues before Dave died? Is there anyone you need to forgive and then consider going a step further to reconcile? Don't wait. Today is the day for a fresh start.

Acknowledgments

As always, I acknowledge you, the readers. Many of you have gifts and talents that haven't been discovered, developed, or released. Know that you were created for a purpose, and I challenge you to find out what yours is.

I'm grateful to my number-one literary fan, pre-editor, and best friend—my dear husband, Jeffrey Glass. A big hug goes to my daughter for giving me the time and space to write. Kudos to my other amazing pre-editors: Emma (John) Foots, Laurel (Lynn) Robinson, Dorothy Robinson, Attorneys Tammy and Renee Lenzy, K. D. Moseley, and Dr. Leslie (Eldridge) Walker-Harding.

I'm sure to forget names as I reflect on the abundant support from so many people. My expression of gratitude and love starts with my Haley, Glass, Tennin, and Moorman families, especially Fannie, Rev. Fred, Gloria, Frances, Hoyt Freddy Deon, Jeraldine, Dr. Kenny, Tasha, Leslie, Lori, and my godchildren. I extend a special thank-you to my dear friends who are also family: to my sisters of Delta Sigma Theta Sorority, especially the Valley Forge (PA), Rockford (IL), and Schaumburg-Hoffman Estates (IL) Alumnae chapters; my New Covenant (PA), Beulah Grove (GA), and Greater Bellwood (GA) church families. Thank you to a long list of booksellers, media contacts, book clubs, and to Jade Design for the awesome website. I also honor the memories of those who continuously inspire my characters—my beloved brother Erick Haley, Joan Walker, and Aunt Lottie Tennin Flowers.

Special thanks to my agent, Andrew Stuart, and super editor Brigitte Smith at Simon & Schuster, for embarking upon this journey with me. Thanks T. Davis Bunn for challenging me some years ago on point of view. You've helped me become a better writer.

P.S. Happy 80th birthday to Bob Thomas and 75th to Earl Rome. Congratulations to the graduates Roslind Burks and Michelle Tolbert. I extend sisterly love to the Deltas of Omicron Chi and the other charter members as we celebrate twenty-five years of being on the Stanford University campus.

Author's Note

———— ◆ ————

Dear Readers:

Thank you for reading a copy of *Chosen*. I hope you enjoyed the story and found it entertaining as well as enlightening. Take a moment and join my mailing list or post a note on my website letting me know your thoughts about *Chosen*.

Look for *Destined*, the next book in the series where the battle over DMI shifts to the international stage.

As always, thank you for the support. Keep reading, be blessed, and I look forward to hearing from you online at www.patriciahaley.com.

Don't miss out on

DESTINED

by Patricia Haley

as the Mitchell family drama continues . . .

Available from Pocket Books
Spring 2010

Securing financing, dropping sales, Abigail, Madeline's schemes—Joel was juggling a list of issues with little support. As expected, Sherry was on his side, but she's his mother. Joel exited his car in the company's circular entrance and began approaching the company's entryway. His eyes were fixated on a woman fleeing the building. Silky black hair framed her caramel-colored face. She blazed past him in a whirlwind, but not before his gaze zoomed in on her eyes during their fleeting glance. A sense of familiarity overcame him, but Joel shook it off. Between DMI and the exhaustive media attention he'd claimed over the past three years, there was no telling where he'd met the woman. He was prepared to squeak out a hello but she didn't allow a single second for socializing. In a swoop she was in a cab, barreling out of the complex. Joel shrugged his shoulders, thankful for the brief distraction while equally intrigued about why she looked so familiar.

A moment later, Madeline came tearing out of the building, running smack into Joel. "Get out of my way," she stated, practically plowing him down. "Where is she?" she belted out.

"Where is who?"

"Never mind," she said agitated, and walked back inside.

Today wasn't making much sense for Joel. He walked through the revolving door and stopped. The lobby was filled with employees, but his gaze was drawn to Abigail, Attorney Ryan, and Don. That's when it clicked—the lady outside was Tamara, his half sister. His knees buckled as he understood the significance of her visit. She'd left Detroit when he was a child. With the strain between his father's two sets of children, Joel didn't have much interaction with Madeline's four children. He knew Don best, but Tamara was pretty much in name only, except for a few family photos his father had kept. In all these years, to his knowledge, she'd never returned to Detroit—not even for their father's funeral or for the reading of the will.

As he reflected on the will and the specific terms outlined by his father, he knew there was only one reason for her to show up now—to sign her stock ownership over to somebody. It didn't really matter to whom if it wasn't to him. Joel wanted to panic but he beat down the notion. Business had to be handled first, and then he could deal with his fears in private later, if he chose to do so.

Don approached Joel and extended his hand. When Joel was in Detroit for their father's funeral, Joel had reached out in an effort to make amends. Don had been cordial but not receptive to fostering too much brotherly love. The brothers' attitudes were reversed today. Joel wasn't in a friendly mood and he shrugged at Don's handshake. He needed answers.

"What's going on here?" he asked Don.

"We have a board meeting."

"Come on, man, you can do better than that. You haven't shown up in three years for any other board meeting and all of a sudden I'm supposed to believe that you and Tamara just happen to be here on the same day for an emergency board meeting." Joel's blood was pumping fast, racing through his veins. His thoughts wanted to get ahead of his words, overcome with the massive number of possibilities threatening his position in the company. They were out to get him. He knew it. He had to think, and think quickly.

Who could he trust? He panned the room, logging in the face of each employee lining the lobby. They were to be watched, too. No one was going to blindly knock him out of the CEO position, not without a serious duel to the death. The job was his. He was chosen by his father and by God.

Joel pushed past Don and Madeline in search of Abigail. He found her and aggressively grabbed her arm. "What's going on here?"

"Joel," she cried out, startling him. He let go of her arm. His thoughts had taken him into a state of confusion, a place he was frequenting more often.

"Are you turning on me?" he demanded.

"Joel, get a hold of yourself. There is a lobby full of your employees here. Don't make a scene. This isn't like you at all," Abigail whispered as she pulled her jacket down on both sides.

Don broke into the conversation with Madeline in tow. "Joel, you need to back off from Abigail. If you have a concern, address it with me."

"What is this, you have to protect Abigail from me? Come on, you can't be serious."

"That's not what he meant to do, Joel," Abigail said.

"Joel, let's everybody take a breath and let's go talk," Don said.

"Okay, big brother, since you're speaking for the entourage, you tell me what's going on, as if I don't already know."

"Let's step into the waiting room. Everybody out here doesn't need to know what we're discussing," Don said.

"Oh, and who are you, the new boss giving orders and taking charge?" Joel chuckled, having no other way to relieve the mounting tension.

"Come on, Joel, let's talk," Don offered again, and pointed to the waiting room off to the side of the lobby.

"I don't need a private room to hear your lies," Joel told Don. Then he turned to Madeline. "I know this is your doing. You just won't give up. When are you going to get this in your head?" he said, tapping his index finger on his temple. "I'm CEO, not you, not your son, not my father, me. Deal with it." He began to walk away.

"Mistakes can and will be corrected," Madeline said.

Joel was instantly yanked back into the heat. Before he could hurl a word, Don stepped between Joel and his mother.

"I said, back off," Don said. "This is between you and me, leave my mother and Abigail out of this."

As Joel and Don stood, squaring off, face-to-face, Joel growled, "Or what, big brother, what are you going to do? You've taken me on before and lost, each time." Joel didn't want to ignite a duel but he couldn't show any signs of weakness. If Tamara had signed her stock ownership to Don or Madeline, then that meant they had controlling interest with fifty-five percent and enough weight to oust him from the CEO role at the upcoming board meeting, not counting Abigail's five percent. His thoughts were jumbled, his emotions were frantic, but they couldn't know.

"Joel, what's gotten into you? This is not you. Don't you see what's happening?" Abigail said in an emotional tone not easily hidden. "Ever since you started pursuing

Harmonious Energy, you've been a different person. You have to see this," she pleaded. He didn't want to hear anything she had to say. She was in the other camp, a traitor. Joel bypassed the elevator and stormed up the stairs, three at a time. He needed time and space to figure out how to stay the coup d'état that was obviously brewing among his so-called family and friends. Six flights up wasn't enough time, but it was a start.

~

A pound of elation had been crushed by a ton of disappointment. Don was baffled. He tried to put the pieces of the day together, to orchestrate a scenario that justified him leaving the comforts of his home and willfully thrusting himself into the family feud again. "I must be crazy. What was I thinking coming back here?" he said to Abigail, the last remaining person in the lobby besides the security guards. The other employees and people with good sense had left, obviously a better judge at recognizing when it was time to abandon a situation.

"I should have stayed in Cape Town and left DMI to crash and burn on its own."

"Your being here right now is not a mistake. God has you here for a reason," Abigail said as she reached out to him.

"If this is God's plan, I sure wish I knew what it was."

"Don, some battles have to be fought. They can't be avoided."

He wasn't accustomed to seeing Abigail speak against Joel. The surprises of the day were endless.

"What happened to your loyalty to Joel, or, I should say, your love for him?"

She removed her hand from Don's shoulder and let her gaze dip and drag across the floor before regaining eye contact. "My mind is clear for the first time in three years, no more living in the clouds and hoping for a fantasy. I'm being realistic now. Joel has lost his mind and there's no need for DMI to be put at risk while he gets himself together."

"That's what you say today, but that's your hurt talking. You won't feel that way in a few weeks or maybe months." He slid his hands into his pants pockets but maintained eye contact. "Take it from me, I know. It's taken me time to let go. You're mad at Joel, but it's not over. My gut tells me that you still want a life with him," he said, gently lifting her chin with his index finger.

She chuckled. "There are plenty of things that I want, like cheesecake. I'd like a slice every day, but it's not good for me. Apparently, Joel isn't either." Don didn't speak. "What?" Abigail asked. "What's that look on your face?"

"What look?"

"I know you don't believe that I'm moving on without Joel. However, I don't have a choice. He's already moved on. Besides, it's different for you. You have the choice to go back to South Africa and live your happy little life and ignore God's calling or stay and fight this battle that you were probably created to win."

" 'Probably' isn't exactly convincing."

"You know what I mean. I know the Lord, but I'm not prophetic. I can tell you what I feel in my heart and in my spirit, but you have to hear God on your own. That much I learned when Joel and I were serving the same God."

Don took a seat in one of the cozy sitting areas. "So I should stay according to the great Ms. Abigail Gerard?"

She followed him and sat down. "If you ask me, I

truly believe that you were destined to run DMI at this point in time. This is your season."

"What about Joel?"

~

Going around in circles wasn't familiar to Joel. He was motivated by directness, action. When he spoke, people moved to carry out his requests. Why couldn't the company recognize that he knew what he was doing? He wasn't some random, aloof guy making whacked-out decisions without merit. He was Joel Mitchell, a primary heir to the Mitchell family dynasty. He was the one, out of a long line of contenders, who was left holding the keys to the palace. He was CEO, the one worthy to run the company. Not Don, and definitely not Madeline.

Joel grabbed the phone on his desk. His reality check deposited a sufficient boost of energy to his weary bones. Two rings got him where he wanted to be, on the line with the personal DMI banker.

"Mr. Mitchell, I've been expecting your call. How can we assist you today?"

Joel didn't have the entire cash situation figured out, but getting what he could from the bank would be a huge help. He'd secure funds from the credit line and worry about the rest next. "I'm ready to complete the merger that we discussed previously. I'll need the entire $250 million from the credit line, and I'd like to discuss other options for securing the rest of the money that we need."

The banker didn't hesitate. "Based on the account hold, the only funds available to you are through the credit line that can be executed solely on your executive order. Any further funding will require a new valuation in the DMI assets and approvals from two members of the board, as we've discussed."

Joel was clear about the other signatures stemming from the board's attempt to hold up the merger, but the valuation was a surprise. "Why do you need a new valuation? You have the most current value."

"Mr. Mitchell, there has been a perceived change in your company's value."

There was no way Madeline had gone this far with her cancerous lies. DMI hadn't booked triple-digit growth last quarter but the ten months prior would surely have offset the dip. He wasn't going to be discounted, not when he was so close to realizing his dream on an international expansion plan. "DMI is solid. You have balance sheets for nearly three years. I don't see the problem. Either you want our business or you don't."

"We absolutely want your business. We've been working with you, or, I should say, DMI, for thirty years and value you as a key client."

"Then why are you giving me such a hard time when I'm trying to throw a significant chunk of business your way?"

"Well, the problem is that for the first time since the line of credit was established, the perceived DMI value has dropped sizably. As a result, the credit line has been reduced to fifty million."

"You can't be serious? That's not nearly enough."

"Mr. Mitchell, I really am sorry. I wish there was some way to meet your business needs, but my hands are tied. I can't extend additional credit to you without a dramatic increase in your company's value."

"Since we're at an impasse, we can consider this discussion to be over," Joel said, bitter.

"What about the fifty million, should I wire that to an account?"

Joel hesitated. Fifty million was fifty million less that

he would have to scramble to find. On the other hand, his pride was worth more, at least another two hundred million more. "No, we prefer to do business with an institution that values a mutually beneficial long-term relationship."

"Mr. Mitchell, I'm sorry you feel that way. Your business has been and continues to be very significant to us. I'm sure this is a temporary situation and will be resolved very quickly, and we can continue doing business together."

"I don't think so." The banker tried wedging a pathetic line of empty rhetoric before Joel cut him off. "Have a good day," Joel concluded, and ended the call. He held the receiver for a while until the dial tone hummed. The fury burned within him.

The bank was an inconvenience, not a showstopper.